STARSHIP ETERNAL

WAR ETERNAL, BOOK ONE

M.R. FORBES

Published by Quirky Algorithms
Seattle, Washington

This novel is a work of fiction and a product of the author's imagination.
Any resemblance to actual persons or events is purely coincidental.

Cover illustrations by Tom Edwards
tomedwardsdesign.com

XENO-1

There are a lot of things looking at the sky. Radar. Telescopes. Cameras. The human eye.

When that thing appeared halfway between the Earth and the Moon, seemingly falling into existence out of the vast emptiness of space as though God himself had created it in that very spot, there were millions who witnessed its fall.

Their stories would diverge, of course. The mind has a way of filling in the blanks with its own measure of ingenuity. Some said it was like a bolt of lightning. Others said it was more akin to a stone sinking in a pool. The dash cam, the helmet cam, the phone cam, the body cam... so many damn cameras, and even then the stories ranged far and wide, becoming legendary, a new mythology in the hearts and souls of the people.

What did I see? A dark black mass with white-hot flames at its head hurtling down at the world. The fist of God striking the planet in a fit of judgement day. Not a satellite. Not an asteroid. Not a damn trick of chemical reactions in the atmosphere, even if the government tried to spin it that way before the truth overwhelmed them.

We knew what we saw, and we would swear the same to any who would listen.

It wasn't a UFO. There was nothing unidentified about it, and it certainly wasn't flying.

An alien spaceship.

The war to claim it started soon enough.

- Paul Frelmund, "XENO-1"

[1]

"TELL ME, Captain Williams. How *did* you discover the weakness on the Federation dreadnought?"

Captain Mitchell "Ares" Williams shifted in the pillowy expanse of his seat, getting the bright stage beams out of his eyes. He faced his interviewer. Her name was Tamara King. She was known on Liberty as the Queen of Talk, her morning stream the highest rated within the Delta Quadrant. She was a willowy blonde, dressed in tall boots and a fashionable high-cut sweater that hugged her curves like a second layer of skin. She was bombarding him with a smile that could make its way past even the most reluctant guest's defenses better than a well-placed nuke.

"It was simple, Tamara," he said. He shifted towards the camera opposite him and returned her smile with a version of his own that was nearly as disarming. "We were watching the fighter formations, tracking the density equations. It was clear they were clustering near a service portal close to the aft, trying to keep our fire away from that portion of the ship. When I saw one of their Kips move into the line of fire and sacrifice itself to prevent one of our tactical's from reaching the boat, I knew there had to be something to it."

He'd practiced the lines so many times. On the transport, in front of the mirror, and in the hundreds of other interviews he'd given in the two months since the United Planetary Alliance had stopped the Frontier Federation's attempt to overpower Liberty and claim the planet.

"And there was something to it, wasn't there?" Tamara asked. She shifted in her chair, getting close enough to him that he could smell her. She was light and sweet.

Mitchell made eye contact, maintaining the smile. "There was, Tamara. A flaw in the design. Weak shield coverage and a direct path for a projectile to hit the reactor. Of course, I didn't know at the time that it would be so effective. I was just taking a shot."

"The Shot Heard 'Round the Universe," Tamara said, drawing cheers and clapping from her audience. She put the tips of her fingers on his leg, resting them there while the crowd quieted. "Your 'twisted snake' maneuver is already legendary. In fact, my nephew likes to pretend he's Ares Williams, and he runs across the lawn yelling 'twisted snake' until he makes himself dizzy and falls over." She paused, waiting while the audience laughed. Mitchell faked a chuckle through his doll-smile. "What's it like, saving an entire planet, everyone here in this studio included, from certain death? How does it feel to be the greatest hero of our time?"

The first few times, questions like these had caused him to blush, to stammer, to threaten to break under the pressure. Time, experience, and training had cured him of that. He still wasn't sure how he did it, how he still managed to do it after all of these weeks, all of these tours along the media circus. Circuit. He only did what he had to do. What he was ordered to do.

"It's what I was trained for. That's all. I don't really think I'm a hero." He looked away from her and felt the heat rush to his cheeks. It had taken a lot of practice, a lot of repetition, to master blushing on command. They'd even hired a coach to help him get it just right. "Only a pilot trying to do his part."

"That's very modest."

Mitchell tilted his head to look out at the live audience. Two hundred bodies filled the seats behind the bright lights, hanging on his every word. They weren't all from Liberty. Some had obviously traveled from other planets in the Delta Quadrant, from Kappa and Gavone among others. They were a mixture of cultures and backgrounds, descendants of the settlers who had left Earth four hundred years earlier and began the process of spreading to the stars. There was a lot of interest in seeing him in person and hearing him recount the decisive battle. And why not? He had saved their lives, and saved the Alliance from being drawn even deeper into a war they still hadn't proven they could win. A war they would have already lost if the dreadnought had been as impervious to their assault as it was supposed to be. If Liberty fell...

"It's true," he said. "I lost eight-hundred brothers and sisters that day. People I served with, ate with, laughed with." He stopped, remembering Ella. Slept with. Loved. "They're the real heroes. They gave their lives to protect this planet. They made the ultimate sacrifice."

Tamara was silent for a moment, playing the crowd perfectly. She moved her hand to his, tracing the back of it with her fingertips while she spoke.

"I'm sorry for your losses, Captain. Every one of them died a hero, and all of them deserve our honor and respect."

The crowd cheered again.

"Thank you, Tamara," Mitchell said, once they had quieted down.

Tamara turned her head, her eyes finding one of the floating cameras, a small sphere hanging a dozen feet away. "When we come back, Captain Williams will tell you how you can be part of the continuing fight for Liberty, and we'll be treated to a special sneak peak at the Alliance's latest campaign."

A small red square popped up in the center of Mitchell's field of vision, a notice that the feed was being paused projected on his retina. Like every other soldier in the galaxy, Mitchell had been outfitted with a neural implant and a p-rat - a cybernetic enhancement more commonly known outside the barracks as an Advanced Reality Receiver, or ARR. The twin pieces of tech were used for most forms of communication, from watching streams to encrypted video and voice transmission, and physical monitoring and control. For Marines like Mitchell, it was also a link to the CAP-NN system, the AI that helped them pilot fighters and mechs.

He started to lean back in the chair, fighting to keep the tide in his stomach in check. He paused when Tamara put her hand on top of his, suggesting he should stay close.

"Do you have plans after the show?" she asked.

It only took a thought for him to access the p-rat and pull up his itinerary. He almost laughed at the idea of it. Two months ago he was only free when he wasn't making drops into hot zones or escorting VIPs with the rest of his squad from the Greylock. Now? He hadn't been in a cockpit in weeks, and the only training he did consisted of acting and etiquette lessons. If he wasn't on camera or shaking hands somewhere, he had nothing but free time.

"I'll be on Liberty another two days, and then they're shipping me off to..." He scrolled through the list behind his eye. "...Cestus for a recruitment drive. After that-"

"I said after the show, Captain," Tamara said. "Immediately after." She stroked the back of his hand. "I've never been with a celebrity Space Marine. You can consider it a thank you for your service to our planet."

Mitchell bit his lip, and then smiled. He'd always thought of himself as a somewhat handsome man. Six feet tall, in good shape, a nice face, and hazel eyes. He had the outgoing personality to go with it, and his job as a Space Marine pilot only added to his attractiveness to the opposite sex.

After the brass had propped him up over the Shot... The rise in that attractiveness, and the resulting attention, was ridiculous.

"I'm free right after the show. What did you have in mind?"

They were interrupted by a stage hand. Tamara leaned back in her chair and sat stone-faced while he worked on removing some of the growing sheen from her face. The streams were filtered to help make the people displayed on them look better than they did in real life, but it was apparent Miss King didn't like the idea of appearing less than perfect to her audience.

"How are you holding up, Captain?"

Corporal Evan Kwon sidled up to him, wearing the crisp, dark blue uniform of the Alliance Space Marines. He was half-Korean, short and thin, well-spoken and well-groomed. He looked like an officer, and he had a lot of decorations on his chest, but they didn't mean much of anything. He was Public Relations. Mitchell's handler.

"I'm fine," Mitchell said, his eyes tracking over to Tamara. He would be even better after the charade was over.

"Hey, I was thinking maybe we could swing by this place downtown after this. It's really popular with the student population, and it might be good to get in there, shake some hands, transmit some-" He noticed Mitchell wasn't paying attention to him and stopped talking. He stood silent for a moment before knocking on Mitchell's p-rat. "This again?" he asked once Mitchell answered.

"It's not my fault. You know women have a thing for Marines to begin with, especially pilots. Even our fellow female thruster jocks."

"Like Ella?"

Mitchell's eyes shifted. His dark glare caused Evan to back up a step.

"Sorry, Captain. I should keep my mouth shut. So, you're good?"

"Yeah." It was almost enough to break his concentration. A countdown appeared behind his eye. Ten seconds. "Get off the stage."

"Okay, okay. So, no to dinner?"

Mitchell shook his head. Evan continued to back away.

"Great. I'll hit your ARR again later so we can coordinate for the trip tomorrow morning."

The stage hand scurried away from Tamara, and she leaned forward again, putting herself back in her pre-break position.

The countdown reached zero, and a green square appeared.

"We're back with Captain Mitchell 'Ares' Williams, hero of the Battle for Liberty." She waited while the crowd cheered. "Captain Williams, you've been doing a lot of interviews in the media lately, and bringing what some would say is arguably the highest level of attention the Alliance military has ever received. And it isn't just here on Liberty but on Alliance planets across the galaxy. Can you tell us a little bit about why that is?"

Mitchell smiled and patted her hand, using the motion to remove it so he could get to his feet. He turned to meet one of the cameras as it angled between him and the audience.

"We may have defeated the Frontier Federation here on Liberty, but the Alliance forces took heavy losses. And the Federation is only one of the threats we all face on a daily basis. The New Terrans have been rattling their sabers for months, piracy is up across the galaxy, dozens of smaller rogue states are doing their best to create upheaval and, let's be honest, we discovered a flaw in the dreadnought design. You can bet the Federation is already working to fix it and get another one built. We need to make a concerted push into their space before that can happen, and at the same time maintain the safety of the rest of our territories. We need new recruits training here on Liberty and across the more than forty planets that make up the Alliance. We need pilots, engineers, admins, officers, everything, and let me tell you, it's a great career and a great way to make a difference. What other profession gives you the chance to say you were responsible for saving the lives of billions of people?"

Tamara stood and joined him near the front of the set. She draped her arm over his shoulders, squeezing his bicep. "I'm not a warrior like you are, Captain Williams, but I'm ready to do my part," she said. She gazed out into the audience. "Take a look at this promotional video starring Captain Williams. Then, if you or someone you know is between eighteen and forty-five years of age, consider heading down to your nearest recruitment center and find out how you can help. Enlistment isn't just a privilege; it's an honor."

[2]

MITCHELL SAT with his back against the headboard, his head tilted so he could look up at the virtual sky displayed on the ceiling. He was still sweaty from the exercise, and the cool air on his naked flesh left him feeling crisp and awake.

"I have to go," Tamara said. Her left eye twitched, showing that she was looking into her civilian version of an ARR. "Thank you."

She leaned up to give him one last kiss, and then rolled out of the bed. He shifted his eyes so he could watch her bend over to retrieve her clothes.

"You have an ARR, I assume?" she said, pulling up her panties.

"Every member of the military does. What's your sig?"

"I'll knock."

She paused for a second. Mitchell heard a slight tone somewhere in his inner ear, his neural implant signaling that someone was trying to transmit to his p-rat. As military, he was forbidden to expose his signature under any circumstances. Civilians could call in, and he could accept, but he couldn't call out unless he already had the key stored. The setup made it possible for the brass to keep control over their classified intel, limit communications at whatever unit level they wanted for a given mission, erase anything they needed in the event of capture, or to force their grunts to conveniently lose access to anything they considered a distraction.

Freedom wasn't free, after all.

He accepted the knock. Tamara's key appeared behind his eye, a six-hundred character string of letters and numbers that he filed under her name. He never needed to remember it. His brain and the implant would handle that.

"Got it," he said. He watched her button her blouse. She had been a lot of fun.

"You're as good as I thought you'd be. Get in touch the next time you're in the capital." She found her purse near the front door, picked it up, and waved as she slipped out.

"Yeah, sure." He stared at the closed door for a few seconds. He didn't think anyone would have labeled him as good before Ella. She had taught him everything he knew, in more ways than one.

He sighed and pulled himself out of bed, checking the time. Eight-thirty. Plenty to spare. He made his way to the bathroom, slipping into a small stall and closing his eyes while being doused in anti-bacterial light and then tickled by sonic blasters. He'd been to a hotel on Earth once that still used water. Now *that* was an experience.

He stepped out of the stall, exited the bathroom, and found his travel pack, digging out his casual uniform. Dark blue pants, a tight, white, high-collared shirt, a wide-rimmed hat and a pair of genuine leather shoes that he had received as a gift from some politician or another in thanks for saving the galaxy. He also found his AZ-9 high capacity hand-rifle and strapped it to his side under his jacket. He had never liked to go anywhere without it before the Shot, and now? Evan tried to keep word from reaching him about the threats the Federation was making on his life, but he wasn't about to take any chances. Especially not when they refused to give him any kind of special escort. "Command thinks it makes us look weak," the Corporal had said.

He was riding the lift down to the lobby when the tone alerted him to an incoming message.

Ignore.

The signal came again in a different tone. Military and important.

Ignore.

"You could be court-martialed for refusing a flagged knock," Evan said, his voice ghostlike inside Mitchell's head.

"I think I'm pretty bullet-proof on the court-martial at this point. Besides, I knew it was you. I don't appreciate you bypassing the block, by the way."

Evan laughed. "You know I wouldn't bother you unless it were important. I'm sending you a new itinerary."

"Why?"

Evan was silent.

"Evan?"

"The Governor of Cestus has fallen ill, so we're shifting some of the dates around. No big deal. This is coming right from Command."

Mitchell knew he was lying. A death threat or some intel pointing towards an attempt on his life. He knew the Federation was eager to see him cut down, and he didn't blame them. He was broadcasting their failure across the entire galaxy, helping the Alliance run their propaganda machine day and night. They didn't seem to care if he wound up being martyred, and the enlistment ranks swelled. It was a matter of vengeful pride to them.

So far, the Security Department had done a good job steering him away from potential attacks, so if they were diverting from Cestus he was certain there was something in the works there. He pulled up his new itinerary. They were leaving in two hours. It was going to cut his plans short, but it was still enough time.

"Fine. Got it. Meet me at the hotel."

"Did you know Tamara King is one of the richest and most famous people on Liberty?" Evan was impressed with things like that. Mitchell had been more impressed with her agility.

"No. I didn't know that. I haven't had much time to pay attention to local celebrity gossip, with the war and everything."

In his life before the Shot, he had been stationed on the Greylock, one of the most elite Space Marine units in existence. They were the last line of defense and first line of response in almost every critical conflict that popped up inside Alliance-owned space. In the last five years he'd been to thirty different planets, done over four hundred space sorties, and seen action more times than he could keep track of. Greylock had been his true home, the small jumpship as good as any planet in the galaxy. The members of the company had been his friends, his brothers, his sisters, and his lovers.

Well, only one lover.

He missed her like crazy.

"Yeah, well, she is. Did you... you know?"

"Evan-"

"What? I'm just asking. I'm the one who has to follow you around like a worried mother instead of having a life of my own."

The lift reached the lobby. Mitchell stepped out and started walking. "Yeah," he said. There was no harm in throwing the Corporal a bone once in a while.

"I figured. I was jealous enough of you after that supermodel on Kepler. Was it good?"

"What do you think?"

Evan's laughter was an annoying buzz in his head. "I think you might be the luckiest man alive."

Eight-hundred of his family, dead. The number wasn't an exaggeration. Mitchell held back the choice words that threatened to make their way through the p-rat. Every word that moved through the implant was monitored, and Command wouldn't like him losing his cool.

"Yeah. Sure. I'll see you when you get here. Have someone grab my travel pack from my room, will you?"

"Of course, Captain."

"Good. Now get out of my head."

There was another signal when the connection closed. Mitchell decided he would have to speak with his CO about Evan's level of permissions. If he couldn't block the rep's knocks, he'd like to at least be able to kick him out when the conversation was over.

He pulled his hat down, trying to obscure his face. He exited the hotel and headed up the street. The traffic in the capital was only just starting to get back to some form of normalcy, though the signs of war were still everywhere. Dark scars marred the facades of a number of buildings around town, while countless heavy machines helped clear demolished buildings, and crews worked day and night to put the city back together. The hum of reactors and the heavy vibrations of mech feet were a constant reminder of the activity, even when their presence was obscured by the tall buildings that had managed to escape the bombardment.

He stopped in front of one of the smaller buildings, a thirty-story construction of poly-alloy and carbonate that was untouched by the war. He glanced through the window at the bar inside, an old-fashioned style pub fitted in dark wood and gold accents. He'd seen it when the limo had dropped him at the hotel in the morning, and he'd been anxious to pay it a visit. He stepped forward, and the glass parted at an invisible seam, drawing aside to let him in. He breathed in the heavy scent of oak and booze and licked his lips in anticipation.

Two hours would be plenty of time.

He did his best to go unnoticed, sitting in a dark corner of the bar by himself and taking a regular stream of Liberty's Finest from an overly friendly waitress. She had called him out on his identity the moment he'd walked into the bar, her face lighting up at the chance to meet and serve the hero. He accepted her phone number and transmitted fifty credits and a government approved holograph to her in exchange for her silent service. She was faithful to the deal, dropping off the drinks and retreating without trying to chat him up too much.

On the outside, Mitchell was everything most men dreamed of being. A decorated Space Marine, a starfighter and mech jockey, a war hero, a celebrity, and a fine piece of meat for any forthcoming member of the opposite sex.

On the outside, during most of his waking hours, he forced himself to buy into the hype, to believe what the Alliance marketing team was selling and drink it in with full abandon. It helped him ace his acting lessons and pass through the media circuit without cracking from the pressure. It helped him stay confident and macho when he took a woman like Tamara King to his bed.

He lifted the glass and downed the clear liquid, feeling it burning the back of his throat and warming his gut. He would have loved to be the man that everyone thought he was. He would have loved to be nothing more than the pilot who took the Shot Heard 'Round the Universe.

It would have made his life that much easier to live. It would have made it that much easier for him when he had no one to sit with but himself.

The problem was that he knew the truth.

He picked up the bottle and poured another shot. Then he cradled the drink in his hand, staring through the glass and the clear liquid inside. He watched the other patrons through it, sitting at their tables, drinking and eating and laughing. The refraction of light left the scene bent. Distorted. Like his life.

Ella.

He put the drink to his lips and downed it in one swallow. His head was spinning a little, his heart racing. He drank to forget, but he didn't know why he bothered. All it ever did was make him remember.

[3]

"ARES, WATCH YOURSELF," Ella said, her voice stern and sexy in his p-rat.

He turned his head, the HUD behind his eyes sending dots and circles scattering around his field of vision, finding the enemy fighters mixed in among the debris. The Federation dreadnought loomed a few thousand kilometers in front of them - a long distance in atmosphere, no distance at all in space. Sharp blue bolts flared up all around it, and longer streamers of red flame exploded from its batteries, raining hell towards them, and down at the surface of the planet. He knew the cause of the shield explosions was somewhere behind him, the Greylock doing its best with its much more limited missile and laser positions. As a Space Marine jumpship, it was meant to launch fighters and belly-up at low orbits for drops, not go head-to-head against a monster like the one at its stern. Unfortunately, all of the other assets they had jumped into the system with were already part of the debris field.

"I've got him," Mitchell said. He recognized the target of his wing-mate's warning, one of the nimble Federation fighters that they had nicknamed a "Kip." It was making a run towards him, angling for a clean shot.

He used his p-rat to place a marker on the target. It made it easier to keep an eye on his enemy through the smaller flashes of blue along the clear carbonate of the cockpit, where the shields vaporized and deflected bits of metal and other junk that had been created by the insanity around them.

"First Squadron," the voice was calm in his head, coming in as a special transmission from the Greylock. "Liberty is taking a pounding. We need to break through their defenses and deliver our payload, and we need to do it now. Mop up your targets and head for the dreadnought."

"Roger that," Ella said. There was a minor tone change, a switch to the team's private channel. "You heard the General."

Mitchell watched her Moray's port vectoring thrusters fire, and her ship rolled and changed course. More of the small thrusters along the fuselage helped to correct the heading, and then the mains burned once to shoot her ahead.

A simple thought sent his ship vectoring after her, the CAP-NN interface responding instantly to his intentions. Inside a mech, the CAP-NN link tended to be a bare plug that went from the back of the head, right into the CPU of the onboard AI. In a starfighter, it connected first to a sleek and frightening helmet, and then from the helmet to the head. It didn't just allow the user to control their shell with their brain. It made them part of the shell. It extended the senses outward to the frame, whether it was a ninety ton mech or a thousand meter battle cruiser, providing a connection that gave the pilot an intimate feel of his ride. It was the only way a human could handle the complexity of the mechanics and steer accurately, especially in space.

A throttle and stick were still standard in the cockpit of the Morays, but it was a backup; a last hope, desperate effort to somehow steer the ship if the CAP-NN was damaged. In truth, it was garbage. Losing the link meant having no feel of the beast you were riding, and even if you could keep the thrusters firing, or the joints moving, you were like a man with no arms in a fistfight.

"You're falling behind, Ares," Ella said.

Mitchell checked the marked Kip, finding it still tracking him, trying to keep up with his evasive maneuvers. An overlay on the outer glass of his helmet kept him apprised of predicted laser fire, right under the shield monitor. He cursed when he saw his integrity was near fifty percent, no thanks to all of the debris that had been generated in the battle. A few quick hits from a pulse laser would knock it to nothing in no time.

"Just getting the monkey off my back, sir," Mitchell replied. The top thrusters fired hard, and he dropped and spun about, rolling and vectoring back in the path of his enemy. The Kip tried to adjust for the maneuver, only to find itself losing composure in the difficulty of the sudden move.

Mitchell opened up on it, firing both forward lasers into and through the enemy ship. There was no sound, no explosion. Not out here. The fighter just stopped. The CAP-NN scanned it, measuring power outputs and life signs. The pilot was alive. His ship wasn't as fortunate.

Mitchell spun his Moray around again and found his squadron making an arcing line towards the dreadnought. The fight still raged around him, the other six squadrons mixing it up with the Kips while missiles arced and exploded across space. They were outnumbered two to one, but the Moray was the best the Marines could provide, and the Federation had put more of their energy into making super destroyers than they had starfighters.

Right now, that seemed to be the better decision.

"What's the plan, sir?" Achilles' voice echoed in his head.

"The Greylock needs a clean shot, which it can't get while that big fat bastard is firing back. We need to get in close and take out some of those batteries."

"Roger."

"First Squadron, form up, stay close. Evasive maneuvers only, don't get dragged into a fight. Keep your focus on the dreadnought."

"Roger," Mitchell said. His rear thrusters burst again, adding enough speed to get him in line close to Ella.

"It sure is messy out here," he said, sending the message over their private channel.

"I don't know about this, Mitch," she replied.

"About what?"

"Surviving. We're completely outmatched here."

"You're killing my morale, El. We've gotten through worse than this."

The squadron swung almost as one, spreading apart to evade an incoming strafing run, and then closing up again as the enemy fighters went past.

"I don't think we've ever been sent out against anything like this."

The dreadnought was drawing closer. It was a behemoth, nearly three kilometers long, sleek and angled, with laser, gun, and missile batteries tracing along almost every flat surface, most of them showing signs of activity. Sensor arrays sprouted at regular intervals, along with shield generators and thruster ports. He could see the light of a hangar bay near the front.

"Remember that time on Avalon?"

"Yeah."

"We got out of that."

She laughed. "Yeah, we did." A pause. "Hey, check your HUD."

Mitchell brought his eyes into the glass of his helmet, the third of his four layers of vision. The CAP-NN was tracking the enemy fighters, highlighting their positions around him. Whether he looked out with his own eyes or glanced at the overlay, it was easy to see that they were in trouble. The single dreadnought carried more firepower and more support fighters than the entire Alliance combat group combined.

"What about my - oh, shit."

The beeping was shrill in his head, the CAP-NN warning him of a new heat signature coming from the base of the dreadnought. It was followed by a dozen more.

"What the hell?" Ella said.

Blooms of flame poured from the enemy warship, hatches popping open across the port side. Larger missiles exploded out of them, high-velocity motors bringing them to speed in a matter of seconds.

"Nukes," Hercules shouted.

The missiles accelerated, their thrusters spewing heat as they powered past the surprised squadron. The dreadnought had already destroyed four Alliance cruisers and a battleship without resorting to nukes. That it was using them now suggested they were sure the fight was just about done, their heavy ordnance no longer needed for new, potentially more dangerous threats.

"They're headed for the Greylock," Ella said. "First Squadron, reverse course to intercept."

The tone changed. An emergency signal from the Greylock.

"Athena, retract that order," General Hill said. "You need to stay on the dreadnought."

"General?" There was obvious panic in her voice. It was a panic they all felt.

"That's an order, Major. Get in close, do what you can. With any luck, we can weaken it for the next attempt at bringing it down."

"The next attempt?"

It was an impossible thought. There were no other Alliance ships remaining in the Delta Quadrant. The next assault on the Federation's latest weapon wouldn't come for weeks. Weeks during which the Federation could put it back together, using resources from the planet they were about to seize.

Time seemed to hold static while Mitchell stared at his HUD. It was tracking the missiles on their arcing path towards the Greylock, adjusting ever so slightly with each refresh, correcting for the jump-ship's evasive maneuvers and remaining locked on the target. Fourth and Fifth moved to intercept, firing on the warheads in an effort to stop the inevitable.

The missiles were fast. Faster than anything he had ever seen. Another new technological achievement? The Federation was small, barely a dozen planets, and yet their advancements had stymied the Alliance for years. How did they do it?

"You heard the General," Ella said. She tried to sound strong, but she cracked on the words. It was the same fracture Mitchell was feeling, the sudden and obvious truth of the situation threatening to break their focus and ruin their composure.

First, the Greylock would be destroyed.

Then they would die, too.

Spaceborne nuclear weapons weren't anything like those designed for atmospheric use. Out here, the warheads were heavy and reinforced, shaped to penetrate the thick armor of a destroyer or a battleship, piercing the hull of the target before detonation. This allowed the exploding warhead to find some measure of atmosphere, which was promptly sucked in and used as fuel for the blast. When the target's shields were still available, the EMP radiation of the warhead's explosion would tax the generation systems, threatening to bring them down.

The Greylock's shields had already been hammered, and her hull was nowhere near as heavy as a battleship's. The first two nukes detonated against them, causing large blue flashes that skittered along the outside of the entire ship and vanished in a flash. Eight more nukes were right behind, dropping quickly in the storm of the jumpship's point defense batteries.

Only two of the warheads made it through.

All it took was one.

Flame burst from the impact point, jetting out into space in a tight line before losing the air to feed it. The Greylock began to break from the inside out. The heat killed the crew first, and then melted through the jumpship's super-structure, compromising hull integrity and pushing against it from the inside out.

The explosion was small and silent.

The end result was the same.

The Greylock was nothing more than another field of debris in a theater already bathed in it.

Their voices were tight whispers over the squadron's comm channel.

"Son of a bitch."

"Frigging bastards."

Mitchell fought against his own desire to cry out, holding back his sudden fury, keeping it in check before he did something stupid. He reached out and clenched the joystick, squeezing it until his hand hurt, needing to direct all of the energy somewhere.

"We're dead," Achilles said.

"Shut up, Private," Ella replied. Her voice was calm, resolute. Mitchell was certain she was feeling the same as the rest of them on the inside. Her ability to control it was what made her such a good Commander. "Stay professional. Ares, check your HUD, a quarter click along that beast's ass."

Mitchell straightened up. If he was going to die, he was going to die on the offensive. He went back to the HUD, looking at the tail. Two dozen Kips floated nearby, completely out of the fight. The battle was nearly over, but they shouldn't have retreated already.

"What the hell are they doing, just sitting there?" Hercules asked.

"I don't know, Herc," Ella said. "Why don't we go find out?"

"What?"

"You heard the Major," Mitchell said. He shifted his eyes forward. The HUD sat ahead of his focus, giving him an augmented view of the field. He looked past the Kips to the side of the dreadnought. Why would they be sitting there like that, out of all the places to wait in reserve?

His eyes traveled the area. His Moray shuddered around him, and new targets appeared, the enemy's forward wings regrouping and coming back to mop up the stranded Alliance fighters. There was no time left. What was he even looking for?

His eyes crossed a raised section of the hull where a shield generator was visible. He swept his eyes across and found the second. He looked downward, to where a third generator rested. He looked back up, taking note of the first.

There was something about it. Something... wrong. His p-rat beeped, alerting him to the enemy fighters that were working to get a lock on him. He took evasive action almost subconsciously, keeping his eyes on the dreadnought.

Too wide. The space between the shield generators was too damn wide! The generators formed a net, a lattice of energy that functioned as both a repulsor and a secondary point defense, working to vaporize and push against anything that it came into contact with. In space, even the smallest molecule could punch through the strongest hull if it had enough velocity. Even out of war zones shields were needed to prevent random space junk from threatening hull integrity.

For some reason, the dreadnought's generator positions were too wide. It meant that the net was inherently weaker in that area. Orders of magnitude weaker. That was why the ships were arranged around it. They were guarding a massive mistake in the design.

Mitchell couldn't believe it. How could it be real? How could they make a mistake like that? The Federation? How could they have done that math wrong? It denied any sense of logic, any attempt at reason.

It was a miracle.

All they had to do was take advantage of it.

"Athena, the shield spacing is off. There's a weak point behind those fighters."

If they could get through them. If they could get to that spot... Each Moray carried a single small warhead in its belly. The ship was too big to suffer the same fate as the Greylock, but the trouble spot was close to the reactor. If they could get a shot at that point, they might be able to cause catastrophic damage.

"First Squadron, engage the fighters," Ella said. The tone changed, signaling that she was sending the message out to whoever was left. "All remaining fighters, form up and engage at these coordinates. This war isn't over yet. Ares, you're with me. Let's go plant a nuke up their ass."

"Roger," Mitchell said.

They split from the squadron while the remaining ten Morays raced ahead towards the enemy defense. The Kips came to life, opening fire at the same time they began vectoring forward to intercept.

"You need to keep my ass clear," Ella said over their private channel.

"You know I love to watch your ass."

"We'll circle around and drop down on it, and try to take them by surprise."

"Roger that."

The two fighters dipped and thrust forward, streaking beneath the belly of the dreadnought. They slipped left and right around the point defense batteries, using their size and agility to pass more quickly than the targeting computers could adjust their aim. They reached the other side and vectored up along it, and then spun and came back the other way. An enemy Kip greeted them on the topside, launching a salvo that they easily outmaneuvered. Mitchell swung wide around the fighter in a looping roll, coming within a few dozen meters before firing pulse lasers at the ship. The blue flashes of shields caught the first few strikes before the fighter's small generator was overwhelmed and the next strike poured into and through the cockpit.

"Are you ready for this?" Ella asked.

"Affirmative," Mitchell replied. "Let's bring them hell."

They returned to the port side of the dreadnought where the fighting was the most intense. Twenty of the Greylock pilots remained, their Morays darting and skittering among the Kips, trading laser fire and missile salvos. Mitchell clenched his jaw when he saw Achilles' fighter go dark, a critical system pierced by a laser, leaving the ship to float out into space. It would only be a matter of time before something in the heavy field of debris pierced his cockpit and sent him to his final end.

They folded over the dreadnought.

A dozen of the Kips rose up to meet them.

They hadn't been surprised at all.

"Shit," Mitchell shouted. He thrust forward, cutting ahead of Ella and opening fire, his line of sight blinded by the flashes from his shields. The integrity monitor in the HUD plummeted.

When the shield ionization cleared enough for him to see, there were two dead Kips floating away from them and ten more still in their path.

"I can't get a clean shot," Ella said. "The warhead has to detonate in that frigger or it won't have the blast power to do anything."

"I'll get you closer," Mitchell replied.

Vectoring thrusters fired along the port side, rolling and throwing him around, orienting him on the enemy fighters. He opened up his gun battery, letting the slugs continue to fire as he rocked and rolled the Moray. It was cover fire, poorly aimed and likely not enough to breach their shields. The ammunition would only last a few seconds. He hoped it would be enough.

"Mitchell." Ella's voice crackled over the p-rat on their private channel. It was soft and tinged with sadness.

"Ella, no," he replied. He knew immediately by the tone of her voice what she intended.

"There's no other way," she said. "I won't let us lose."

He found her on his HUD. The cover fire had cleared a few of the Kips, but there were more, so many more. She was the most amazing pilot he had ever seen; the elite of the elite. She danced between them, her Moray twisting and moving in a way that nobody could match. She drew closer to the dreadnought, keeping the fighter so nimble that the Kips couldn't get a bead. His heart pounded, ready to burst with respect and love and pride and fear.

She drew ever closer to the dreadnought, an avenging angel on the wings of fury.

"Damn it, Ella," he whispered across the channel.

"I love you, too, Mitch. Take care of yourself for me."

It was impossible. Amazing. Terrifying. Her Moray burst through the line of fighters, a hundred meters from the dreadnought.

The CAP-NN caught the signature of her warhead activating.

Inside her fighter.

Mitchell stopped breathing. Everything froze at that moment except for the streak of thrusters from the rear of Ella's ship. Then it too was gone, joined with the chink in the behemoth's armor and then expanded by the force of the nuclear explosion.

MITCHELL WAS STILL SITTING at the table when Evan entered the bar. The Corporal didn't even need to scan the floor, his eyes shooting right to the corner.

"You were supposed to meet me at the hotel," he said. He found a chair, slid it over to the table, and sat down.

"I didn't invite you," Mitchell said. His eyes were red and his voice was dry despite how much he'd already had to drink.

"Can I join you?"

"No."

Evan leaned in, keeping his voice low. "Look Mitch, I know you've been having a hard time since Ella died. This stuff," he waved at the empty bottle of whiskey on the table, "It isn't going to help."

Mitchell didn't react. They'd had this conversation before. Two days ago. He was tired of hearing it.

"She's the hero," he said. "She died to save this planet, and all she gets is a posthumous Medal of Courage and her name on a plaque. What the hell am I doing to honor her? I'm running around pretending that I took the damn Shot Heard 'Round the Universe and screwing rich celebrities."

"Beautiful, rich celebrities," Evan said.

"That's not the point."

"You've heard this before, Captain, but it seems when you're fuzzy you need to have it spelled out. The Alliance got owned by *one* Federation dreadnought. One. Try to let that sink into your neurons again. The fact is, we've been under-budgeted and stretched too thin for decades. Jeez, outside of the Moray and maybe the Zombie, our equipment is inferior, and getting more inferior every year. Corporations running economies? They're spinning figure-eights around us, and testing the value of things like freedom and choice with every new piece of tech they put into the field. Do you know what it means to public relations to have you running out there and building support? Do you know what it means to enlistment numbers, or when budgets are set next year? We can't do that with a corpse."

Mitchell's drunk, angry glare was only slightly less threatening than his regular angry glare.

"All I'm saying is that this is bigger than you and me. I know the brass is feeding you the bullshit to spill on live streams, but you can't tell me you don't believe in any of it."

"You don't think I know all of this. I'm tired of being a pony. I'm more useful out there, as part of this thing. I'm a frigging pilot."

"Not anymore. Now you're a figurehead. There are a lot of perks."

Mitchell thought of Tamara. It was fun, but it didn't mean that much to him when his guard was down. That she was a rich celebrity? There were plenty of poor, unknown prostitutes with nice bodies and a lot of enthusiasm. "I'm a fraud. A complete fraud."

"That wasn't your decision to make. The Space Marines own you. The Alliance owns you. They want you to be their poster boy. You don't have to like it, you just have to do it. Soldier up, Captain."

Mitchell sighed and tried to decide if he should punch the Corporal or not. "Tough love again?"

"I keep trying a different approach. You're a stubborn son of a bitch, and I'm tired of having this conversation."

"I want to get back in a cockpit."

"We both know that isn't going to happen. You're done with combat."

Another sigh. "I need another drink."

Evan put his hand on Mitchell's shoulder. "We have to get going, Captain. We're running behind schedule as it is. The transport's waiting at the spaceport, the car's waiting at the hotel."

Mitchell was still for a few seconds. He stared down at the empty shot glass, and then nodded. When he was drinking, he always decided he preferred to be sober. When he was sober, he always wanted to be drinking. "Trapped like a rat in a cage."

"A well-fed rat in a gilded cage."

That one earned a small smile. Mitchell put his hand down on the table and shook his head lightly, feeling the world start to spin. The alcohol inhibitor in his gut let him get just wasted enough to be vulnerable, but not enough to completely lose his senses.

"Which planet are we headed to?" he asked, circling around the table. He had seen it pass by on his p-rat, but he hadn't paid much attention.

"Kolmar."

"Really?"

"I know, it's a mining planet. We get some of our highest enlistment rates from there. I mean, given a choice would you rather pilot a digger or a Zombie?"

He put his arm over Mitchell's shoulder and shifted in front of the Marine, looking him in the eye and preparing to give him advice as if they were friends. If Mitch had been sober, he might have punched him for it.

"Look, Mitch, I know the situation isn't what you-"

A shrill tone sounded in Mitchell's inner ear. Evan's head pitched forward at almost the same time, the front of it breaking apart and spraying him with flesh, blood, and bone.

He reacted out of pure instinct, his years of training working faster than his mind could figure out what had just happened. He took a tighter hold of Evan's corpse and ducked beneath it, at the same time feeling his body begin to warm. His neural implant flooded him with adrenaline, pushing away the inebriated haze. He looked past Evan and watched more holes appear in the clear carbonate, feeling the shock of each slug burying itself deep into the Corporal's flesh. If the force hadn't been reduced by the window, the shots would have gone right through both of them.

Mitchell dropped Evan and rolled to the side, finding his AZ-9 and bringing it to his hand. He came up behind a table, looking out the window and up towards an office on the other side of the street. His p-rat showed him the residual signature of a high-powered rifle. Both it and its user were gone.

He connected his p-rat to central dispatch. "Command, this is Captain Williams. Corporal Kwon is down. I'm under attack."

A clinical, emotionless voice replied. "We have your position, Captain. The authorities are being notified, and a team is being deployed."

"Like I'm going to wait for a team," he mumbled, dropping the connection. He stayed crouched behind the table, his eyes scanning the street. A dark car slid to a stop in front of the building, black window descending to reveal the end of a heavy rifle.

"You can't do that with a corpse," Mitchell spat.

The assassins might have expected him to run away, to try to evade their fire. He did the opposite, breaking from behind the table and sprinting towards the door.

The rifle opened fire, spraying the front of the bar. The bullets screamed around him, his aggressive maneuver throwing the shooter's aim just enough. A bullet tore clean through his right shoulder, his p-rat showing the damage in the corner of his eye, assessing and sending stimulants and healing drugs from a second implant in his buttocks. Another shot hit him in the same arm. If he hadn't been left-handed, he would have dropped his gun.

Instead, he brought it up and took two shots into the car. The rifle stopped firing. The driver's side door opened, and a man slid out and started aiming. Mitchell rapid-fired six more rounds. The first four skipped off the roof of the car, the last two hit the driver in the face.

He could hear sirens now, the York police dispatched ahead of the military for faster local response. He thought about stopping and letting them handle the cleanup. No. Someone across the street had killed Evan, and he wasn't about to let them get away.

He kept running towards the dark car, jumping and using the open window to vault up and over it. He shoulder-rolled on the other side, a little awkward on his left, and got to his feet, running for the front of the office building. Everything had happened so fast, he doubted the shooter could have gotten down from their perch yet.

He pushed his way past the bystanders who had paused in the street to watch, shoving a man in a suit aside and squeezing through the door before it could finish opening for him. His eyes tracked across the lobby, finding the banks of lifts near the center. A security guard was standing to his left, his hand on the butt of his gun, hesitating to draw on a man in military dress.

"Where are the stairs?" Mitchell asked. He knew he must look frightening. His right arm was a bloody mess, his shirt soaked through. He didn't feel the pain at all. Space Marines were trained to take a beating.

"That way," the guard said, pointing to the right of the lifts.

"Is there another way out from there?"

"Service entrance is in the back."

"Is it guarded?"

"Yes."

"Show me. As fast as you can."

The guard started running towards the back. He led Mitchell into the stairwell, where an opposite door had been kicked open, leading into the service area. It was a large room with four loading bays and access to the thermal systems below. A second guard was on the floor not far from the door, blood pooling around his body.

"Oh, damn," the guard said.

Mitchell didn't hear him. He crouched and entered the room,

sweeping the area with the AZ-9. He found the rear exit. The door was closed.

He charged ahead, leaping down the raised service platform towards the door. He shoved his shoulder against it, slamming it open at the same time the soft whine of an engine sounded to his right. He turned his head to see a figure mounted on a bike. He tried to rotate around to get his left hand, and the AZ-9, up to fire at the same time the bike began to accelerate away. He took four shots, scuffing the side of the building across the alley but missing the assassin completely.

A moment later they were gone.

"Damn it," Mitchell cursed. He stared down the empty alley for a few seconds, until his vision was blurred by a drop of blood that rolled into his eye. He used his finger to wipe it away, confused when his entire palm came back red.

He didn't remember being shot in the head. He hadn't felt it, and the p rat wasn't showing it.

He blinked a few times. The p-rat wasn't showing anything. When had that happened?

He started to feel dizzy. He put a hand to his chest. His heart rate slowed. Everything was getting warm. Flashing lights bounced off the windows, filling his blurring eyes. A shape headed towards him. Law enforcement.

"Captain?" the officer said. "Are you okay?"

Mitchell tried to speak, finding it impossible. The stimulants should have been keeping him up and alert, but they couldn't do that if the implant were malfunctioning.

"Captain?"

Mitchell collapsed.

[5]

EARTH. May 17, 2035

"Give it back."

Kathy darted across the field, a baseball cap in her outstretched hand, shaking it to tease her victim.

"Kathy, stop."

Michael chased behind her. He was big for his age, overweight, too slow.

"Come on, beluga. You can catch me," Kathy said, turning around and running backward, waving the cap at him.

"I can't. Nobody can catch you."

She laughed and stopped the chase. It was true. She was the fastest runner in her class. Maybe in her whole school. She was lean and lithe, her young body already in top shape from a rigorous after-school schedule that included martial arts, yoga, ballet, gymnastics. Anything that was physical and challenging. That and violin lessons. She hated violin lessons.

"Here," she said, walking back to Michael and handing him the hat. "You're no fun."

"I am fun," he said. "Just not when you make me run."

They both laughed at that.

"Let's go back with the others," Michael said, pointing back to the playground where the other ten-year-olds were on swings and slides, or kicking a ball between them.

"Okay."

They started walking back. They'd gone about halfway when Kathy stopped.

"Kathy?" Michael asked, noticing she had paused. She was standing completely still, not even blinking. "Are you okay?"

She turned slowly, her body twisting, her head arching up towards the nearly cloudless sky. She had stopped because she had heard something. No, she had felt something. Something familiar. Something that told her she needed to look up at that precise moment.

There was nothing.

Blue sky, the glare of the sun in the corner of her left eye. Her imagination running away with her again.

"Kathy?" Michael repeated.

Still, she didn't look away. She couldn't. She could feel something. A charge in the air that hadn't been there a few seconds ago. A strange pressure in her ears.

She felt a hand on her shoulder.

"Kathy, come on. What game are you playing now?"

She reached up and shoved it away. "Just wait."

"What are you looking at?" A moment later, "There's nothing up-"

Except there was. She saw it now. So did Michael. A dark spot against the ocean, a sliver of void.

"What is that?" Michael said. "An airplane?"

She didn't know what it was. Not an airplane. It was something. Something big.

It was getting closer.

A rumble sounded from up there. Way, way up. It was gentle at first, as soft as a purring cat. It seemed to be ahead of the spot, and at the same time trailing it, or maybe circling all around it. As the spot got larger, the rumble got louder.

The playground fell silent.

The others had noticed now. They heard the sound and they looked up. The dark spot had grown and shifted into a longer shape, more like a bullet or a spear.

Seconds passed.

The front of it lit like a match, a small red spot at first, and then a flare of sparks, red and blue and white that spread around it, wrapping it like a blanket. The rumbling grew louder, loud enough to shake the ground they were standing on.

Then it was silent.

The thing was still there. It was still falling. From space, Kathy knew. It had to be entering the atmosphere to be burning like that. She stared at it in wonder, eyes wide and unblinking, heart racing in the excitement. It was trailing across the sky now, sparks and smoke and small bits of debris flowing out behind it. It was coming faster and faster, outpacing the sound of its travel, rocketing across the sky, reaching the face of the sun and momentarily blotting it out in its mass.

She could almost see it, rounded and sleek in its speed. It was approaching the horizon in a hurry, reaching the edge of her sky almost as fast as it had arrived. For all its size, it was still so high. She knew it wouldn't stay there. It was going to come down. It was going to crash somewhere, whatever it was. An asteroid? A satellite? A secret military weapon? An alien? There were too many possibilities.

It was the most amazing thing she had ever seen.

It vanished over the edge of some trees and houses that rested outside the school grounds, a massive hulk of a form. Too big to be a satellite. Too big to be anything manmade, and she hadn't seen anything online about any asteroids passing close by anytime soon.

Kathy closed her eyes. The thing had passed them by, spared them from the fury of its impact. Would everyone be so lucky? Where was it going to hit? How many would be killed?

The sound caught up to them, a deafening roar that shook the trees and caused some of the children behind her to start screaming in fear. She felt Michael take her hand in his, and for once she didn't shake him off. Not because she was scared. Because she was happy. All of her life she had dreamed of the stars. All of her life she had felt that there was something out there. She had read every e-book she could find about the space program and the moon landings. She idolized the astronauts who had made their way off the planet and out there, before budget cuts and fiscal restraint had caused a once curious species to resort to small, unmanned exploration and leave the people glued to the planet.

This. This was something. She knew it. She had been training her body, training her mind as if she would one day become one of those astronauts she had read about. As if she would one day make the trip up there. To her, there had never been a question of if, only one of how.

Something told her she had her answer.

6

"Ares."

"Ella? Am I dreaming?"

"Not exactly."

"Where am I?"

"Find it."

"Find what?"

"Goliath. They're coming. Find it."

"What? Who's coming?"

"They're going to fix it. Don't forget."

Mitchell opened his eyes. He could see the robotic arms of the medical bots positioned over him, rotating and shifting around his right side, picking shrapnel from his wounds, cleaning them out, and gluing him back together. He was too drugged up to feel any pain from it. In fact, he couldn't feel anything below the neck at all, a sensation that might have panicked a civilian.

It wasn't the first time he had been shot. He was a Space Marine.

He didn't remember how he had gotten here. He remembered the gunfire, the chase. He remembered passing out.

Evan was dead. Damn.

"You're lucky," a man said from his left.

Mitchell couldn't move his head, but he shifted his eyes so he could see the doctor in his peripheral vision. An older man with a white flattop and a beard on a narrow face.

"The arm. One more inch down and the bullet would have exploded your elbow joint. We would have replaced it with a bionic."

"That's lucky?"

The doctor grunted. "I bet you've heard bionics are the best thing since the cure for cancer? I won't say they don't have their benefits, but they have drawbacks too."

"Like what?"

"They aren't the real thing. Flesh and blood." He came closer to Mitchell, moving to his right side and leaning down to inspect his head. "You were doubly lucky. One of the bullets grazed your temple. It managed to short your implant, but you didn't die. I'm Dr. Drummond, by the way."

They're going to fix it. Don't forget.

Mitchell blinked. Had he imagined the voice in his head? Ella's voice. It had felt like she was talking to him through his p-rat, as though the damaged implant had given him a conduit to the afterlife.

It was a stupid idea.

"Nice to meet you, doc. I heard a voice. While I was out."

"Mmmhmmm. I'm not surprised. Like I said, your implant was damaged. A crew was already rushed in to repair it, but sometimes the new circuits and the reset causes a bit of bio-feedback. I wouldn't worry too much about it."

"So, it's normal?"

It certainly hadn't felt normal. It had been so real. Like she was here, instead of gone.

"Perfectly." He went over to the side of the room, out of Mitchell's vision. He returned a moment later with a small patch on his fingertip. "I'm going to put this over the wound on your head. It should seal everything up back to normal within the next few hours. Normally, we'd keep you here for observation, but Command wanted you out of sickbay an hour ago." He pushed the small patch to Mitchell's head.

Mitchell blinked again, feeling a jolt of electricity run through his brain.

"Why the rush?" he asked.

"Beats me," Drummond said. "I'm just the doctor."

The three sets of robotic arms finished patching the rest of him. They retreated along a rail towards the back of the room. Dr. Drummond moved to his side and checked their work. "Mmmhmmm. I don't know why they still have us verifying the medical bots. It's not like they ever make a mistake. That's government bureaucracy for you."

He moved out of view again, and a moment later Mitchell's whole body began to feel warm, the feeling slowly returning to his limbs. He flexed his fingers, the pins and needles beginning to subside.

"Good as new," Drummond said. "Once you can sit up, access your ARR and confirm that it's functional."

Mitchell pushed himself up, forcing his muscles to work despite their weariness. Shocks ran all along his body in protest, but he didn't let that stop him. He turned and swung his legs off the side of the gurney, unconcerned with his nakedness. He focused on his left side, to where the p-rat was displaying his vitals.

"Everything appears to be normal," he said.

Dr. Drummond was staring at him. "Mmmhmmm. I've never seen someone come out of paralyzation that fast."

Mitchell smiled. "I've done this a few times before. You get used to it."

"No, Captain. Most people don't get used to it."

Mitchell shrugged and pushed himself to his feet. His legs felt a little bit weak, but he shook them until all of the prickliness faded.

"I could use some clothes."

Dr. Drummond pointed to the left. "In there. Get dressed, and then come back and sign your discharge."

Mitchell went through the hatch on the left, into a sparse dressing room. A new uniform was waiting for him there. He started putting it on at the same time he accessed the p-rat.

"Ella?" he whispered, sending the thought through the neural implant.

There was no reply. Of course there wasn't. He was being stupid. Drummond said it was normal.

He finished dressing, enjoying the feel of the new, pressed uniform on his skin. He checked himself in the mirror. They had shaved his head in order to clean the wound, a look he hadn't sported since his last mech drop on... He struggled to remember. There had been so many planets. He knew it had been six months ago.

It felt like a lifetime.

He put his hand to the patch on his temple. Dr. Drummond was right that he was lucky to be alive. If the bullet that grazed his skull had been an inch to the left...

"Captain Mitchell Williams?"

She was standing in the sick room when he came out. She was a serious woman, fit and pretty. Dark hair tinged with wisps of gray that fell to her shoulder-blades, a narrow face and sharp features. A beige complexion matched with bright blue eyes. Her uniform was crisp, newly pressed and positioned just-so on her lean frame. She had opted for the skirt, revealing long, smooth legs that ended in a pair of standard issue pumps.

"You aren't Dr. Drummond," he said.

"Did you make that assessment on your own, or did your ARR help you with that?"

"Cute. Let me guess, you're my new handler?"

"My name is Major Christine Arapo. And yes, I'm your new handler."

"Major?" They had sent in someone who outranked him.

"Let me be blunt with you, Captain," she said. "I know what

happened at the Battle for Liberty. I know what Command is making you do. And, I know that you don't like it."

"I especially don't like the part where I get shot."

Her eyes narrowed. "I also know you were supposed to be on a shuttle off Liberty thirty minutes before the attempt on your life. An attempt that would not have been made if you had been on that shuttle. An attempt that left Corporal Evan Kwon and four civilians dead. The fact that you were shot was an avoidable situation that you created. Do you follow me, Captain?"

Mitchell stared at her for a moment, feeling his heart skip. Corporal Kwon dying was bad enough. He hadn't known about the civilian casualties. "Yes, ma'am."

"Good. I'll continue to be frank, Captain. General Cornelius sent me this assignment himself, but that doesn't mean I'm happy about it. I didn't spend the last twenty years working my ass to Major only to have my reward be to babysit a Space Marine whose diaper is too tight."

Mitchell was silent. It was the best thing to do in the situation.

"You signed up for this, Captain. For the next ten years, your life belongs to us. That means you're property. Command tells you to go onto streams with your pretty face and work the crowd, that's what you do. Command tells you to screw the Queen of Talk, that's what you do."

He wondered how she knew about that already.

"You don't go and cry into your beer. You don't get your fellow officers killed. And you damned well don't put civilians in the line of fire. Is that understood, Captain?"

"Yes, ma'am." He barked it out, putting himself at full attention.

She softened then, just a little. He wondered if she'd been expecting him to protest. "There's a reason we change your travel plans last minute, Captain, and it isn't because we like paying expediting fees. Security wasn't clear on whether the threat was on Cestus or Liberty, so we tried to get you far away from both."

That explained why they were heading to Kolmar. The planet was right near the inner edge of the Rim.

"Permission to speak frankly, Major?"

She caught his eyes with her own. "Granted."

"If Command were more transparent with me on the threats, instead of treating me like a baby whose diapey is too tight, we could have avoided this, ma'am. I may enjoy the occasional drink. I don't enjoy getting people killed."

She nodded. "I've advised Command of the same. Obviously, you knew something about the threats. The AZ-9 isn't exactly a subtle choice."

"As I've said, ma'am. It doesn't take a genius to suspect that the Federation might be a little bit pissed at me for blowing up their prized starship. Thanks to Command, they don't know they have the wrong guy."

"Which is how it will stay. At ease, Captain. What can you tell me about the one that got away?"

Mitchell let his body relax. "Not much, ma'am. All I saw of them was their back. They were wearing black riding skins, and they were tall. Six feet, maybe?"

"Gender?"

"I don't know. They were wearing a helmet. I would guess male by their build, but I've seen female Marines with that kind of stature before."

"Age?"

"I don't know. I'm sorry, Major, I didn't get much of a look. What about the two I killed?"

"No prints, no identification. They had military p-rats, but they'd been updated with black market firmware. Our best guess is mercenaries. We're working with the Liberty government to figure out how and when they made planetfall."

"I wouldn't mind going after them, ma'am. I owe them for Corporal Kwon."

"I'm sure you know that won't be possible. How is your arm feeling?"

Mitchell lifted and rotated it. The bots had done their job. "A little stiff. I'll be good as new in a couple of days."

"Excellent. I'm sure you know, we can't afford to have you out of action for long. Fortunately, your shootout downtown has only added to your cachet. The media hasn't even mentioned the bystanders that were killed, only that you single-handedly stopped a terrorist attack by the Federation."

"Terrorist attack?"

"Yes. That was my idea."

Mitchell tried not to draw back when she smiled. There was a predator that lived in the jungles on Kepler that the scientists had named an Osset. It was a frightening large, blue, cat-like creature that displayed the unusually human characteristic of hunting purely for sport.

That's what she reminded him of.

"I'll send Dr. Drummond back in so you can finalize your discharge. Report to the officer's barracks. They'll set you up with a room for the remainder of the night. I'll meet you in the morning, oh seven hundred, and we'll review your itinerary moving forward."

"Yes, ma'am," Mitchell said.

Major Arapo took a couple of steps towards the exit, and then stopped. She looked back at him. "We're going to be spending a lot of time together, Captain, so please, call me Christine. As long as you behave yourself we can remain casual. That doesn't mean we're friends, or that I won't shake you down if you test me. I hope you'll work with me because I'm looking out for you, and for the Alliance, and not because of my rank."

Mitchell forced a smile. He wasn't convinced she wasn't focused on what was best for her and her career. "I'll do my best, Christine."

"See that you do better than that."

She closed the door behind her, leaving him alone. He heard her voice for a minute through the hatch, and then Dr. Drummond returned.

"She's a beauty, isn't she?" he said.

"Major Arapo?" Mitchell asked. "Are you familiar with the praying mantis?"

Dr. Drummond laughed. "At least it ends on a good note."

"She might be right for you. She's a little old for me."

"I prefer the word 'experienced,' Captain."

Mitchell felt the doctor's knock on his p-rat. He accepted the discharge form and attached his sig to it, and then sent it back.

"A woman like that... I don't think I want her experience," Mitchell said. He put out his hand. "Thanks for putting me back together, doc."

Dr. Drummond took it. "The bots did all the work, but you're welcome."

Mitchell was standing at the open hatch to the sick room when he felt Dr. Drummond's hand come down on his shoulder.

"Mmmhmmm. Ares. Find Goliath."

Mitchell spun around so fast that the doctor stumbled away from him.

"What did you say?"

"What?" Dr. Drummond asked.

"What did you just say?"

"I said take care of yourself, Captain." The doctor stared at him. "Are you sure you're okay? I can run another diagnostic."

Mitchell shook his head. He hoped the bullet hadn't done more damage than they realized. "No. I'm okay. Just a little jumpy, I think."

Dr. Drummond didn't look convinced. It didn't matter. Mitchell had already signed the discharge.

He left the infirmary without another word.

7

Major Arapo knocked on his p-rat the following morning, at precisely oh seven hundred hours. Mitchell had been awake for three hours prior, the thirty-four hour days on Liberty offering him a little more recuperation time than he might have been granted on Earth. He'd used the time to go through his typical morning run followed by a round of intense PE that helped him try to work his arm back into its normal range of motion. The run had given him a chance to clear his head. By the time he'd returned to his room sweaty and awake, he had come to the conclusion that the voice in his head was exactly what Dr. Drummond had said it was - nothing more than a minor glitch caused by the repair of his neural implant.

A quick clean up and a new uniform, and then he was left waiting on a gel sofa, using his p-rat to scan through the local news. Of course, the attack from the day before was splashed everywhere he looked, followed by election polls and updates on rebuilding projects around the city. The media had completely bought into the whole terrorist plot angle, playing it up as if all of Liberty had been under siege.

"Good morning, Mitchell," Christine said when he opened the

hatch to his room. The Major looked exactly the same as she had the night before, as though she had spent the entire time since he had last seen her frozen in suspended animation.

"Good morning, ma'am," he said.

"Christine. Please, Mitchell." She continued to stand at the entrance to his room.

"Right. Since we're on friendly terms, Mitch will do. You can come in whenever you're ready."

She didn't lose her stoic expression as she crossed the threshold. A signal in his ear sounded when she pushed a document to him.

"I'm sending you an updated itinerary."

Mitchell scanned it. "We're staying on Liberty?"

"Yes. For another four days. It was Security's recommendation, based on the data models."

"They already tried to kill me here and failed, so this is where I'm the most safe."

"Yes. Something like that."

"What about the one that got away?"

"We found the bike abandoned at the spaceport. We're operating under the assumption that they fled."

"Do you think that's the right assumption?" he asked.

"No. We'll have a team trailing us while we're here on Liberty. They'll keep you safe."

Mitchell smiled. "You want them to try again." It was a statement, not a question.

She shrugged. "Let's just say Command wouldn't be disappointed to have a shot at capturing the assassin. If there's a chance at learning where and how they were hired, it might give us a vector to plant someone."

"Into the Federation? Good luck with that."

"In the meantime, arrangements are being made to host a gala for you tomorrow night, in recognition of your heroism yesterday."

"What heroism? Five people died because of me. A fact that you didn't hesitate to point out yourself."

"And I reprimanded you accordingly. As far as the people of Liberty are concerned, you saved them. Again."

Mitchell shook his head. "What will Command do if the truth ever finds its way out to the public?"

"It won't."

"How do you know?"

Christine was silent. Mitchell waited for an answer, and when it didn't come, he returned his attention to his new schedule. They would spend the rest of the morning visiting campuses around the city, and then the afternoon at a heavy equipment manufacturing plant, cheering on the workers who were pumping out the mechs that were rebuilding the planet's infrastructure. He had another interview later in the evening with a local stream in Bethesda, a smaller city on the other side of the globe. Then they would circle back to Liberty to prepare for the big party.

"I did get shot yesterday, you know," he said, closing the list, and his eyes. He suddenly felt tired.

"That's hardly a grueling schedule, Mitch. Show up, shake hands, say a few words, eat, drink, and... on second thought, don't drink."

"I wouldn't dream of it."

Her left eye twitched as she checked her p-rat. "Transportation is here. Are you ready to go?"

"Almost." He stood and entered the bedroom. His AZ-9 had been left at the base of his bed, cleaned and reloaded, along with a small magnetic clip to help him hide it more efficiently beneath his uniform. He mounted it in easy reach and returned to the living area, flashing it to the Major. "I got the feeling you wanted me to keep carrying this."

"We can't let you run around defenseless."

He followed her out to the waiting transport. It was a long-range personal carrier, a long, windowless rectangle with a wedge-shaped nose that rested on a pair of repulsor nacelles, making it able to move in both ground and aerial lanes of traffic. The hatch opened as they approached, and they hopped inside and took up positions in the rear pair of cushioned seats. High-resolution cameras transformed the solid walls into windows on both sides of them, offering a view that scared people who didn't do much flying. Mitchell glanced forward in search of a cockpit. More and more carriers were returning to human pilots, part of the Alliance's economic initiatives to reverse a centuries-long trend of automation and robotic replacement. This one was still completely AI controlled.

The hatch slid closed and the transport rocketed forward and up, inertial negators absorbing the g-forces for the passengers. It felt like they weren't moving at all, though the view from outside made it obvious they were.

"First stop is Liberty University," Christine said. "We arranged a quick recruitment fair. We'll set you up at the front of it to sign autographs and answer questions about life as a Space Marine. World Stream will be by at some point for wider coverage."

"If I don't look excited, it's only because I'm saving it all for later," Mitchell said. It was meant to be a joke, but Christine didn't show any signs of a sense of humor. "Never mind."

They continued the trip in silence. Mitchell could tell the Major was using her p-rat the entire time, probably handling whatever business she had been forced to drop to attend to him. She was more than public relations. That much he was sure of.

"What branch?" he asked, breaking the silence.

"Excuse me?" she said.

"I was just wondering what branch of the military you did field duty in, before you moved to PR. You're too..." He tried to think of a word that wouldn't come across as offensive. "Fit... to have always been in marketing."

She paused, trying to decide whether or not to answer him.

"Army," she said at last. "I wanted to be a Space Marine, but I failed the neural testing."

All of the military's neural implants were equal. The Marine's version was just a little more equal, and a Marine pilot's was even more equal than that. The Marine's base model required an ability to handle an increased power draw on the body due to the added support systems and more robust algorithms. Mitchell's version also contained the interface for the CAP-NN system that helped him pilot the fighters and mechs with better skill and efficiency than the automated systems that had come before him; like the one flying the transport. Either way, neural aptitude was a genetic trait, not really a failure. You were either born with the juice or you weren't. You either had the right makeup to communicate with CAP-NN or you didn't. Mitchell had heard rumors there were initiatives underway to change those facts, but it was too late for the Major.

"Being a ground-pounder is nothing to be ashamed of. It takes a lot of guts to run around in an exosuit without mech support."

"Who said I was ashamed?" She glared at him with angry eyes. Defensive. "For that matter, where did you get the idea that I was in public relations?"

"You said you were my handler. Corporal Kwon was PR."

Christine started laughing. "I'm not PR."

"Then what are you?"

"Not PR."

"Come on, Chris-"

"Stow it, Captain."

Mitchell closed his mouth. He was used to secrets. Besides, he could guess what she was by looking at her. Command didn't want him surrounded by security. Planting a Special Ops agent as his rep was the next best thing.

8

"CAPTAIN WILLIAMS, it's an honor to meet you."

He couldn't have been more than eighteen, fresh-faced and wide-eyed to be in the presence of the Alliance's newest and most visible celebrity. He was wearing a high collar and tight gold vest with three-quarter length pants and molded boots, a popular fashion on Liberty at the moment.

He held out his hand. It was pale and delicate.

Mitchell took it and shook, careful to squeeze hard enough that the Space Marine machismo was communicated, and soft enough that he didn't break the kid's hand.

"Great to meet you, too. Thanks for stopping by," he said. "What's your name?"

"Aldus, sir."

"Aldus. That's an interesting name." A stupid name.

"It's the name of the first scientist who entered XENO-1. My parents are huuuuuggggeeee history lovers. Especially XENO-1. They had so many books on it, and I read every one."

Mitchell smiled and nodded, glancing to his left. Major Arapo had positioned herself near the rear of the small enclosure, keeping an eye on him and the students who were filing in to meet him, take a poster and enlistment packet, and walk back out. There was a Private at the door making sure only one person could enter at a time.

Excellence University was the third of the five schools on their itinerary for the morning. Mitchell accessed his p-rat and checked the time. Another hour here, and then an hour at the other two campuses, which were each less than a five minute transport ride.

"XENO-1," Mitchell parroted, not really listening to the student. "I'm not that familiar." He pulled up a stream in his p-rat, some kind of romantic comedy or something. He switched streams.

"Really? The alien starship that crashed on Earth? The reason we're even standing here?"

Mitchell kept nodding, playing along. "Oh. Yeah. I remember now." He didn't. "Do you have anything you want me to sign?"

"No, but I did want you to remember Goliath."

Mitchell dropped the p-rat overlay and glared at the boy, who smiled sheepishly, his face turning red.

"What did you just say?" Mitchell asked.

"I didn't bring anything. I was in a rush to get here before the line got too long."

"No, you said something else. Goliath?"

"No, sir."

"You did," Mitchell insisted. He leaned forward, and the student shied away.

"I was talking about XENO-1. The Goliath was the first starship that was built from the tech that was recovered from it. I didn't say anything about it though. Maybe you just extrapolated it in your mind?" He kept retreating towards the door.

Christine was at his side a moment later. "Is there a problem, Captain?"

Mitchell looked at Aldus. The boy was terrified. He straightened up and spread his friendliest smile.

"No. No problem. Aldus and I were just discussing history. Did you know he's named after the first scientist who entered XENO-1?"

"Mmmmm. Did you get an enlistment packet, Aldus?"

Aldus shook his head. "No, ma'am. I don't want to enlist. I'm studying to be an engineer. I have a full scholarship from Kurida Heavy Machines."

"Are you sure? We have a contract with Kurida. They allow their engineers to work on military projects after five years of employment. You can enroll into the program now if you want."

He kept backing away. "Not today, thank you, ma'am. Captain Williams, thank you again." He ducked out of the enclosure, giving Mitchell a few seconds to regain his composure.

"What was that about?" Christine asked.

"Nothing," Mitchell said. He fixed his posture and held the smile. He sent the message out to the Private at the door that he was ready for the next visitor.

She was nineteen or twenty, with short, spiked brown hair and a clear, carbonate nose ring that held the tiny broken abdomens of flash bugs piled inside, causing it to flicker. She wore a shirt that barely covered her breasts, and shorts that could have been easily mistaken for panties.

Or maybe they were panties?

"Wow, you're more gorgeous in person than you are on the streams," she said.

He wasn't sure how that could be. The streams were sharper than real-life, their filtering designed to minimize atmospheric interference, even skin tones, and balance lighting.

"Thank you," he said, maintaining his composure. They had prepared him to handle all kinds of people making all kinds of comments.

She held out her tablet, a foldable piece of e-paper that currently sported a picture of him completely naked, a heavy rifle slung over his shoulder and his CAP-NN helmet in front of his groin. He fought not to laugh as he took it from her and swung his finger along the picture to sign it. It was a photoshop, a fake. They'd taken his head and attached it to another model. The physique was pretty close, and the helmet had been well blended. As for the rifle... He would never carry anything that big. There was no room in the cockpit for something like that.

"You know that isn't really me?" he said.

"It is when I'm alone at night," she replied.

Mitchell smiled. "You dream about me?"

"While I play with myself."

He fought to stay neutral. Maybe they hadn't prepared him well enough? "Oh. I'm flattered. Are you interested in enlisting?"

"Shit, yeah. I want to be a pilot, like you. I already went down to the center for the neural testing. They said I passed."

"You know they won't let you keep the decorations." He leaned back to grab the packet from the table. It was special e-paper that contained all the forms and an easy, secure transfer up to Alliance databanks.

She put her hand to her nose ring. "Yeah. Easy come, easy go. Anyway, I just wanted to see you for real. Thanks for the autograph." She took the packet and extended her hand. He shook it, impressed with her grip. When she took her hand away, he found she'd left him a folded up note.

"Just in case you want to let me try the real thing," she said. She winked at him and left the enclosure.

Mitchell looked down at the e-paper. Not everyone had an ARR, which meant they had to resort to less technically advanced means of passing information. She could have knocked him from her tablet, but he guessed she didn't trust the privacy of it. He unwrapped the paper, expecting to find her signature print.

They're coming. Goliath. Find it.

He felt his heart rate pop. He glanced back at Major Arapo. Her left eye was twitching, but the other one noticed him. She tilted her head in silent question.

He looked back at the paper. Was he losing his mind?

They're coming. Goliath. Find it.

It was still there in a messy print. He started towards the front of the enclosure. He had to find the girl and ask her what the hell this was about. He only made it two steps before Christine's arm was on his shoulder.

"Mitch?"

Her eyes were on the paper. He closed his hand over it. Dr. Drummond had told him his experience was normal. If that were true, why did the word "Goliath" keep forcing itself into his mind?

"What is it?" Christine asked.

He opened his hand and gave her the strip. "What does it say?" He held his breath, bracing himself for the answer.

"You're freaking out about her sig print? I didn't take you for being into the grungy type, but as long as she comes to you and it's consensual-"

"That's not it, damn it," he said. "I think I may be having some residual symptoms." He put his hand to his head. The patch had fallen off while he slept, leaving the wound completely healed. "I'm done for today."

"You're done when the day is over, Captain," she replied.

"Christine, I said-"

"Major Arapo. You can call me Christine when you're being cooperative."

"Are you joking?"

She grabbed his arm and pulled his face close to hers. "Property, Captain. That's what you are. Did you ever bitch at your CO that you couldn't make a drop because you had a headache?"

"That was life or death. This is... this is all bullshit."

"Lower your tone, Captain."

"Or what? What can you do? Lock me up? Court-martial me?"

"We made you. We can break you."

"No. You can't. That's what I'm trying to tell you. I'm already broken." He tapped his skull. "I'm hearing things, seeing things. Something's messed up in there, and it happened after I got shot yesterday. I'm not trying to be a problem, Major, but unless you want to risk me freaking out on World Stream, you need to get me the hell out of here."

She let him go, her face turning rigid. "Okay. I'm bringing you back to Drummond. Whatever happens, whatever he tells you, you're not getting out of the gala. General Cornelius is going to be there to give you the medal himself, and I'll be damned if you're going to miss that."

Cornelius was one of the top ranking officers in the Space Marines and a legend in his own right. The last thing Mitchell wanted was to embarrass himself in front of the man. "Yes, ma'am."

"Wait here. I'll clear the queue. We leave in five minutes."

Mitchell watched her exit the enclosure. He noticed she'd dropped the strip on the floor. He picked it up and looked at it. He could see the sig print clearly now. Why had he seen a message before?

There was something wrong with him, but what?

[9]

"Mmmhmmm. I don't see anything wrong with your brain, Captain," Dr. Drummond said. "At least, nothing that wasn't there before." He brought a pair of scans up onto the wall behind him. "The one on the left is your gray matter during your last physical, about eight months ago. The one on the right is today."

Mitchell shifted between the two. They were nearly identical, save for a small spot in his prefrontal cortex. "What about that?" he asked, pointing.

Drummond examined the scan. "That's the wire that connects your brain to your implant. It was damaged yesterday, so the techs replaced it. From what I've been told, it's a standard upgrade. All the new recruits are getting fitted with it by default."

"They didn't change anything else, did they?"

"Let me see." His eye fluttered as he read the data projected onto it. "Minor system updates, three percent improvement in CAP-NN routing. Compatibility with the Carrion, whatever that is."

Mitchell knew what it was. A new mech, still in testing phase. If they were adding the compatibility routines to drive it, that meant it was on the verge of being approved for purchase. That wasn't exactly good news. Greylock had been sent a Carrion to test out. It was a small, thirty ton mech, nimble as anything, but also a brittle piece of shit. They'd brought it down to a training ground on Cestus and disabled it inside of five minutes with standard infantry fire.

It was being approved because the cost was as low as its usefulness. Having a hundred of them wandering a theater as peacekeepers would work out just fine, as long as nobody actually attacked it.

"So, nothing that would cause me to be seeing things? Or hearing things?" Mitchell put his hand up to his temple again.

"Nothing obvious. Personally, I think it's just stress. You've been getting run ragged the last couple of months. I submitted a request to have you moved to inactive for a few weeks for some R & R, but it was denied. It seems Command doesn't think there's anything difficult with being a celebrity. They aren't accounting for the fact that you watched your entire squad get blown away."

Mitchell winced. It wasn't the most sensitive statement, but his heart was in the right place. "Thanks for trying, doc."

"I'm just doing my job. So you know, Major Arapo requested copies of all the records, as well a full write-up. If you hear or see anything else, just try to ignore it, and definitely don't try to convince her. The more I have to talk to her, the more apropos your praying mantis analogy seems."

Mitchell laughed. "Is that your professional opinion?"

Dr. Drummond got to his feet. "I'm seventy-four years old, seventy-eight in Earth time. It's my experienced opinion."

"I don't suppose you can tell me anything else about her?"

"Like her birthday?"

"Like who she's reporting to? What branch she's out of? I have my hunches, but..."

"They don't tell me much. What I can tell you is that I was surprised to find out someone like her was already stationed on Liberty. I'm pretty confident you're the reason for that."

It wasn't anything Mitchell didn't already know, but it was nice to have confirmation. "Thanks again, doc. I hope I don't see you again too soon."

"Me, too, Captain. Me, too."

Major Arapo was waiting for him outside, her flat expression betraying her tense posture.

"I know," Mitchell said, cutting her off before she could speak. "Nothing on the scan. No abnormalities anywhere. Dr. Drummond seems to think I'm stressed."

"We're all stressed. It's part of what we do."

"I don't suppose I could get a week off sometime?"

"I'll bring it up with Command. Right now, we have to get you ready for the gala tonight."

"Get me ready?"

"There's a new dress uniform waiting in your room. You need to try it on. We used the measurements from your scan this morning, but when you're going to be meeting with General Cornelius and the Prime Minister of Delta, you take extra precaution."

Mitchell stopped walking. "Wait. Did you say the Prime Minister?"

"Yes."

"Of the entire quadrant?"

"Yes. Why do you think there was such a rush to put this thing together? It's going to be great for publicity to have you up there getting awarded by the Prime Minister."

"And I'm not supposed to be stressed?"

She stopped a dozen feet ahead of him and spun around. "I thought you were a Space Marine?"

"I'd rather drop into the middle of a nuke field than make small talk with the Prime Minister."

"There's nothing to be afraid of, Captain. He pisses the same as you do."

"Just into a nicer bowl?"

"Yes. Come on."

Mitchell caught up to her, and they continued walking.

"So, after I try on the uniform, then what?"

"Don't you ever check your ARR? We canceled everything else today ahead of time, in case your scan came back problematic. Command didn't want to take chances on this one. You have a whole seven hours to yourself." She smiled sideways at him. "Of course, you're locked down to your room until then."

"I figured as much. Are you going to be standing guard outside my door?"

"I have better things to do than babysit you all the time."

"Like what?"

They reached the officer's barracks. Mitchell followed her to his room near the center of the long, flat building. There were two MPs already waiting outside, ready to ensure he stayed put. They were both larger than him, with square jaws and thick muscles. They came to attention when they approached. Maybe she wouldn't be standing guard. Someone would.

"This is for your protection, Mitch," she said, ignoring his question. "Since you're not sure about your own stability. It's only until after the gala."

"Not taking chances. I get it. Howdy, boys."

"Captain Williams," one of them said in greeting.

His hatch opened and he stepped into the room. "I'll see you later then, Major," he said, turning around. She was already on her way back out.

Mitchell closed the hatch and went into the bedroom. The uniform was laid out on it, and he ran his hand over the decorations pinned to the chest, and the space that had been left for the new one. He considered trying the uniform on right away, and then decided against it. It had taken almost a full day for him to get a minute alone.

He retreated to the living room, dropping down onto the gel sofa and leaning his head back on one of the arms. A thought brought up the p-rat interface, and a second started a query for "Goliath." The voices in his medically cleared head kept telling him to find it. He figured it couldn't hurt to learn what *it* actually was.

The first result was called *The History of XENO-1*. Aldus had mentioned the name, and he had a feeling that somehow it had been what set him off. He scrolled the table of contents, skimming through the menu, with titles like The Arrival, The Discovery, First to Antarctica, The Beginning of the Xeno War, The Xeno War: Year 2, The Xeno War: Year 3, The Xeno War: Year 4, A Time of Peace, and The Goliath.

He stopped when he saw it, moving into that section with a thought. It was mixed media: video, imagery, and text all floating in the center of his left eye with enough transparency that he could see the ceiling behind it. He closed his eyes and spread the p-rat display across both of his retinas, finding himself immersed in a three-dimensional space, surrounded by floating boxes containing the content, all neatly organized. He held his hands out and reached for a section labeled "Construction."

The rest of the contents shrank away, while the photos in the Construction section flew out and expanded into a giant wall of imagery. He pulled the first image, and it shrunk down into a stack he could flick through.

The first picture was nothing but a shell, a frame of what appeared to be an earlier form of poly-alloy - a nano-scale material based on carbon, graphite, and iron. It was an extremely durable and light metal that along with carbonates, aerogels, and ultralight cement was used in just about everything these days. The caption beneath the photo read "A skeleton ship. First successful application of new alloy."

A starship? He checked the date on the image. September, 2043. Over four hundred years ago. He turned off the display for a moment, leaving himself in darkness.

Goliath. He tried to remember his history lessons. He had never been a particularly attentive student, preferring to watch the girls in his class rather than attune himself to the droning of his professor. Now he wished he had at least listened a little bit. He smiled, wondering if that was the day Keely Masterson had worn that skin suit with the dynamic patterns that flowed across it, the one that had been banned a couple of months later due to a glitch that would cause parts of it to randomly turn transparent. He didn't know if anyone else had seen it when the chest had gone clear. If his professor had, he didn't say anything. A sly pervert. Who could blame him for not paying attention that day?

He turned the display back on and flicked the graphic away. The next image was a few months later. More of the frame was completed, revealing the massive size of the ship. It wasn't quite as large as the Frontier Federation's dreadnought, but it was bigger than anything in the Alliance's stable. Two kilometers long, and half as wide. It was bulky for a starship. Not that aerodynamics mattered in the vacuum of space, but it would be an awfully big target, and impossible to lay shield coverage over. Mitchell wasn't sure they even had shields back then.

Four hundred years. He put his hand up to his head again, feeling the smooth skin where he had been shot. Dr. Drummond told him he was fine, and the scans backed him up. He didn't feel fine. Why was he seeing things, and hearing things? What did they all have to do with this antique starship? If it were still around, he was sure he would have heard about it.

"The bullet messed me up a little, that's all," he said out loud. "It shorted the implant, and somewhere in my subconscious I pulled back the memory of my history class. Probably focused on a strong emotional response. Probably because of Keely."

He flicked out of the image gallery. "Doc's right. Just leave it alone. Keep up the good work as a performing monkey, and maybe you'll get a few days rest somewhere down the line."

He felt stupid for even making the effort to do the search. He backed out to the results and decided to scan them, just to see what else he could find. There was no harm in scanning a list.

He scrolled through thousands of results. He found some references to an old Earth comic book that predated XENO-1, but everything else pointed right at the starship. It made him feel better to see it, as though it proved his hypothesis. It also meant it was time to drop the whole idea. The more he obsessed over it, the more obsessed he would become. He wasn't about to take something that could have been harmless and turn it into psychosis.

Mitchell opened his eyes and cleared the display from his right eye. He looked over at the time in his left eye. He still had five hours until the gala. He wanted a drink. That wasn't going to happen. He wanted to head over to Training and hop into a simulator. He doubted the MPs would be too agreeable to that idea either. He sighed and returned to the bedroom. He stripped down and tried on the uniform. Of course, the fit was perfect, and he had to admit he looked damn good in dress blues.

He took it all off, careful to keep it in perfect condition. He couldn't afford to be wrinkled in front of Cornelius or the Prime Minister. Then he laid down on top of the bed and closed his eyes.

Despite all of his years of training and experience, he had never gotten quite used to the idea of being out of control during a jump. There was a tight lightness in the stomach that came from plummeting to the ground in the cramped confines of thirty to eighty tons of metal, carrying thousands of pounds of ordnance and relying on boosters, aerofoils, and finally foot thrusters to make the landing an arguable degree of gentle. It was an uncomfortable feeling, one that he had never seemed to be able to master.

Ella had taught him how she managed to stay so calm. It was the only thing that had ever helped.

"It's all in the breath," she said. "Slow, deep, steady, focused. Mind over matter."

"Slow. Steady," he said to himself, taking control of his breath.

He wasn't joking when he told Christine he would rather drop into a nuke field. It would have been bad enough to meet the Prime Minister straight up. He was going to be getting an award from the man. An award predicated on a damn lie.

"Slow. Steady."

[10]

EARTH. *February 9, 2036*

Kathy was glued to the television. Her entire family was. Maybe even the entire world.

Almost nine months had passed since it had fallen from space, the gigantic craft that someone had labeled "XENO-1." It had crossed over the northern hemisphere, sending shockwaves for hundreds of miles around it, rattling windows and houses and people on its cruel descent before finally touching down in the Antarctic. It slammed into the surface of the ice with enough force to leave a trail of debris nearly a hundred miles long, and wiped out the permanent field station of more than one nation along the way.

Chaos had followed in the immediate aftermath. Tsunami warnings were issued, the disruption to the southernmost continent creating a slew of environmental concerns. An EMP leak from the crashing ship knocked out power for hundreds of thousands for over a week and a half. People died, the causes too numerous to keep track of. Drowned in the floods, hit by distracted drivers, heart attacks from surprise and shock, heatstroke from losing their AC.

They tried to lie about it at first. They said it was an asteroid. They thought they could get away with it. They were old men trying to tell old tales. Cameras were too good, too sharp. Pictures and videos flooded the internet, detailed shots that clearly showed a structure that was organized and made of some kind of metal. More pictures showed it was charred and scarred, broken and burned, though how it got that way - if it happened on entry into the atmosphere or had been battered on its journey - was anybody's guess.

An embarrassed government updated the lie. People were fired. Life went on. Antarctica was nobody's property, and it now contained something that everyone wanted.

The United States was the first to arrive on the scene, only a day ahead of Japan, Russia, China, Iran, and the rest. They each wanted to claim the wreck as their own. They all wanted the secrets everyone on the planet knew that it held. The secret to traveling in space. The mysteries of how to build something so immense and send it to the stars. A demilitarized zone was formed around it, guns pointing in every direction, the actual crash site off-limits. To enter it was to die, and more than a few tried. Their bodies remained to be buried under fresh snow and ice. The bulk of the ship suffered the same fate.

The news coverage had been running non-stop in Kathy's house since the day the ship came down. She was enamored with the mystery of its origins, and the potential that it held to carry her beyond the blue sky. She stayed up late watching interviews with soldiers who served at the site, with politicians who were part of the arguing over how to best claim it, or share it, or figure out some way to actually do something with the opportunity other than watch it get buried under the cold. She listened to the pundits, the celebrities. She went online and searched the back channels for conspiracies and clues. She even convinced her parents to buy her a t-shirt that read "I saw the crash" and had a blurry satellite photo of the site pressed onto it.

Today was different, though. Today was the day she had been waiting for. A decision from the President, from Congress, from the most powerful nation in the world on how they would solve the quagmire and move civilization forward and into a new age.

Her parents were on the couch beside her. Her father, tall and strong, an electrical engineer. Her mother, a chemistry professor at the nearby community college. They had instilled in their daughter the love of science, the desire to learn. Her younger brother was somewhere in the house, probably his room, disinterested in politics and tired of hearing about XENO-1.

Kathy checked the time. 8:59. She kept her eyes glued to it until it switched over to 9:00. The commercials on the television paused midstream, and the United States seal appeared in their stead. A moment later, that too vanished, replaced with a camera view of a podium.

Their house was silent. The room at the White House was also quiet. Kathy could almost feel the tension through the thin layer of diodes. There had been an incident two days earlier. A bomb had gone off in the camp of the Alliance of Nations and killed almost a hundred soldiers.

The President was an older woman, with gray hair and a taut face wearing a conservative blue suit. Her posture was confident and composed as she gained the podium.

"My fellow Americans," she said, her voice solid and strong. "These past months have done nothing, if not proven that there is life beyond this Earth, intelligent life that is not so unlike our own. Life that sought to learn, to grow, to reach for the stars and attain them. Life that ended tragically in the snow and ice of the Arctic." She paused, drawing in a deep breath. "We have made every attempt to honor the lives of these travelers who we do not know, and have not met. At the same time, we have worked tirelessly to honor the lives of our fellow humans here on Earth by coming to a peaceful and reasonable resolution to the question of ownership of the stricken craft. It has become abundantly clear in these months that there are those outside of the Alliance of Nations who are unwilling to settle for anything less than complete control of the site, to the extent that two days past they carried out a cowardly terrorist attack to disrupt our peacekeeping operations outside of the demilitarized zone. Intelligence sources have identified the source of this attack as that of the so-called Federation of Allies. While we have made every effort to negotiate with the Federation in good faith over the past four months, it has become clear to me that the leadership of the Federation does not share this non-violent view."

She stopped then, holding the pause for at least ten seconds. She glanced to her left, offstage to where her husband waited and offered encouragement. Kathy leaned forward on the couch, her heart skipping, her fear and excitement building.

"It is with the utmost sadness that I am to announce that the Alliance of United Nations has voted in favor of abandoning our talks with the Federation and reinforcing our claim to the crashed starship, using whatever resources and force is required.

My fellow Americans, I regret to inform you that tonight, we are at war."

11

"Do you always sleep naked, Captain?" Major Arapo asked.

Mitchell opened his eyes. The Major was standing next to the bed, unimpressed.

"Do you always walk into people's quarters without knocking?" He tapped his head, and then blinked a few times. Christine was wearing a little black dress that accented all the best parts of her.

"I did knock. You didn't answer. I thought you Marines were supposed to always be alert." She glanced down towards his midsection. "I see one part of you is."

Mitchell refused to be embarrassed. "That isn't because of you," he said, sliding off the bed right next to her and making her back out of the way to avoid him. "I guess all of this excitement is wearing me out. Or maybe being a statue is making me soft. Hand me my underwear?"

She kept backing up. "Making you soft?" she teased. "Get your own diaper. I'll be waiting outside. You have ten minutes." She turned on her heel and left.

Mitchell grabbed the clothes and carried them into the bathroom.

He cleaned himself off and got dressed, and then met the Major in the hallway. The MPs had already been dismissed.

"I'm sure you have special instructions for me," he said as they started walking.

"You've done all the training. I shouldn't need to tell you how to smile and wave."

"No words of wisdom on talking to the Prime Minister?"

She thought about it. "Ask him about his dogs."

"That's your advice?"

"Yes. Ask him about his dogs. He has two golden labs, Butter and Margarine."

"Butter and Margarine?" Mitchell rolled his eyes.

"Ask him without doing that, or laughing. He thinks the names are clever."

"Right. How many times have you been one-on-one with the Prime Minister?"

"Three."

"Why?"

"Why what?"

"Why were you meeting with him?"

"It's classified."

Mitchell stared ahead of them, deciding if he should try to needle her a little. He doubted she would tell him much of anything.

"Which department of Special Ops are you in, Major? Intelligence? Security? Infiltration?"

The look she threw him made him flinch.

"That's none of your business, Captain."

"Were you ever in the Army? Or have you always been Spec Op?"

"I didn't say I was Spec Op."

"You didn't deny it either."

She surprised him by smiling. "You're a real pain in the ass, Captain."

"Yes, ma'am."

"I'm still not going to tell you what department I'm in, but yes, I swear I was in the Army. I was on the field during the New Terran's invasion of Antares. Your company didn't leave us with much to do."

"I didn't make the drop on Antares. It was my first tour with Greylock, and I hadn't finished the Zombie training. That was ten years ago, and I'd put you around forty-three? That would make you old for Spec Op."

They left the barracks. A transport was waiting outside, and they climbed in.

"You think I look forty-three?"

"Give or take."

"I'm thirty-seven," she said. "And yes, I am too old for Special Operations. Maybe now you'll drop it?"

"Yes, ma'am." He could feel the heat in his face, regretting his comment on her age. He forced a smile and leaned back in the seat. He caught Christine glancing over at him, a wry smile at the corner of her mouth, before she turned her head away and moved her attention to her p-rat.

Mitchell closed his eyes and focused on his breathing.

"By the way, Captain," Christine said, interrupting him a minute later. "You can look up the report on Antares if you don't believe me."

He opened his eyes and looked over at her. "Do you care if I believe you?"

"There's a lot I'm not at liberty to say, but I think our relationship will work better if you trust me."

"Okay. I trust you."

"Liar."

"I don't need to know anything about you to jump when you say jump. You obviously haven't led a team before."

She glowered at him again. She was offering him an olive branch, and he had returned fire.

"I'm sorry, Major," he said. "Enemy fire is one thing. Rubbing elbows with the rich and famous? I've done basic, but I'm still pretty green."

"Apology accepted."

The gala was being held at the top of the Millennium Towers, the most luxurious hotel in downtown York. It was a four-kilometer-tall wonder of architecture, a twisted sculpture of metal and carbonate that glittered when the planet's sun hit it just so. It rose near the south end of the city, offering visitors to the grand ballroom an unbeatable view of the surrounding landscape, from the majority of York to the north, the Caspian Sea to the east, and the faint rise of the Lincoln mountains to the west. Rumors had it that the hotel and the area around it had escaped the Federation bombardment only because they considered the building too beautiful and too valuable to risk damaging.

"How are you feeling, Captain?" Christine asked.

They were riding alone together in the lift to the ballroom at the top of the tower. Mitchell watched the ground shrink beneath the carbonate floor.

"I'll survive," he said. He was pleased to find the breathing exercises were as effective for parties as they were for combat. "You look beautiful, by the way."

She seemed surprised by the compliment. "I... Thank you." She paused as if considering whether or not to return the compliment. "You clean up well."

It wasn't much in the way of praise, but he would take what he could get. "Thanks. If you thought I was messy before tonight, you should have seen me after a mission. Mechs get insanely hot once you start firing lasers or launching ordnance."

"I can imagine."

"Butter and Margarine, right?" he asked.

"What?"

Mitchell stared at her. She still seemed a little shaken by the fact that he had noticed the way she looked. Or was she nervous about something else?

"The Prime Minister's dogs?"

"Oh, yes. That's it."

"Are you okay, Christine?"

"I'm fine." She pointed at her eye. "Multitasking. I'm on the comm channel with the security team for the event."

They reached the ballroom. The lift slowed to a stop and the hatch slid to the left, revealing the inner party.

It was everything Mitchell had been expecting. A huge room laid out with a bunch of round tables, a dance floor, an old-fashioned brass band playing really old songs. Women in heavy gowns, men in military dress uniforms and tuxedos, servers dashing around with trays of food and drink. The open view of the world from this height was mesmerizing and sad. The Federation bombardment had left whole chunks of the city in scarred ruin, dotting the landscape with patches of dark browns and blacks.

He stowed the thought and put out his arm. It was showtime. "Major?"

She wrapped her hand around it, allowing him to escort her in. They only made it a few feet when the band stopped playing, the room quieted, and all attention was on them.

A single clap broke the silence. Then another, and then another. Within seconds, the entire room was cheering for him. Mitchell smiled and waved at them, looking at the floor in practiced humility. He stood up to the barrage for a few minutes, and then it died down and the band resumed playing. Christine led him into the throng, and he paused to shake hands and accept the accolades of the men and women who offered them.

"I don't know who most of these people are," he whispered to Christine.

"Rich, famous, and powerful within the Alliance. That's all you need to know."

Their table was near the front. Two men and a woman were already seated there. Mitchell recognized the man in uniform immediately, having seen him in person on a number of occasions, and through streams many times over.

"General Cornelius, sir," he said, coming to attention.

The General turned his head away from his conversation. He

was an older man with a white flattop and a strong jaw, his body fit despite his years. He was the kind of man who could pull off the rare feat of being both grandfatherly and hard at the same time, a gift that made him beloved among his soldiers.

"Captain Williams," he said, getting to his feet, a growing smile washing across his face. "At ease."

Mitchell relaxed and took the General's hand when it was offered.

"It's an honor to sit at a table with you, sir," he said.

"Nonsense," Cornelius replied. "The honor is mine. Mitchell, let me introduce you to my wife, Sarah."

The woman stood and held out her hand. She was around Christine's age, a couple of decades younger than the General, with a thin frame and a surgically enhanced face. Mitchell took her hand and brought it to his lips. "Ma'am."

"Captain Williams." The other man stood. He wore a long black jacket with a high collar, a gold pin resting near the tip. He had longer white hair and a tired look around his eyes. "I'm David Avalon, Prime Minister of the Delta Quadrant."

Mitchell shifted to face the Prime Minister. The man didn't offer his hand, instead waiting while Mitchell bowed to him.

The Prime Minister returned the bow, and then smiled warmly. "I'm happy to see you up and well, after the incident the other day. Your courage is already a thing of legend."

Corporal Kwon and the civilians that died might have disagreed. He forced himself to stay in character. "It was what any good Marine would have done, Your Excellency."

"Perhaps, but you were the one who was there. I'm looking forward to presenting you with the Medal of Courage. You certainly deserve it. I can only imagine where the Federation would be right now if you hadn't destroyed that dreadnought."

Mitchell glanced at General Cornelius. He had to be careful with his words, so as not to upset either one of these men. "I'm confident the Alliance forces would have found some way to stop it."

"Of course."

"Ah, David," Cornelius said, "where is that wife of yours this evening?"

"Not feeling well, I'm afraid. She said she might come down a little later. She really wants to meet you, Captain. I think she has a bit of an understandable crush on you."

Mitchell could feel his composure cracking at the statement. He wasn't sure how to answer that.

"Major Arapo tells me you have a pair of golden retrievers, Your Excellency," he said. The words felt awkward spilling from his mouth.

The Prime Minister's smile was practiced and perfect. "Labradors," he corrected. "Yes, I do. Butter and Margarine. I would have brought them with me, but the hotel has a thing about dogs in their ballroom."

Mitchell was silent again. A few seconds passed before Christine saved him.

"I believe it's almost time to begin the proceedings, Your Excellency."

His eye twitched while he checked the time. "You're right. Thank you, Major. General, Captain, shall we?"

12

MITCHELL SURVIVED the first few hours. He made it through the ceremonies, offering smiles and handshakes, and giving a short speech on humility, courage, and the value of enlistment in, and support of, the Alliance military. He made small talk with dignitaries from half the planets in the Delta Quadrant, and found himself on the dance floor more often than not, putting his training to the test to please the rich and powerful.

He noticed that Christine kept an eye on him no matter where he went. She managed to cut him off from the bar twice and shook her head sternly whenever he reached for a glass as a server went by. She followed him to the bathroom, and she found her way to his side whenever he got involved in a conversation with anyone who wasn't working the gala. At first, he found it somewhat humorous that the secretive special operations officer was assigned to almost literally babysitting him.

After a while, he just found it annoying. He wasn't about to confront her and risk making a fool of himself, so he tried to ignore her, focusing on his dance partners and doing his best to charm them. He had varying degrees of success depending on where the Major chose to position herself, but even when she was out of his sight, she wasn't out of his mind.

He was returning from a trip to the bathroom when a woman in a sparkling silver dress approached him. She was younger than anyone else in the room, a beautifully constructed work of art with blonde hair that fell in ringlets around her face, soft, full lips, and big, brown eyes. She was easily the most attractive woman at the gala, a fact that she seemed to recognize by the way she was carrying herself.

"Captain Mitchell Williams?" she asked, putting herself directly in his path.

He came to a stop. "Yes?"

Her smile was perfection. "My name is Holly. Holly Sering. I never thought I would actually get a chance to meet you."

"It's a pleasure," Mitchell said. He kissed her hand, as he had so many others.

"Do you want to dance?" she asked.

She was blunt, assertive. He hadn't even noticed the band was playing. "Sure."

She led him to the corner of the dance floor, away from the tables. He followed the music for a few beats, and then wrapped one hand around her waist and took her other hand in his. She followed his steps effortlessly, flowing into him and submitting to his lead.

"I don't remember seeing you earlier," Mitchell said. "I would have noticed you in the crowd." He was certain she hadn't been at any of the tables when he'd accepted the medal.

"I was late to the party," she said. He twirled her around, causing her to smile. "You're a wonderful dancer for a pilot."

"They made me take lessons," he said, "so I could charm rich women. My Commanding Officers think that it will help them get more spending bills approved."

"You're joking."

"I'm not. Is it working?"

She laughed. "Yes."

"Did you come here with someone?"

"No. I came alone."

"What about your husband?"

She pulled her hand away, showing him she wasn't wearing a ring before returning it to him in time for a few more steps. "No husband."

"All the better for me, then."

She laughed again. "Getting ahead of yourself, Captain?"

It was his turn to smile. He had no idea who she was, but in two minutes this woman had turned his night from torture to pleasure. He didn't know what it was about her, but he liked it. "Am I?"

"We'll see."

They continued dancing, chatting as they did. Even though the floor was crowded around them, Mitchell could always find Christine near the edge, talking to someone or another or nursing a drink, but constantly keeping one eye on him.

"So, you know what I do," Mitchell said. "What about you? Government? Industry?"

"I'm a musician," she said.

"Famous?"

"You would probably have recognized my name if I were."

"Not really. The military keeps me on a pretty short leash. They're worried the Federation will try to kill me."

"From what I gather, they did try to kill you, and a lot of other people."

"It was nothing I couldn't handle. I'm just sorry innocent people died."

The song wound down, and the band paused for a breather. He stood facing Holly, his heart pulsing from the exercise, and from the sight of her. He was about to ask her to join him at his table when she leaned in and kissed him on the cheek.

"Well, it was fun, Captain," she said. "Thank you for the dance." She started walking away.

"Huh? Wait. Where are you going?" He followed after her. She was the only thing that had brought any life to this party.

"I'm not much for crowds," she said. "I just came up because I was invited, and I really wanted to meet you."

"I can't convince you to stay?"

"No. I'm sorry, Captain."

"Mitch."

"I'm sorry, Mitch. You seem like a great guy, and I don't know, I feel electrified being around you. I just... I have this thing about large groups."

"I don't like crowds much myself," Mitchell said. "Do you have a p-rat?"

"A what?"

She didn't know the slang.

"An ARR?" he asked.

"Oh. Yes."

"Why don't you knock me, so I can at least get your sig? Maybe we can get together some other time?"

"I'm going off-world tomorrow. I doubt our paths will cross again anytime soon." She looked up at him, considering. "You know, you already got your medal. Why don't you come down to the lobby with me? We can grab a drink."

Mitchell found Christine across the room, in the middle of a conversation with General Cornelius. He was speaking to her, which meant she couldn't pull her attention away at the moment.

"I want to. I really do. Do you see that woman over there?" he asked.

"The one in the black dress?"

"Yes. She's my bodyguard or something. If she sees me trying to leave, she's going to do her best to stop me."

"So don't let her see you," Holly said.

Mitchell kept watching Christine. She wasn't going to be happy if he disappeared. He imagined she would chew him out again, and find some way to punish him. At the same time... "Service elevator?" he asked. He turned his attention to the swinging door the servers were keeping busy. He doubted they brought all the food and booze up through the main, clear carbonate lifts.

Her eyes sparkled mischievously. "Good idea."

He took her hand and started moving through the crowd, keeping to the far side of the room, away from Major Arapo. A few of the guests stared at them as they wandered past, about to say something before thinking better of it. More than once, Mitchell stopped walking and turned away from Christine, leaning down to pretend to tie his shoe, or taking a bite from one of the trays. Holly mimicked his motions, her face bright the entire time, clearly enjoying the subterfuge.

They reached the kitchen unnoticed. Mitchell pulled Holly through the door, nearly crashing into a server with a full tray of champagne. He laughed and pulled Holly close to him, squeezing them around while the server stared at them in surprise.

"You aren't supposed to be back here, Captain," one of the chefs said, noticing them passing through.

"I'm looking for the service lift," he said.

The man looked from him to Holly, and back. "Right. Out that door, turn left, three doors down, turn right. You'll need clearance."

"What level?" Mitchell asked. Most military had override access to public security systems, depending on how locked down they were.

"Two."

"Won't be a problem. You didn't see me."

He laughed and waved as they exited the kitchen, following his directions to the service lift.

"Everybody seems to know you," Holly said.

"I've been plastered all over every stream for the last two months, and there are shots of me displayed everywhere around the city. It's crazy, really. There was even a girl who asked me to sign a photoshopped picture of me that she said she masturbates to."

"Really?"

"I'm not kidding."

They reached the lift. Mitchell scanned the id number on it, and then knocked from his p-rat. It recognized his credentials and opened up. They stepped inside, both laughing. Mitchell touched the screen to send it to the ground floor.

"Do you like it?" she asked. "Being famous?"

"I don't think of myself as famous. I'm popular now because of the battle, but give it a year or two and people will forget about me. But no, I don't like it. I'm a pilot who can't fly. A warrior who can't fight. There's going to be a push into Federation space, and I'll be sitting on the sidelines, watching people I convinced to join the Alliance military go out there and do what I should be doing. Not only that, but I have almost no control over what I do, or when I do it. It's only gotten worse since yesterday."

"That sounds awful."

"It's frustrating, but it isn't all bad. You wouldn't have come up to the party to see me if I were just some Joe Mechjock."

"Am I enough to make it worthwhile?" The mischievous look in her eye had returned.

"You might be."

She reached over and hit the 30 on the lift's touchpad. "I have a feeling your bodyguard or something is going to be looking for you. Let's skip the drinks. You have something else I want right now."

Then she was pressed against him, her head tilted back, her lips finding his. Her kiss was forceful, aggressive, and it took him a moment to recover from the attack and launch his counterstrike. He wrapped his hands around her, lifting her up and pushing her back against the side of the elevator. She giggled under the kissing, hands tightening around him.

"Are you always so straightforward?" he asked, pulling his head away for a second.

"When I see something I want, I go right for it. I call it smart." Her hand found the back of his head and pulled him in again.

13

SHE BROUGHT him to her hotel room on the thirtieth floor. It was nothing special, a standard suite with a king sized bed, a bathroom, and a dresser. A funky piece of artwork hung behind the bed, painted in color-changing ink that moved in whorls that changed color depending on the way the light was hitting it and the position of the viewer.

Mitchell noticed it almost subliminally as he sat on the bed with Holly in his lap, holding her close, kissing her neck and shoulders, pressing his naked body to hers. She rocked against him, purring and moaning, her hands scratching his back in her pleasure.

He had been with at least a dozen women in the last two months, and while they had all been great partners they had each held onto a certain demureness, as though their public status carried over into the bedroom. He didn't know what Holly's public status was. Maybe she didn't have one at all. Either way, she wasn't hindered by it. She wasn't hindered by anything. She was assertive, aggressive, fearless.

It was amazing. Mind-blowing. Even Ella, in all her confidence, had never quite merged with him so well.

It was perfect.

Too perfect.

He shouldn't have been so surprised when the door to the suite opened, and the lights flashed on.

"What the hell is going on here?"

Holly froze in his lap. He stopped kissing her and lifted his head, looking straight at the painting and feeling his already rapid heartbeat move to triple-time. He recognized that voice.

What the hell had he just done?

"Wait out here," he heard the Prime Minister say.

Holly shifted off him, breaking their connection, putting her back against the bed. Her face was flushed, her hair sweaty. She glanced at him, her eyes trying to transmit a nervous apology.

"Captain Williams?"

Mitchell turned slowly, putting his hand over his quickly deflating groin.

"Your Excellency," he croaked. "What are you doing here?"

The Prime Minister's face was rigid, every muscle clenched tight. Mitchell could feel the anger building behind it as the man did his best to maintain the composure of his status. He was the Prime Minister of Delta, he couldn't very well resort to throwing punches. Not that Mitchell would have any choice but to let them land.

"I should ask you the same thing," he said, in a low whisper that fought to not be a snarl. He looked over at Holly, and Mitchell saw the anger flash to sadness for an instant. "Did you know that the woman you were just screwing is my wife?"

It was worse than a punch to the gut. Mitchell looked back at Holly. She was thirty years the Prime Minister's junior, at least. She was staying in a plain, ordinary hotel room, not one of the VIP suites. She wasn't wearing a ring and had told him she didn't have a husband.

"Sir, I-"

"Get out."

He slid off the bed, reaching down and grabbing his pile of clothes off the floor. He held it in front of his midsection. "Sir-"

"I said get out," the Prime Minister screamed.

Mitchell bowed his head and took a wide angle around the man. The door to the room was closed, but he knew the Prime Minister's guards would be right outside of it.

"David?" he heard Holly say. "Uh... what? Captain Williams? What was... What were we just doing?"

Mitchell stopped and turned his head. Holly was looking back at him, her eyes suddenly fearful, as though their prior activity had been anything but consensual.

"Holly, what's the matter?" the Prime Minister said.

"I don't know," she replied. "I..." Tears started running from her eyes. She reached down and grabbed the sheets, pulling them up over her body, covering herself in front of him. "What did you do to me?" Her look was accusing and angry. What the hell was going on?

The Prime Minister spun around, his anger boiling over. "Guards," he shouted.

The door opened. Two men in dark suits entered, blocking Mitchell's exit.

"Sir, I didn't. I swear," Mitchell said. How could everything have gone so bad, so fast? His whole body felt cold.

The Prime Minister didn't look at him. His eyes were on his wife. When he spoke, Mitchell could hear the pain in his voice. "Bring him to a vacant room and keep him there. Call a doctor."

A strong hand fell on Mitchell's shoulder. He kept his eyes on Holly, who had buried her face in the sheets. How could she be doing this? He was going numb with disbelief. He didn't resist when the guards pulled him from the room.

"Are you out of your damn mind, Captain," one of them said. The other was silent, his eye twitching. Probably getting access to another room.

"I didn't do anything," Mitchell said. "Check the surveillance. She threw herself at me."

"We'll pull the surveillance as a matter of course. If you're telling the truth, it will be plain enough."

"Do you believe me?"

"If I didn't think something was up, you'd be out cold right now. I'm a former Marine myself. You can't possibly be dumb enough to throw away a rep like yours over a piece of ass."

"Forty-second floor," the other one said. "The whole thing is vacant for remodeling. Room 4218."

They ushered him back to the service elevator, giving him the courtesy of not parading him naked in front of the other guests.

"Why the hell is he staying in a random room in the middle of the hotel?" Mitchell asked, still trying to make sense of things.

"Standard operating procedure," the guard replied. "More attractive to the taxpayers, and harder for assassins to find him in a place this big."

"She told me she was single."

"Look, Captain, you need to just shut it for now, okay? We'll bring you to a room. Clean yourself up, get dressed, and wait. Security will get their hands on the feeds, and if you're telling the truth this whole mess will go away in a couple of hours. I can't say the same for the future of the Prime Minister's marriage."

Mitchell stayed quiet. He put his clothes on in the elevator on the way up and then marched to room 4128. The guards deposited him inside.

The door locked behind him.

14

MAJOR ARAPO SHOWED up two hours later. Mitchell had cleaned himself up and managed to calm down by then, reasoning that the hotel surveillance was sure to clear him of any wrongdoing, even if Holly insisted that she had been coerced instead of accepting responsibility for her actions.

Still, her confusion had been awfully convincing. If he hadn't been there, and known better, he would have believed her himself.

He heard the door unlock right before it opened. She walked in, and he stood to meet her. Her face was as tight as he expected, her posture stiff. Furious.

"Captain-" she started.

"Did you review the feeds, Major?" The best defense was a good offense.

She froze. "I did."

"Then you know I didn't do anything wrong."

She laughed. An unpleasant, sarcastic laugh. "Didn't do anything wrong? Are you kidding me, Captain? You snuck out of the gala with a woman you barely knew. You purposefully avoided me, because you knew I would try to stop you, and, oh, what's this... You got your-self in trouble!"

"How was I supposed to know that-"

"You weren't supposed to know. You weren't supposed to leave the gala or my sight. I tried to give you some breathing space. I tried not to have to watch every move you made like you're some kind of unintelligent infant. Obviously, my assessment of your mind was completely off base. One night, Captain. One night you needed to be on your best behavior, and not only did you screw up, but you did it in the worst possible way, with the worst possible woman. You weren't supposed to know, but if you had stayed put, you wouldn't have had to. What if she had been the Federation assassin who tried to kill you the other day?"

Mitchell had been preparing a retort. The last sentence stole it from him. He felt the heat of his embarrassment on his face. "I didn't think about-"

"You didn't think at all, except maybe with that cock of yours. My assignment is to protect one of the Alliance's most valuable assets. It's a lousy assignment, let me tell you. Even so, I put one hundred percent into everything I do. That's why Cornelius trusted me to do it. He's going to have both of our asses for this."

Mitchell was frozen, his offense abandoned. He had screwed up, big time, and was taking the Major down with him. He didn't have to like her to feel guilty for that. They were on the same team. It was just as bad as if he had left her wounded somewhere.

"I-"

"Don't," Christine said. "Don't say anything. I'm sure you're sorry, now. You should have been sorry ahead of time. To be honest, I can't for the life of me figure out how you got onto Greylock."

"Excuse me, Major?" Mitchell's anger started flowing back. "If I was on a ship preparing to invade the Federation, instead of here trying to be something I'm not, we'd both be happier. I got onto Grey-lock as a pilot, not a salesman."

"I agree with you. I do, Captain. That's not the hand we've been dealt. Even so, I expected a little more tactical planning from someone with your background and experience."

He heaved out a sigh, letting all the fight go with it. "Yeah, I messed up. What happens now?"

"Now we try to keep everything quiet. The Prime Minister saw the feed. He's confused as hell because he said his wife's never acted like that in her life. It doesn't help that she doesn't seem to remember any of it."

"She doesn't remember? Are you sure she's telling the truth?"

"We brought Dr. Drummond in with a portable medi-bot to scan her. She's telling the truth. Or at least, she thinks she is."

"How can that be?"

"I don't know. The Prime Minister suggested that you might have drugged her."

"I didn't-"

"I know. I vouched for you myself."

"You did?"

"Yes. I don't like you, Mitchell, but we're in this together, and I really don't think you'd resort to rape when you have so many women literally throwing themselves at you."

"Thanks, I guess."

"The good news is that thanks to this incident, I got you cleared for some time off. The Prime Minister doesn't want you anywhere near Delta for a while. We're leaving for Earth tomorrow. You'll have a week to yourself, and then we'll be doing a promotional tour there."

Mitchell nodded. "Sounds great to me. I wouldn't mind getting out of Delta."

"I'm having your things brought from the base, we'll leave from here in the morning." She started backing towards the door.

"Major," Mitchell said, catching her hand. "Christine. I'm sorry."

She looked down at their clasped hands for a moment, and then up at his eyes. "I believe you. Try to start using your brain, Mitch. Goodnight."

She vanished out the door. Mitchell noticed that the Prime

Minister's security detail was gone, and when the door closed it didn't lock. He was a free man again, Christine trusting him to be smart enough to stay put.

He couldn't help but wonder what had happened to Holly. She had been so into him, so sexy and charismatic, and yet when the Prime Minister had walked in on them she had seemed frightened and insecure. How could someone be one person one minute, and someone else the next?

How could she not remember it?

He didn't know and couldn't guess. He decided to just drop it. One more night and he would be on his way home on a vacation he desperately needed. He hadn't been back to Earth in four years. His parents were there. His sister. Maybe he could even get his brother, the Admiral, back from patrolling the Alpha Quadrant? With such a big galaxy to play in, in-person family gatherings were near impossible.

He sat down and accessed his p-rat, prepared to tell his folks he was coming home. He thought about what to say, and then ditched the idea. If he sent a message now, it would probably leave with him tomorrow morning, piggybacking on his transport for a ride through the galaxy at faster-than-light speed. It would have been great if he could use the military's more efficient relay system of advanced communications drones, but they were reserved for urgent messaging, not so Mitchell could tell his folks he would be stopping by.

He flopped back onto the sofa and closed his eyes.

There was nothing to do but wait.

[15]

EARTH. *July 14, 2040*

Kathy woke up at five every morning, the same as she had for the last five years - ever since she had joined the Air Force. She used a small LED to navigate her way to her footlocker and threw a pair of sweats over her panties. Then she found her running shoes, laced them up, and silently abandoned the rest of her squadron, leaving them to sleep another hour before Reveille.

She slipped out the door of the barracks and onto the flat expanse of concrete that covered most of the base. It was a cold morning, colder than she had expected, even inside the massive balloon that protected them from the worst of the intense winter that raged across Antarctica at this time of year. She guessed it was probably forty degrees inside. A hundred degrees warmer than outside.

They did their best to mimic the light of the outside here on the inside, which meant that it was still pitch black. She slipped her LED against her ear so it pointed straight ahead, illuminating the area in front of her. Not that she needed it. After all this time, she knew the layout of the base by heart.

She started jogging. Slowly at first, and then picking up speed as she made her third circuit of her route, the same one she had been making since the war had ended almost eight months ago. Her squadron had been grounded, but Command had decided to keep them here on the southern pole in reserve, just in case the Federation decided to change their mind about the truce. That was just fine with her. It kept her close to the wreckage, close to the thing that had changed her life the moment she had looked to the sky, even before it had appeared to her while she stood on the playground grass.

They were going to build a ship. That was what Captain Johns had whispered to his mates. Using the alien technology they had found, as soon as they figured out how it all worked, which they were doing more rapidly than anyone had expected. Of course, they had the finest minds in the world working on the problem - scientists from over a dozen nations. Their research was already bearing fruit, including the small, experimental generator that rested in the corner of the huge, enclosed space and powered pretty much everything.

She wanted a chance to be on that ship. It had been her dream for over a dozen years and was the reason she had joined the Air Force to begin with. How she would get that chance? She still didn't know.

She didn't need to check her watch to know what time it was. Her schedule was so perfect, so rigid, that as she crossed the twenty lap marker she knew she had ten minutes to Reveille. She took a different path then, crossing towards the center of the cement to where the three rows of fighters waited. They were F-70s, the latest and greatest, the first and only fighter developed entirely during the timeline of the war. They were incredible machines, radar avoiding, maneuverable, and faster than fast. She had flown over two hundred missions in hers without incident, registering more hits than any of her squad mates. They called her "Swooping Death" because of her favorite move, a crazy high-G maneuver that made the entire fighter rattle like a snake. It was a move that none of the other pilots were even willing to try. Swoops for short. She liked the full name better.

She approached her fighter, putting her hand against the cold metal side and lowering her head. A quick prayer to her parents, her mother dead from cancer, her father killed overseas after he joined the war effort. Another prayer for keeping her safe and alive, and a third a wish to see her way to the stars. It was all she had wanted for as long as she could remember.

"Second Lieutenant Asher."

The voice came from behind her left shoulder. She flinched a little, surprised by it, and then slowly turned around.

"Yes, sir?" She didn't recognize the officer standing in front of her. He was older. Tall, with salt and pepper hair and a nice smile.

"My name is Colonel Buford, I'm a liaison for what we're calling Project Olive Branch."

"Where did you come from?"

He smiled. "Originally? Idaho."

She returned the smile. "No, sir. I mean, I didn't know we added another head."

"Technically, you didn't. I arrived a few hours ago from Camp Alpha."

Camp Alpha was the base closest to the main wreckage site. She felt her heart begin to beat faster.

"Oh. Isn't that a weird time to be traveling, sir?"

"It is, but I have my orders. Anyway, I had heard from your XO that you like to get up early, and seeing as how my visit is sensitive in nature, I thought it was best to strafe you from the darkness."

"An ambush? How long have you been watching me?"

"Long enough to know your form is perfect, and I mean that in every non-sexually harassing way." He reached into his pocket and unfolded his data board. "Your combat record is impressive."

"Thank you, sir."

"So is your physical training. Black belt in three... no, four different martial arts?"

"It's like learning multiple languages. It gets easier the more you know."

"You're also an accomplished cellist?"

"That's an overstatement, and trust me, I'm nowhere near as perfect as your docket is making me out to be."

"Modest, too. I understand why he recommended you."

"Who recommended me, sir? For what?"

"Your squadron commander, Captain Johns. He thought you would be an excellent candidate for Olive Branch."

"What's Project Olive Branch?"

He glanced down at the board. "Sorry Lieutenant, I don't have enough time to go into detail, and in any case you need to tell me you're interested before I can get you security clearance. All I can say right now is based on what Captain Johns told me, this is straight up your alley."

She felt her heart pulsing, her body tingling from excitement. If Colonel Buford was here from Camp Alpha, there were only so many possible reasons. "I have to tell you I'm interested, before you can tell me what I'm interested in?"

"You gotta love the military."

"I do, sir. I'm interested."

He glanced down at the board, tapped it a couple of times, and turned it towards her.

"We don't have time for you to read the whole thing. It basically says keep your mouth shut, there are no guarantees, we're not responsible if you die, etcetera. Sign on the red line, and you'll be transferred to Alpha by tomorrow afternoon."

She put her finger to the board, sliding it across the line.

"I'm honored, sir," she said.

He smiled. "You should be."

[16]

HE'D BEEN DREAMING about Holly. It had started well and gone downhill from there, until the petite woman had morphed into the Major, her scowl and angry barking stealing every bit of his aroused thunder.

A hand jostling his shoulder woke him up.

"Mitchell," Christine said. Her voice was worried.

His eyes snapped open. "What's going on?"

"We have a problem. We need to get you out of here."

He bounced to his feet, his soldier's instincts catching up to his bad civilian habit. "Why?"

"Do you remember when I said nobody would find out about what really happened at the Battle for Liberty?"

There was a knock on the door. A physical knock. Then another on his p-rat. Tamara King.

"Shit," Christine said. "That son of a bitch."

"Tell me what's happening."

"The Prime Minister. He has access to classified data banks. He pulled yours."

Tamara King knocked his p-rat again.

"He told the Queen of Talk that I didn't take the Shot," Mitchell said, his voice flat.

"Yes."

Mitchell looked at the door. He expected he might have been afraid, or angry, or something.

He laughed instead.

"What's funny?"

"I don't know," he said. "I always worried about the truth coming out. I'm more relieved than I thought I would be. More relieved than scared." He realized it was true. He'd been living the lie for the last two months, and he'd been miserable for it.

"That won't last," she said. "General Cornelius is five minutes away from finding out about this, and he's going to be quick handling damage control."

"So?"

Tamara King's knock came again. Mitchell deleted her sig, cutting her off.

"So whose side do you think he's going to take? Yours or the Prime Minister's? In five minutes, he's going to label you a fraud who sexually assaulted the Prime Minister's wife."

"I didn't-"

"It doesn't matter. She thinks you did, and you can bet if the Prime Minister is upset enough to out your involvement in the battle, he's going to back her story. Especially now that your integrity is in question."

"In question? It sounds to me like it's already been flushed. I'm going to be court-martialed and sent to prison on Kolmar. Not to mention becoming the most hated man in the galaxy."

"If you're lucky. I think he'd just as soon have you shot before you can get out of the building." She looked back at the door. "The bitch is outside your door, and its the only way out. Do you have your sidearm?"

"What do I need my-"

"Do you have it?"

Mitchell shoved his uniform jacket to the side.

"I'll distract her, you make a run for it."

"Christine, what the hell are you talking about? Where am I going to run to? The second General Cornelius gives the order to have me arrested, every military and law enforcement unit on the planet is going to be looking for me. I'm not exactly inconspicuous."

"Get to the spaceport, find a transport off the planet."

"Who's going to take me?"

"Sneak onto one. You survived three months stranded in a Delphi jungle. I know you're more resourceful than you act."

"You're serious about this?"

"Dead serious. We don't have time to argue."

He grabbed her by the shoulders, pulling her face close to his. "Who *are* you?" he asked. "And why would you help me run?"

Her eyes stared into his. They were intense, so intense. "The Goliath. Find it. They're coming."

"What? What are you talking about?" He clenched her shoulders tighter beneath his hands. His initial resigned calm was threatening to turn into panic.

"Find it." She leaned forward in his grip, her lips pressing to his. She kissed him quickly. "Now."

She pulled herself forcefully away, moving to the door and opening it. Mitchell ducked to the side, out of view of Tamara, who was standing in the hallway with a recorder at her back.

"Where is Captain Williams?" he heard her ask.

"Whoever leaked his location to you gave you the wrong room number," Christine said.

"I don't think so," she argued. "Please move aside."

"You can't tell me what to do."

"That's why I said please. I'm already aware that Captain Williams lied to the military about his actions during the Battle for Liberty, an offense punishable by life in prison. Are you protecting him, Major? What do you think the fallout of that would be?"

Mitchell kept himself pressed against the wall. Christine was only a couple of feet away.

"Fine. You want to come in? Come in. He isn't here." She moved aside to let Tamara and her recorder enter, positioning herself in front of him. The Queen of Talk charged into the room, and Christine stayed right on top of her to keep her from turning his way.

"Captain Williams?" Tamara shouted. "I know you're here."

Mitchell crept forward, slipping past Christine and out the door. He ran to the end of the hallway, even as he heard the Major fighting with Tamara again.

He had five minutes, maybe less.

He needed to get out of the building and onto the street. The spaceport was only a couple of miles away, he could run that in no time.

Why was he running?

He didn't want to die. No. It was more than that. The Goliath. It wasn't his imagination. It couldn't be. Could it?

He reached the lift, pausing before he summoned it. They could find him through his p-rat. He brought it up and flipped through the menus until he reached the hard reset option. It would reboot the interface, give him a minute of invisibility before he would have to do it again. They could still track him, but not as easily.

He eschewed the lift for the emergency stairs, moving around behind the shaft and opening the manual door. It was a long way down. He kept going, his feet quick on the steps.

He had covered almost ten floors by the time his ARR rebooted. He got a knock the minute it came back online. Then a second.

"Christine," he said, answering the first.

"The order just went out, Mitch. They're look-" The communication cut out.

"Captain Williams," the voice echoed in his head. It was General Cornelius. "We have a situation. Deliver yourself to base immediately."

Mitch paused on the steps. He could do as the General said.

Return to base and take his chances. He looked up towards the forty-second floor, and then moved his p-rat back to the reset screen. Once he rebooted again, he couldn't go back.

He remembered the image of the Goliath, the massive structure, and the feeling of familiarity that had washed over him. He didn't know what it meant. He didn't know what any of this meant, but he had to find out.

He hit the reset.

[17]

THE FIRST OFFICER caught up to him on the ground floor, opening
the door to the stairs at the same time Mitchell reached the bottom.
They were in one another's face for only a second before Mitchell's
fist hit the man hard in the gut, doubling him over. He knocked the
gun from the officer's hand and threw him to the ground, rushing
through the door and out into the lobby.

He didn't want to kill anyone.

There were a lot of civilians in the hotel, waiting on nearby
couches, talking to the concierge, or crossing to the lifts. A squad of
police were moving in through the front, a precursor to the military
that would follow.

Mitchell ducked back into the stairwell. It continued down
another dozen floors, into the basement and a garage below it. He
kicked the first officer again, knocking him out and keeping him
down, and then returned to the descent.

The ARR finished resetting.

"Third floor parking."

The voice was clear in his mind. It was muffled but familiar.
Who had spoken to him without a knock signal? How?

Christine had helped him escape. She had even kissed him, as if that wasn't strange enough. Now someone was giving him directions? He navigated the p-rat back to the reset and hit it again.

The door to the stairwell opened above him.

"Captain Williams! Stop, or we will shoot."

He drew the AZ-9 and kept going. He wouldn't shoot first, and he wouldn't hit them if he did. They were only following orders.

The bullets pinged the steps and railing around him, whizzing by his head, coming dangerously close to ending the chase before he even discovered who had sent him the message. Mitchell turned his head and fired back, keeping his aim high, hoping to push them off. The officers' volley paused while he unloaded a few rounds and reached the third floor, and then resumed as he hit the touchscreen to make it open.

It didn't.

"What?" Mitchell said. He hit it again, and then ducked into the corner, squeezing against the wall to avoid the gunfire. He should have expected this. The entire building was on lockdown.

The bullets stopped coming.

"You can't get out, Captain. Please, just come out with your hands up."

They were coming down the stairwell, slowly enough to back away if he started shooting at them again. Mitchell cursed silently and glanced over at the door. He wasn't going to be getting out that way. The only escape from the stairwell was in the officers' custody.

"Ok. Don't shoot. I'm coming out." He put the AZ-9 on the ground and kicked it out where they could see it. "I'm unarmed."

He started inching away from the wall. The officers were still up a couple of floors, leaning down, weapons trained on him. One broke away, descending faster to bind him.

His p-rat came back online.

"Get out of the way," the voice said. "Now!"

Mitchell's combat training took over. He reacted instantly, dropping and rolling forward, his hand going out to where the AZ-9 was resting on the ground. He grabbed it at the same time something hit the door and it exploded inward in a screeching cacophony of grinding metal. The officers fell back in surprise.

The door was reduced to mangled slag. Mitchell hurried to his feet, ignoring the burning in his back from a piece of shrapnel that had skimmed him. If he hadn't reacted as quickly as he did, he would have been dead. He took a pair of stumbling steps and then dashed out into the garage. The soft woosh of a bike approached from his left, and then it was next to him, the rider holding out a helmet and beckoning him to get on.

He recognized the bike and the rider right away. The assassin that had tried to kill him. Now they were helping him? He paused, unsure, until he heard the sound of boots on the steps behind them. He took the helmet, pulled it over his head, and swung onto the back of the bike. The repulsors whined as they worked to hold it steady at the new unbalanced force, and then they were off, racing across the parking lot well ahead of the police.

"Whatever happens, don't take off the headgear," his rescuer said through speakers in the helmet. A man, judging by the solid shape of him beneath Mitchell's arms. "It's jamming the transmissions to and from the ARR."

"Who are you?" Mitchell asked.

They hit the ramp up, and the bike skidded on pads of air, drifting around the turns towards the exit.

"Later," came the reply. "Once we're safe."

The bike reached the ground level. The gate was closed, a police cruiser parked in front of it, four officers positioned behind the car with their rifles aimed forward.

They slowed but didn't stop. The assassin pulled something from in front of him and tossed it up into the air. It was a small, flat disc, and it spun stationary for a split-second before zipping forward.

It exploded when it hit the gate, the force strong enough to push the car and the police behind it back, tearing them apart and clearing the wreckage from their path. The bike sped up, whizzing past the carnage and out into the street.

"You killed them," Mitchell said, feeling nauseous at the idea. These were the good guys. Men and women with families that were only doing their jobs and trying to keep the city safe.

"They would have killed you."

He turned to look back at the smoke pouring from the side of the hotel. Whatever happened from here there was no going back.

They zoomed onto the street, the agility of the bike keeping them at a good pace as they looped around and between the mix of piloted and automated vehicles, threading their way in the direction of the spaceport. They made it three blocks before the first of the military air support arrived in the form of a small, wedge-shaped drone with a rotating laser cannon slung between the repulsors on either side.

It moved in above them, following their path but not risking a shot in the density of the city. It was no doubt recording their position, helping the other units determine a way to box them in.

The assassin picked up another of the discs and threw it upwards, in the general direction of the ship. It hovered for a moment and then rose towards it. The onboard computer must have identified it as a threat because the laser cannon swiveled and fired a single shot at it. For the AI to fire, it had to be certain it wouldn't hit any civilians.

Somehow, the disc avoided the Shot. The laser hit a car in front of them, burning through its engine and dropping it to the pavement like a stone. A moment later, the disc hit the ship and exploded, knocking the craft from the sky. The largest piece of debris plummeted onto the street behind them, leading to crashes and screams.

The destruction seemed to spur the defenses into more aggressive action. Two more of the drone ships fell into the space between buildings, cannons rotating towards them and preparing to fire. The assassin skidded to the left and down an alley before they could take the Shot, cutting into a space too narrow for the ships to follow. He came to a stop halfway through, dropping a small device onto the street before returning to the original path.

"Dummy signature," he said, explaining the maneuver. The device would fool the AI into thinking they were still sitting in the alley, a trick that would buy them a little bit of time.

"It's still a kilometer to the spaceport," Mitchell said. "It's going to be crawling with military."

"We're not going to the spaceport. We just want them to think we are."

They burst back out onto the street, finding the traffic stalled in the mayhem and the pedestrians retreating to the safety of the buildings. It made it easier for them to travel, the bike able to climb the hoods of the other vehicles, or ride along the sidewalks. They cleared another four blocks, still headed in the direction of the spaceport.

An armored Suppressor moved out into the street in front of them, the turret on top rotating and opening fire. Bullets kicked up pavement in front of them, and the bike swerved back and forth in an effort to stay ahead of the targeting computers. Mitchell watched it coming, wincing as the bullets drew ever closer to them, waiting for the moment they began to sink into his flesh. The ping of slugs against the frame of the bike was cut short when the bike reached another alley, getting out of the line of fire and escaping the storm.

They crossed the alley onto another street, turning and lurching forward, cutting across before the Suppressor could catch up. It fired at them from behind as they moved away.

More drones began flowing in from overhead. If they managed to lock on with their lasers, they were as good as dead.

"We aren't going to make it," Mitchell said. He didn't even know where his rescuer was taking him, but the net was closing fast.

The bike continued to accelerate, weaving around stopped cars, bouncing over the sidewalk. He stayed as close to the civilians as he could, knowing the AI wouldn't take a shot as long as innocents were at risk.

"We already did," the assassin replied. He shifted his weight and turned the handle of the bike, forcing it into a leaning skid that brought them out onto the edge of an overpass. Stretching below them were the hyperlanes, fully autonomous highways that carried ground vehicles from city to city at ultra-high speeds.

Mitchell felt his heart stop. He couldn't possibly...

The bike zipped forward, straight towards the divider that separated the above-ground city lanes from the hyperlanes below. A third disc came to his hand, and he threw it forward at the wall.

Mitchell closed his eyes. The AI would sense the debris and stop the traffic, but would it be fast enough to keep innocent people from being killed in a horrific crash? He didn't think so, and he didn't want to see his fear confirmed.

He heard the explosion, felt the heat of it. The whine of the bike's repulsors changed as it shot out into open air, twenty feet above solid mass. Then they were angling downward, dropping to the ground below at the same time he heard the din of the destruction at their backs. The repulsors scraped along the ground and the bike wobbled and almost fell out from beneath them before the rider straightened it up, and the automated systems caught the new vehicle. His rescuer hit a button, and a weak energy shield wrapped around them. It wouldn't be enough to stop a bullet or a laser, but it protected them from the elements as the lane system pulled them to speed.

Mitchell couldn't believe they had made it.

[18]

THEY EXITED the hyperlanes twenty minutes later, nearly eight hundred kilometers from York. The spot wasn't a designated exit, but a stretch of open air surrounded by fields. The assassin had done something to override the autonomous control of the bike and impressively steered them off the grid.

They had ridden through the fields, over an embankment that separated the hyperlanes from the land and into a massive growth of wheat. The farms on Liberty were corporate owned, thousands of acres across, tended by huge machines that towered over the crops and were surrounded by smaller drones that did more delicate work. Mitchell could see a couple of them off in the distance, but their own path was clear.

"They won't expect that we ditched ahead of an exit," his rescuer said. His voice sounded strained. "We should be safe."

"Where are we going?"

"There's an old hangar fifty klicks east of here. It's going to be torn down in the next couple of weeks, but it's there now. So is our ship."

"Our ship?"

"Yes. It isn't pretty, but it will get you off Liberty."

"Who are you?" Mitchell asked again.

"Not yet. When we reach the hangar."

They sped through the field in silence, the energy shield throwing up sparks of brighter light as the wheat bounced off. They reached a narrow road and raced along it, headed east. Mitchell sat behind the assassin, focusing on his breathing, trying to clear his head. What the hell was he doing on this bike? The man he had escaped with had killed an untold number of people getting them out of York, not to mention Corporal Kwon and four civilians two days earlier. And he had tried to kill *him*.

Or had he?

He had been shot in the side of the head. Grazed, right at the place where his neural implant was located. It had been damaged, shorted, and ever since then...

He put his hand to the side of his helmet and wondered at the implications. Had the whole assassination attempt been a ruse? Had the engineers who fixed the implant done something to it in the process? The implant was a direct link to his brain, and it had routines built in that could both monitor and assist in controlling nearly every basic function.

Could he trust his own mind?

The idea almost frightened him more than the thought of his impending public implosion when Tamara went live with her report of his fraud, when the Prime Minister called him out as a rapist, and when General Cornelius sang in tune to all of it and denied the military's involvement in the lie.

It all felt so surreal, and at the same time so oddly familiar. As if he had known this was going to happen.

Or, as if it had happened before.

What about Christine? He hoped she had managed to get through it with her own integrity intact. He still didn't get why she had helped him escape, or what was with that kiss. He also didn't get why his mind kept going back to that, of all things. The Major was physically attractive, sure, but there was so much about her he found grating. Why did he care that her lips tasted like honey? That her mouth was soft and warm and perfect.

He stopped himself. It was those kind of thoughts that got him into this mess to begin with. If he survived, if he managed to get off Liberty and make it through another day...

He was done with women.

The bike pulled off the road a few minutes later, making a beeline down a small path between overgrown brush until finally reaching the abandoned hangar. It was made of poly-alloy and ultra-light molded concrete, a grayish-rose color that looked like a pimple in the middle of the green field that surrounded it. There was rust showing around the edges, and part of the back corner had either collapsed or been knocked down by vandals. The doors were closed, a magnetic lock bolted to it and keeping them that way.

His rescuer stopped the bike, and they both dismounted. Mitchell noticed the man was the same height as him, with a build that was probably very similar beneath his rider's padding. He reached up to take his helmet off.

"Don't," the other man said. "Inside." He walked up to the lock and put his palm against it. It deactivated, and he pulled the doors halfway open. Then he turned and headed back for the bike.

That was when Mitchell saw the blood.

"You were hit," he said.

It was thick on the man's chest, flowing steadily enough that it had stained the entire front of the padded suit he was wearing.

"Yes. Three times." He grabbed the handlebars and led the bike into the hangar. Mitchell followed behind him.

A single light went on when they entered. It was resting on a simple metal table in the corner, a bright diode that bathed the entire building in a daylight glow, including the ship the assassin had mentioned.

It was a starfighter. Not a Moray. Older. A dual-purpose configuration, intended for use in space and atmospheric missions. He stared at it, trying to remember the model. A pair of vectoring thrusters on the top and bottom and fixed gun mounts facing front, a long beak with seating for two in the cockpit, a wedge-shaped set of wings with small missile launchers extruding along them, and a flat tail that sported a pair of thrusters at the rear. Compared to the Moray, the thing was a brick.

"An S-17," the man said. "It's more agile than it looks."

He stood at the table, picking up a tool from it that Mitchell didn't recognize.

The S-17. That was it. The ship had to be sixty years old, at least.

"We need to disable your implant," his rescuer said.

"What?"

"The helmet you're wearing is jamming the signal, but as soon as you take it off the Alliance will know exactly where you are. You don't want to get caught, do you?"

Mitchell stared at the device.

"Trust me, you don't want to get caught." The man walked over to him. "Take off the helmet."

"Why don't you take off yours?"

"I don't have a fixed implant. The helmet is a surrogate. I need it to help me zoom in on your skull. Now lean down and let me do this. We don't have a lot of time."

Mitchell leaned down, and the man positioned himself next to his head.

"Now, take off the helmet. Quickly."

Mitchell grabbed the sides of the helmet and pulled it off. The moment he did he was greeted with a shrill tone that forced him to clench his jaw. Then he felt a sting and the warmth of his blood on his cheek. The tone vanished.

"Remote disable," the man said. "Nasty. It won't bother you again."

"I didn't know they could do that," Mitchell said.

"If they used it, it means they have no intent on bringing you back alive to tell anyone else about it."

He returned to the table, bending down and reaching under it. He came up holding a jumpsuit similar to his and a pair of boots.

"Lose the uniform, put this on."

Mitchell didn't question. He stripped out of the jacket, shirt, and pants, and then slipped on the jumpsuit and boots. They were both a perfect fit.

"You obviously know who I am, where to find me, what size clothes I wear," Mitchell said. "Isn't it time you told me what all of this is about?"

The man paused. Then he reached for his helmet.

"Yes. I think it is."

He lifted the helmet from his head.

Mitchell found himself looking back at... himself?

[19]

EARTH. *October 21, 2055*

"Smile team, you're about to make history."

Kathy smiled, careful not to squint her eyes when she did. It was hard enough to keep them open with the glare from the New Mexico sun. Rising up a kilometer behind her was a massive block of alloy and carbonate. It was spread almost two thousand meters long and two hundred meters tall across the plains, bolstered another twenty meters by the repulsor sled that had been built beneath it.

A starship. An honest to god, made in the U.S.A. starship.

And she was one of the pilots.

It was a dream she had known since she was able to recall dreaming about anything. A path she had been so sure of since the day that XENO-1 had plummeted from the sky. A future that had been so clear, so straight, that in the back of her mind she had somehow always known that this day would come. Somehow.

There were thousands of people lining the viewing area out on the plains, the dignitaries from nearly every nation in the world getting the front row seat to the event. The ship had been built here on the New Mexico flats, but the workers had arrived from dozens of countries to add their own skill and expertise to the design and construction. It truly was the work of an allied world, one that had overcome so many of the past squabbles over the last few years in exchange for a piece of this history.

And she was going up in it.

"One more."

The cameras didn't flash. Not in this light. There were so many of them.

A roar of engines, and a squadron of F-70s split the sky, trailing colored smoke as they cut overhead and away. Kathy looked up at them, watching them until they vanished into the skyline.

"Major Asher," Bonnie said. "Smile."

Kathy put her eyes straight again and smiled. Bonnie was the ship's navigator, an Irish woman with a round face and a great singing voice. The ship's computer would be handling the course for this test run, but she still needed to be there - just in case.

One hour to liftoff. She'd survived the two years of training, the black tie gala two nights ago, and a dozen speeches from a dozen heads of state today. Now she just wanted to get on board the Dove, to get up there and out among the stars. She wanted to get on with her mission, a mission that was more important than any of them may have realized.

"Time to go," Rear Admiral Yousefi said. He was the CO of this mission, and of the Dove - a position that had been more highly sought after than any that had ever come before. That he was a former member of the Federation, a former enemy, had been forgotten over the last few years. They were all in this together, now, regardless of country or branch of the military.

"Yes, sir," Kathy said, along with the others. They broke their photo formation and lined up behind him, facing the Dove, more affectionately known to them, and the media, as Goliath. The whole thing had been orchestrated ahead of time, every detail given the suitable pomp. A live band started playing over nearby loudspeakers, and the crowd began to cheer.

They weren't going to walk the kilometer to the ship. Instead, they walked a few hundred meters to a waiting transport, itself a sample of their newfound technology. It floated a few inches from the ground, the repulsors keeping it steady, the engine nearly silent. A platform telescoped out from the rear, allowing them to climb up onto it, remaining in the open air so that the bystanders could see them.

"I feel like a sheep in the summer," Bonnie said.

The transport accelerated steadily, lifting further into the air, six feet or more to show that it could. The repulsor technology was almost as impressive as the FTL engines that had been reverse-engineered from what the scientists had discovered on XENO-1. She didn't understand much of the math, but she knew it had something to do with harnessing dark matter to fight the pull of gravity.

The crowd cheered louder. The transport moved steadily towards the Goliath, which rose higher and higher above them until it blocked the sun behind it. Kathy had been in it over a hundred times already, and even now she gasped at the sheer immensity of the ship, her mind boggled by the impressiveness of humanity's undertaking. That they had been able to work together to build such a thing was unbelievable.

Soon enough, there was nothing to see but the cold alloy sides of the ship. A hatch opened in front of them, leading into what was intended as a hangar. Assuming the FTL engine tests were successful, they would stock the ship with smaller ships that could spread out and search for E-type planets, other signs of life, or other valuable resources before returning to the Goliath. Their primitive application of the alien technology wasn't the only reason the ship was so large.

For now, the hangar was empty, except for the transport. It landed smoothly and they disembarked, heading out a side hatch and moving down an open corridor.

"Welcome home," Yousefi said.

Even after the FTL test, they were to be the first crew of the Dove, and would spend two years aboard her. Thankfully, however the engines worked they didn't affect relativity the way Einstein had predicted. Time in what they had decided to call hyperspace, in honor of the science fiction that had coined it, passed the same as time on Earth. They called the travel faster-than-light, but it wasn't technically accurate. Kathy didn't understand exactly how it worked, and she didn't really need to. FTL was good enough to describe that they were traveling maximal space in minimal time.

"Dove, we are at T-minus forty-five minutes," the voice said through the ship's comm system.

"Roger, Command," Yousefi said.

They continued to walk, reaching the central hub of the ship. It was a small, round space, with a lift in the center and four hatches that branched out around it, a setup that was repeated across all of the Goliath's decks. The crew paused for a moment while the lift hatch opened, and they all climbed in.

"I'm so excited, I think I'm going to pee in my flight suit," Bonnie said.

"I already did," Kathy joked.

"Let's save the urine for the recycling system," Yousefi said.

The lift carried them up to the center of the ship, a hatch on the opposite side sliding open and leading them to the control room. They walked towards it in anxious silence. It slid open as they neared, revealing a design that looked like it could have come from a sci-fi movie and had certainly been at least partially inspired by one. A central command station with a large captain's chair was positioned near the center while other stations circled it, each surrounded by its own set of semi-transparent screens.

It all seemed to float in the middle of the open New Mexico air. The entire room was a massive projection system, capturing data from hundreds of cameras mounted around the Goliath's hull and merging them together into a nearly seamless three hundred sixty-degree view of the ship's surroundings. It was impressive to see, and to experience, and every time Kathy entered the room she felt like she was taking a giant leap of faith that the floor was really there, and she wouldn't go tumbling down into the dirt below them.

The designers had originally wanted to install a bridge at the top of the Goliath, with a clear carbonate bubble through which they could observe space directly. They hadn't perfected the process yet, and efforts to produce something of that size had all ended in failure during stress testing. There were smaller viewports in different areas of the ship, but most were head-sized at best. It was a little disappointing that they had to rely on mechanical eyes, but at least they were ultra-sharp mechanical eyes.

They took their seats, strapping themselves in. The ship was equipped with "repulsor repulsors," an engineering joke term for artificial gravity, which was essentially the reverse polarity of the repulsor technology. The straps were there just in case that tech failed.

"Nothing to do now but wait," Captain Pathi said. He was one of the five engineers on the crew, who were in charge of trying to fix anything that went wrong in-flight, including the artificial gravity.

Kathy stared out through the view feed. She was leaving her planet behind. She wished her parents were alive to see it.

The minutes seemed to pass so slowly. They all sat on the bridge together in tense silence. Maybe some were praying, maybe some were running through their own duties over and over in their mind. Kathy sat in silent contentment. This was what she was born to do.

"T-minus one minute," Command said.

That brought her back to attention. The computer was supposed handle the liftoff, but she had a stick in front of her, just in case something went wrong. If it did, it was her job to keep them going up and out, to get them into orbit. She put her hand on it. The feel of the familiar shape was comforting.

"Twenty seconds," Command said.

"All systems are operational," Pathi said. "Generators are purring like happy cats."

"Ten seconds."

"Nine."

"Eight."

Kathy took a deep breath, letting it out slowly, feeling the tingling in her nerves, the butterflies in her stomach.

"Four."

"Three."

"Two."

"One."

"Flipping the switch," Yousefi said. In truth, he pressed the enter key and initiated the launch sequence.

The ship began to rise.

"Not as impressive as the old way," Bonnie said with a nervous laugh.

The repulsor sled beneath them wouldn't make much noise at all, unlike the rockets that used to get things into space. Instead, they floated upwards almost silently, the massive sled bringing the even more massive starship up into the sky.

"Command, we have liftoff," Yousefi said with a satisfied smile.

Command cheered over the comm channel. Kathy could picture the thousands gathered to watch the moment cheering, along with the billions who were seeing it on screens around the globe.

They rose ever higher, the sled gaining momentum over time. By the third minute, they were approaching the atmosphere.

"All systems optimal," Captain Pathi reported.

"Kind of boring, really," Bonnie said, though her face betrayed her. She was wearing a huge smile, her eyes like saucers.

And then they were out into space.

Kathy watched her screen and waited for confirmation that the sequence had gone as programmed. "Sled released, Admiral. Standard thrusters firing." The thrusters would pull them out of orbit.

"Congratulations, team. We're in space," Yousefi said.

Kathy stared out the view screen. They were facing away from Earth, but it was true. There was nothing in front of them but stars - open space that was a whole new frontier for them to explore. A tear of joy made its way to her eye, and she left it to run down her cheek while she said a prayer of thanks.

"FTL engine is coming online," Captain Pathi said. "Two minutes to FTL test."

It was the moment of truth. All of the simulations had been successful, but the nature of FTL meant that it couldn't be tested without sending something up to actually do it. They had wanted to use a non-piloted ship, but the countries in the Alliance complained. They all wanted to send a crew member of their own up in the inaugural voyage, and there was certainly no shortage of volunteers willing to risk their lives on the missions. Since the ship had to be large to house the engine anyway, the Alliance had decided to go all-in and build something reusable, and trust the scientists that were certain the technology was viable and functional.

They were about to find out.

"One minute," Pathi said.

The ship began to vibrate slightly, a pressure building around them.

"Is this normal?" Yousefi asked.

"Nobody knows what normal is." Pathi sounded nervous.

The ship's vibration grew.

"Thirty seconds," Pathi announced.

Kathy closed her eyes, absorbing the feel of the vibrations. She was accustomed to the shaking, it had always happened to the F-70 when she swooped in on a target, the force threatening to tear the fighter apart and leave her to fall to her death. She had never worried that it would happen. She had never worried that she might die.

She wasn't worried now.

The shaking increased, forceful enough that their bodies shifted in their harnesses. The stars began to blur in the viewscreen, coalescing together into a solid, blinding white light.

"Twenty seconds."

There was creaking from the joints, and red data flowed across the walls.

"Abort," Yousefi said. "Abort."

Pathi was at his keyboard. "It isn't responding, sir," he said. "Ten seconds."

Kathy looked around at the crew. They were scared. She glanced at the view screen. It was completely white, as if they had fallen out of space and into sheer nothing.

Or everything.

The view screen went out.

"Five seconds."

Yousefi leaned forward in the command chair, his eyes wide and his mouth open in a silent scream. His knuckles were white against the armrests.

"Two... One..."

To the people on the ground, the Goliath was a dark speck that was there one moment, and gone the next.

They would wait for it, a countdown timer showing them the five minutes that the ship was supposed to be gone.

They would wait, silent and anxious, as that clock ran down to zero.

Then they would wait, silent and fearful, to see if the ship would ever return.

Then they would go home, in small groups at first, and then a flood, witness not to mankind's greatest success, but its most visible failure.

20

"IT CAN'T BE," he said. The man in front of him wasn't just similar in appearance. He was identical, right down to the small notch in his ear that Mitchell had gotten in boot camp during a live fire exercise.

It couldn't be, but he knew it was.

"You can call me M," the man said. "I know this is a little shocking. The important thing to know is that I'm not you. Not exactly. I'm a clone of your DNA, an identical twin in a sense. A replica, except one with all of your memories - past, present, and future."

Mitchell wasn't sure he had heard him right. "Did you say future?"

"Yes."

"As in time travel?" He would never have even entertained it, except he was looking in a mirror. A living, breathing, speaking mirror.

M shook his head. "Not exactly. We don't have a lot of time, Mitchell. The damage I've sustained is fatal. I've lost too much blood, and my heart rate is already beginning to slow. I'm here because I'm desperate. We're all desperate. We need your help."

"Who needs my help?"

"The human race."

"I don't understand."

M's eyes traveled the hangar, as though he expected someone, or something, to be listening.

"Have you ever heard of eternal return?"

"No."

"In simple terms, it means that time is circular, not linear. That everything which is happening today will happen again at some time in the future, whether it is a billion years, a hundred trillion years, or some greater length of time that can't be easily fathomed or understood. To think of it in a more analytical way, given infinite time and a finite number of potential events, these events will repeat infinitely, starting and ending and starting again with what you know as the Big Bang. For millennia it was only a theory, a religious belief, a footnote of potentiality. Then we created the eternal engine."

Mitchell stared at M. It was the craziest thing he had ever heard. "You're saying that you made an engine that can travel billions of years into the future? That this, all of this, has happened already?"

"Yes. And no. It's a long story, and I won't be alive to tell it. I know this is difficult for you to believe, but consider that humans once thought the Earth was flat, too. Ask yourself, if time is a loop, what happens when one is able to traverse the loop, either by moving infinitely forward in infinite time, or standing infinitely still for infinite time? The problem with time travel on a linear plane is that it creates paradoxes, questions that are impossible to resolve. Once you've accepted eternal recurrence as the universal truth, all of this will begin to make more sense."

Mitchell spent a few moments thinking about it, trying to understand. "If time is a loop, and you injected yourself into that loop, that means this couldn't have happened before. You threw the entire loop of events askew. How does the universe handle that?"

"The minute I arrived here, every loop that occurs after this one will have the me from the prior loop injected into it at the exact same place and the exact same point of time. The nature of the engine requires that it traverse one cycle at a time. The nature of the time loop means that the minute I arrived here, I closed off every instant of past time within this cycle. Locking it, so to speak. When I say I have memories of your future, that isn't quite true. I have memories of the future you experienced in my original timeline, the source loop. I can tell you everything that happens in that future, but with any luck none of that will come to pass here, now. My presence here, their presence here, has assured that."

"So then tell me, what happens in your future?"

"Humanity is destroyed."

"What?"

"They're coming, Mitchell. The ones who created me. I escaped ahead of them. I came back here to warn you, and to get to you before they did."

"Before who did? Why me?"

"You're the only one who can stop them."

"How do you-"

"You almost did. You came so close." M put his hand to his bloody chest. "I don't have enough time to explain it all. I wasn't expecting this. I didn't know this was going to happen." He smiled. "I couldn't see it."

"The Goliath," Mitchell said, the image of the massive ship's hull blinking into his mind. "This has something to do with the Goliath."

M looked pleased. "Yes. It has everything to do with the Goliath. When time loops, you retain a distant subconscious memory of your prior existence, because the bulk of the matter that makes you who you are has reassembled in the same place, at the same time, to create you once more. Most people never recognize this, they never connect to it. But some do. It is the reason people believe in things like reincarnation or love at first sight, even if they don't understand it.

"The other night, when you were in the bar. There was an attempt on your life, an attack arranged by the Frontier Federation in retaliation for the Shot. I knew the time and place from your history. I knew when to arrive to get the best vantage point."

"You shot me."

"One time. One bullet. There were four shooters that night, Mitchell. There should have only been the two in the car. You killed them. I killed the other, who was under their control. The bullet I fired was not a normal projectile. It was electromagnetically charged, designed to short your neural implant and hopefully trigger your latent subconscious. I wasn't sure it had been effective until you ran a query for Goliath. I was certain you were remembering, but you gave up so quickly. I've been trying not to affect the loop too drastically because every change moves us further from the past I wanted only to nudge. I was still debating whether to risk confronting you in person when they forced my hand."

"You're talking about Holly?" He knew there had been something to her sudden memory loss. He would never have guessed someone else had done something to her.

"Yes. The Prime Minister's wife."

"How did they do it?"

"Your neural implant is connected to a receiver. That receiver is connected to a number of channels, both public and private, which feed transmissions into the implant, and from the implant directly to your brain. The signals are massively encrypted, but that encryption is useless when the enemy has the keys. Instead of images or words, they passed binary through the channel. Commands."

"They hypnotized her?"

"That's one way of looking at it. More accurately, they used her like a drone."

"The come-ons, the sex?"

"Don't underestimate them, Mitchell. They are very different, but also very alike. Faking sexual interest is not a difficult task, especially when it comes to a man like us."

Mitchell felt his face flush at the inference. "I still don't understand why?"

"To stop you. And to stop me before I could help you again."

"Help me with what?"

"Your future. You fought them, and you lost. I traveled across timelines to stop you from making the same mistake. I thought I had escaped unnoticed, but they followed me, and now they mean to ensure that humanity still loses. Everything in this timeline is different now, altered beyond any but the basest understanding of what events might recur. Every infinite future is changed. I don't know what will happen now. Your one hope, your best hope, is that they don't either."

Mitchell put his hand on his head. This couldn't be happening. This couldn't be real.

"What about Christine?" The thought came to him suddenly. She had helped him. Why?

"Who?"

"Major Arapo. She helped me escape. She told me to find the Goliath. I can't figure out how she knew, or why she did it. She doesn't even like me, and she kissed me."

M shrugged. "It may have been a residual transference from the implant. I don't know."

"You didn't drone her or anything?" He knew it sounded stupid. He knew he was stupid for even thinking about her at a time like this. He had a feeling there was something to her actions, something to her. Something just out of reach.

"No," M repeated. "It was not my doing. It doesn't matter now, Mitchell. I've provided you with a ship. I'm sorry I won't be able to make the journey with you. Go. Now. The Goliath is waiting for you, hidden among the stars. It holds the key to your salvation. To mankind's salvation."

"How am I supposed to find it?"

"You will. You have to. It's the only way mankind will survive them."

Mitchell growled, his frustration beginning to wear through. "Damn it, survive who?" he shouted. "Who or what the hell are you supposed to be?"

M didn't answer. He started coughing, and then he dropped to his knees. His face was pale, his forehead sweaty. The blood had soaked through his shirt and jacket, and ran down his leg to pool at his feet.

"Be careful who you trust," he said, his voice fading. "Our technology is more advanced than yours. The normal encryption isn't safe, and you aren't safe around anyone who has a standard receiver."

"How can I believe you? How can I believe any of this?" He stared at his clone. It was ridiculous, insane. Maybe he was insane? "Who are they? How do you know that they're coming for me, or that they caused all of this?"

M looked up at him, their eyes locking. "Take the ship. Get out of here. Find Goliath, or you will all die."

He pitched forward onto his stomach and didn't move again.

21

MITCHELL STARED down at M. For everything he had just been told, for everything he had just experienced, looking at his own dead body was the hardest part.

"What the hell do I do now?" he said, his skin cold and clammy, his heart pulsing. He looked back at the S-17. Did he really have a decision to make? Did he have a choice? If what M had said about their intent to kill him was true, and he was certain it was after they had rampaged through the city, he could either get in the starfighter or die. "Find the Goliath. How am I supposed to do that?"

M hadn't given him an answer or a clue, and space was a big, big place. The Goliath could be anywhere within a galaxy millions of light years around.

If he couldn't find it, the war was already lost. What war? One that didn't exist, against an enemy that didn't exist?

Mitchell put his hand to his head, feeling the cut the device had left in it, and the crusted blood around the edge. He questioned whether any of it was real. Was the dead man at his feet real? He bent down and rolled him over, looking away from the face, his face, staring back at him with blank eyes. He smacked his head, feeling the burn of the wound being reopened. If there was a short in the implant, would this fix it?

When he looked at M again, the face was still a replica of his own. He flopped back onto the ground, sitting and staring out into the daylight through the crack in the hangar door.

"You wanted to fight, Mitch," he said to himself. Either he had gone mad and didn't know it, or he was completely sane, and the threat was real. In the end, it didn't matter. His only option was to live in the world that he believed existed around him, and hope he didn't hurt too many innocents.

He sat there for another minute, letting the stark reality sink in. Then he got to his feet, dusted himself off, and began undressing M. It was a macabre process, made all the more sinister by the man's appearance. It had to be done. Once M was naked, Mitchell grabbed his uniform from where M had stashed it on the floor and clumsily dressed the dead man in it. When he was finished with that, he prodded at the wounds until they oozed more blood out onto the clean shirt, and then wiped the original bloody one against it for good measure.

Satisfied that M was a convincing enough stand-in, he made his way to the hangar doors and finished pulling them the rest of the way open. He scanned the sky, noticing a dark spot against it some distance away. He started to pull up his p-rat to magnify it before remembering his implant was dead. He hoped he could fly the fighter without it.

He returned to the inside of the hangar and picked up M's helmet. He had said he used it as a substitute for an ARR. Hopefully, it would work some magic for him, too.

He walked over to the S-17. A small hatch in the side beneath the cockpit slid open and a line of small, narrow lifters organized to the ground. Mitchell furrowed his brow in confusion. As far as he knew, nobody had managed to create lifters that small, never mind install them into the nose of a fighter. M hadn't mentioned any upgrades. He had barely mentioned the ship at all.

Mitchell climbed the steps. The cockpit slid silently open at his approach, and he swung himself inside. It was old and worn, the safety straps faded, the textile seat torn in places. A joystick sat on his right side, two pedals rested near his feet, and a series of controls ran along his left. The front of the cockpit was filled with instruments, buttons, and dials, a throwback to the days when ship designers were afraid to leave pilots without control, or at least the feeling that they had some control, in the event of a critical systems loss. Mitchell had to think back to the first trainer he had flown to remember what most of them were for. The newer fighters like the Moray didn't have a dashboard - everything was delivered to the p-rat.

The clear carbonate slid closed over his head, and he felt the pressurization in his ears. Mitchell scanned the cluster for the ignition, finding the switch on the right side of the panel. He flipped it.

Nothing happened.

"Are you kidding?" Mitchell said, staring at the dashboard. He toggled the switch again.

Still nothing.

Was the fighter broken? Dead? He searched the panels for the toggle to open the cockpit again. He found it on the left. When he hit it, the clear shell began pulling back. A soft hiss alerted him that the cabin was depressurizing, followed by the clearly audible whine of an engine and the rhythmic echo of a running mech.

They had found him.

"Of course they did, because I can't get this old piece of shit to work," he said, toggling the cockpit closed again. He'd watched similar scenes in movies plenty of times before. It was supposed to be drama, not his actual life.

He hit the ignition a few more times. "Come on, you bastard."

The first drone became visible in front of the hangar, still a few miles away. Too far for its laser to do any serious damage. He hit the ignition again.

"Come on, come on, come-"

He glanced down at M's helmet in his lap, feeling like an idiot.

He lifted it up and over his head.

The entire world around him changed.

In an instant, every incoming vehicle was painted in front of his eyes, along with speeds and vectors that flew into his brain faster than he could have consciously processed. A second later, the familiar connection to the ship he was sitting in became obvious to him. Somehow, the old bucket had a CAP-NN link that didn't require a direct contact. The helmet was enough.

Mitchell brought the engines online with a thought. The reactor was silent, but he knew he was up and running.

A huge, metal man moved in front of the open hangar door. A Zombie, the military's favorite eighty-ton mech. It was all sharp angles and odd surfaces, meant to reduce its signature on scans. It was humanoid shaped, with articulating hands and feet, burst jets mounted over its shoulder blades, and weapons interspersed at various points along the frame. There were twin missile launchers embedded in the chest, a pulse laser on each wrist, and a heavy machine-gun protruding from its belly. It also carried a massive railgun cradled in its hands. There was no sign of the pilot. The cockpit was positioned at the back of the machine, inside a shell of poly-alloy and nano-composite that could absorb a lot of punishment. It meant Mitchell could fight back against the mech and not have to worry too much about killing one of his own.

If he could fight back.

He thought about the weapons systems and the neural link returned the data on his offensive potential. He nearly lost his focus. The steps hadn't been the only upgrade M had made to the old fighter.

The Zombie started raising the railgun. One shot from the heavy slug at this range would go clear through the fighter, shields or not. Right now, he was a sitting duck.

A well-armed sitting duck. He fired at the Zombie, blinded by the flash of blue light that flowed from the front of the ship and blasted into the mech, slicing clean through the right leg as though it were nothing. The mech wobbled for a second, the pilot and the AI both fighting to keep it upright.

They failed.

The mech rocked and tumbled away. Mitchell fired the rear thrusters and the smaller vectoring jets, and the S-17 skipped forward and into the air. He launched past the downed mech and out into the sky, urging the fighter into a steep climb, feeling the effects of the G-forces despite the efforts of the negators. A tone in his mind alerted him to the drones readjusting to track him, and he threw the ship into a winding roll.

He couldn't hold back his smile as he pushed the S-17 harder, forcing it into a quick rotation that strained the structure and would have challenged most pilots. He fired on the drones, two of the flat discs shooting out from the launchers in the wings and flying towards them, nearly invisible in the daylight.

Both exploded a moment later.

Another tone sounded. The mech pilot was good, and had managed to get the disabled Zombie into a one-armed kneel. It raised the railgun towards him and fired.

The fighter swung left, narrowly avoiding the Shot. Mitchell dove downwards towards the mech, closing the distance so fast his opponent's synthetic musculature couldn't keep up to reposition the gun. Small missiles launched from its chest, and the fighter responded with a series of quick laser bursts that burned through and detonated each one before they could land.

The mech turned green in Mitchell's helmet. He had a lock but didn't fire. The shell might protect the pilot from conventional weapons. He wasn't sure about this fighter's ordnance, and he didn't want to kill anyone. Instead, he urged the ship back up, pushing hard against gravity and firing the rear thrusters at full. The S-17 came level a dozen feet above the Zombie's head and rocketed low across the wheat fields, spreading them with the force. Mitchell rolled and flipped, shifting and launching into the air, going straight up towards the outer atmosphere.

More targets appeared on the helmet's overlay. Two more Zombies and a full squadron of drones. They had probably expected him to be running to a transport, not a starfighter. By the time they got a few Morays on his tail, he'd be well into orbit and ready to move into FTL.

Assuming the ship had FTL. The original S-17 didn't. No starfighter did. Humanity had made immense progress in reducing the size of the engines over the last four hundred years, but they still couldn't fit them in a package as small as a fighter and provide it with enough power to move into hyperspace.

M had said the enemy technology was much more advanced. Whoever they were? M was a replica of him. Were they all clones? Replicas? Copies? Were they some kind of other human? Or something else entirely? If the modifications done to the S-17 were any indication of their capabilities, there was one thing he was certain of:

Humankind was in a lot of trouble.

Mitchell kept climbing, pushing easily into the upper atmosphere and then finally out into space. He was able to let off the thrusters then, allowing his momentum to keep him moving further from the planet. The neural link continued feeding him information, showing him the positions of the other starships resting in Liberty's orbit. One of them was moving in his direction, a Navy frigate. It wouldn't waste its heavy ordnance on him and would only be carrying two squadrons of fighters.

He asked the CAP-NN for FTL. A moment later a star map appeared inside his helmet as a three-dimensional rendering of the galaxy. A sphere appeared around the fighter, showing him what the ship had the power to reach.

He stared at the map. He had no idea where to go. No idea where to start looking for the Goliath. What he did know was that he needed to shake the frigate. He would get himself somewhere relatively safe, and then he would worry about the rest.

He zoomed in on the map, moving to the outer edge of the sphere. It would deplete the reactor to dangerous levels to make the trip, but he had to risk it. It was the only place in the galaxy where a man whose likeness as well known as his could disappear.

He set a course for the Rim and vanished from the universe.

22

Hyperspace was a lot more fun on a battle cruiser.

That was the thought that kept cycling through Mitchell's mind as the ship traversed hyperspace, leaving him staring at a wall of solid black for what felt like an eternity.

In truth, it was twenty-seven hours. Twenty-seven very long hours.

Long enough that he had been reduced to closing his eyes and trying to recall scenes from his favorite streams in a futile effort to fall asleep.

Long enough that he had to empty his bladder into the flight suit four times, letting the material soak up the urine and distribute it for storage. It kept him dry, but it didn't do much for the smell of the cockpit.

Long enough that he was running out of air.

The ship had calculated the circle based on its power capabilities, not his ability to continue breathing. Or, perhaps M had been much more accomplished at slowing his heart rate and using less oxygen. Or, maybe M hadn't actually needed to breathe at all.

Either way, after twenty-seven hours the fighter fell out of hyperspace, a warning beep sounding in his mind and alerting him to the decreasing levels of oxygen that remained in the system. A fighter pilot was intended to spend a maximum of eight hours on sortie, with a decent backup air supply in case the ship became disabled and needed to wait for a tow. Twenty-seven hours was well beyond the planned use-case and it was a small miracle of its own that he had stretched it as far as he did.

He checked the star map as soon as the ship dropped, noting that it had cut him short of his initial destination in the Rim, and instead left him near a large, barren planetoid. There was no settlement, no refueling station, and no atmosphere to skim for a reload of air. As near as he could tell, he was in the middle of nowhere with about two hours of oxygen left in the tank and no way to replenish it.

"It figures," he said. "Why did you drop me here?"

The ship answered by cutting the main thrusters and using the smaller ones to bring him into a short orbit with the planetoid. He considered overriding it and forcing it back to FTL, but he knew he was still too far away from anything that could help him.

He really was going to die here.

He put his head back and closed his eyes, keeping his breathing as light as he could manage. He was going to die. It was like a cruel, cold joke. He wondered what M would think if he were still alive? Would he be amused by the outcome of his interdiction in time?

Time. Mitchell thought about what M had said, replaying it in his mind over and over again. Eternal return. The idea that everything in his past before M had shown up had happened before and would happen again. Did that mean there was no such thing as fate? Did it mean that people had no control over any aspect of their lives? That it was all predetermined by the last pass through? It couldn't be, could it? Not when nobody knew that they were reliving an endless cycle. It was all unique to him, and to everyone else.

No, not everyone. M said that some people remembered, at least a little. He had remembered the Goliath. Did that mean that he had been on the ship before? That he had found it in a past loop, or a potentially infinite number of past loops? Did it mean that in a different timeline it had never been lost in the first place?

Then there was Major Arapo. The way her kiss sat on the edge of his thoughts, when there had been so many other women, when there had been Ella. Was she a bigger part of his past life than he realized? If so, then how?

It was a lot to process. A lot to try to come to some kind of rational coexistence with. He had a million questions and no answers, and now it wouldn't matter. He didn't need answers anymore.

He only needed air.

What was the likelihood of that? He was a single speck of dust in a universe of infinite dust. It was over, before it had even begun. He should have died with the Greylock, with Ella, or at least instead of her. He'd been gifted extra time to experience another side of life, and he decided it was better to feel grateful for that than to lament what he was about to lose.

He stopped breathing easy, returning his cycle to normal and putting himself into his familiar meditative state. He cleared his mind of thought and worked at easing the tension from his stiff limbs.

He waited to die.

23

He didn't die.

He wasn't sure how long he was meditating for. An hour? Two? He had fallen into a state of calm so deep that he never noticed the dot that appeared on the helmet's overlay. He never saw the ship that moved into position above him.

He only came around to the idea that he wasn't alone when something pounded at the exterior of the cockpit's clear carbonate shell, and he opened his eyes to see a woman in a spacesuit waving at him.

He was still for a moment and then waved back. He could see her face behind the tinted faceplate of her helmet. It was a little pudgy, with a short nose and big lips. Her smile was warm enough. She raised her hand in a thumbs-up sign. He mimicked it, and then clenched his fist to his chest to signal that he was low on air. Her smile vanished, and she motioned away, turning and firing her thrusters.

Mitchell tracked her through the helmet, only then noticing that a ship had arrived and that there were three people tethered to it, moving about around him. Was it a miracle, or had the AI somehow known that another ship was coming to this spot? How could it?

He smiled at the realization. Because it had already happened. Except when these people, whoever they were, had arrived the first time there had been only the planetoid. Now they had found a ship, found him, and all of the future surrounding them had changed again.

It was a heavy thought. Did M know he might run into trouble? Had he arranged for the ship's AI to understand such fine details of his history? Either way, he was thankful.

The fighter turned slightly when tow lines were magnetically sealed to it, the cockpit swinging around and giving him a better view of his rescuers' vessel. It was a salvage ship, a rectangular block with an ugly profile - low-slung thrusters, a bulbous bridge, and all kinds of drilling and cutting equipment hanging from the sides like parasites.

The fighter swung again, tilting to become level with the ship. He couldn't feel the motion of being reeled in, but he could tell the salvager was drawing closer. He turned his head as far as he could, looking up and back until he could see the three people, each holding a line, and the light of the hangar above them. He kept his eyes on them while he was brought inside, the hangar doors closed, and the artificial gravity was activated and he was lowered to the deck.

The woman who had knocked on the glass stood in front of the fighter, holding her hand up, telling him to wait for the room to pressurize and fill with air.

He took the time to look around. The hangar was not quite what he expected. For one, it was clean. There was no sign of the stores of salvaged metals and materials common to ships like this one, held in large nets to keep it contained during zero-g.

For another, there was already a second fighter sitting in the corner, an older model Pirahna, along with a mech. They had a mech? It was a Knight, another older design, sixty tons, with a head shaped like a medieval Earth helmet. It was painted black, and the faceplate had a large, gruesome smile stenciled onto it.

They also had an orbital transport - a means to travel from the ship to atmosphere and to tow their salvage hauls to waiting collection vessels. It was the newest piece of machinery of the bunch, its alloy shell reflective in the bright lights of the hangar.

Mitchell turned his attention back to the woman. She raised her hand and tapped her helmet, and then pulled it off.

He had been right, she was a little pudgy, with small eyes and wild brown hair. She was joined by the other two crew members a moment later - an older man with a mohawk and a scar near his left eye, and a younger guy with red hair. They kept their eyes glued to him as he toggled the cockpit open and got to his feet. Blood began flowing through his legs once more, and he shook them out before extending the small lifters from the nose of the fighter.

"What the-" he heard the younger man say, at the sight of the ladder. The other two remained silent.

Mitchell climbed down, still wearing the helmet. The moment he reached the floor of the hangar, he found a gun pointing at his face.

"Take it off," the older man said. "Now."

"He smells like piss," the woman said, her Russian accent heavy in her words.

Mitchell put his hands up, moving them slowly towards the helmet. The gun stayed on his face while he took hold of the sides and lifted it off. The moment it left his head the cockpit of the fighter slid closed again, and the whole thing shut down.

"Who are you?" the man said.

"Not a threat," Mitchell replied.

"Hey, I know that guy," the younger one said. "I seen him on the streams." He came towards Mitchell, stopping a couple of feet away and examining his face. "Sure, you do smell ripe. You're him though, aren't you? Captain Mitchell Williams, the hero of the Battle for Liberty."

"Yes. I am. Thank you for the pick-up."

The older man kept staring at him. "You're sure you know this guy, Cormac?"

"Yes, sir. I know a face when I see one." Cormac put out his hand. "Good to meet you, Captain. My name is Cormac, Cormac Shen." His smile was large and crooked. "I can't believe I'm touching a celebrity, especially one who met Tamara King, Bethany Daniels, Lin Xiang. You didn't get to do any of them, did you?"

"Cormac," the woman said, smacking him on the shoulder.

Mitchell took his hand, ignoring his question. "Mitchell. You can call me Mitch." He looked over at the older man. "I'm really not a threat. I'm not even armed." He had left his AZ-9 back in the hangar. He was going to miss that gun.

The man was still hesitant.

"Come on, Anderson," the woman said. "Cool it with the firearms."

Anderson lowered the gun.

"My name is Ilanka. They also call me Rain."

"Rain?" Mitchell asked.

"I rain hell," she said with a smile, motioning towards the mech in the corner.

"You're a pilot?"

She turned and spread her hair, showing him the CAP-NN link. "Alliance Navy. Former."

"What about you, Cormac? Are you a pilot?"

"No sir. Army. Former."

"You're all ex-military?"

"Enough with the questions," Anderson said, finally walking over to him. "We need to bring him to Millie."

"You're definitely military," Mitchell said. "Marine. I can tell by the way you walk."

Anderson glared at him but didn't speak.

"Come on, Mitch," Ilanka said. "He's right, we need to bring you up to the Captain."

"I don't suppose I could get cleaned up first?" he asked.

She laughed. "How long were you in that thing, anyway?"

"And how did you get out here, in a starfighter of all things?" Cormac said.

"Rain, Cormac, stow it," Anderson said. "You can tell your story to Millie. You can get cleaned up after she decides whether or not to kill you."

Kill him? Not because of what had happened on Liberty. There was no way this group could know about that... yet. "Whatever you say. You saved my life."

"We wanted that fighter of yours. I was kind of disappointed when we discovered you weren't dead. Let's go." Anderson raised the gun again, using it to point him in the direction of the airlock.

"Stop being an asshole, Anderson," Ilanka said. "He's not even armed."

"He's in the middle of nowhere in a damn starfighter. You two may think you can trust him because he's a hero or something. Whatever. I don't, and I won't until Millie does. Since I outrank both of you, you can either shut the hell up or stay here."

"You don't outrank me, Anderson," Ilanka said.

"I have seniority on this ship, that's good enough. I repeat - shut up or get lost."

"I'm not missing this," Cormac said.

Mitchell followed behind Anderson, with Ilanka and Cormac trailing him. The older Marine led them out of the airlock and into a long, narrow corridor. The smell of synthetic lubricants and burning was thick in the air, and the normally whisper-quiet pulsing of the main reactor vibrated along the walls and floor, leaving a constant buzzing in his ears.

They didn't cross paths with any of the other crew on the way, though they did pass one hatch that was open a couple of inches at the bottom. Mitchell thought he saw the shadow of a face kneeling against the crack, watching them go by. Either the ship was running a skeleton crew, or none of the other workers wanted to get involved with this business.

They reached the end of the corridor. A hatch opened to a lift, and they stepped in. Anderson continued to keep the gun leveled at Mitchell, and he stared at him as if daring him to try something. Mitchell had come across his type before. Guys like that were usually only tough until the trouble started and things got intense.

Mitchell thought about trying to make small talk during the ride up but decided against it. He had a feeling it would only result in another threat from Anderson, or maybe the man would stick his pistol up his nose. There was no point in starting trouble.

The lift stopped and the hatch opened, leading directly out onto the bridge. It was a cluttered, dirty affair, the screens marred with dust and grease, and food trays stacked on one of the consoles. A pile of dirty clothes lay in the corner, and Mitchell noticed with surprise that the clear carbonate that protected them from the vacuum of space had a noticeable crack in it.

There was a captain's chair in the center of the bridge, a ratty thing with wires hanging off the back and tears in the surface that allowed the gel innards to ooze out. A narrow, female hand with long fingers tapped a rhythmic cadence on one of the arms.

Millie waited until Anderson was standing right behind the chair before getting to her feet.

She was younger than Mitchell expected. She was also prettier than he expected. Not gorgeous, not a Tamara King type, but possessing a simple, natural beauty that was teased out even more by the contrast of her appearance against that of the ship.

She was wearing an Alliance Navy uniform, freshly cleaned and pressed, crisp and tucked in all the proper places. Her face was cool and neutral, her blue eyes curious, her auburn hair wrapped in a bun and tucked under a perfectly shaped cap. Her nails were manicured, painted, and flawless, as was her posture.

"Lieutenant Anderson," she said. The Lieutenant stood at attention, having lowered the weapon in the Captain's presence. "I see you brought me a gift."

Cormac started to giggle, until Millie's eyes found him.

"Captain Mitchell Williams, ma'am," Mitchell said. "Thank you for hauling me in."

She gave the slightest nod. She either hadn't noticed his smell or was doing a great job of ignoring it. "Captain Mildred Narayan. No offense, Captain, but we thought we were hauling in a derelict S-17 that had been floating through space for entirely too long. That is, after we thought we would be mining ore from the rock below us. Your rescue is a fortunate coincidence for you."

"Very fortunate."

"Tell me, Captain. How did you wind up out in the middle of nowhere in an S-17? If I remember correctly, that particular fighter has a twenty-hour air supply on board."

"Twenty-eight if you breathe slowly enough," Mitchell said. "I was in hyperspace. Headed for the Rim."

He heard Ilanka gasp behind him.

"An experimental fighter?" Millie asked.

"I don't know."

She started tapping her fingers on the back of the chair. "Captain, I don't want to sound crass, but your situation at the moment is very tentative. You see, that S-17 of yours is valuable to us. More so if it's experimental, or if it's been modified in any way. The problem is, we can't claim it as salvage as long as someone was found inside it, still breathing." She glanced at Anderson. "Do you understand?"

"Perfectly," Mitchell said. "You can have the ship if you promise to take me to the Rim." Or at least he would let her think she could have the ship, and buy himself some time.

"Why do you want to get to the Rim so badly?" she asked.

"I'm trying to get away."

"From what? You're the most famous soldier in the galaxy."

He was surprised. He hadn't thought she knew who he was. "Exactly." He paused, trying to decide what to say next. "And you're not a soldier at all anymore, are you? Not to be out here, mining ore from planetoids. I mean, you're dressing the part but-"

Cormac coughed behind him. Millie's face was turning red, her jaw tight with anger. Her fingers stopped tapping, her hand clenching the back of the chair instead. Mitchell noticed that her fingers sank right through it, past the cushioning to the metal frame.

"That's none of your concern. Let's be clear, Mitchell. I have the power. I have the control. You tell me what I want to know, and maybe I won't throw you out of the airlock."

He had touched a nerve, telling her they weren't military. There was something strange about this Captain and her ship. He glanced back at Ilanka and Cormac. He might get those two to talk to him if he survived long enough.

"I didn't take the Shot Heard 'Round the Universe," he said. "The brass propped me up to help rally the Alliance and boost recruitment efforts. They wanted to create a celebrity of their own, a superstar that would make war look glamorous. The media found out about the lie, and now they're pinning the whole thing on me. They have orders to kill me on sight."

"What?" Cormac said.

"You didn't take the Shot?" Ilanka added.

Mitchell stared at Millie. "No. I'm not a hero. It was my wing-mate, Ella, who sacrificed herself to destroy the Federation dread-nought. The Alliance made me take credit for it."

The color had drained from her face, leaving it a porcelain white. She kept staring at him, leaving a thick silence hanging in the air. He waited for her to speak. To order him to the airlock, or to ask Anderson to shoot him and be done with it. He wondered if he should have been so honest. She would have heard eventually, and if he lied and they kept him around... then what?

"I need to get to the Rim, Captain," he said. "I need to get away from the Alliance. To disappear. I'll do whatever it takes to get there. You want the ship, it's yours. It's fair payment. Nobody needs to know you ever saw me."

She still didn't speak. He could almost see her mind working behind her eyes, calculating her next move.

"You're in it for the salvage, right? That fighter is more than what it looks like. The ordnance it's packing could blow this bucket apart with one shot."

She didn't react to his comments. Finally, her hand came away from the chair. The frame was bent beneath it, mangled by the force of her discontent. A bionic. "Anderson, take him to the head and let him clean up, and then bring him to the storeroom on E-Deck. Cormac, go and get basics from Lopez, and bring them down."

Mitchell hadn't realized he was holding his breath. He let it go, relieved that she wasn't going to kill him just yet.

"Yes, ma'am," Cormac said. He backed away from them and vanished in the lift.

"I could take your ship, Captain," she said. "I don't need your permission, and nobody would ever know you had been here if I did. That isn't why I'm sparing you." She reached out, putting her bionic hand against his cheek. He could feel the slight vibration of the synthetic fibers beneath the layer of real skin and poly-alloy. "You want to go to the Rim? I think I might have another way you can pay for passage there."

[24]

ANDERSON LED Mitchell off the bridge, down the lift to B-Deck. These were the ship's berthing quarters, small rooms sectioned off from a long, straight, narrow corridor, many with two-tiered bunks embedded into their walls, and even more of them obviously not in use. Judging by the lived-in look of the quarters, Mitchell guessed there were fifty to sixty people on the salvage ship at most.

"It must be tough, running a mining op with so few hands," Mitchell said.

"That's none of your business," Anderson said. He was walking behind him, keeping the gun pressed against his back. Mitchell had no fear that the man would use it, not after Millie had decided to keep him alive. It seemed the old Marine just felt better holding it.

"I did a two-month tour guarding a military uranium mining operation. The rock they were working was bigger, but they must have had three hundred souls on the job and half that again in bots."

"I said it's none of your business."

There was a hatch near the middle of the berths. It slid open at their approach, revealing a larger room of toilets and secondary half-wall with a shower behind it. A woman was already in it, washing off her hair amid a spray of water and steam.

"Water?" Mitchell asked. Other than posh retro-hotels, he didn't think anyone still used it to clean themselves.

"It's more effective at removing small particles. It also uses less overall system power and is easier to recycle. We don't have unlimited access to heavy fuel. If you're going to be spending a lot of time in the Rim, you'll want to get used to it. Strip and clean yourself up. Towels are over there. You can wear one down to E-Deck."

Mitchell shrugged himself out of the flight suit, thankful to be rid of it. He slid off his underwear and circled around the half-wall.

The woman turned to face him as she ran her hands through long, dark hair. She had dark skin and almond eyes, a lean figure with large breasts and wide hips.

"Who are you?" she asked.

He'd been in the service for too long to be bothered by communal anything. There was no consideration of gender in the military. You weren't a man or a woman there. You didn't have a sex at all. You were a warrior, a fighter, a tool.

"My name is Mitchell. I was picked up an hour or so ago." He approached one of the spouts. It went on as soon as he stepped under it, blasting him with water that was hot enough to scald. He gritted through it.

"You're the damn fool they found floating out in the middle of nowhere?" She walked over to him and put out her hand. "Ensign Wanda Briggs, Navigations."

Mitchell took her hand. "Good to meet you."

She laughed. "Have you met the Captain yet?" She glanced over to where Anderson was standing, his arms folded, his posture rigid. "I guess you have. You must be important."

"Why do you say that?"

"She didn't kill you." She reached over to a cutout in the wall and handed him a bar of soap.

"Does she kill a lot of people?" Mitchell asked.

"Nah. I'm just messing with you." She laughed again. "I mean, she's done some dirty business, but that's the name of the game, right?" She moved closer to him, positioning herself under his spray. "Don't get the wrong idea. Just getting some hot water."

"Dirty business. I assume you aren't talking about mining."

"Yeah, sure I am, sweetie." She winked at him. "I think you're lucky we stopped by here when we did, and if the Captain thinks you can be useful, and I'm guessing that she does since you're standing here and not floating on your merry way out there, then you're even luckier. She can be hard, but she's fair. All the ones who didn't make it..." Her face turned so quickly Mitchell felt a chill despite the hot water. "They didn't deserve to, may they rot in hell."

"Williams, stop screwing with Ensign Briggs and get a move on," Anderson shouted.

"Better do as the man says, sweetie," Wanda said, backing up to her original head. "I'm sure I'll be seeing you around."

Mitchell nodded and started lathering himself up while he tried to decipher the meaning behind her words. It was obvious from the moment he stepped out into the hangar and saw the mech that there was more to this ship than mining. Between the small population and Wanda's comments, he was beginning to wonder if excavation was on their true agenda at all.

They were all former military, and at least some of them were still acting the part. Mercenaries? Pirates? They had no loyalty to the Alliance, he was sure of that much. Unless Millie was holding him in order to turn him in. Maybe she was hoping the Alliance would offer a bounty for him? Not likely, since they probably thought he was dead. He wondered who they thought they had chased out into space. An accomplice?

He finished soaping himself down. Ensign Briggs abandoned her shower and waved to him on the way out, grabbing a towel and passing Anderson without comment. Mitchell quickly washed himself off and stepped out of the shower, taking a towel of his own and drying himself.

"There are a lot of berths up here," he said, wrapping the towel around his waist. "How come we're going down to E?"

"That's where the doors with the locks are," Anderson said. "You aren't a guest just yet, pretty boy. Right now, you're a prisoner." He motioned with the gun, and Mitchell stepped in front of him, taking point out of the head and away from the berthing. The tip of the pistol was cold against his back, and he briefly considered trying to take the weapon from the soldier, if only to show him that he could.

E-Deck was almost completely designated for storage, a fact Mitchell found amusing because there was next to nothing being stored on it. There were plenty of rooms with manual seals on them, but most of the doors were hanging open, suggesting that maybe they had held something of value once, but that had been a long time ago.

The room Anderson led him to was in the back corner, as far from the lift as they could get. It was blank and nearly empty, save for a portable bodily excretion device - more often called a "pisspot," a stack of clothes, and a tray holding two large metal cylinders of water and a dozen cans of field rations. The water was good enough for a few days if he was careful. No doubt they expected the pisspot to keep him somewhat hydrated.

"Not planning to visit?" Mitchell said, dropping the towel and slipping into the clothes. They were standard grays: cheap cloth pants, a t-shirt, and shoes that were typically distributed to new recruits in boot camp, or to prisoners who had elected to service in exchange for a shorter sentence.

"Don't know. Don't care," Anderson said. "Ration your water and food, and I'm sure someone will be by before you starve."

He smiled for the first time as he closed and locked the heavy door.

[25]

HE WASN'T ALONE that long.

The door opened a couple of hours later. A heavyset man peeked in around the corner, his face red, his forehead sweaty, his nose running.

"Captain Williams?" the man said.

"Do you have anyone else being held down here?" Mitchell asked.

The man smiled and pulled himself the rest of the way in. He was bigger than his face had suggested, his stomach a round ball beneath his oversized pecs. He had dark hair and three chins, each sporting a few days' growth. He wore coveralls and a heavy apron - protection against intense heat. A tool belt was wrapped around his massive waist.

"My name is Watson," he said.

"Engineering?" Mitchell asked.

He nodded. "One of them. Singh is the other. She's busy with the reactor right now."

"The shuddering?"

"No. That's normal. Well, not ideal. We can't do much about it though, not unless we can get some new bearings. Even if we got new bearings, we'd need a new mount. Or at least a rebuilt mount. Hell, we could use a new reactor. Or a new ship. That would be great. Have you been to the bridge?" He spoke fast, his voice nervous. He had an accent that Mitchell couldn't place.

"I've been to the bridge. Are you New Terran?" Mitchell asked. He hadn't talked to more than a handful of New Terrans in his life. They were mostly a reclusive bunch, though every so often a ship would show up orbiting an Alliance planet and request asylum. The New Terrans were pretty strong on religion, in a way that didn't sit well with all of their populace.

"I was born on New Terra One. My parents defected when I was four. Well, my mother did. My father was killed helping us escape. You've been to the bridge. Did you see the crack in the carbonate? I've been taking measurements. It's been growing point zero-zero-zero-three-tenths of a centimeter per week."

"That sounds bad."

"It is. By my calculations, at the current rate of spread we're looking at complete structural failure between fifty-three and ninety-seven years from now. The service life of a standard Salvage class starship is rated at three hundred years. Verdict: this thing is a death trap." He closed his eyes, as if he were re-running the calculations in his head. He opened them a few seconds later. "Oh. The Captain sent me down to adjust your ARR."

"What do you mean, adjust?"

Watson pulled a small device from his tool belt. It bore a vague resemblance to the device M had used to disable the implant.

"You have a standard issue Marine jockey ARR, yes?"

"I did. My implant is disabled."

"I'm going to shut it down and upload a patch that will- wait, did you say disabled?"

Mitchell turned his head and showed him the wound. "Completely offline."

He took another tool from his belt and put it to Mitchell's head. "It is. How did you... who... what?"

"It's a long story."

Watson tapped his fingers on his lips. "I'm not sure what to do with this."

"What are you trying to do?"

He didn't answer right away, distracted by his thinking. "Oh. The patch. It's a black market hack that removes all of the military control signals, and switches the encryption bands over so they can't listen in on your communications. It also opens up the ability to upload fresh ID scenarios. I've also added a few subroutines to the data feedback flow that increases target accuracy a little bit. It's all pretty useful stuff." He shook his head. "It's also useless if your implant is broken."

"I didn't say it was broken, I said it was disabled."

"Someone turned it off?" He said it with a level of excitement that didn't match the news.

"Yeah. Is that a big deal?"

He started giggling. "A big deal? Well, only if you consider the big bang to be a big deal. Otherwise, no." He kept laughing at his joke, then stopped suddenly. "You can't 'turn off' a military implant. At least, nobody I've ever heard of knows how. Who did it?"

Mitchell shrugged. "What does it matter? It's off."

He looked hurt. "I just wanted to know. Of course, I have to report this to the Captain. She'll want to know why I haven't given you the update."

"Of course. I guess I should take it as a good sign that she wants to go through the trouble? She isn't intent on getting rid of me just yet?"

Watson headed for the door. "I wouldn't make too many assumptions when it comes to the Captain. She can be a little moody sometimes." He shifted himself out of the room and locked the door behind him.

Mitchell leaned back against the wall and closed his eyes. He figured that either someone would be along shortly to grill him about the ARR or he'd be by himself for some time.

[26]

EIGHT DAYS.

That's how long Mitchell estimated he spent locked in the storage room. It was hard to be precise without his p-rat to check the time, but he got used to his cycle of eating, drinking, sleeping, and using the pisspot.

It was almost enough to make him insane, and maybe that was what Millie wanted. He fought to stay focused, to use his meditation skills to hold the boredom and loneliness at bay. He tried not to think about Ella or his predicament, and as a result found himself thinking about Major Arapo more often than he thought was healthy.

In an effort to get his mind away from that, he increasingly found himself ruminating on the Goliath. M had said the damage he had done to the implant would cause him to remember his past life. Although it couldn't exactly be called past life. Past history? Past future? What had he done, and how did it relate to the ship that was built on Earth over six hundred years earlier?

It was hard to stay patient, sitting alone in the empty room, knowing that there might be some threat approaching that according to the clone was destined to destroy humanity.

Unless he stopped it.

Somehow.

The train of thought was as circular as M claimed time to be. He did loops around the arguments, broke himself of them by doing any kind of physical exercise he could manage, and then swung back around again once he was exhausted, starting with Ella, and then the Major. He had a feeling he had known her before. Had they been lovers once?

He could hear the sounds of the ship at times, the docking clamps releasing on the mining equipment, the internal shuddering of the vessel when the hangar opened and closed. He knew the moment they went back into FTL, spending only three days near the plane-toid, only one and a half actually mining it. They could have collected a few tons of ore at most in that short amount of time. Not nearly enough to make the trip profitable.

It was enough to make it look like they were mining, though. What was Captain Narayan really about?

Mitchell was doing pushups when the door to the room unlocked and opened. Anderson stepped in, looking the same as he had the day he had left Mitchell down there.

"Let's go," he said. He was brandishing the gun again.

"Where?"

"Captain wants you cleaned up. Back to the shower."

Mitchell got to his feet. He was filthy again. The smell of old sweat wafted from him. At least he had opted for the Marine-offered laser treatments to permanently remove his facial hair.

"Where are we?"

"Hyperspace."

"Where are we going?"

"None of your business."

Mitchell walked out ahead of Anderson, making his own way back to the lift. They took it up to berthing, and then back to the shower. Both the bunks and the head were conspicuously empty this time around.

"Two minutes," Anderson said.

Mitchell washed himself down in a hurry. Anderson gave him a fresh pair of grays on his exit, along with a Navy-issued flight suit.

"A suit?" he asked.

"Captain's orders."

Once he was dressed, Anderson marched Mitchell away from the berthing and back to the lift. He thought he was going to be returned to his prison, but instead the former Space Marine sent the lift up to A-Deck.

The lift opened out to a long inner-hallway. A conference room sat on his right, a communications array on his left. A man sat at the comm station, leaned back in his chair with his eyes closed, ignorant of the men in the hallway. He wore a Navy uniform, though he had torn the sleeves from the jacket to keep his muscular arms bare.

Mitchell stared as they passed, confused by the room's existence. It was way too much equipment for a mining ship like this one. It would have been out of place on a ship like the Greylock.

"Keep walking," Anderson said.

He had slowed while he tried to figure out what the array was doing there.

Anderson pointed him to a door a little further down. It was identical to the rest, though there was no clear carbonate window into the contents of this one. When they reached it, Anderson knocked.

The hatch slid open. The muzzle of the gun pressing into his back enticed Mitchell to enter.

The room was clean and warm. A sofa rested near the center, a lounge opposite. Colorful rugs were laid across the metal floor, paintings hung on the walls, and a grand view of the blackness of hyperspace was visible through small portholes arranged along the far side near a dining table. Two places had been set, and the smell of real food brought Mitchell to an immediate salivation.

Millie walked into the room from an adjoining doorway. She was still wearing her uniform, though she had lost the hat and let her hair down. It fell in ringlets to her shoulders, the small change revealing her to be more attractive than he had initially guessed. She was still plain, but there was an edge to it now.

"Mitchell," she said. She looked at Anderson. "You're dismissed."

"Captain, are you-"

"Dismissed, Lieutenant."

Anderson bowed slightly, shoved the gun into Mitchell's back one last time for good measure, and then left the two of them alone.

"I know you haven't eaten actual food in a few days. Our stores are running low, but Lopez found some pheasant hiding in the back of the freezers." She smiled. "Pheasant meaning some kind of edible bird from some planet or other. We can't afford to be that choosy. Please, come have a seat."

Mitchell stood there. He didn't trust her or her hospitality. "I don't understand this."

"I told you I had an idea how you could earn your way to the Rim. I brought you here to discuss it."

"Why didn't you just drop by my cell?"

"I know you had a run-in with Ensign Briggs in the shower. Whatever you think you know, Mitchell, I'm not a monster. I have a job to do, and I do it to the best of my ability. That's all."

"I doubt that's all."

"Sit. Eat." She made her way over to the table, taking one of the spots. "You should be thankful I'm being gracious. I could have killed you days ago."

Mitchell followed her to the table and sat. His eyes latched onto the slices of cooked bird and the small potatoes that surrounded it. She motioned for him to take some, and he did.

Millie stared at him while he took the food. She kept staring when he offered to serve her, lifting slices of meat and placing them on her plate. She stared while he took the first few bites and a sip of the wine that had been delivered with it.

She waited until he was starting to relax. Then she sprang it on him.

"I know what happened on Liberty," she said. "Not just the Shot, but the Prime Minister's wife."

Mitchell had to force himself to not react too strongly. "Lies," he said.

"I don't care if they are or not. You saw the array on your way here?"

"Yeah. A bit upscale for this tub, isn't it?"

"It is. I'm also guessing you're smart enough to realize that we didn't spend much time mining the rock we found you circling?"

"You aren't miners. Or salvage. I got that much. Mercenaries?"

Millie laughed. "Not quite. I'm going to tell you our secret, Mitchell. First, I want you to tell me yours."

"Why?"

"What do you mean, why?"

"Why do you think I have a secret? I told you, I'm trying to escape the Alliance."

"Yes, I know. And you want to go to the Rim to hide. Whatever you heard about the Rim, it isn't as lawless as the rumors suggest. It's just a different kind of law. Step foot on any of the planets there, and the first person who sees you is going to sell you out." She laughed. "Except you don't actually need to hide, do you Mitchell?"

She knew more than she was saying. She had just told him as much. "Make your point, Captain."

"You can call me Millie," she said. She took a sip of her wine, her eyes refusing to leave him. "I have an advanced communications array on board. Three days after you showed up in my path, an autonomous envoy fell in about a thousand AU from our position with a transmission."

She paused, waiting to see him sweat. Mitchell made himself breathe steadily. He knew she wanted something from him, and she had a plan on how to get it. This was all leading up to the pitch.

"It seems that Captain Mitchell 'Ares' Williams was found dead in an old hangar near a Gentech farm. They tracked a starfighter leaving the same hangar, one that disabled a mech and destroyed a few drones before launching into space and vanishing before a frigate could intercept. They don't know who was flying the fighter, or how the pilot was connected to Captain Williams." Her eyebrows lifted. "Do you want to finish the story, or shall I?"

"They ran DNA analysis on the body," Mitchell said. He knew how the story went. "They're certain that the corpse they found was Captain Williams because they got an exact match. He was killed by gunfire taken during his attempt to escape York after he was accused of rape. Now you're wondering - if the dead man was Captain Mitchell Williams, who the hell am I sharing this meal with?"

She nodded, the smile remaining on her face. "There's also the matter of the FTL-capable fighter which you claim to have stolen, and which the Alliance says isn't theirs. Which brings us back to the beginning. You have a secret, and I want to know what it is."

"But you don't want to kill me over it, or we wouldn't be here."

"I think we can help each other, Mitchell. Or whatever your real name is. We don't need to dogfight one another with lies and half-truths."

"Then you tell me a truth, Millie," Mitchell said. "The drone that came out of FTL nearby. Did you intercept its transmission, or was it aimed at you?"

"You first," she replied. Her poker face was impeccable.

"You won't believe me."

"Is your story that unbelievable?"

"Truth is relative."

"Relative to what?"

"What you already believe. What you pray to. What you're predisposed to think. Did you know I scored a 1570 on my aptitude exam during enlistment screening? Top one percent, and I was supposedly going to be fast-tracked right through officer's training. A shooting star. My brother is a Navy Admiral, and he said I was going to make General before I was thirty. I didn't."

"Why not?"

"I wanted to be a pilot. I didn't believe in the score because it didn't suit me. You won't believe my story because it won't suit you. Hell, I'm not even sure if I believe it, or if the bullet I took on Liberty caused me to lose my mind. I'm not wholly convinced any of this isn't a hallucination or fever dream or something."

"Trust me. I'm very real." She took another sip of wine. "Tell me your truth, then. You've already guessed that I don't want you dead."

Mitchell picked up his glass and downed the wine in one swallow. Liquid courage? He was hoping it would help clarify reality for him.

"My real name is Mitchell Williams. The body they found in the hangar was a clone. My clone. I don't know who made him, all I know is that he claimed to be from an alternate timeline. Have you ever heard of something called 'eternal return?' "

"It sounds like reincarnation. Is it like that?"

"Kind of, but on a much, much bigger scale. The way the clone explained it to me, it's like the entire universe being reincarnated exactly the same as it was the last time. It goes on and on this way for eternity. That is until something changes it. He said they created an engine, he called it an 'eternal engine,' that can transport them from one cycle of time to another. He told me that his kind, whatever they are, for whatever reason, want to destroy us, and that this whole thing is somehow connected to the first starship humankind ever built. Have you ever heard of the Goliath?"

She thought about it. "It sounds familiar, but I'm not an expert on Earth history."

"Me neither. Supposedly this ship holds the key to our salvation, and I'm the one who's destined to find it. Or at least, I may or may not have in past loops, except I screwed something up and we all died anyway."

"So your clone told you to go and find a lost starship, gave you an FTL-capable starfighter, and sent you on your merry way? Was this before or after you got in trouble with the Prime Minister?"

"After. They set me up to become public enemy number one in order to stop me from the future I might have had."

She stared at him in silence.

"I told you that you wouldn't believe me."

"You have to admit, it sounds impossible."

"I know."

"It does explain a few things, though. For instance, how you can have a starfighter with an FTL engine. Or the fact that neither Watson or Singh has been able to do so much as get the damned cockpit open. Even the access doors are incompatible with any of our tools. They were going to take apart the helmet you were wearing, but after Watson said your ARR was offline, I told them to hold off. I was worried they might not be able to put it back together again."

"It uses a wireless neural network link with the ship's AI," Mitchell said.

"Amazing." She put her hand to her face, supporting her head and continuing to stare. "I want to believe this."

"But you don't."

"No. Not completely. Clones from the future? Right now, I'm working on keeping an open mind."

"Technically from the past. Is that so impossible though? Every time we move into hyperspace we're breaking relativity."

"Not breaking. Bending. Anyway, you're talking about an entire shift in the way we as a species consider time. That's a pretty big thing."

Mitchell shrugged. "Well, believe it or not, Millie, that's my story. I hope to God that you're a real thing, that this ship is real, and I'm not passed out in a field somewhere, or that this isn't Hell. Either that, or I hope I wake up right now. Let me tell you, it hasn't been fun since the Prime Minister walked in on me with his wife in my lap."

"So that part is true?"

"No. These... I don't even know what to call them... travelers? They can send transmissions through the implant. Suggestions. Did I have sex with the Prime Minister's wife? Yes. One, I didn't know she was his wife. Two, it was consensual, believe me."

"I do believe you. I got access to your records. You were one of the top jockeys in the most elite company in the Space Marines. Liberty wasn't the first time you earned a commendation, and you have zero marks against you over ten years of spotless service."

Mitchell had been reaching for another slice of the bird. He dropped his fork, his own suspicions drawing nearer to resolve. "How did you get my records?"

She smiled. "To answer your earlier question: the drone that dropped out of FTL sent us the transmission. I'm the lone Admiral in the one-ship Navy known only as Project Black. Welcome to the Riggers."

27

"THE RIGGERS?" Mitchell asked. He was frozen in his chair, eyeing Millie as though she might sprout fangs and tear into him.

"From the root term 'frig-up,' which got slang-shortened to 'frigger,' and then just 'rigger.' We're the Alliance's dirty little secret. A small black ops team of some of the best of the best who just happened to run afoul of some galactic law or another."

He was dumbstruck. He struggled to find words. "I.. How? I mean... I never heard of-"

"Here's the deal, Mitchell. Everyone on this ship has been court-martialed. Some of the reasons aren't at all pretty or forgivable. Some of us should have been jettisoned into space. The thing is, we have undeniable skills, skills that the Alliance spent a lot of money on providing us and aren't exactly keen to lose. So, about five years ago they started a program under the table - Project Black. The idea was to bring all of us frig-ups who have at least some concept of chain of command and patriotism together and send us off to do all the low-down dirty that the Alliance can't afford to be connected to. In exchange, we get to continue to live, breathe, and soldier on."

"This is a military vessel?" Mitchell said softly.

"Yes. You already worked out that the whole mining thing is a front. Good for you. There's a reason we have a Knight and a Piranha in the hold. We also have a couple dozen of the most ferocious Army grunts in the universe on board. We do what the Alliance can't do. We drop in where the Alliance can't go, including the Rim. You wanted to disappear, Mitchell? This is your chance. Your best chance. The Alliance thinks you're dead, and I want it to stay that way."

"If I join you."

"If you join us."

Mitchell leaned back in his chair. His first thought was that he couldn't believe his luck. His second was the realization that there was no luck involved. The starfighter's course to the planetoid had nothing to do with the air supply. He hadn't programmed the thing to take him anywhere. The destination was preset, his control an illusion. M wanted this ship, the Riggers, to find him. It was the only thing that made sense.

He started laughing. Even if the future had changed the moment M arrived into the time loop, that didn't mean there was no advantage to knowing what might have been.

"What about Goliath?" he asked.

"We have operational orders," she said. "We can't go hunting for a lost starship."

"I need to find the Goliath. Don't you get that? If what my clone said was true, we're all dead without it."

"I told you, I'm still on the fence with believing your story. I don't need to believe you to want you on board. To want you as part of the team, badly enough that it's going to be my neck if any of the top brass ever hears that I've got you stowed away here."

"What if I say no?"

"You become a security risk that I won't take. You won't say no, not when push comes to shove."

"How do you know?"

"Because you're a pilot. A warrior. You said so yourself."

Mitchell stared at her. She was right. They both knew it. Still, M had warned him to find the Goliath. How was he going to do that trapped on this ship?

"The S-17 and the helmet will only work with my brain, and I know that's a resource you aren't going to want to waste. It also has an FTL engine. How do you know I won't cut and run the first chance I get?"

She tapped the side of her head. "Watson's working on a replacement for your implant. We don't have the standard issue or we'd be outed as military any time we went near an outpost. It has a kill switch built in that I can activate from here. If you give me any reason at all to think you're planning on going hyper, I won't hesitate to drop you." She got to her feet and walked over to his side of the table. She put her hand on his arm and looked down at him. "Besides, you know the value of discipline and the chain of command better than most of the cons on this ship. I know you won't abandon your team."

He wouldn't. They both knew that, too. "There may be an enemy out there. One that's going to overpower us before we can act, if we don't act with the information we've been given."

"There are real enemies of the Alliance out there, Mitchell. Threats we already know about. We're in a unique position to try to stop them." She paused for a few seconds while she thought. "Tell me you'll become one of us and I'll do my best to get you whatever information I can on the Goliath. If you get me a concrete lead on its location, either we'll go and check it out as soon as our docket is clear, or maybe you'll earn enough trust that I'll allow you to go on your own. I don't have to make you this offer, but I'm smart enough to know how valuable you can be to our mission."

It wasn't as though he had an abundance of options. "Fair enough," Mitchell said. "I only have one other condition."

"Trying to bargain? I've already been more than generous."

"You have. Consider it an ask, then. I want to report to you directly."

She smiled. "That was a given. You're the second-highest ranking officer on this ship."

Mitchell returned her smile and waved towards her empty chair. "In that case, Admiral, please, sit. Eat. We don't want to waste a perfectly good whatever-it-is."

"Please, call me Millie when we're alone, and Captain when we aren't. The crew responds better to me that way." She returned to her seat while Mitchell picked up his fork and grabbed another slice of the pheasant.

"Have it your way. So, Millie... You know my history. What are you in for?"

He figured it was something white-collar. Money laundering, tax evasion, fraud, that sort of thing. Despite Ensign Brigg's veiled warning, the Admiral seemed too together to have done anything violent.

She didn't hesitate to answer. Maybe it was because she was used to the question from being a criminal in charge of a ship of criminals. Maybe it was because she had no regrets. Either way, the answer sent a chill through his spine.

"Murder."

28

SHE DIDN'T SAY anything else about it, and Mitchell was afraid to ask. They finished their meal, with Millie doing most of the talking, taking the time to explain what was expected of him, and what life on her ship was like. It wasn't too different from life on the Greylock, a life he had been missing so badly. The main adjustment would be in his need to learn different aspects of the ship's operation in order to help the too-small company keep it all running as efficiently as possible.

Afterward, she sent a knock to Anderson, to have him escort Mitchell back down to B-Deck and his new berthing.

"Once you've settled in, you're free to roam the Schism as you will. Just make sure you find your way to engineering before you bunk for the night so Watson can install your new implant."

"You named this ship the Schism?"

"I didn't. General Cornelius did. It was to remind us that we're in this together. It's a word that symbolizes the constant threat to our cohesiveness. As I said, some of the crew are here for some very ugly crimes, and we tend to hold our own opinions more strongly than the typical soldier."

Crimes worse than murder? He wasn't sure he wanted to know what they were.

"So Cornelius knows about Project Black?"

"Of course. It was his idea."

"What time is it now?"

"Eighteen-hundred Earth-standard. I'll be holding a mission briefing at oh-six-hundred."

Twelve hours. It would be plenty of time to explore a little bit. "How soon can you get me the data on Goliath?"

"Not until we come out of hyperspace. I'll have to be subtle with the request. We don't want to draw any unwanted attention, and believe me when I say we're under more constant scrutiny than the rest of the armed forces. The only reason we have any autonomy at all is because we require custom implants."

A heavy fist rapped on the door. It opened a second later, and Anderson stepped in. His glance crossed over Millie and landed on Mitchell. He still had the gun in his hand.

"You won't be needing that any more Lieutenant," Millie said. "Captain Williams is one of us now."

He scowled at Mitchell.

"Holster your sidearm, Lieutenant," Mitchell said. "That's an order."

Anderson looked like he was going to explode. His face turned beet red, the muscles on his neck throbbing below his collar. He slowly put the gun away, remaining silent.

"Captain Williams doesn't exist. Do you understand, Lieutenant? He's a ghost on this ship."

"I don't have to take orders from a ghost."

"You'll take orders if he gives them," Millie snapped. "Don't test me, Anderson."

His forehead wrinkled and then he bowed to her. "Yes, ma'am!"

"Good. Take Mitchell down to berthing. He'll be getting Yasil's quarters."

Anderson was silent, but by his expression he didn't look happy about that decision either.

Millie turned to face Mitchell. "I've already sent a message to Lopez to bring down enough grays for a week. If you want something fancier, you can find your way to supply. You might want to stop by there anyway, we have a few replica paintings and things like that you can use to decorate your room."

"You're giving me a whole room?" He had never had his own quarters. The idea made him more uncomfortable than he would have guessed.

"That was my plan."

"No offense, Captain, but no thank you. I know Ilanka is one of your pilots. Just put me near her."

"Are you sure?" Millie asked.

"Positive. I don't want special treatment. I told you I was in. I'm going to earn my keep."

She smiled. "Okay. Ilanka is in B-23. The bunk above hers is open. We had a second pilot, but we lost him during a mission three months ago."

"I'm sorry."

"Don't be. He was a stupid asshole. He died because of it."

Mitchell didn't know what to say, so he just started walking towards the hallway. Anderson glared at him as he passed.

"Good night, Captain," Mitchell said, turning and giving her a slight bow. She returned the gesture.

"Good night, Mitch."

The door closed behind them, leaving him alone in the hallway with Anderson.

"Well, Anderson?" Mitchell said. He expected the older Marine to have something to say, or maybe to try to level him.

"Well, what?" Anderson replied.

"Do you want to have it out here and now, or are you going to pull some kind of passive-aggressive bullshit when people's lives are on the line?"

Anderson bit his lower lip and shook his head. "No, sir. I expected you to be all full of yourself. Forget Liberty, Greylock was still the envy of every Marine. You didn't take Yasil's quarters. You want to be one of us. I respect that."

Mitchell buried his surprise and put out his hand. "No hard feelings then, Lieutenant?"

The man took his hand. His palm was calloused and rough, his grip firm. "No, sir."

They walked to the lift and took it down to B-Deck. Anderson led Mitchell to B-23, one of the smaller berths with just enough space for a bunk, a pair of footlockers, and room to maneuver to each. Ilanka was laying on the top bunk, her eyes closed but shifting beneath them.

"Lieutenant Kalishov," Anderson said, loudly enough that he was clearly making an effort to surprise the pilot.

Her eyes opened slowly. She smiled when she saw Mitchell. "Captain Williams," she said. "What brings you to my bunk?"

"Captain Narayan offered me a job," Mitchell said. "We're going to be roomies."

Her face lit up at the news. "Really?" she said. She sat up and slid off the bunk, hopping to the floor. "I was worried about you, when you vanished like that. Millie has reputation to uphold, after all." She wrapped her arms around him in a friendly embrace. "Do you like top or bottom?"

"I'm fine with either."

She pulled away from him. "Then, I'll take top. You don't snore, do you? Sevrin snored like bear."

Mitchell assumed she was referring to the lost pilot. "No, the Marines corrected that when I enlisted."

"Good. Good."

Mitchell felt the new presence behind him, though he didn't hear the man approach. He looked back and found himself face-to-face with a frail-looking bald man with a large tribal tattoo running across the entire right side of his face. He had a bundle of clothes in his hands.

"Lopez, I assume?" Mitchell said.

"Private Alvaro Lopez, sir," Lopez said. "I brought down the grays as the Captain requested. Where would you like them, sir?"

"Put them in there," Ilanka said, pointing to one of the footlockers. "Okay."

"I have to finish my rounds," Anderson said. "If you need directions, Ilanka knows where everything is." He headed off before Mitchell could thank him.

"There you are, sir," Lopez said. "Knock if you need anything else, anytime. I don't sleep much."

"Thank you, Private."

Lopez bowed and vanished from the room.

"So, Millie told you all about our little family?" Ilanka asked.

"She did. To be honest, I didn't see that one coming."

She smiled. "It's all very mysterious. I was hoping she would try to recruit you, when you said you wanted to disappear."

"It would have been nicer if she had decided right away. I spent eight days locked in a storage room."

"You're fortunate she wasn't as direct with you as she's been with some of the others."

"What does that mean?"

Ilanka paused as if she regretted the statement. Then she shrugged. "The military sends all of their top rejects to us. Anyone who has high skill but occasional, shall we say... lapses in judgement." She laughed at her joke before turning eerily serious. "Not all of the rejects are a good fit for our mission, and Millie doesn't like to take risks. The way I see it, this ship is a sheet of ice, and the people on it are cracks. If one of those cracks gets too big, or goes too deep, the entire sheet falls apart. She makes sure those cracks are never made."

"How?"

"How do you think? These people have already been court-martialed and sentenced. If there's no life for them here on the Schism, there's no life for them at all."

The thought was a chilling one. "How long have you been on board?"

"Since the project was launched. Five years. Anderson, Millie, Watson, and me are the only original crew members left. We've had a lot of memorials, a lot of eulogies. The nature of our mission means a hard life with a short expectancy. Even so, I've made it longer than I expected to after I was found guilty."

"What did you do?"

She put her hand up and patted his cheek. "Mitchell, I'll share this advice one time, because you're new. If someone wants to tell you why they're here, they will. If not, it is offensive to ask. I'm here because I'm here, and that is all there is to it."

"Understood," Mitchell said. "I'm sorry for asking."

"It is not a thing," she replied. "Are you hungry?"

"No. Millie fed me before sending me down here."

"The pheasant?"

"Yeah. How did you know?"

She chuckled. "She gives that to all the new recruits their first night. I hope you enjoyed it. It's the last good meal you're going to have for long, long time."

29

"COME IN."

Watson's voice was muffled from the other side of the doorway, disguised even more by the shuddering of the walls around engineering. Mitchell pushed open the hatch and stepped in.

The engineer was sitting on a stool at a small workbench, his mass overflowing the tiny seat and leaving Mitchell to wonder how it was supporting him. He had his face right up against a tiny transistor that he was cradling in a pair of tweezers, a small tool pressed to it.

"Ah, Mitchell," he said. "Millie told me to expect you. I was just putting the finishing touches on your implant."

"What is that?" Mitchell asked. He looked around the room. It abutted the engine room near the rear of the ship, a workshop filled with what looked to him like nothing more than debris, but was probably everything the two engineers needed to keep them online.

"This?" Watson asked, holding up the tool. "It's a nano-laser. I didn't have a high-qubit micro-controller to match your existing implant, so I had to devise my own upgrade. I'm not actually guiding the laser though, just holding it over the chip. It's programmed to do the rest."

He put the chip down on a black surface. His hands moved in front of his face, working an overlay that Mitchell couldn't see.

"That's better. Give me two minutes to update the firmware and we'll get you ready for surgery."

"Surgery?" Mitchell scanned the room again. There were bits of wire and metal everywhere, and grease stains lined the walls and floor.

"Not here," Watson said with a laugh. "Medical is down on G-Deck, near the belly where it's most protected. I'd introduce you to the ship's doctor, but we don't have one."

"No doctor?"

"I'm afraid we don't rate medical personnel," Watson said. "We have some high-quality bots. The military sends them to us for testing. We're better than any guinea pigs."

It wasn't a reassuring thought.

"Fifteen seconds," Watson said, watching the progress of the update. "Once we confirm the update is working, I'll have to flash it to the rest of the crew. Millie insisted that we change our encryption schemas."

Mitchell smiled. She had at least believed him strongly enough to not take any chances with their implants.

"There we go." Watson picked up the implant with the tweezers again and placed it in a small dish of clear liquid. "Follow me."

"I was hoping Singh would be around," Mitchell said as they left Engineering. "I haven't gotten to meet him yet."

"Her. She usually bunks down pretty early and takes the morning shift. There are just the two of us trying to keep all of the systems running. It would be easier with a little less ship."

Mitchell was curious. He had just come from B-Deck, and Ilanka was the only crew member he had seen. "She has her own quarters?"

"I know what you're thinking. She isn't on B-Deck. We have berths right outside engineering, to keep us closer to the action."

They reached a nondescript part of the corridor. Watson put his hand to it, and a hidden hatch slid aside, revealing a small lift.

"Service shaft," he said. "I'm not supposed to take you this way." He shrugged and they piled in together.

It was a tight fit, but a fast ride, dropping them off deep in the ship's center, somewhere above the hangar. Another corridor greeted them. This one was spectacularly clean and well-kept, the poly-alloy reflective from the embedded lighting in the ceiling. A bot crawled slowly along the wall, continuing its endless task of keeping the area sanitary.

"Have you ever experienced a clean tube before?" Watson asked when they reached a hatch along the corridor. It had a glowing red cross to the left of it.

Mitchell shook his head. "I don't know what that is."

"Experimental tech. Uses nano-scale bots to remove one hundred percent of contaminants from the surface layer - your clothes, your skin. We're the only ship that has one right now." He smiled. "At least the side effects have been minimal so far."

"Side effects?"

"Itching mainly."

The hatch opened into a dark room constructed of clear carbonate. A small vent rested to the left, and Mitchell could see the medibot station in front of him. They stepped in.

"The hatches on both sides won't open again until we're clean," Watson said. The rear hatch slid closed, leaving them in dim silence.

"How long does it take?"

"A few minutes."

"Where are the bots?"

"Already on you. They're nano-scale. Invisible to the naked eye. Once your ARR is back online, you'll be able to see them. It's pretty cool to watch them swarm over you."

Mitchell thought he felt something on his eye. He blinked a few times.

"It's a very impressive system. The nano-bots collect the contaminants, and then carry themselves out to a tiny airlock and are jettisoned into space. There's a machine behind the vent there that continually builds new ones."

"Why not just let them loose on the whole ship?"

"They can't be replaced quickly enough to keep everything in this tub germ-free."

A soft tone sounded, and the clear hatch ahead of them slid open. "Shall we?"

Mitchell followed Watson through and into the infirmary.

"I assume you know what to do?" the engineer asked.

Mitchell stripped off his clothes and laid down on the padded machine. Even though the work was being done on his head, the medi-bot wouldn't activate as long as he was clothed.

Padded arms fell across his chest and his groin, offering a small amount of patient decency that doubled as a restraint system. The arms on the track above him came to life, small, dextrous fingers opening and closing. Watson placed the small tray with the chip in it on the counter and hit a few buttons on the machine. The routine to remove a faulty neural implant was pre-programmed.

Mitchell closed his eyes. He heard the arm sliding along the track, and then felt a soft prick in the side of his head. Everything went numb in that area immediately after, and when he shifted his eyes to look over in that direction all he could see were the limbs of the robotic arms making the smallest of adjustments.

A few minutes later an overlay appeared in front of his left eye, a blinking cursor signaling that something was happening. Lines and lines of text sped by, pausing during "diagnostic daemon" and then resuming. Soon after, three words flashed in front of him.

Ready.

Set.

GO.

A patch was applied to his head, and the arms retreated. The restraints shifted, and Mitchell sat up.

"Well?" Watson asked.

Mitchell brought the system menu into his vision. He settled on "self-diagnostic" and watched the overlay switch to a layout of his body and information about blood pressure, heart rate, and the levels of the synthetic hormones stored in his backside.

"Seems to be working. Try to knock."

"I can't yet. You're the first with the new encryption. I'll start updating the rest of the crew after we're done here. You feel okay?"

"Yeah, fine. Why?"

"I overloaded the main routing board to squeeze a little more speed out of it. You probably won't notice it day-to-day, but I think you will in combat."

Mitchell slipped off the table and grabbed his clothes. "The ship I came in, the helmet. It has its own link. Is this going to interfere?"

"Good question. We won't know until we try."

"If it does, can I turn this off?"

"Not without the Captain's key."

"Kill switch?"

"She told you about it?"

"Yeah."

He nodded and motioned towards the door. "I've got to go find Goliath. Your ARR has a map of the ship. No need to get lost."

Mitchell stared. He was going to ask Watson what he had said, but he stopped himself. "You didn't just say Goliath, did you?" he asked.

"No, Captain," Watson said. "Maybe I should double-check my enhancements."

Mitchell put up his hand. "No, I'm okay. It's a pre-existing glitch." He slid his clothes on and headed for the door, Watson trailing behind him.

"Let me know right away if you have any problems," the engineer said. "I'm going to update my comm system first, so I'll be available within the next half hour."

"Definitely. Thanks, Watson."

"Any time."

Mitchell took the long way around to the main lift and then back up to B-Deck. He explored the p-rat while he walked, switching through the different functions, impressed with the increase in responsiveness. By the time he returned to his bunk, he had already found an old stream to watch before getting some shut-eye.

Ilanka was still there when he arrived, but her open mouth and slight snore told him she was sleeping. He whispered a goodnight to her and settled on the bottom bed. After sleeping on the hard floor of the storage room for the last eight days, he was grateful for the simple comfort.

He was asleep within minutes.

30

"BIND HIS HANDS."

It was the first thing Mitchell heard before he felt himself being grabbed and flipped. He opened his eyes and tensed, ready to fight back, only to feel something get wrapped over his head, and a pair of hands grip his neck while it too was tied to him.

Three sets of hands held him tight while a wire tie was used to hold his wrists together behind his back. Then he was lifted from the bunk and shoved forward, smacking into the wall.

"What the hell is this?" he said. He sensed someone to his left, and he kicked out that way, catching what felt like a stomach with his bare foot. An *oomph* of air followed by someone crashing into the bunks confirmed his suspicion.

"Get a grip on him, damn it," someone said. He recognized the voice.

"Captain?"

"Good morning, sunshine," Millie said.

"I thought we had an arrangement?"

"We do have an arrangement, Mitch. You're one of us now."

He was shoved forward again, out of the berthing.

"You treat all of your men like this?"

"You already got the warm welcome. This is the other one. I call it a team-building exercise."

He knew there were other people with her, but they stayed silent, letting her do the talking.

"Hazing?" Mitchell asked.

"Not exactly."

A fist cracked into his gut, and he gritted his teeth, refusing to react. Hazing had been banned from the military for years, and with the advent of the implants and ARR, it had become easy to track and identify, despite participant's unwillingness to rat out their squad mates.

Except he was on a ship of criminals whose p-rats weren't connected to the main military grid. Which meant it was fair game, and apparently an honored practice.

"Okay," Mitchell said, taking another fist on his shoulder. "Show me what you've got."

"That's the spirit, Captain," Millie said.

Hands gripped him and threw him into the lift. He smacked against the rear wall hard enough to lose his air. The lift headed down.

His p-rat was active, and he used it to position himself in the ship. They dropped down to the hangar deck, and he was forcibly shoved and kicked until they reached the starship's belly. At that point, the bottom of the bag over his head was lifted, and someone tilted a cup against his mouth.

"Drink it, Captain," Millie said. "That's an order."

Mitchell opened his mouth and took the stuff in. It was alcohol or something like it, crude and strong. It burned his throat going down, but he refused to cough. He swallowed what they offered.

"More," he said. They wanted to see how tough he was? He had been a Space Marine a lot longer than he had been a face in the media.

"Mitch-"

"Be quiet," Millie said.

Mitchell recognized that voice, too. Ilanka. A moment later, the cup was against his mouth again. He swallowed what was offered.

"Strip him," Millie said.

Hands grabbed his clothes and tore them away, leaving him bound and reduced to his underwear.

"You keep a tight figure, Captain," Millie said.

He didn't answer. The drink was stronger than what he was used to. Much stronger. He checked his vitals on the p-rat. His blood-alcohol had spiked in a hurry, and he felt a little bit dizzy. The implant should have been working to balance out his system, to keep him from getting too wasted.

That function must have been removed.

"More, Captain," Millie said, putting the cup to his lips again. He tried to turn his head aside and was rewarded with another punch to the gut. "I said more."

Mitchell drank it, fighting against the wave of nausea that rolled through him as a result. His levels continued to rise in a hurry, and when he felt the tie fall away from his hands he tried to hold them out and almost fell over.

"Take off the hood," Millie said.

The hood was lifted away. They were in the hangar. It was dark except for a spot of light being cast down from a searchlight mounted on the mech's shoulder. Millie was standing directly in front of him, having traded her full uniform for the grays. Ilanka was on his left, Briggs on his right, and a new person, a muscular black man, at his back. Behind them were a few bystanders - Watson, Cormac, a woman he assumed was Singh, two more muscle-men, a foppish blonde, and another petite woman with long, black hair.

Where was Anderson?

"Hello, Mitch," Millie said. She was smiling, excited. All pretense of stuffiness and superiority had faded from her, and he couldn't help noticing her curves beneath the simple clothes.

Her eyes dropped down. "I hope that isn't just because you're drunk," she said with a laugh.

"Now what?" he blurted, blinking his eyes. Millie split into two, and the hangar started to spin.

"The main event. Come on out!"

Anderson stepped out from behind the huge leg of the mech. He too was stripped down, his old body still in good shape, covered in tattoos and scars. He grinned as he approached them, and then reached out and took an offered cup of the alcohol, downing it in one gulp.

"How many did he have?" he asked Millie.

"Three."

"Three?" Anderson sounded surprised. "Fine." He quickly gulped down two more cups of the stuff.

"The rules are simple," Millie said. "Winner is the one that's still conscious. Loser gets hung to the Knight for the evening."

"What?" Mitchell started to say, looking over towards the mech. He had just enough time to see there was a crossbar welded to the armor plating on the knee, and then he was stumbling backward, trying to recover from a heavy fist to his jaw. The onlookers cheered around them.

"Cheap shot you bastard," he said. There was no way Anderson was as wasted as he was already.

"You heard the rules," Anderson replied, closing in. He grabbed Mitchell's shoulders and threw him under the light.

Mitchell stumbled and fell, unable to keep his balance with the alcohol in his system. He couldn't remember the last time he had been so drunk. It had happened fast. Too fast.

Anderson was on him in a second, kicking him in the ribs. He coughed as the blows poured into his gut, hitting the already bruised skin. Whatever Millie thought of him, whatever her desire for wanting him to join her Riggers, it was clear that she was setting him up to lose this particular fight.

"Come on Anderson," she yelled. "Finish him if that's all he's got."

Anderson stopped kicking, reaching down for Mitchell's shoulders. As disoriented as Mitchell was, he somehow managed to get his hands out and bat the older man's grab away, reversing on his knees before falling over onto his back again.

The drunken haze was starting to make him angry.

"Where are you going?" Anderson mocked. "There's nowhere to run. Get up, you coward."

Mitchell rolled over and forced himself up. His feet shifted and everything was spinning around him. He could hear the other crew members cheering and whistling, and he was sure they were taking bets on who would win this ridiculous fight.

It was going to be Anderson. Mitchell was sure of it. He was doing his best, but he could barely stand, and the older Marine didn't seem to be feeling the booze at all. Of course he wasn't. Mitchell had no doubt he was accustomed to the drink.

"Come to daddy," Anderson said, moving towards Mitchell, knees bent, hands out. Mitchell threw an awkward punch at the man, stumbled back a step, and put his arms up to deflect a flurry of incoming blows. He managed to defend himself from the first set before a sharp elbow caught him in the temple, and he spun around and hit the deck again.

Anderson circled around him, laughing. Mitchell lay on his stomach, fighting a wave of nausea that threatened to force him to spit up whatever drink remained. As fast as it had affected him, it couldn't have been much.

"Anderson, do it." Millie's voice was a harsh snarl. If he had doubted she had the temperament to commit murder before, he didn't now.

The older Marine reached down and took Mitchell's shoulders again, pulling him up and holding him in a tight choke, slapping him in the face with his free hand over and over again.

"How do you like that?" the man spat. "Frigging Greylock."

Mitchell tried to turn his head away, his anger replaced with humiliation. Wasn't that the point of this? To humiliate him? How did Millie think this was going to bring him closer to his new teammates?

"Come on, Mitchell. I knew you were a wimp, but this is embarrassing," Anderson said through his laughter. He heard more laughing from a few of the gathered crowd, Millie's loudest of all.

He had a decision to make. He could let Anderson continue to embarrass him, or he could just give up. He fell limp in the man's grip, closing his eyes. Anderson held him up for a moment before realizing he had passed out.

"I guess I win," he said. He lowered Mitchell to the floor, rolling him over so that he was face up. "Loser gets strung up."

Mitchell held his eyes closed, listening to the soft sound of Anderson's feet on the cool metal floor. The losing was the humiliating part, not the hanging. He was a Marine, he had suffered worse than spending a night dangling by his wrists.

He could feel the softest brush of air when Anderson bent down to gather him by the shoulders again.

Then he made his move.

Head pounding, every muscle feeling leaden, Mitchell gathered himself in one motion, reaching up and grabbing Anderson's legs. He pulled as hard as he could, shifting the Marine, yanking hard enough so that his feet wound up skidding along the floor and continuing forward.

Anderson tried to find his balance, but there was no purchase for his heels and he cursed as he fell, hitting the ground hard on his back. Mitchell gritted his teeth, rising and tackling him before he could recover, throwing angry punches into the Marine's head. Anderson tried to get his hands up to block, but Mitchell had gotten his knees on them and was using his weight to hold him down. He rained the blows in, one after the other, opening old scars along Anderson's face and creating new welts and cuts.

"Stop. Stop. I submit, damn it," Anderson said, his face open and bleeding.

Mitchell heard him give up, and still continued punching.

"Captain," Millie said sharply, her officer's visage returning in an instant. Mitchell ignored her, continuing to hit Anderson in the face. She had wanted to teach him some kind of lesson. He was going to teach her, and Anderson, one instead.

"Get him off," she told the black man.

Mitchell finally stopped when he saw him approaching. Anderson lay beneath him, his face bloody and battered, his consciousness gone. Mitchell looked over at Millie and then spat on the Marine. Only then did he get to his feet.

"Loser gets strung up," Millie said. He had been wrong. She didn't care who won or lost, just that they danced to her tune.

Mitchell looked down at Anderson, and then back at Millie. Then he looked over at Ilanka, who seemed embarrassed to be part of the whole bizarre ritual.

"Go to hell, Captain," he said. He walked past them all, forcing himself not to stumble despite his drunkenness and anger, heading out of the hangar without another word.

[31]

MITCHELL WAS STANDING in the shower, leaning against the wall and letting the hot water run down his face and over his chest, when Millie arrived. She didn't announce herself. She didn't call out to him or say anything at all. Instead, he heard the shower head next to him begin sputtering water, and he glanced over to see who was there.

"Captain," she said, smiling at him as though none of the bullshit in the hangar had just happened.

"There's a free head down there," he said, pointing to the furthest part of the shower. He did his best to ignore her nakedness, finding it half-easy, and half-hard. He decided it had to be the drink still messing with his brain.

"I thought we could talk for a minute," she replied.

Mitchell took a deep breath, ready to use it to scream at her. The action made his entire gut throb. At least one cracked rib, he guessed. He needed to get down to medical and have the bots fix him up.

"I've got nothing to say," he replied quietly.

"It was nothing personal," she said. "I had to do it. The crew expected it."

Mitchell was silent. He stared at the drain below him, collecting the water for recycling.

"This ship isn't like any other ship in the galaxy, Mitchell," she continued. "I have to somehow keep control over a crew of rapists, sadists, pedophiles, hackers, mad scientists..." She trailed off.

"Murderers?" Mitchell said.

The anger flashed across her eyes. "Yes. These are tough men and women, people who fall outside of what anyone would consider social norms. You might think there's something to your rank, but not here. Their pecking order has nothing to do with the bars on your shirt. If you want respect, if you want them to follow you into a dogfight, you need to earn it."

He turned his head towards her again. "By putting me at a massive disadvantage? By setting me up?"

"Yes. They had to see what you're made of for themselves. They don't give a shit what your duty record says." She reached out and put a hand on his arm. "What you did down there? You bought yourself the respect of every one of the crew. You showed them that you don't give up, you don't give in, you keep fighting. In ten minutes you taught every single member of this squad that if they mess with you they're going to find themselves bloody and beaten."

He pulled his arm away. "And you had this whole thing planned out the whole time? You were sure it was going to end the way it did?"

"Not at all. I couldn't be sure you would win, but if you didn't... Then I would know something about you, too, and your place on Riggers would have been set. It didn't matter if you won or lost, it was how you played the game."

"You have some crazy ideas on how to run a ship, Captain."

"I've learned the hard way. It wasn't always like this, Mitch. When the project first launched, I tried to be fair and honest, stern yet lenient. It was a nightmare. A total nightmare. I had no authority, no power. There were three murders and two rapes in the first week, and General Cornelius was threatening to can the whole thing before it could become enough of a disaster that the rest of the brass would ask questions. I need this ship, this gig. It was either this or execution. Them or me. I did what I had to do, and figured out how to make it stop in a hurry. The new recruit gets tested, the crew gets out a little extra energy, the hierarchy is organized, and we all go on living as cautiously normal as any powder keg family like this one can."

"Including Anderson?"

"The bots will patch him up. It's all no hard feelings."

"No hard feelings? That works for your crew?"

"So far. I lost ten people in my first month as the head of the project. I've only had to put half a dozen to death in the years since."

"You've killed six of your own soldiers?"

"Do you think I'm happy about it? Pleased with myself? Every single one of them would have killed me or anyone else here if they had the slightest inclination. I have to be the strongest, the meanest, the coldest. If I'm not, if I show one thread of weakness, it's all over for everyone here."

Mitchell kept his eyes down, thinking about what she had said. He had underestimated everything about this ship. "Fine," he decided. "You say it's over? Then it's over. I have to tell you, I'm not a fan of your methods."

"Understood." She put her bionic hand on his shoulder again. It purred against his skin. "Let me make it up to you."

She softened when she said it, just enough that there was no question as to what she was suggesting. The still-tipsy part of him was tempted, very tempted. He took her hand away again and stepped out from under the water. "No, thanks."

"Are you sure? No commitment, no emotional garbage. We don't get too many opportunities out here, and to be honest, the rest of the crew is too unstable to trust. You? You aren't like the rest of us." Her eyes fell to his midsection again. "I can see at least one part of you is saying yes."

He shook his head. "I think that part has gotten me in enough trouble already. Maybe some other time." He checked on his p-rat. Oh-three-hundred. "Briefing in three hours?"

"Yes, Captain," she said.

"I need to head down to medical, and then catch some shuteye. If you need to wake me up, do me a favor and spare the wire ties."

Mitchell grabbed a towel and left.

MITCHELL ARRIVED for the briefing at exactly oh-six-hundred, dressed in his grays, his body still recovering from the beating he had taken. The medi-bots had put his two fractured ribs back in place and injected him with painkillers, but there wasn't much they could do for the smoldering anger he was still feeling. He had accepted what Millie had said about how things worked on the Schism. That didn't mean he liked it.

The briefing room was located next to the hangar, across from the armory. It was a standard setup - enough chairs for a hundred people, a podium, and a holographic monitor up at the front, a UPA flag hanging in the rear. It was nowhere near full when he arrived, though he thought most of the souls on the ship were present save for Watson and Singh. There were still a number of faces he didn't recognize, and a few he had seen at the fight but not met.

He could feel their eyes on them when he stepped into the room. He could sense the hush in their conversations. He fought against the renewed feeling of embarrassment, pausing in the entrance and scanning them deliberately, making sure they knew he was sizing up every last one of them.

"Captain on deck," Cormac shouted from his place near the center of the room. There was a uniform thump as the entire room shifted to attention. For a second Mitchell thought it was for him. Then he felt a hand on his arm.

"Ares," Millie said. "I'm glad you could join us."

Mitchell looked at her over his shoulder. She was dressed in her full uniform again, her hair and makeup just so. Anderson was trailing behind her, his face bruised but otherwise intact. He caught Mitchell's eye with his own. There was no malice there, no anger. Maybe he had been hoping to win the fight, to prove something, but he had also accepted that he lost.

"Captain," Mitchell said, coming to attention.

"There's a seat next to Rain," she said, pointing over to the front corner where the other pilot was sitting.

"Yes, ma'am." Mitchell bowed slightly and took his place. Ilanka flashed him a smile as he sat.

"I'll keep this simple because I know your little brains can't handle too many big words," Millie said, gaining the podium.

Her left eye twitched, and the holographic projector switched on. Displaying on it was an image of a stardock - a massive, ringed and spoked station where starships rested at measured intervals like knobs on the wheel of an ancient sailing ship. It orbited a massive red and brown gas-giant as a world unto itself, an entire ecosystem devoted to the economy of starships, be it in refuel, repair, trade, or providing for the needs of the thousands of hands on board.

"This is SD Nine-Three. Also called Calypso, after the planet that it's orbiting. We're currently about three hours away from dropping from FTL nearby." A bright dot showed where they would fall out of hyperspace, a few hundred AU from the dock. "As you know, we undertook a small mining expedition about a week ago, in order to gather enough ore to pass a routine inspection and get the Schism cleared for hookup with the station."

The image on the projector faded out and was replaced with a new visual. Mitchell recognized the face immediately.

"This is the target," Millie said. "Alliance intelligence has it on good authority that Chancellor Ken and his retinue are scheduled to be carrying out an inspection on the dock, in preparation for its conversion to a military platform. Our mission is to make sure that doesn't happen."

Mitchell sat up straighter in his chair. Chancellor Ken was one of the top leaders of the Federation, famous for his aggressive rhetoric and war-mongering. If he was visiting the star dock, that meant the Schism was going to be falling out of hyperspace in Federation territory.

Millie seemed to notice his new level of alertness. Her eyes passed over him, and the hint of a smile played at the edge of her lips. "Command has ordered that we're to make an initial effort to capture the Chancellor. I don't think I need to tell you how valuable he would be to the Alliance as a hostage. Failing that, our objectives are, in order of value: assassinate Chancellor Ken, destroy his personal cruiser, disable the dock."

The image of the Chancellor was replaced with one of the Federation cruiser, a pill-shaped starship bristling with weaponry. While destroyers were more heavily armed, they were brawlers. Cruisers were quick and dirty, their usual assault vector being a drop from hyperspace to unload their heavy ordnance, and then a massive thrust to clear their initial drop location. Once the warheads hit their targets, the cruiser would go back into hyperspace and either rendezvous with the formation point of the attack group, or move away and return for a second run.

It was the starfighters that would work to keep the cruisers in line, using probabilistic models designed by top military intelligence to calculate the most likely assault vectors and arrange for a squadron or two to intercept the cruisers when they fell out of FTL. A starfighter at existing velocity could easily outpace a cruiser that had to thrust from "hyperdeath" - the relative standstill required before and after hyperspace travel. This allowed the pilots to fly rings around the cruiser, weakening shields, inflicting damage, or forcing it to launch its own smaller ships, which in turn served to prevent them from leaving the field.

"Sunny, you'll be leading the ghost team onto the station," Millie said. "I'm transferring your specific mission orders and data now." Mitchell glanced back, finding the petite woman with the black hair. She nodded almost imperceptibly, and then put her hand on the arm of the person sitting next to her, an unassuming, younger man with a mop of blonde hair and a sharp face. Was she Sunny, or was he?

"Shank, your grunts will be on standby for extraction, full exo. If things go bad in a hurry, you need to make sure the ghosts get back alive."

"Yes, ma'am," Shank said. Mitchell saw he was the big black man from the fight.

"Rain, you and Ares will be suited up and running hot. If this thing blows up, you can bet we'll be hit like a hornet in a beehive. The Schism only has a few fixed projectile positions, a couple of laser batteries, and minimal shields. We won't last two minutes against a Federation cruiser."

"Yes, Captain," Ilanka said.

"I'm transmitting mission data to the rest of you now. Most of you have done this before. You know the stakes." She turned her head, looking directly at Mitchell. "To be clear for the benefit of our newest member: my direct orders are to vaporize the Schism and send kill signals to all of the crew the moment I believe mission secrecy has been compromised. Remember, we don't exist, and nobody will miss us when we're gone."

Mitchell stared back at her, keeping his expression flat while he shivered on the inside. The truth of his situation hadn't truly hit him when M had removed his helmet and showed himself a clone. It hadn't struck him when he spent eight days in confinement. It hadn't sunk in before, during, or after the initiation. Only now, only after hearing those words, did his mind finish the calculation.

This was his life for the rest of his life, for as long as it lasted.

What surprised him was that after everything that had happened surrounding the Shot, he was almost happy about it.

"Yes, Firedog?" Millie said, looking back at Cormac. The private must have knocked her p-rat with a question.

"I couldn't help but notice we're launching this little bit of mayhem on a Federation dock. I know Sunny looks just like one of them bastards, but Shadow is going to stand out like a boil on my cock. How exactly are they going to infiltrate security to get a shot at the Chancellor?"

"Shut it, Dog," Shank said, turning towards his soldier. "You know that's need-to-know, and you don't."

"I know, but-"

"I said shut it."

Cormac lowered his eyes. "Yes, sir."

Millie turned her attention to Ilanka. "Yes, Rain?"

"I just wanted to publicly welcome Ares to the squad, especially as my wingmate." She turned her head to look Mitchell in the eye. "It's an honor to fly with you, Captain."

"Thank you," Mitchell said.

"Yes, Captain, welcome to the Riggers," Millie said. "Here's to good hunting on your first mission with us."

The response from the gathered crew was uniform. "Riggers! Riigg-aaah," they all cried as one. Mitchell noticed even Anderson joined in.

It seemed maybe there was something to the so-called team-building exercise after all.

[33]

"I HATE THIS PART," Ilanka said.

Mitchell tilted his head over to where she was sitting, strapped into the cockpit of the Piranha. He raised his hand up so she could see him waving at her from his own position in the cockpit of the S-17.

"If we're lucky, we'll get to spend a nice evening hanging from the launcher."

Millie had decided the two pilots would be running hot, which meant that the fighters had been hooked up to the ship's launch system and suspended from the ceiling, facing straight down towards the bay doors. The air and gravity had already been removed from the space. If their services were needed, the hangar doors would open and the launcher would give them a solid push forward, a small boost before they fired their own thrusters and cleared into space. The position and the strategic placement of a mechanical false ceiling had also served to hide the fighters from the Federation inspectors that boarded the ship to assess the cargo of ore.

"We've cleared inspection," Millie said, her voice echoing in his mind through the p-rat. All of the crew had been outfitted with the updated software, and the new encryption scheme that Mitchell could only hope the enemy, any enemy, couldn't crack. "Sunny, your team will disembark in five."

Mitchell had managed to catch a little bit of the scuttlebutt that was surrounding the mission in the three hours between the briefing and the moment they dropped out of FTL. He had learned that Sunny was First Sergeant Sang Yi, a former Army Special Forces sniper, and that the blonde was Private Caleb Smith, Mouth, her voice and lover. It seemed that for as much of a stone-cold killer the woman was, she had terrible social anxiety whenever she wasn't running a mission.

Their plan was to have the two soldiers, plus two others in their assault group, go on leave from the ship, armed with carbonate blades that would avoid detection from both frisking and scanning. They would make their way to the Federation Plaza - the hotel where heads of state always stayed. Once they were there, they would use a scanner that Watson had surgically implanted into Mouth's calf and connected to the neural implant to scan for the Chancellor, using readings that had been provided by intelligence.

When they found him, they would have to improvise on how to reach and capture him, most likely trying to infiltrate his security team, or take control of his transportation. If that failed and they were caught, Shank's team would be dispatched to raise havoc on the station and give the ghosts the distraction they needed to attempt a retreat. The fighters would be launched to cover an attack on the Schism. Once everyone was back on board, the Schism would tear away from its moorings, back off a little bit, and launch its two warheads at the station. Surviving that would be questionable, because they had to keep close range to fire inside the shield web. They were banking on the hope that either their own shields were enough to deflect the resulting force, or that they would be able to disable the web and get far, far away from the dock.

It was the best plan possible for an impossible mission that was only half a step above suicide. Like Millie had said, the members of the Riggers knew the alternative. Project Black existed to try to execute on bold, stupid ideas, and so far they had somehow come away intact.

"I don't know what I would have done if you hadn't shown up," Ilanka said. "This mission is crazy enough, and to be running support on my own? Bezumnyy."

The whole idea was that they wouldn't be needed. If they were, things were already beyond desperate.

A tone sounded in his mind. "Sunny, you have a go," Millie said. Mitchell hadn't expected to have a line into the full squad communications, and was surprised to find that she had grouped him in.

"Roger, Captain," Mouth replied. "Wish us luck."

"Good luck. Good hunting." A new tone sounded, the channel switching. "Shank, is your team in position?"

"Ready and waiting with itchy trigger fingers," Shank said.

Another change in tone.

"Rain?"

"Reactors are online, all systems are nominal."

"Are you having fun yet, Ares?" Millie said.

"I'm hoping I won't have the chance to, ma'am."

The comm switched off, leaving Mitchell in complete silence. He kept his eyes on the helmet's display, which was showing him a map of the star system, the station, and all of the ships both parked at it and orbiting nearby. The dock could hold forty large starships at a time, and it was currently filled with a mixture of traders and military. Frontier Federation military. There were another two dozen or so ships within sensor range, mostly transports and merchants.

It was the cruiser that worried him. The other military vessels were smaller frigates and patrollers - armed and dangerous, but not nearly as much.

"So Rain," Mitchell said, trying to break the silence and ease some of the thick tension. "What squadron did you fly with, before you landed here?"

"The Black Knights," Ilanka replied. "I'm surprised you didn't guess."

The mech was a Knight.

"Did you steal it?" Mitchell asked.

Ilanka laughed. "No. The Captain requisitioned it for me. I have A-plus rating on it. She's been my baby for almost ten years."

"Have you seen a lot of combat?"

"Not as much as you have, I think. Navy doesn't launch many ground assaults these days. I think that's why Millie was able to get it transferred."

"What about the fighter?"

"Purchased in the Rim. It was stolen, just not by us." She laughed again, a hearty, throaty laugh. "I know you were with Greylock. How did you wind up a Space Marine? I think you could have been actor, or model."

"Me? I think my mother might be the only one who would agree with you on that."

"Don't be silly. You have pretty face, nice body. I know. I saw."

Mitchell was glad he was wearing the helmet. She wouldn't be able to look over and see how red his face was getting.

"Thanks, I guess. Would you believe I lost a bet?"

"I don't believe you lose very much."

"I did that time. A bet with my younger brother, Steven. I grew up on Earth. The original Earth. In Arizona, the United States. We had these old-fashioned off-road bikes, the kind with wheels instead of repulsors, the ones they make for nostalgia. We picked a spot, and he bet me he could beat me out to it and back. It was over rough terrain, lots of inclines and obstacles. We're lucky we didn't get ourselves killed then and there. Anyway, if I won, he joined the Marines. If he won, I joined."

"So he won?"

"Affirmative. Then he joined the Navy. He commands a destroyer now, a few thousand light years closer to home. Rear Admiral Steven Williams. He's prettier than I am, too."

"Is he married?"

"Are you interested?"

"I might be."

It was a joke they both got. Mitchell knew the only way he was getting off this ship was to either die or figure out a way to escape, and he didn't want to escape unless it meant reaching the Goliath. Being here, sitting in a cockpit, ready to die in an attempt to kill a Federation VIP... It was all he had ever really wanted. It was something he was sure he'd lost.

He could only hope the price wasn't as high as M had suggested.

"So anyway," Mitchell said, "I signed up the next day. Took the physical, and then went in over the weekend for the testing."

"Did you score well?"

"Average," Mitchell lied. "How about you?"

"Same. I think I would have done better, but I've never been very good at math."

"I don't even know why they still have that on the test. AI takes care of any calculation we could ever want."

"In event of system failure," Ilanka said in a deep, monotonous voice, mimicking the training streams they had all been forced to watch.

"At which point, you're already unconscious and sucking space," Mitchell said. "God, I hated that series."

Ilanka was laughing heavily, enjoying their banter. Mitchell couldn't help but smile. He was enjoying himself, enjoying loosening them both up and regaining the camaraderie he had lost the day the Greylock, and Ella, had died.

That was the moment everything went to hell.

THE TONE in his ear was shrill, an emergency signal. A woman's voice followed after.

"Damn trap... They were waiting for us... Son of a bitch... We've been had... Mouth is dead. Coming home."

He didn't recognize the voice. He assumed it had to be Sunny. Her breathing was hard, her anger obvious in her voice.

"Shank, get your team out there," Millie said, across the emergency channel.

"Already on the move, Captain," Shank said.

"Ilanka, hangar doors are opening now. Track your targets, buy us some time."

"Roger," Ilanka said. The mirth was gone. She was stone cold.

Mitchell felt his heart rate increasing. He watched the display on the helmet. The Federation cruiser had changed color, indicating that its main engines were warming.

A flashing blue light issued a warning, and then the hangar doors began to part beneath them, silent in the vacuum. They opened quickly, faster than was probably safe, likely another modification added by Watson or Singh. As soon as the doors were open enough for them to squeeze through, the launchers fired, releasing them and shoving them ahead.

Mitchell hit the throttle with a thought, pushing the ship forward, careful not to lose course and hit Ilanka on the way out. The Piranha was smaller than the S-17, more narrow and tight, with rounded stubs for wings. It was made for space combat only, so there was no need for a configuration that provided lift.

"The patrollers are the primary targets," Ilanka said. "We won't be able to do much against that cruiser. Stay close to the Schism."

They shot out of the hangar and shifted their vectors, rocketing up and over the top of the salvage ship. Mitchell looked down as they passed, catching a glimpse of the bridge with the cracked viewport and Millie sitting in the captain's chair, her head back and linked to the Schism's CAP-NN.

"We lost Rover," Sunny said. There was a grunt over the comm, and then a man's scream. "They just lost somebody."

"Shank, sitrep," Millie said.

"Clamping bay, ma'am," Shank said. "Pinned down. Security is in full exo. This was one hundred percent trap. They knew we were coming."

"How, damn it?" Millie shouted. Mitchell could hear the frustration and anger in her voice.

They were dead. They were all dead. His first mission.

"Sunny, sitrep."

"Trapped between the Federation ambush and the security detail. There's no way through."

"Shit," Millie said. She was losing her cool, fast. "We're going to shred the clamps. Shank, you have sixty seconds to punch through that detail, and then I want you falling back."

"Captain, the inception team is going to be caught."

"Don't you think I know that? There's nothing we can do."

Mitchell winced, his jaw clenching. How had the Federation known they were coming? How could they know anything about them, when only a select few in the Alliance knew the ship existed at all?

"Ares, incoming," Ilanka said.

Mitchell checked his display. A patrol ship was rounding the top of the dock, getting into position to open fire.

"I'm on it," Mitchell said. "Stay with the Schism."

He pushed the thrusters harder, flipping over towards the patroller. The Federation versions were much simpler than the Alliance patrol ships. They looked like cubes that had been rotated, stacked, and merged together into a hundred meter long spear, with projectile batteries embedded in the top and bottom, and laser turrets running along the sides.

"We don't have shields yet," Millie said, noticing the incoming ship.

"Not a problem," Mitchell said. He was moving towards the patroller at a crazy velocity, as though he were planning to ram it.

A blue bolt extended from the ship, a laser aimed in his direction, made visible by the helmet. The targeting computer was behind on calculating his trajectory and rotating accordingly, the small size and high velocity his best defense. Mitchell knew the missiles would come next.

It was standard defense against fighters. Six vectoring warheads dropped from the patroller, their thrusters igniting. They spread out in front of Mitchell, each missile moving into a calculated position where the AI and the gunner expected him to be. It was a tough calculation to make against a human pilot and one of the reasons why fully autonomous warfare had yet to be achieved. Years of research had revealed that when the best AI paired off against one another, they became so chaotic and erratic in the maneuvers that they actually arrived at a highly predictable state.

Mitchell was anything but predictable. He flipped the S-17 up and away from the missiles, a quick change that left the ship vibrating from the force of the thrust, threatening to bend the structure. He angled over the warheads at the same time the defense system fired dozens of lasers towards them, detonating them hundreds of meters away.

"My turn," Mitchell said. A single thought launched two of the explosive discs from the wings of the fighter. He was within a half a kilometer from the patroller now, and he had to do a quick reverse and full rear thrust to shoot away from the resulting explosion. "One bogey down."

"Nice work, Ares. Two more on the starboard side," Ilanka said.

"On my way."

"Shank, any progress?" Millie asked over the p-rat.

"We're at a stalemate, ma'am. They're under too much cover to punch through."

"We're out of time. Shank, pull your men back. Sunny, you're on your own."

"Understood, Captain," Sunny said, her voice flat.

Mitchell cursed under his breath. This wasn't going well.

A flashing icon in his helmet caught his attention. The cruiser was starting to pull back from the dock.

"Cruiser is active," he said. He found the two patrol ships circling towards the Schism from opposite sides. Ilanka was racing towards one. He would have to clear the other.

He used the neural link to check his ordnance, and was surprised to find that the ship was reporting the supply of the explosive discs as nearly full, minus the one he had just fired. He remembered the clean room down on medical. Could it be that this unassuming S-17 was capable of manufacturing its own weaponry?

He swept under the Schism, coming up at the patrol ship from below. It fired on the salvage ship, its laser scoring a direct hit on the rear, near the thrusters. The armor was thick enough to hold for a few seconds of burn. It would have to be enough.

Mitchell launched three of the projectiles at the ship, turning away and heading towards Ilanka's position before they even struck the patroller. A few seconds later it vanished from the display.

"Two down," Mitchell said. He tracked the cruiser again. It was backing away from the dock, but it had to vector along the same rotating orbit in order to avoid hitting any of the other ships. That meant that it was positioned around the curve of the dock, giving them a little more time.

Mitchell watched Ilanka maneuver around the patrol ship, the Piranha flipping and spinning, turning and twisting. She expertly avoided the defensive fire, taking pot shots at the patroller that whittled away its shields. He was certain with time she would break through and destroy the ship.

Time wasn't something they could spare.

"Rain, back off," Mitchell said. "I've got the firepower."

"Roger," Ilanka said. "Don't wait for me. I will clear."

Mitchell went into a corkscrew spin to throw the targeting systems, getting close and firing two more of the projectiles. This time he followed them with his eyes, tiny slivers that slipped past the shields and sank into the hull, exploding an instant later.

Blue flashes surrounded him, his shields catching the smaller debris and vaporizing it while he angled around the larger pieces. They hurtled towards the surface of the dock, only to be pulled apart by its own near-field shielding. One of the docked transports wasn't so lucky, its own shields down, not expecting an attack from within the dock's outer defensive shell. Shrapnel tore into it, breaching it in silence and causing it to vent both air and crew out into space.

"Three out," Mitchell said.

"We're back on board, Captain," Shank said. "Taking heavy fire on the docking port. Airlock is closed, but it may be damaged. We lost Gremlin."

"Ensign Briggs, bring us out," Millie said.

"The seal may be damaged," Briggs replied.

"Then they'll die," Millie snapped. "We have to move, now!"

"Yes, ma'am."

The forward vectoring thrusters began to fire, pushing the Schism away from the dock. It was caught on the harness, the locking mechanism only able to be released by dock control. The thrusters gained power, fighting against the connection. Either the ship would tear free or the operators would release it before it pulled the entire station out of position.

"That cruiser is still coming," Millie said. "ETA thirty seconds. Briggs, how long to reach safe firing range for the heavy?"

"Forty-one seconds, Captain," Briggs replied.

"Damn it, we need this piece of shit to move faster. Shank, are you still alive down there?"

"Affirmative, Captain. The seal has a small leak. Firedog is welding it now. We won't be going out that way for a while."

"At least something went our way."

"Ares, with me," Ilanka said.

Mitchell found her position and altered his thrust, vectoring towards her. They stayed close as they maneuvered around the curve of the station, heading towards the cruiser.

A dozen fighters poured from the warship's belly, their thrusters glowing in the blackness, turning them in their direction.

"Getting hot out here," Mitchell said. His shields flashed as laser pulses started striking against them.

"Go through, target the cruiser," Ilanka said. "You might be able to damage it with that thing."

"Roger."

Mitchell threw the fighter to the side, then jerked it up and over. He got lock on one of the Federation's fighters on the way by, launching a disc into it and smiling at the explosion. He caught sight of Ilanka as he looked back, her shields taking heavy fire as she attempted to fight eleven to one. She wasn't going to last long out there.

He looked back at the cruiser. He could hit it, sure. Maybe damage it. Meanwhile, she was going to die.

"Pulling back," Mitchell said, turning around. Three of the enemy fighters had been trailing him, and he snaked through them, hitting one with the forward lasers and two with the projectiles. All of his weapons bypassed the shields as though they didn't even exist.

"Ares, the cruiser," Ilanka said.

"Sorry, Rain. I outrank you. Either the cruiser is going to blow the Schism or we're going to get away. I'm not leaving you for dead."

"You are stupid asshole," she said.

"Tell me about it."

He came at the Federation fighters from behind, the neural link targeting and locking much faster than any other ship he had flown before. It would have been amazing and impressive to dogfight that many enemies and come out of it alive.

Except their time was up.

The cruiser rounded on the Schism, still reversing clear of the dock, trapped between it and the outer shield web. More Federation ships waited in the space beyond, kept out of the fight by the shields, which the operators must have been ordered to hold up. They were still trapped, still stuck, with no way out.

That wasn't completely true. He had a way out. The S-17 was FTL capable. If he could stay alive, hide, act derelict, he could get out of there the moment it was all over.

And live a coward. He dropped the thought from his mind.

A barrage of missiles launched from the cruiser, aimed directly at the Schism. Mitchell cursed as he vectored towards them, pushing hard to add thrust. At these speeds and distances, the Schism would be nothing but dust within seconds.

He found himself in the center of the salvo, alarms ringing in his ears because he was directly in the path of one of the projectiles. A nuke would fry the dock at this range, which meant the warheads had to be conventional.

He let the CAP-NN take over, tracking the warheads and firing the defensive lasers. The missiles were close, too close. They detonated around him in balls of escaping gas, silent and deadly. The forces jostled the fighter, the shields fighting to absorb the energy. More alarms went off, the integrity monitor dropping.

Then it was clear again, white stars and the rounded curve of the gas planet against a black backdrop in front of him. He had saved them from the first shot. He wouldn't survive another.

"Ten seconds to clear," Briggs said.

"Preparing to fire," Millie replied. Mitchell knew she would be arming the onboard nuke and setting the target. From this range, there was no way they could miss.

A new alarm went off inside Mitchell's head. A new dot appeared on the display. Then another. And another.

"I'm picking up a huge energy spike," Briggs said suddenly. "New targets incoming."

Mitchell's heart thumped, something in him finding recognition in the readings. "Captain, shields up, now," he shouted.

"What?" Millie said.

"Do it." It wouldn't be enough. The shields on the Schism were minimal. They wouldn't survive the hit.

A blinding white light streamed from deeper space, from beyond visual contact with the new targets. It arced towards the dock with an edge of blue fire, a massive ball of energy rolling unstoppable towards the station.

The outer shields lit up, attempting to catch the ball. The front end of it pushed in for a second, slowed by the web of repulsive energy, before shattering it into nothing, bursting through and continuing its flow towards the circular dock.

It hit in the center, the energy spreading as it struck the center spoke, racing outward like a wave swallowing a boat. Within seconds, the entire structure and all of the ships attached to it were coated in an iridescent glow.

Seconds later, they began to crumble.

The center spoke went first, the structure literally falling apart, venting atmosphere and leaving pieces of the suddenly disintegrated dock drifting outwards.

"Holy shit," he heard Millie whisper. A moment later she was composed. "Ares, Rain, get back on board. I'm lowering the shields around the hangar."

They both raced for the Schism, the cruiser that nearly destroyed it turning to engage the new threat.

A second ball of energy sped towards it. The captain tried to vector around, and he managed to get most of the ship clear.

Not all of it. The edge of the weapon caught the side of the cruiser. It spread along it, and pulled it apart.

"Alliance?" Ilanka asked.

"No," Mitchell replied.

A latent, vague understanding of the time before.

A warning from a stranger who looked just like him.

They had arrived.

A third ball of energy swept behind them, aimed at the ships that had been positioned beyond the station's shields. They scrambled to clear the space, but it was too late. Pieces of the fireball caught each of them, spreading to the poly-alloy and breaking them apart.

"Drop the mains, ready the FTL," Millie said.

The Schism continued to float backward. Ilanka and Mitchell reached the hangar, vectoring in, their CAP-NN systems working to adjust their thrust and keep them from slamming into the walls. The doors closed behind them, the artificial gravity pulling them to the floor, the AI firing heavy thrust to land them on their feet.

The alarms still sounded inside the helmet. A fourth power spike, a fourth firing of the energy weapon that had decimated the station with one blast.

This one was headed right towards them.

Mitchell watched it coming, breathing in and holding it. Had they known he was here? Was he the target? Or was it just coincidence that they arrived here, now? Was it related to the fact that the Federation had known they were coming? Was there a clone, a replica, one of them, already on the Schism, or buried deep enough in the ranks of the Alliance military that they knew about this operation?

All those questions and more flowed through his mind as he waited once more to die.

A new dot appeared in his helmet. The nuke. Millie had launched it, but why? To where?

He watched it approach the energy ball. It vanished right ahead of it, the force of the explosion countering the force of the Shot. The ball broke apart, turning into a stream like water from the shower, its velocity slowed by the impact.

"I can't believe that worked," Millie shouted in excitement. "Briggs, status."

"FTL engine online, ma'am."

"We're getting out of here."

Mitchell felt a slight shift, and then all of the targets in the helmet were gone.

[35]

MITCHELL DIDN'T GET out of the fighter right away. He took a minute first to catch his breath and calm, and then slid the cockpit open, removing the helmet and jumping down without waiting for the ladder. Ilanka was already standing on the hangar floor, surveying the Piranha. It was scuffed and dark from a few soft hits from enemy lasers, adding to its already worn patina. It was otherwise unharmed.

"I don't think I've ever been so happy to be alive," she said.

Mitchell's first instinct was to tell her not to get used to the idea. He didn't say it out loud. Instead, he turned and looked at the S-17. The onboard AI had positioned it caddy-corner to the Piranha, it's wing only inches from the other fighter. It had been a closer call than he realized. He eyed it for damage, finding none.

"That ship is amazing," Ilanka said.

"Amazing to us. I don't know how fantastic it is against whoever just obliterated Calypso."

The statement stole her excitement. "We made it out alive." It was the only defense she had.

"Watson, Ares, Rain, Shank, Anderson, meet me in Olympus asap," Millie said, her voice echoing through the p-rat.

"No time to shower even," Ilanka said, raising her armpit and giving it a sniff. "I think I pissed myself in the excitement."

"I didn't need to know that."

They made their way to the lift and then up to A-Deck, passing by the communications array to the conference room that he had noticed earlier. Watson and Shank were already there. Watson looked calm and thoughtful, while Shank just looked tired. His face was sweaty and marred with grease, his clothes grimy and torn. A small bloodstain had formed near his left knee.

Anderson was there, too, standing in the corner, his face dark.

"Captain," he said when Mitchell walked in, coming to attention.

"At ease, Lieutenant," Mitchell said. He took the seat next to Shank, noticing that the textile was already stained. With blood? Sweat? Tears?

"Officer-"

"Stow it, Anderson," Millie said, entering the room like a whirlwind. Ensign Briggs trailed behind her.

The Admiral took a seat at the head of the table. Her hat was off, her hair was down, her eyes red and face tight. She was silent for a minute, staring at each of them.

"What the hell was that?" she said, in barely more than a whisper. It was a simple statement, but the way it escaped her communicated everything they were all feeling. "We lost a lot of people today."

Nobody spoke. There was no clear answer. Only a lot of questions.

"Williams," Millie said, looking at Mitchell. "Any ideas?"

Mitchell tried to collect his thoughts and figure out what he wanted to say, and how to say it without sounding like a complete lunatic. He settled on a question of his own. "Do you believe me now?"

Her face paled. He could see her jaw clenching, sending ripples across the surface of it. "I was afraid to, and hoping you were delusional. I do."

"Believe what?" Shank asked.

"You weren't keyed into the full theater," Mitchell said. "You didn't see them."

"See what?"

"I didn't see them either," Millie said. "I only saw the weapons they fired. It was more than enough."

Shank smacked his hand on the table. "Will someone tell me what the hell you're talking about?"

"The mission was accomplished," Millie said. "The dock is destroyed. So is the cruiser. Except not by us. A new threat. Three ships. They fired energy weapons that punched right through the station's shields and broke down the structural integrity of the shell. It literally fell apart."

Shank didn't say anything. He didn't need to.

"The nuke managed to slow the velocity and break down the weapon," Watson said. "We have to assume it's at least partially susceptible to radiation or EMP."

"Not susceptible enough. We barely made it out," Millie said. She wiped a strand of hair from in front of her face. "What are the odds of them showing up at the same place and time as we did?"

Her eyes were back on Mitchell again, as if he had the answers.

"How do we know that is case?" Ilanka said. "Could be enemy is attacking all over."

"Yes," Millie agreed. "We won't know until we get into position to send a message back to Command. We're on our way to the rendezvous point now. ETA six hours. Until then, let's assume that it's just a really bad coincidence. The fact remains that there is nothing in the Alliance arsenal that can stand up to a weapon like that. Throwing nukes a round at a time is a losing proposition."

"Goliath," Mitchell said. "M believed it could help us."

"Who's M?" Watson asked.

"Permission to speak freely, Captain?" Mitchell said.

"Granted," Millie replied.

Mitchell got to his feet and proceeded to tell them everything about what had happened to him, from the moment he had been shot to the present. He described the conversation with M in the best detail he could, and they responded with the usual emotions: fear, shock, disbelief. The disbelief was minimal. The whole story was a lot more acceptable after what they had witnessed.

"I thought fighter was experimental," Ilanka said. "It makes more sense that it is from the future."

"Not from the future," Watson said, his eyes alight at the possibilities. "The past. Billions or even trillions of years in the past. This whole concept is very intriguing, especially since it flies in the face of a lot of accepted science."

"I don't care about the past or the future," Millie said. "I care about right now. Mitchell, I still don't see how Goliath can help us? Talk about outdated technology."

"Nobody even knows what happened to the Goliath," Anderson said. He had been quiet until then, standing in the corner like a silent guard dog. "I'm a little fuzzy on my history, but from what I remember the launch was successful, and they always assumed the FTL drive test was good because the ship vanished off sensors when it should have. It was only supposed to be gone for five minutes. It never came back."

"It never came back?" Mitchell said. He hadn't known that. There was still so much about the starship he hadn't gotten a chance to learn. "That sounds pretty important. Where did it go?"

"Nobody knows," Anderson said. "It disappeared. The military assumed it was either lost in space or destroyed."

"Obviously, it wasn't destroyed," Shank said. "Your twin wouldn't tell you to find something that was already dust."

"Even if the Goliath is out there, even if it could somehow be useful against this enemy, how are we supposed to find it?" Millie asked.

"I don't know," Mitchell replied. "Somehow, I'm supposed to figure it out. The whole thing is insane."

Shank laughed. "At least you're in the right place for that. What's the plan, Captain?"

"Make the rendezvous and see if Command has anything to report. We'll be close enough to Caldera that we can latch onto their databanks and download a few terabytes of archival data. Watson, we need to be sneaky about it. I don't want anyone knowing that we're pulling old data on the Goliath."

"Yes, Captain," Watson said with a mischievous smile. "Consider it done."

"Did you say Caldera?" Mitchell asked.

"Yes. I know what you're thinking. Yes, our meeting point is in the Rim. No, I'm not going to tell Command about any of this, not right away. They don't know you're here, or even alive, and I intend to keep it that way for as long as I can. Somebody ratted us out to the Federation. I don't know if they're on this ship, if there's a spy in Command, or worse, if the enemy has already infiltrated our ranks. Whatever the reason, we don't take risks." Her eyes flowed to the rest of the present crew. "All of this is to stay in this room, do you understand? If one word leaks to anybody else on this ship, I'll have all of you out of the airlock before you can stammer a pathetic apology. We all have our pasts, we've all done things we may or may not be proud of. We're still loyal to each other, and to our origins. At this moment, we're not just black ops. We may be the Alliance's best chance at stopping a war."

"Riigg-aaah," Anderson said.

Millie got to her feet. "Services for the fallen will be held in the mess in one hour. Anderson, with me."

"Yes, Captain."

"Dismissed," Millie said.

[36]

MITCHELL WAS SURPRISED to find a dress uniform waiting for him when he returned from the shower with Ilanka. It was laid out on his bunk, neatly pressed, two new ribbons resting over the heart. He didn't recognize either of them.

"We aren't technically military," Ilanka said. "We don't get actual medals, so Millie made up her own. It helps keep crew motivated."

"What did I win?"

"That one is called 'bad-ass award.' It is for your first kill. The other is a medal from one of the fallen crew, to be worn to the memorial service. That one was Sunny's Medal of Valor."

Mitchell felt the punch in his gut. He picked up the jacket and fingered the medal. "This is an actual medal."

"Yes. Sunny got that one before she was court-martialed. They took it from her, of course, but Millie got it back somehow."

Mitchell's respect for the Admiral grew at that moment. She was emotional, chaotic, unorthodox. But she knew how to bring people together. "I'm honored to wear it."

"You should be."

Mitchell starting dressing himself, surprised when he got a knock on his p-rat.

"Cormac?" he said.

"Captain," Cormac said. "I'm sorry to bother you. I just had to ask... is it true?"

"Is what true?"

"Aliens!" The word came out loud enough in his head that Mitchell put his hands to his ears. He wondered who had started passing the rumor, right after Millie's warning about venting them for having a big mouth.

"Yeah, I guess it is. I'm glad you made it out of Calypso."

"Me, too. You should have seen it, mate. Friggin' Frontier shits just waiting to ambush us. It was the worst firefight I've been in since Babylon."

"You were on Babylon? During the New Terran invasion?"

"Yeah. I was just finishing boot camp. Green as a blade of grass. They dumped a dozen mechs and three hundred exos right on top of us. I was lucky because my squad was out on maneuvers at the time, and we were carrying full ordnance. Even so, we spent three days pinned down, trading shots with the NTs before the counterstrike sent them home."

Mitchell had heard that there was a rogue squad who had used the confusion of the invasion to do some very uncivilized things to a number of the civilians. Cormac was here on the Schism. He couldn't help but wonder if the man had been part of it.

"So, about those aliens," Cormac said. "What do they look like? What color are they? Do they have more than two arms? Do-"

"Cormac," Mitchell said.

"Yes, sir?"

"Are you always like this?"

"Most of the time, sir. And I've always fantasized about aliens. I mean, we've settled what? A hundred planets across millions of light years? And no other intelligent life. We really are alone out here, which is a bloody shame, if you ask me. I always pictured it like the movies. Women with green skin and three tits, six inch tongues-"

"Cormac," Mitchell said again. "I think you watch too much porn."

"Sorry, sir. Anyway, the idea of aliens gets me a little excited. Even if they aren't sex-starved."

"I don't know what they look like. The only one I met was a replica of me. They might all be like that. Or they might be completely different."

"I wouldn't mind a replica of your roomie. Only in my dreams."

"You have a thing for Ilanka?"

"Oh, yeah. I have since I was dropped onto this boat. I try to time my showers so I can be there with her. Not every time of course. I don't want to make it too obvious that I'm only there to get a look." He stopped talking for a couple of seconds. "Oh, bloody hell. You won't tell her I just said that, will you?"

Mitchell glanced over at Ilanka. She was still in her bra and panties, slipping on her blouse. She was in decent shape, and she did have a nice chest. Even so, she wasn't his type. "I think Rain can take care of herself."

"Thank you, sir. I better go finish getting ready. See you there."

A soft tone signaled that he was gone. Mitchell finished pulling on his own shirt and pants, and then the jacket. "How do I look?" he asked.

"Very handsome," Ilanka said. "Like your commercial, but more real."

"You've seen the commercial?"

She tapped her head. "We don't get to download new streams very often. Last time was month ago. I have seen your face every day since then. Now I see it twice as much. Is not a bad thing."

They finished dressing and headed down to C-Deck. The mess hall was a large, open room on the starboard side, one of the few spaces with views to the blackness of space beyond. Normally it was filled with more rows of tables than there were people on board, but all of them had been shoved to the back except for one. It was placed at the front of the room, a black cloth laid over it, and a small screen displaying each of the lost soldier's faces spread across.

Seven. They had lost seven.

It was another punch in the gut.

"It's a strange place to hold a memorial service," Mitchell said as they entered. Half the crew was already present, standing in small groups or alone using their p-rats.

"It is cleanest place in the ship after showers and medical," Ilanka replied.

"Captain Williams?" A hand tapped his shoulder. Mitchell turned around, finding a small, balding man standing there. He didn't recognize him from the hazing or the briefing.

"Yes?" Mitchell said.

"I'm Ensign Philip Hubble. I'm in charge of supply."

That explained why he hadn't seen him before. "Nice to meet you."

"I heard you really saved our rears. I just wanted to thank you. Death isn't high on my list of priorities."

"Mine, either."

Philip smiled. "Yes, well, if there's anything you need, just knock. I have access to a number of suppliers." He winked as he said it, trying to be subtle, and failing.

"I'll do that." Mitchell shook his hand, and the man wandered off to speak to Ensign Sao.

"Be careful what you ask for," Ilanka said. "The only things that are free are provided without asking."

"I figured as much."

Anderson entered the room with Millie.

"Officer on deck," he shouted.

"Riigg-aaah," the crew replied, breaking up and arranging themselves into formation near the center of the room. Ilanka helped Mitchell find his spot near the front and center. He glanced back, guessing that they had put themselves in rank order.

Mille walked to the center of the room. She was organized, composed, and serious. She paused at the table, running her eyes along each of the images there. She made the sign of the cross in front of them, and then turned around.

"Riggers," she said.

"Riigg-aaah," they replied. Mitchell caught on quick enough to join them.

Millie let a small smile escape.

"Sunny, Mouth, Talon, Ahab, Pissface, Lolita, Gremlin. Criminals, yes. Soldiers first. Friends to some. They gave their lives for the Schism. For our mission. For our family."

"Riigg-aaah!"

"I don't need to tell you what their skills have meant to this team. Most of them were good people, too." She let the smile slip then.

"Riigg-aaah!"

"Keeping with tradition, each of you has been given something belonging to one of our fallen comrades." Her eyes fell on Mitchell's chest, to Sunny's medal. "I ask that you keep these things and add them to your footlocker with the rest. Keep them somewhere that you'll see them, that you'll always remember the sacrifices our teammates make for us and for our mission. Gone. Not forgotten."

"Riigg-aaah!"

Mitchell put his hand to the medal, running his fingers along the etched surface. He didn't need to be told of sacrifice. He had seen it first-hand, lost the most important woman in his life. It didn't matter if he had been with the Riggers for two days or twenty years, they were his family now, and he felt the anger over the loss of their teammates. Seven of them. He glanced around the room again. The entire crew was here, close to fifty strong. Fifty. The number was so small to begin with.

"Sunny, Mouth, Talon, Ahab, Pissface, Lolita, Gremlin. Their names will be etched into the bulkhead on the bridge, joining the others who have given their lives for the Alliance. Bow your heads, and offer a prayer to whatever you believe in for the souls of our departed."

They all bowed their heads. Mitchell closed his eyes. The souls were out there, one with the universe. They would reform one day, brought back to their past state, eternally returned to the place and time when they laughed and loved, when they were ambushed and died. Unless their future was changed. The timeline may have locked when M arrived, but what about the next? Or the one after that? Could the so-called eternal engine move infinitely for infinity?

The thought of it kept Mitchell with his head bowed until Ilanka elbowed him in the ribs. He lifted his head, seeing that Millie was watching him curiously.

"Are we going to get even with those Federation bastards, Captain?" Cormac asked from his place near the back.

She looked away from him. "I don't know. We're currently headed towards the rendezvous point near Caldera. We'll make our report and wait for our next orders."

"I hope we do," Cormac said.

"Riigg-aaah," the crew shouted in reply.

Millie smiled. "Does anyone have anything they'd like to say about any of our fallen comrades?" she asked.

"I do," Shank said, stepping forward. Millie motioned for him to join them at the front of the room. The big man looked back at the images, lingering on Gremlin, the only member of his team to lose their life. "You all know me. I've been on this ship for three years. I've seen almost a hundred people come and go, either because of the rigors of this job or because they were bigger assholes than Command had guessed when they shipped them here. It doesn't matter. The point is, after a while you start to get numb to it. You start to expect it."

A tear formed at the corner of his eye, and he wiped it away angrily.

"I wasn't expecting this. Gremlin was one of the best. Shit, he was here longer than me. Frigging lucky pot-shot." He paused, gritting his teeth. "Don't let yourselves get numb. Don't forget, and don't forgive. We're the lucky ones to be here, and we have a duty to the people who came before us, who come after us, anyone who died when we didn't. We get even every time we complete a mission. We get our revenge by working together to send a big frig you to our enemies."

"Riigg-aaah!"

Shank returned to his place in the line, the anger still visible in the tension of his body.

"Anyone else?" Millie asked.

Cormac started forward.

"Not you, Firedog," Shank said.

"But-"

"Remember the last time?"

"Yeah, but I-"

The grunts started laughing first, followed by the rest of the crew. Mitchell hadn't been there the last time, but he could imagine the Private making any number of inappropriate remarks.

"Well then, if nobody else has anything to say, you're all dismissed. We'll be dropping from FTL on full alert. If the Federation knew we were headed to Calypso, they might know about the rendezvous point as well."

The laughing stopped. They shifted back to full attention, ready to receive new orders.

"Thank you all," Millie said. "Riggers!"

"Riigg-aaah! Riigg-aaah!Riigg-aaah!"

Millie left the room without another word, Anderson trailing behind.

"What were you thinking?" Ilanka asked. "During moment of silence?"

"This may just be starting," Mitchell said. He paused, feeling sick to his stomach. "This may never end."

37

MITCHELL FOUND himself back in the cockpit of the S-17 when the Schism dropped out of hyperspace. Ilanka was to his left, suited up and ready in the Piranha, able to see him quite clearly from their position on the hangar floor. There hadn't been time to re-mount the fighters to the launchers, and so leaving the ship would mean opening the doors and letting the evacuating air carry them out into space.

It was a tense moment, watching the clock hit the drop point and feeling the slight shift of the change. Then the ship fell dead, the hyperspace engines being replaced with thrusters, a speck of dust drifting in an ocean of nothing.

Not quite nothing.

"Shields at full," Millie said, her voice loud in his inner-ear. She had patched him directly into her own comm channel, giving him full access to everything that was happening on the bridge. She wanted him to hear what Command had to say, even if they weren't allowed to know he was on board.

"Shields up," Briggs said. "Forward compartment on G is breached."

"Damn it. It's a mess out here."

She gave him a display then, a view from beyond the cracked carbonate on the bridge. The entire area was littered with debris - bits and pieces of metal, textile, and flesh.

There were bodies out there. Dead bodies, of people dressed as though they had no idea they were about to be exposed to naked space. Some were well-dressed. Some were in uniform. Others had been caught with their pants down. There were a lot of them. Too many. Hundreds. They would float into the web of energy provided by the shields and be reduced to ash.

"What the hell..." Mitchell closed his eyes. It was hard to look at.

"I'm not picking up any readings from the area, Captain," Briggs said. "There's nothing larger than a person out here. No ships, no satellites."

"No ships?" Millie said. "Not one?"

"No, ma'am."

"What about the planet?"

"I'm receiving a communication, Captain."

"Put it on."

"Please," came the voice, deep and haunting and frantic. "If you can hear us. We've lost contact with the Sabertooth. We've lost contact with everyone. What's going on up there?"

There was silence while Mitchell waited for Millie to respond.

"Who is this?" Millie asked.

"Stanis Lem, President of the Dark Side Trading Company. Please, can you tell me what's happening out there?"

"This is Captain Alison Caine of the salvage vessel Pyrite," she replied. "Stanis, I don't know how to tell you this. There's nothing alive up here."

The pause was painful. Mitchell glanced over at Ilanka. He could just make out the tears in her eyes beyond her clear helmet.

"What? I... There were ships. Four ships. They appeared from the shadow of Gusav-3 two days ago. Our sensors picked up huge energy spikes, and then all of our near-surface electronics went out. Even the ones that are EMP shielded. We were lucky our generators survived, or we would all be dead. We just got communications back online a few hours ago and we've been calling out. No one has answered. Not for me, not for anyone. Not until you."

The dark form of Caldera swung into Mitchell's view on the port side. It was an E-type planet, but only barely. It was dry and rocky, ninety percent mountains and crags, with only a small deposit of water and a small belt where rain would ever fall. It was there that the planet's only city rested, hidden among the dark spires of stone and ore, a bastion of safety for the lawless activity it sheltered. It was a planet known to the Federation, the Alliance, and the New Terrans. Most of the planets of the Rim were. It was allowed to exist because it served as a jump point for the starships who reached out into the galaxy beyond the Rim, searching for new worlds, new resources, anything that could make them rich. It was allowed to exist because it was a known quantity and, in the case of the Schism, it was needed to keep their true mission secret while providing supply.

"I don't know what to tell you, Stanis," Millie said. "We were coming to Caldera to trade. It seems you have nothing for us. We can pass a message along for you, for a price."

"Those are my people that are dead," Stanis screamed back through the comm. "A settlement ship with two thousand souls on board was about to go beyond the Rim when these ships appeared."

"Do you want me to weep for those I never knew?" Millie responded. Mitchell wondered how much of it was an act. "Your misfortune isn't my concern. Feeding my crew is."

"You cold bitch," Stanis said. "If my systems were online, I'd have already fired on you." There was silence, as Millie decided not to respond. "Damn you, Captain Caine. What's your price?"

"Fifty-thousand. I'm transmitting the account id now."

"Fifty? Maybe you aren't completely frozen. Information received. I'm making the transfer."

It was a lot of credit, but not nearly as much as she could have wrung from the desperate man. Then again, Mitchell had no idea if she intended to deliver his message or not.

"What's your message?"

"It's private."

"No, it isn't. I don't need you telling your parent corp to hire mercenaries to hunt me down. I didn't start working the Rim yesterday."

Stanis laughed across the channel. "Sending the transmission codes. The message is simple. Attacked, disabled. Send immediate assistance."

"That's all?"

"Yes."

"Very well. I'll be leaving the area in the next few hours. I'm going to scout the debris for anything of value first."

"What?" The anger returned to Stanis' voice.

"Your misfortune is my gain in more than one dimension," Millie said. There was a soft tone as she closed the communication with the planet. "Ensign Briggs, is there any sign of the drone out there?"

"No, Captain. I don't think it's arrived yet."

"It should be-"

Mitchell's helmet picked up a new ship. It was the only other one out there. It had a different color to it, purple instead of the typical red and green.

"And there it is," Millie finished.

"Receiving data," Ensign Sao said.

"Transmit across the secure channel."

A new tone alerted Mitchell to another communication signal opening up for him. The video of the stream filled into the front of his eye, slightly transparent so he could see the theater grid in front, and the hangar behind.

"Admiral Narayan," General Cornelius said. He was sitting in a large chair, one that looked as though it was located on a massive Navy battleship. "I trust you'll have good news to report. I've prepared your next mission briefing, which should be uploading to your databanks as I speak. I understand this last mission was difficult, and I expect this next to be more so. The truth is that the Council of

Prime Ministers is beginning to question the value of a number of different special operations teams, and your designation is opening the door to a lot of difficult questions that I'm beginning to struggle to adequately respond to. The only way I can keep this project alive is to prove that your team is the absolute best and most efficient way of striking our enemies in secret. Even so, I expect that you'll need fresh meat aboard, and to that end, I've arranged for a ship to meet you with a stock of new recruits. Coordinates for the drop are also being provided. Cornelius out."

The screen went dark. Mitchell sat and watched the emptiness of the grid for a few seconds. The video feed returned.

Cornelius' face was close to the recorder, and he whispered into it. "Millie, I'm sorry to do this to you. I am. You know what the other option is, and I can't bear the thought of it. I'm doing all I can to keep this program running. I know you'll survive. You always-"

The stream dropped again, the connection closed. What was that about?

A new connection opened.

"Send the transmission we prepared, and add this message," Millie said. "Enemy has reached zone seven of the Outer Rim. Caldera left disabled, all ships in orbit destroyed. Assume enemy is moving into Alliance occupied space. Destination unknown. Four ships reported."

"Is that all, Captain?" Sao asked.

"That's all."

"Yes, ma'am."

The channel closed. Millie knocked on his p-rat directly.

"Mitchell. Please come and see me in my quarters immediately."

38

MITCHELL WAS in Millie's quarters fifteen minutes later, sitting across from her in a small office adjacent to the living area. They were separated by a simple desk whose top was currently displaying a grid of the surrounding space, similar to what he had been receiving from his helmet.

She had waved him in when he arrived at the doorway, her eyes twitching beneath the data she was reviewing, no doubt the orders they had received from Cornelius. He had taken his seat and remained silent until at last her eyes stopped moving, refocusing on him.

"Admiral-"

"Millie," she said. "We're alone, Mitch."

"Millie. What do you need?"

"I wanted to explain."

"You don't have to explain anything-"

She cut him off again. "Yes, I do. The message from General Cornelius-"

Mitchell put up his hand. "Permission to be frank, Millie?"

"Of course."

"Why me?" he asked.

"What do you mean?"

"Why are you opening secured channels for me? Why did you even let me hear that message? You didn't have to. I wouldn't have questioned it."

She leaned forward in her chair, putting her arms on the desk. The Schism was a blue spot between her elbows.

"I need you, Mitch. I've needed you for a long time."

Mitchell had always wanted a woman to say that to him. He'd pictured it a little differently. "Okay."

"You know the makeup of this crew. You don't belong here, Mitch. You're a straight shooter, a here-in-the-flesh white knight. If not the Battle for Liberty, than of over a hundred other missions and interdictions. I told the General that we picked you up. He was confused as hell about the body they found and how you wound up halfway across the galaxy, but he knew who you were. He told me to keep an eye on you, and if your story turned out to be straight..." She paused, the chill running between them both. "He's smart enough to keep his mouth shut on this one. When he finds out what happened at Calypso, and here-"

"He'll what?" Mitchell asked. "Send the troops out to meet them? Alliance battleships have nothing on that weapon."

"Nukes."

"Can slow them down. Maybe. You can't count on closing the distance and getting a few shots off, or some fighter squadrons up into their rear. You've seen what the S-17 is capable of, and that's a modification of an Alliance design."

"I hear you, Mitch," Millie said. "I agree with you. Which only proves my point. The people we have, they're the best of the best of the broken. You're just the best of the best, and the only person I've had on this boat in five years that I can trust."

"I'm not a hero," Mitchell said. "I survived because I was surrounded by the elite. I survived because of Ella." He paused.

Talking about her always lowered his shield integrity. "What about Anderson? He seems loyal."

"He is loyal," Millie replied. "Almost too loyal. Do you know how many times I've had to forcefully throw him from this room, or the bridge? He sticks to me like a lovesick puppy. It has its uses, but it isn't all wine and roses. I told you earlier, you're the second highest ranking officer on this ship. I need you to be my XO. I need you to know what I know, hear what I hear, because you can. You're stuck like the rest of us, but you aren't damaged like the rest of us."

"I am damaged," Mitchell said. "Maybe not in the same way, but this life, this career; it takes as much as it gives. Probably more." Ella's face flashed through his mind, followed surprisingly by Major Arapo. Why her? "Besides, I'm a pilot."

"Who had tremendous aptitude scores, and could have been telling my father..." She paused, then pursed her lips. "General Cornelius what to do."

Mitchell stared at her. He knew from the message there was something between the two, and it was clear that Millie had wanted him to see it. She was showing him that she was going to trust him, whether he wanted her to or not.

"Is that what Project Black is about?" Mitchell asked. "Your father getting you out of harms way?"

The anger launched to her face in an instant. She somehow held it back. "Honestly? Only in part. The budgetary misappropriation was already underway before I came into the picture. It was just my luck to end up here."

"What happened?" Mitchell said. "A General's daughter? Murder? I know I'm not supposed to ask, but if you're going to trust me, I need to know I can trust you."

Millie shrunk back into the chair. In an instant, she turned from an angry, confident leader to a frightened young girl.

"It's hard to talk about," she said. "I can still see it all so clearly in my mind." She snapped out of whatever past had gripped her, shifting in the seat and regaining her composure. "I met a man during

OTS. The man of my dreams. He was a star in the program, a tactical genius. We dated for a while, and I thought that I had met my future husband." Her smile was part snarl. "He did something to me one night, slipped me something. Then he wanted me to do... things... Not just for him, but for his buddies, too. After a few rounds of no, they decided they weren't going to give me a choice."

Mitchell felt his own jaw tense. "Millie, you don't need to tell me the rest, I-"

"No," she said. "You got me started, so now you're going to hear it through." A tear welled up in the corner of her eye. "I don't know how long it lasted. I don't really remember it. All I remember is the pain, and the violation. The drunk laughter. They gave me something that knocked me out, and I woke up alone in my bed, wearing my pjs like my world hadn't been torn apart. They were all top cadets, Riley was the top scorer in the entire program. I was going to go to the MPs to report it, but I couldn't."

"Why not?"

"They did something to my p-rat. They replaced the biometrics somehow. They were planning the whole thing. They were ready for me to say no. I don't even know if Riley ever really wanted me, or they were just looking for a target. It doesn't matter. Without evidence from the ARR, it didn't matter what my body said. I decided I wasn't going to let it break me. I decided to stay quiet."

She breathed out, a long sigh. The tear dropped from her eye onto her lap.

"I thought I was doing the right thing. I put all of my energy into my training. I excelled in the program, rose to the top of the rankings. I got my revenge by finishing at the head of the class." She laughed and shook her head. "It wasn't enough. The whole time I was just getting angrier and angrier. I wanted to let it go, to move on, but I couldn't. Not while those bastards were still breathing, still able to violate someone else. I didn't break the day they raped me. I only cracked, then. I broke two years after.

"The night before graduation, I tricked the clerk into thinking I had checked in my M-72 at the range. Instead, I carried it back to the barracks with me. Then I hunted them. Quick, dirty, silent. Each and every one. I saved Riley for last. I don't know what was driving me. It wasn't human, it wasn't logical. It felt... amazing. Freeing. Frightening. I found him in one of the simulators, doing a civilian. I opened the door, ready to shoot. Seeing him with a guy's head between his legs let that last inch of sanity sneak in just a little. I hesitated.

"He kicked him into me, knocked me down. The rifle discharged, and I must have hit the civilian because he was limp when he fell onto me. Riley jumped out of the simulator and knocked the rifle away. He had a boot knife. I got the guy off me and we fought. I'd been working hard, I was a better martial artist. I beat him in the end, but not before he did this." She raised the bionic hand. "He took my hand. I took everything. Then it was over. The MPs caught up to me and I was arrested. I might have been dead that night if I was anybody else's daughter."

"They got what they deserved," Mitchell said. He realized the story had caused him to clench the arms of his chair, and he forced himself to relax his hands.

"Yeah. Unfortunately, civilized society doesn't care much for vigilante justice." She laughed again. "Cornelius came to me in holding. He asked me why I did it. He believed me when I told him. He said he would find proof. I told him it didn't matter, and it didn't. Two wrongs don't make right. I don't regret what I did, except for the civilian. I'm still sorry he got caught in the crossfire. Anyway, he convinced the rest of Command that I was too valuable to waste. Project Black needed a leader, and my scores were top notch. Because of the circumstances of my actions, and his intervention, they decided to rank me as Admiral and assign me to the Schism. Now they're talking about shutting us down."

"How can they do that? What's to keep you from hiding out here in the Rim?"

"The Schism has a kill switch, just like you do. Command loads the order to a drone, the drone meets us at a rendezvous, and the Schism self-destructs. Game over."

"Why not disable it?"

"You don't think we've tried? The trigger is a grain of sand in an ocean of alloy. We can't even find it."

"Don't make rendezvous."

"You don't think a rogue ship of highly-trained criminals would attract a lot of attention or a nice bounty for our destruction? We need supplies. We can't hide in empty space forever."

"So you just wait for the CPM to decide that they don't want you anymore, and then we all die? That doesn't sound like much of a plan."

"No, but it's all we've got. I've been on borrowed time since I fired the first shot. I'm fortunate to have had the chance to serve the Alliance."

Mitchell was certain he didn't agree with that perspective.

"What are the new orders?" he asked.

"The General was right about the difficulty, but these were sent before we encountered these travelers of yours. As soon as Command learns about the destruction, I have a feeling the mission parameters are going to change in a hurry. We have four days to get to the midpoint between the Polaris system and our current location. We'll be meeting an unmarked transport there to pick up some new crew members. I can only hope we have new orders waiting."

"What about Goliath?" Mitchell asked.

"There's a reason we aren't leaving for the meeting point right away. Luckily, Caldera's massive databanks are buried down deep with their generators. Singh has been working on getting access since we arrived here. She has four hours to get the data on the Goliath into our onboard storage, which is going to be a trick in itself. She needs to grab much, much more than we need in order to dilute the focus, but either way our friend Stanis is going to be wondering what we wanted the archive data for once he has his systems all up and running again."

Mitchell watched her face. "You think he may be one of them?" he said.

"It would make sense. If you could replicate people, or even take control of them through their implant, why not destroy everything and leave a spy behind? We have to assume that he's the enemy because we can't be sure that he isn't."

"If that's the case, it sounds like the race is on."

"The race was already on, Mitch." She got to her feet and circled the desk to stand in front of him. "You know my story, and I know yours. I'm offering you a promotion if you want it."

"The crew won't mutiny over it?"

"Between what you did to Anderson and your actions at Calypso? I think they would mutiny for you if you wanted my job."

Mitchell shook his head. "Not a chance. I'm happy being a pilot."

"So you're turning me down again?"

"I didn't say that. Whatever we're facing, whoever these travelers are, I know I'm important somehow, and that makes you and the Schism important too. They tore through Calypso, and through this zone like they know exactly what they want and where to go to get it. This is bigger than you and me. If you need a second head to help you work this mess out, I guess mine will have to suit."

"So you'll do it?"

"Yes."

She smiled. "Thank you."

"Don't be too quick to thank me. You might have just sealed our fate."

She laughed, a mischievous look in her eye. "In that case, who knows how much longer we'll be alive? My bedroom is right over there."

Mitchell felt the stirring below his belt. "After what you just told me, you want to-"

She leaned down, putting a finger on his lips. "I made the decision not to let them steal my life from me. That included my enjoyment of more basic pleasures. I trust you, Mitch."

Mitchell was still for a moment. Then he reached up and took her wrist, pulling her gently to him. She fell into his lap, their eyes meeting first, their lips meeting after. Passion, fear, excitement, anxiety. It flowed between them, fueling the desire and lust. He picked her up, still kissing her, and carried her across the living area to the bedroom beyond. He had tried to swear off women, and maybe he would have been successful anywhere else. Millie was emotional, intelligent, unpredictable. She was hot and cold, fire and ice, steel and silk.

She was just like Ella.

39

THE KNOCK from Singh came two hours later. Mitchell was still in Millie's bed, the Admiral's head resting on his bare chest. They were both awake but silent, giving some time to relax in the afterglow of their passion.

She picked her head up and held it there a moment. Then she looked up at him. "The download is almost done. It's time to get moving. You can use my private shower."

She rolled away from him, out of the bed. He watched her for a moment and then followed behind. Her bathroom contained a more modern and standard cleaning system, and she stepped into it, let it remove the dirt and oil and sex from her, and stepped back out. He took his turn, and then returned to the bedroom to retrieve his clothes.

"We need to do that again sometime," Millie said, pulling on her gray shirt.

"You know where to find me," Mitchell replied. He had been with more women than he could remember since the Shot. She wasn't the most skilled lover, but she had more feeling behind her efforts than any of the others. It wasn't just lust. It seemed as though every emotion she possessed poured out in her lovemaking, and it served to heighten the experience in ways he hadn't felt since Ella was killed.

"Your p-rat memory won't hold all of the archives, and we don't have the servers configured with the new encryption yet. You'll have to go down to engineering and let Singh plug you in."

"Plug me in?"

"Through the neural link."

"They can do that?"

"Singh can. She and Watson developed it in the early days to help manage our dark protocols."

Mitchell had been buttoning his own shirt. He stopped and turned towards her.

"Why are you surprised, Captain?" Millie asked. "We're dead to the Alliance. Sometimes we need supplies we can't get from their offline channels. Things we need, or just things to keep the crew happy. We have to find ways of our own. It doesn't matter if we're outside the law because we're already tried and convicted. So, every once in a while we get a short break between sanctioned operations. We have connections, and we use them to pull gray market work. Any encryption can be broken given enough time, so we don't risk putting that data over the air. It's a bit of a throwback, but it works."

It was a little bit of trivia he wouldn't have guessed. It also didn't matter. There wouldn't be time to run mercenary jobs anytime soon.

"I'm heading to the bridge to get us moving towards the next rendezvous point." She walked over to him and kissed his cheek. "I'll be in touch about more private matters. You can see yourself out."

She was smiling as she picked up her hat and fixed it to her head. She breathed in, and in an instant had returned to the stone-faced Captain that he had met a few weeks earlier.

Mitchell left Millie's quarters and headed straight to engineering. When he entered, he was surprised to find Watson kneeling in front of Singh. She was leaned back in a chair, her feet up and bared from their standard issue shoes, the portly engineer rubbing them with large fingers.

"Did I come at a bad time?" Mitchell asked.

He hadn't met Singh yet, not formally anyway, though he had seen her at the hazing, and the memorial. She was a slight, petite woman, with dark skin and long black hair, large eyes and an even larger nose that didn't suit her face.

"Corporal Watson lost a bet," Singh said, explaining the activity. "He didn't think I could pull the data in less than three hours."

"Millie expected it to take four," Mitchell said.

Watson stopped rubbing and pushed himself to a stand. "Captain Williams," he said, turning and giving him a slight bow.

"Of course she did." Singh leaned down to retrieve her shoes, put them on, and stood. "She didn't knock you to send you down here."

Mitchell hesitated for a second. "I thought the channel was encrypted?"

"The messages are," Watson said. "The point of origin is easy to trace if you know how."

"Does Millie know about this?"

Watson shrugged.

"You got here pretty quickly," Singh said. "And she answered my knock from her bedroom." Her eyebrow went up.

"What about it?"

"Nothing," Watson said with a smile. "It's our little secret. Just don't tell anyone about the tracking."

"Why did you tell me about the tracking?"

Singh shrugged.

Watson shrugged.

Mitchell decided to drop it. They were playing some kind of game with him. No, not with him. With each other. They were using him as the equipment.

"Millie said you needed to plug me in," he said.

"To our servers," Singh said. "Follow me. Watson, hold down the fort. And don't forget to check the oscillations again."

"I already checked the oscillations."

"No, you didn't."

"Yes, I did."

"You didn't put it in the log."

"Do you want to check the log?"

"Later." Singh sighed as she ushered Mitchell out the door and across the hallway.

"You two have an interesting dynamic," Mitchell said on the way.

Singh led him into a cold room, dimly lit by a few overhead diodes that created a walkway towards the back of the space. "He's a stubborn ass," she replied.

They stopped in front of a small workstation, a holographic overlay sliding up in front of them. Singh moved her hands along and through it, selecting menus and entering her password. Then she reached to her left and pulled a small stool from the darkness.

"Sit with your face towards me," she said.

Mitchell did as she asked. She circled behind him and he heard a click. Then he felt the pressure of the needle being pushed into his skull.

"You know what to do from here," she said. "Knock me when you're finished."

"You aren't staying?" Mitchell asked.

"To do what? Watch your eyes flicker? I've got a foot massage to get back to."

There was no humor in her voice. Even her accusation about his prior activity had been flat and serious. She thought Watson was a stubborn ass. He wondered what Watson thought of her?

She left him alone in the cold, dark room. He closed his eyes, the data archive immediately spreading out all around him, as though he were standing in an endless room of labeled folders. It was more than just the historical data, it was everything that was stored on the Schism's banks - terabyte after terabyte of intel. Secret contracts for dark operations, personnel files, Captain's log entries... everything. Millie had given him the keys to the kingdom. Out of trust or necessity? Did she have sex with him to try to buy his loyalty?

He eyed the personnel files. He could learn anything he wanted to know about any one of the crew, past or present. He could find out if Millie told him the truth of her past. He could discover why Ilanka had been sent to the Schism. Or Anderson. It was tempting, but who was to say that he could look without leaving a trace? In any case, they didn't have time to waste on curiosity.

He navigated completely in his head, leaving his eyes closed and his hands in his lap. The folders swirled around him, flying past until he reached the one marked "Historic." He slipped into it, getting a new list. He spoke a single word in his mind, "Goliath." He was greeted with a structure of documents similar to the one he had viewed only briefly back on Liberty.

He made his way back to where he had been the first time, to the images of the Goliath's shell. He marveled at it anew, in awe of the sheer brute force of the construction, the technology behind the materials, the repulsors, everything, so rudimentary at the time. He flipped through everything, watching the years pass as the ship slowly and steadily became something more than a skeleton.

He didn't know how long he was sitting there. It was long enough that his feet grew numb from the cold, and his head began to hurt from the sheer volume of data that was passing between the implant and the databanks. He watched every video, flipped through every photo. He even went back to the time before the Goliath was commissioned, to the time when the world was at war over the wreck of an alien spacecraft that brought them such incredibly advanced technology. He watched videos of the battles, the clashes between the United States and its Alliance of Nations and the attacking armies of China, India, and Iran.

He was particularly interested in the air combat. It was a lot different than modern combat, mainly due to the prevalence of high-explosive warheads and comparatively weak defensive materials. That imbalance had been equalized over the centuries and caused a return of more personal, close-range strategies. It was amazing to him to watch fighters duke it out over dozens of kilometers, shooting one another from the sky without ever drawing near.

There was a lot to learn there. A lot to study and understand. A history that was more exciting than he had ever imagined.

It was all useless.

There was nothing in there that would give him any clue about the Goliath's position in space, or any idea where they should go to search for it. He watched the video of its launch day. The commemoration by the U.S. President, the firing of the repulsor sled that lifted it out of the atmosphere and into zero-gravity, the countdown to the firing of the FTL engine for the first time.

He watched it vanish in the clear blue sky of the morning. He felt the tension and excitement of the people on the ground as they waited for it to return. Minutes passed. He held his breath along with them. He shook his head and ground his teeth when the five minutes expired, then ten, then twenty.

The Goliath was gone.

Where? Where did it go? He felt angry and frustrated. He had to know. It was the only thing that mattered right now. The idea of the Alliance falling to this threat, these travelers who decimated Calypso as though it was nothing more than a speck of dust. These travelers who would make their way to the inner sphere of the settled galaxy, who would find their way to Liberty, and to Christine.

Mitchell paused, his emotions falling away, his body feeling the full, sudden brunt of the cold. Why had he thought of her? Why was he worried about her? It didn't make any sense. He barely knew Major Arapo, and their relationship had been nothing more than cordial. Until she helped him escape. Why had she done that? What was her motivation?

He could see her in his mind. What was their connection? Why couldn't he keep her out of his head? M had said that people could subconsciously uncover their past lives, to recognize what went before even if they didn't always understand. He had hoped that learning about the Goliath, seeing it, would help jog whatever latent memories had brought it to his attention in the first place, and give him some indication of where it might be hiding. He had gotten nothing from it except a history lesson, and now he was wasting energy on someone he hardly knew instead. Was she a part of his ancient past?

He pushed her from his head, reaching up and back towards the neural link, ready to pull it out. He needed to rest and refocus his energy on the task at hand, rather than his strange infatuation.

His hand closed around the small connector. He was about to remove it when he paused. Not because he changed his mind, but because the databank had returned an image from a query he hadn't realized he'd made. A single image, an old photograph, still sharp after all these years. It was a group of men and women, twenty in all, wearing dark blue flight suits and holding helmets at their hips. They were smiling at the cameraman, and beneath the photo was a caption.

"The crew of the Goliath, T-minus one hour."

Mitchell didn't notice all of the faces. His eyes went right to a single one, crouched in the front row with a big smile that he thought looked slightly strained. He leaned forward on the stool, even though he didn't need to, zooming in on the face and bringing it up close.

He felt his heart thump in his chest. He felt his mouth go dry. There was no mistaking the dark hair, the small nose, the bright eyes.

He had been thinking of Christine and now she was there, in an ancient photo retrieved as a match on the image of her that he had conjured in his mind.

A crew member on a ship that had been missing for four hundred years.

40

MITCHELL LEFT THE ROOM, closing the door behind him and completely forgetting to knock Singh and tell her he was finished. His heart was still pounding, and his blood was running cold through him, bringing dimples to his skin and leaving him chilled.

It was her, he was sure of it. More sure than he even should have been. He could feel it, a diode in his soul, shining in on the truth. Christine was there the day the Goliath launched. She was a member of the crew. If not her, someone who looked just like her. Identical.

He made his way straight for the bridge. Millie didn't completely trust the wireless communications, even encrypted, and after what Singh and Watson had said, he didn't either. It was better to go to her in person. Especially since the whole idea of it was beyond reason.

Ilanka was in the lift when the doors opened. She was dressed in her grays, her hair and clothes sweaty.

"Comrade," she said. "Are you well?"

He barely heard her, reaching out and directing the elevator to the bridge without using the p-rat.

"Mitchell?"

He glanced over at her and nodded. "I'm okay," he said. He wasn't ready to tell her anything. "Where were you?"

She smiled. "You haven't seen gym yet? It's not the most modern, but it is a good workout."

"You'll have to show me sometime."

"I can show you now?"

"No, thanks. I have to go and speak to the Captain."

"Why not just knock?" She tapped her head and then looked at him sideways. "Making better friends with our fearless leader?"

"She offered me a position as her XO."

"Really? That is good for you, Mitchell. Good for us, too, I think."

"Is she that bad?"

"No, not bad. She does what she must. Maybe a little heavy-handed sometimes, but fair. There has been some fear that if anything happened to her, Anderson would take control of ship. Even if there is resistance."

"Mutiny?"

"Nothing so glamorous. He does have Shank on his side, and inside these walls, the grunts with the exos have the power. Outside? You and me control the outside." She laughed at that. "He won't dare, not after what you did to him. He is bully, but he has respect."

He remembered the personnel files. Now he wished he had at least glanced at Anderson's. What had the Lieutenant done that had landed him here?

The lift stopped, the hatch sliding open.

"My stop," Ilanka said. "See you later, Commander." She hopped out of the lift and waved as the hatch closed.

Mitchell's thoughts returned immediately to the photograph. He had saved it to his p-rat, and he pulled it up again. This time, he examined a few of the other faces in the crowd, half-expecting to find his own. The crew had been made up of people from each country in the new Alliance of Nations, and so each one was as diverse as the last. He wasn't sure where Christine was from. She could have passed as Italian, Middle-eastern, Columbian... It helped her fade into the image as strongly as she had jumped out at him.

The lift reached the bridge. The hatch slid aside. The first thing Mitchell saw was Anderson, standing stiff and straight next to the Captain's chair, arms behind his back. He couldn't see the Lieutenant's face, but his neck was red, the veins throbbing. Was he angry?

He saw Millie's hand resting on the bent arm of the chair, absently tracing the indents and curves she had made with the bionic. He glanced past them, noticing that the bridge was otherwise unoccupied. Where had Briggs gone off to? The pitch black of hyperspace filled the cracked carbonate view.

Anderson's head turned. He saw Mitchell entering, and his already tense face grew even more tense.

"Captain Williams," he said with a slight bow.

"Lieutenant Anderson." Mitchell returned the bow. Then he approached Millie from the other side. "Captain, we need to talk."

Millie looked at him, and then at Anderson. "Dismissed, Lieutenant."

"Captain, I-"

"I said dismissed," she snapped, starting to get to her feet.

"Yes, ma'am," Anderson said quietly. His eyes darted to Mitchell, and then he retreated to the lift.

"Do you have news, Captain?" she asked.

Mitchell waited until the lift arrived and Anderson boarded. "I do. Are you familiar with the events on Liberty before I wound up on the Schism?"

"The Prime Minister's wife?"

"Before that."

"Refresh my memory."

"A few days before the Gala, I was attacked by assassins from the Frontier Federation. They killed my public relations rep and shot me a few times before I killed them."

"Yes, I remember reading about that. Go on."

"After I got out of medical, my rep was replaced. The woman who replaced him was military, but I was certain she wasn't public relations. She was dodgy about it, but she didn't deny it. Her name was Major Christine Arapo."

He accessed his p-rat then, knocking only to send her the picture.

"What is this?" she asked.

"An old photo, taken the day the Goliath was launched into space. See the woman kneeling in the front? Third from the left?"

"Yes. She's pretty."

"That's Christine Arapo."

Millie's head snapped up, her expression finding a path between fear and anger. "What?"

"That's what I thought. Millie, I don't know what the hell is going on, but this Major Arapo turned up at my side right after M said he stopped the Federation, and these new enemies, from assassinating me. She wasn't that friendly, but she stuck to me like glue, and after the incident with the Prime Minister's wife she got me out of a jam before M picked me up."

"You're saying she's one of them?"

"I don't know. I don't know who or what she is. I asked M about her, and he said he didn't know her. She wasn't afraid to introduce herself to Cornelius, and she was doing her job better than my last rep did. I think it's safe to assume if you pull her records, you'll find she's the real deal."

Her eye twitched. "You're certain this is her?"

"It's crazy, I know. I'm sure. There's something about her. I don't know what it is yet. I just know that it is. She's the key to something. It could be the Goliath."

He thought that finding a clue, any clue, might have made her happy. Instead, she stared out into the blackness in silence.

"Millie?"

"Shut up, Mitch. I'm thinking."

Mitchell forced himself to stay slow and steady. He waited for her for a couple of minutes. "Every minute is another minute we're wasting."

Millie got to her feet, turning on him. "What the hell do you want me to do, Mitchell?" she shouted. "Make a beeline straight for Liberty? Drop by and kidnap this Major because she looks like an ancient astronaut?"

Mitchell took a few steps back, surprised at the outburst. "Millie, I-"

"Stow it, Captain. We have orders. Orders to meet a transport in four days. If our orders stay the same, we're to be in Polaris three days later before making a two-week trip into New Terran space. Liberty is ten days at top speed, and not in the same direction."

Mitchell slumped. He understood why she was upset.

"We can't chase this lead without breaking our orders," she said, quieting her voice. "If we break our orders, we die."

"Let me go," Mitchell said. "I can take the S-17."

"You won't have enough air."

"I will. The air shortage was rigged. M set it up so that-" He stopped talking. He hadn't told Millie any of his hypothesis.

"So that what?" she asked, her anger returning.

"So that you would find me," he said. "In his origin timeline, the Schism went to that rock, gathered the ore, and moved on to the mission without ever knowing a thing about me. I think they knew what the Schism was, what it is here in this timeline. I think he delivered me to you on purpose. I mean, what are the odds that a ship is going to turn up in the exact place in space where I am?"

"Stranger things have happened."

"Stranger things are happening. He knew where the Schism would be then. Which means they also knew where the Schism was going."

"You think the travelers set us up at Calypso?"

"I think it's possible. They may have dropped in to blow us out of the galaxy, and ensure that there wouldn't be anyone to stop them."

"Stop them from what?"

"I don't know what they want, other than to destroy mankind. All I know is that I'm supposed to be the one who can beat them." He took a few steps towards her, getting close. "I don't think I'm supposed to do it alone. This timeline is different, it was as soon as M arrived here. I know we have orders, but we have a more important destiny."

"I don't believe in destiny."

"Neither do I. Nobody says we're going to succeed or survive." He put his hand on her arm. "Let me take the S-17, and go to Liberty. I'll find Christine, I'll find out what the hell is going on, and then we'll meet somewhere after the mission."

Millie looked up at him, thinking.

"No," she said at last.

"Millie-"

She put her finger to his lips. "No. I don't know what happened in this origin timeline. I don't know if we succeeded in our mission to kill Chancellor Ken. If we did, then we would have been sent on this second mission into the New Terran space. What if the travelers know about it? What if they planted someone on the ship that we're going to meet? An assassin? Or even a bomb or something? I get it now, Mitchell. We're screwed, whichever way we turn. We might as well try to save humanity and go down in a blaze of glory." She put her bionic hand to his face. He could feel the humming of it against his skin. "If you're wrong, we're all dead."

"We might be all dead anyway."

"That's why I'm trusting you." Her eyes twitched momentarily. "Ensign Briggs is coming up. We'll plot the course and head for Liberty. If we're lucky, we'll have enough time to scan the surface, find your Major, and get back into hyperspace before the drones can send word that we missed the rendezvous."

"What if we aren't lucky?"

"Our blaze of glory is going to be a silent whimper. We'll be detonated the second we come out of FTL."

[41]

TWENTY MINUTES later Mitchell and Millie were back in the conference room, with Ilanka, Shank, Watson, Singh, and Anderson arranged around the table with them.

"You may have noticed we dropped out of FTL ten minutes ago," Millie said. "We're changing our course away from the rendezvous point."

"What?" Shank said. "Away? Millie-"

She shot him an angry glare.

"Captain," he corrected. "If we miss the rendezvous, we're going to be breaking parole. If we break parole-"

"We all die," Watson said.

"That's why I brought you up here. We have a lead on Goliath."

Ilanka put her hand on Mitchell's shoulder. "Really? That's excellent news."

"There's more," Millie said. "We don't have the location or even a vicinity, and the lead is tenuous at best."

"I don't want to die over tenuous," Shank said.

"I don't want to die at all," Millie replied. "That being said, you know the score. You saw what happened at Calypso and Caldera. We have a choice to chase the lead and hope it bears fruit or chase the next mission and hope there's an Alliance left to return to if we survive it. Oh, and I should mention, I've seen the mission specs. That 'if' is a pretty big one."

"What's the mission?" Anderson asked.

"The New Terran's mining complex on Nova-12."

"What about it?"

"We're supposed to destroy it."

The room was silent, save for Anderson's laughter. "With a Knight, a Piranha, and this tub?"

"Exactly."

"Captain, that's straight out suicide," Shank said.

"Not necessarily. Not with Ares' S-17," Ilanka said.

"It's still only one more fighter."

"One more fighter that destroyed two Federation patrollers on its own," she replied.

"Enough," Millie said. "I brought you here because you're my senior crew. I don't need to ask you anything, but considering I'm signing our death warrants I thought I would put it up for discussion." Her eyes crossed each of them in turn. "Now, Mitchell has identified a person of interest on Liberty who may or not be one of the travelers, and who may have information about Goliath. In order to reach Liberty and question this person, we need to break mission protocol and go even more rogue than we already are. You all know the penalty for doing it, and how that punishment can be meted out."

"A person of interest?" Anderson said. "Someone who may have come across the Goliath, wherever it is out there?"

"Better than that," Mitchell said. "Someone who was on the Goliath the day it disappeared."

"How is that possible?" Shank asked.

"We don't know, and we don't have enough information to guess," Millie said. "We'll get to that. First, I want each of you to decide what you want to do. I need all of you in on this one, because I have a feeling its going to get a lot worse before it gets better."

"I'm in," Ilanka said without hesitation. "From what I've seen, we're going to die anyway if we don't stop those ships."

"Hell, I'm in," Shank said. "I think our odds of surviving Liberty are about as good as surviving Nova-12."

"I'm in," Singh said. "The whole idea of travelers from the infinite past... It's very exciting." There was no hint of excitement in her voice.

"Captain," Anderson said. "You know I'd follow you almost anywhere, but this..." He turned his attention to Mitchell. "Nothing personal, Captain. I respect you and where you came from." He looked back at Millie. "You've been infatuated with Mitchell since he boarded this ship, and it's clouding your judgment. I know what happened on Calypso, but the more I think about it, the more ridiculous this whole thing sounds. A clone from the future-"

"Past," Watson said.

"Shut up. A clone from the future? A lost starship? And now a person who was on the lost starship turns up on the very planet that this one came from?" His finger lashed out at Mitchell, betraying the idea that it was nothing personal.

"Not just from the same planet. She was my handler for the last few days before I ran," Mitchell said. "Do you think that was an accident?"

Anderson huffed. "Please. You think that makes it more believable?" He glared at Shank, then Watson, then Ilanka. "You've all bought into this bullshit without much questioning. Do you think there's nothing else going on here? Do you think this is all on the up-and-up? First she screws him and then she wants to make him XO?"

"Lieutenant!" Millie snapped, her expression taut.

"Executive officer?" Watson said. "Were you going to tell us about this, Captain?"

"Right after we decided whether to head for the rock or the hard place," Millie replied. "What I do during downtime isn't relevant to this conversation."

"Not relevant?" Anderson said. "Of course it is. This guy comes out of nowhere and in a couple of weeks he's at the top of the food chain, telling stories and convincing you to do whatever he wants. It's one thing when it's just your ass on the line. It's another when it's all of our frigging lives."

"He kicked your ass during the hazing," Shank said.

"He tricked me."

"No rules, remember? Look, Anderson, I'm usually on your side, but you need to take a breath and sit down. It seems to me you're pissed off because Mitchell got something you've wanted for a long time and weren't good enough to earn."

Anderson's face turned red, and his hands balled into fists. "You son of a bitch," he said. "I'll kill you."

Shank got to his feet. "Come on and try it."

Mitchell watched the two men close in on one another, heads down and ready to come to blows.

"Enough!" Millie shouted again, slamming her hand down on the desk. Shank and Anderson both turned their heads towards her. "You're way out of line, Lieutenant."

"I'm the only one here who's willing to say what everyone else is thinking," Anderson said.

"No one else is thinking like you," Ilanka said.

"No? It never crossed your mind, Shank? That maybe our Captain isn't thinking with her head anymore?"

"I didn't know the Captain and Mitchell had sexed each other," Shank said. "I don't really care either. Ares saved our lives at Calypso, and he's already proven he's more of a man than you are. If the Captain trusts him, then I trust him."

"Screw you, Colonel. What about you, Ilanka? I know you like our pretty-boy here, but can you honestly tell me you never wondered if he's out of his mind?"

"I'm wondering that about you right now. You know we're all criminals of some kind. Except Mitchell."

"He raped the Prime Minister's wife!" Anderson said.

Mitchell felt all eyes turn towards him. He hadn't told anyone but

Millie that part of his story.

"How do you know about that?" Mitchell asked, working to stay calm.

"I have my ways."

"Is it true?" Ilanka asked.

"No," Mitchell said. "It isn't. I was set up."

"Please," Anderson said. "We were all set up." He laughed.

"If you were court-martialed for being an asshole, I doubt it was a setup," Mitchell said. He looked at Ilanka. "I didn't do it."

She nodded and smiled reassuringly.

"You've just opened up another point of discussion though, Lieutenant," Millie said. "Mitchell told me about that in the privacy of my quarters, and I didn't tell you anything."

Anderson's angry face fell, his eyes dropping. He realized he had made a stupid mistake.

"Well, Lieutenant?" Millie pressed. "How did you know?"

Anderson was silent, his eyes downcast. He wasn't going to tell. He didn't need to. Mitchell looked over to where Watson was sitting, silent during the entire exchange. He too had his eyes down, trying to avoid the confrontation.

"You can intercept signals if you have the right tools and know the encryption scheme can't you, Singh?" Mitchell asked.

She considered for a minute. "Yes, I suppose you could. Are you accusing me?"

"No," Mitchell said. "Not you." He had recognized that she and Watson were playing a game, trying to outdo one another. Now he understood that it had gone too far. "Watson?"

The big man kept his head down. The room fell silent.

"Watson?" Millie said.

"I just wanted to see if I could do it," he said. "It's not as easy as you make it sound. You need to build modulators to capture the signal, decryption tools, and a rig that can do the processing as well as the neural implant, which has the brain to help it along."

"How long?" Millie asked, seething.

"I didn't mean any harm. You know sometimes my curiosity gets the better of me. That's why I'm here anyway, because I hacked into confidential systems."

"That isn't why you're here," Millie said, her voice cold and even. "The MPs only discovered that after you got caught with that little boy."

Watson looked stricken to have his past announced to the gathered crew. His face flushed, and he made a strange whining sound that was somewhere between a cry and a howl. Singh pushed her chair back, putting space between herself and the engineer.

"Oh, grow a pair, will you," Anderson said. "You should be glad nobody told me you were a child molestor earlier, or I would have slit your fat throat already."

"Captain," Shank said. "Permission to throw this piece of dirt out of the airlock."

"Granted," Millie said. Mitchell saw it then. The bald reason, the easy calculation. She knew he was forfeit the moment she mentioned his crime. She'd always known. He was too valuable to waste, too valuable to let the truth come out. Until he had crossed her, and betrayed her trust. The reasons why didn't matter. Excuses were worthless.

"What?" Watson said. "Captain? No. You can't. You need me. You need me to keep the engines going. To keep medical running. To handle electrical and plumbing and-"

Shank grabbed him from behind, pulling him to his feet. "I'll learn to do all of it if it means getting you off my ship," he said.

"You might have to," Millie said.

"Wait," Anderson said. "That doesn't change the other facts."

"No, it doesn't," Millie said. "You knew what he was doing, and you didn't tell me."

Anderson paled. "I... You don't rat out your mates."

"I can't believe you just said that," Ilanka said. It was clear to Mitchell there was history - much, much more history - to this entire altercation than he could understand.

"Not when it suits you, is that it, Lieutenant?" Millie asked. "Not when it lets you get into my bedroom. Tell me, did you listen in while Mitchell and I were doing it? Did you jerk off?"

"I..." He fell silent. Was it an admission, or had he realized arguing was a lost cause?

"I'm going to take this shit to the airlock," Shank said. "We can finish up when I get back."

He started dragging Watson for the door, the man not fighting it, but not going easily either. His body fell limp in the soldier's arms.

"Shank, wait," Mitchell said, a sudden thought coming to him. "Watson, you said you built a system to intercept encrypted communications?"

"Yes. It's kind of a hack, and it isn't completely reliable."

"Could you use it to stop a kill signal?"

The engineer raised his head and started nodding. "I should be able to. I mean, it will take some work because the signal is much lighter and shorter than the standard ARR transmission, but the theory is all the same."

Mitchell turned to Millie. "Can we delay the order to have him jettisoned?"

"You want to keep this child molester on board?" Shank asked.

"I didn't say I wanted to. We're all here because we have valuable skills. Right now, we need his. If we can stop the military kill signal from blowing the ship, the odds get a little better."

"Ten-million-to-one to one-million-to-one?" Singh said.

"I can do it," Watson said. "Don't kill me, and I'll make it happen."

"Captain," Shank said. "I'd rather take my chances with the kill switch."

"No," Millie replied. "Mitchell's right. We need him. Sit him down, I'll deal with him in a minute."

Shank looked like he was going to argue again. His mouth opened, his jaw shifted. Then he reached out with one hand to grab a chair, and used the other to shove Watson down into it.

Millie circled the desk, coming around to where Anderson was still standing. She put herself right in his face. "As for you. I trusted you. I told you things that nobody else on this crew knows. I put up with your presence, your smell, your constant begging for a roll with me. I gave you more power than you ever deserved because you gave me something in return. Someone to talk to, someone to confide in. I was stupid. I should have known what I was getting into. All I ask of any member of this crew is respect. For me, for your teammates. Eavesdropping on my private quarters? Throwing it in my face as if you have some kind of rights to anything on this ship?"

She slapped him, hard with the bionic hand. The force sent him falling away, his neck making a sick, wet snap as his head twisted on top of it.

He hit the ground with a solid thud, his body shoving two of the chairs out of the way. He laid there motionless, his eyes open, his jaw shattered. He groaned softly, trying to speak, trying to move. Mitchell watched him there, feeling a strange sense of calm. She'd broken his neck along with his jaw, paralyzed him from the top down. The medical bots could fix it, but he had a feeling they'd never get the chance.

"Shank, take him down to airlock four," Millie said, her voice as calm as Mitchell was feeling. It had to be this way. They both knew it. He was sure Shank and Ilanka knew it. All it took was one dissenter, one teammate they couldn't rely on, and everything was put into jeopardy.

Anderson moaned, his voice becoming more strained and desperate as Shank approached. Mitchell glanced around the room. Ilanka was glaring at Anderson, no love lost between them. Singh and Watson were looking away, trying to pretend the whole scene wasn't happening.

Shank lifted the broken Lieutenant, dragging him from the room without a word. Anderson continued to groan and try to speak, his voice unheard in the aftermath.

"We're going to Liberty," Millie said. "Does anyone else have anything to add?"

"Now TURN YOUR WRIST. That way. Snap it. Hard."

Mitchell snapped his wrist. The sparring stick crackled with energy, more for effect than anything. It held enough voltage to send a nice shot of pain through the target, but not enough to do permanent harm.

"You do this to all the new recruits, don't you?" Mitchell said.

Ilanka laughed. She was standing opposite of him on an old, worn gel mat, barefoot and dressed in her grays. Her hair was tied back behind her head in a pony-tail, her face glimmering with the sweat of her exertion. "Only the recruits I like. You are good fighter."

They'd been sparring for an hour, hand-to-hand, in the back corner of the gym. Ilanka had made him promise to come down with her before they reached Liberty, and after two days portioned between reviewing data on the Goliath and sleeping with Millie, he had made good on his word.

"I'm not," he said. "Bigger, yes. Longer reach. You're just as good as I am." He wasn't being nice. He had been a mid-level martial artist on the Greylock, and Ilanka was giving him a tough workout. His size advantage was the only thing keeping him ahead on the point system they had agreed to.

"Sticks will even things out then, yes?" she said. She was holding her own pair of the sparring sticks, and with the press of a button they extended out just a little further than his, giving her an even reach. The sticks could be used as an extension of the arm, or more like a knife - that was up to the user's discretion. The fact that Mitchell had never used them before left him feeling more than a little overmatched before they even started.

"I think you might have a slight advantage," he replied. He practiced the wrist snap that activated the shock-tip a few more times. Then he slapped himself on the arm with it to test the potency.

It hurt. A tight sting formed where the tip touched him, and then spread up his arm as a shockwave of painful heat. He had to control himself to keep his grip on the other stick, and he clenched his jaw in a successful effort to not cry out. Painful. Survivable.

"That was dumb thing to do," Ilanka said.

"Better than being hit and not knowing what to expect."

"True. Are you ready?"

"As ready as I'll ever be."

She nodded and then charged him, her sticks spinning in her hands. He backpedaled away from her, certain that she had just completely suckered him to get even with his point lead.

"You hustled me," he said as he frantically tried to keep up with her strikes. He felt the stick tapping him on the shoulder, the elbow, the thigh. She hadn't activated the shock. Not yet.

"Is only fair," she said. She backed up a step, making him think she was going to give him a breath. Instead, she flicked her wrist at the same time she extended the stick. The tip caught him on the back of the hand, and the shock made him drop one of the sticks.

"No, it isn't," he grunted. He tried to bend down to pick it up, but she threatened another shock, changing his tactics.

"War is never fair, no?"

"That depends on who you ask."

He stepped forward, trying to get past her guard with his stick, which he held more like a knife - a weapon he was more comfortable with. She batted it aside and caught him on the shoulder, bringing another stinging wave of pain.

"Also true," she replied. "It is all fair to me."

They moved across the mat, trading blocks and attacks. Mitchell took three more hits on his appendages, each strike causing him pain.

"What is score now?" Ilanka asked.

"I thought you were keeping track."

"I am. It is twelve to ten, your lead." She smacked him on the arm with the stick. "Twelve to eleven."

"I don't suppose you want to quit now?" he asked. The stick came in at him again, and he dove to the side, rolling away from her and back to his feet.

"You are supposed to quit when ahead, no?"

"Yes. How about if I quit?"

"Then you forfeit and I win."

He caught her incoming wrist with his free hand, quickly snapping the stick against her thigh. Her face tightened, but she didn't seem to notice the blow otherwise. "Thirteen to eleven."

"Nice," she said. She backed up a step and they faced-off. Then she came at him again, a flurry of blows and three incredibly fast taps hitting him in rapid succession and leaving him disarmed and struggling to shake it off. "Fourteen to thirteen," she said.

Mitchell laughed. "Damn. I quit." He tried to straighten himself up. "This won't leave me impotent, will it?"

"Millie would have my head for that," Ilanka replied. "No."

The mention of Millie having anyone's head drove them both to an immediate silence. While they both knew Anderson's demise had been self-precipitated and necessary, it was still an uncomfortable topic. He was well-liked among the rest of the crew, and it had taken the backing of Shank, Ilanka, and surprisingly, himself to help calm the nerves that had resulted. It didn't help that Millie had informed them of the decision to abandon the assigned mission and head to

Liberty immediately after. If it hadn't been for Cormac standing guard in full-exo and Shanks' reassurances to his grunts, things might have gotten ugly. The scene had shown him how much pull Shank had, and that if Anderson had ever wanted command more than he wanted sex with Millie, he might have been able to pull it off.

"What happened between you and Anderson?" Mitchell asked. "That made you enemies." He hadn't even realized they were until he had seen the look she gave him, once he was paralyzed and broken.

"He was onboard because he went on a rampage after a campaign on Exelon, which is my home world."

"The attempted coup? That was years ago."

"Before I was enlisted, when I was little girl. I was in small town, Stovic, outside the capital where the coup took place. Anderson was part of the Space Marine company that arrived to bolster the government defenses. After the revolutionaries had been defeated, he took it on himself to go to nearby towns and rape some of the women, and kill some of the men."

"He told you all of this?"

"Yes, when he learned I was from Exelon. We got into argument, and he began to brag about what he had done. He told me he might be my father, and I broke his nose and his arm before Millie put a stop to it."

"She should have let you kill him then."

"She might agree with you now. It was the reason he wasn't allowed off ship. He couldn't be trusted not to do it again, but he had other skills, especially training new meat. I think the only reason he never attacked Millie was because of that bionic hand of hers. Your promotion, and your favor in our Captain's bed was more than he could take."

"It was a stupid thing to do."

"It was. I'm glad he did it. I've waited five years to see him get his."

Mitchell wiped some sweat from his brow with the bottom of his shirt. Millie had said they were the best of the broken. Between her story and Anderson's, along with Ilanka's satisfaction at the Lieutenant's death, he was beginning to understand exactly what she meant. Did that fact that he was glad the man was gone make him one of the broken, too? No, he was sure that had happened the moment Ella had taken the Shot and paid the ultimate price.

A knock on his p-rat interrupted his thoughts. It was Singh. "Do you have something?" he asked.

"I do. Come see me in engineering."

"I have to go," Mitchell said to Ilanka. "Singh says she got something. Thanks for the exercise." He leaned in and kissed her cheek.

"We'll try again, yes? You need practice with sticks."

"Rematch. Absolutely."

"I'll ride lift with you. I need a shower."

Mitchell wondered what the engineer had found. He had transferred most of the Goliath data to a separate part of the databank so that she could review it, their need for security reduced in their treason. He had searched for more information on the woman in the photo, the one who appeared to be Christine, but there was surprisingly little in the archive and queries had been fruitless. Singh had come up with the idea to create a new algorithm that would work to locate her in references to the other crew members, or to Goliath in general. To find her needle in the other haystacks.

It seemed she had made hay.

[43]

MILLIE WAS ALREADY in engineering when he arrived. She was standing near the data terminal, perusing a list of operational statuses. Watson had only been incarcerated in storage for two days and already the remaining engineer had to make decisions on which systems to fix, with the hopes that they would catch up eventually. Two of Shank's grunts had been dispatched to help her with simple tasks, but teaching them the complex workings of a starship was not a quick or easy process.

"Captain," Mitchell said on entering the space. Millie looked up at him and smiled.

"Mitch. Are you cheating on me?"

Mitchell grabbed at his sweaty clothes. "If sparring equals cheating, yes." He knew she was joking. They had both agreed their sexual activity was a casual endeavor, even if the time they spent at it was anything but passing.

Singh didn't react to the ribbing. Then again, she didn't react to anything outwardly. Watson's imprisonment and Anderson's death had both seemed to leave her unaffected.

"What do you have?" Mitchell asked the engineer.

She knocked his p-rat, opening a channel between the three of them and transmitting a dataset of images and videos. "Pick one," she said.

He did, selecting a video of the crew of the Goliath during a routine simulation. The view was focused on the Commander, but he could see Christine's head in the top left corner of the stream.

"Not your best choice," Singh said.

The video disappeared, followed up with a photo. He wasn't sure where it had been taken, but it showed a couple of the members of the crew talking in the foreground. Christine was visible in the background. They were all wearing uniforms with name tags pinned to them.

"Taken at a black tie gala, two days before the launch of the Goliath. There were only candid shots, and somehow she avoided being in the foreground of any of them. I only found this one, but it was enough. I employed an algorithm to extrapolate the name from her badge, using the color variations in the shadows around the embossing."

"That sounds hard."

"Not really."

"Who is she?" Millie asked.

"Her name is Major Katherine Asher," Singh said. "She was an Air Force pilot. From what little I found on her in our archives, quite a good one. She served in the Xeno War."

Mitchell stared at her. She was blurry in the background, but the resemblance was unmistakable. If she wasn't Christine Arapo, there had to be a connection somewhere in the family tree.

"What else do you know about her?" Mitchell asked. "You didn't find much?"

"No. Less than I would have expected. Much less. There are thousands of photos and videos in the archives, and each of the crew members turns up as the subject hundreds of times. Except for her. She isn't the focus in any of them, and as the pilot of Earth's first starship, it would be expected she would draw a lot of attention. Especially because she's beautiful."

Mitchell glanced at Singh. He had never seen Christine as beautiful. Pretty, maybe. "So why isn't she?"

"If I had to guess, I would say that someone tried to remove her from the archive."

"Who?" he asked.

"That's a stupid question."

Mitchell bit his lip. Singh certainly wasn't afraid to be blunt. "I won't ask why either, then. She's important to this whole thing, here and now. We need to get Major Arapo off of Liberty and find out what she knows."

"That's not good enough," Millie said. "Christine Arapo can't be Katherine Asher. That would make her four hundred years old." Mitchell started to argue, but she put up her hand to silence him. "Yes, I know you see a strong resemblance. Maybe she's a great-to-the-nth-power grandmother. Maybe it's just a cosmic coincidence. Maybe it has something to do with the whole idea of eternal reincarnation. Or, maybe she's one of them, like your replica was. I don't know, but we can't assume that Major Arapo does either."

"She knows something. She helped me escape."

"Which is why we are still going to try to pick her up, but we need to cast a wide net to make sure we get what we're after."

"What are you suggesting?"

"Data. As much as we can grab."

"Liberty has public databanks we can-" Singh started to say.

"Not public," Millie said. "Military."

"Military?"

"They have historical records that stretch back to the twenty-first century, copied into the main banks of every major installation on every settled planet. Katherine Asher was military. She'll have a record."

"How do you know it hasn't been erased?" Mitchell asked.

"I don't, but military security is much stronger than civilian. There's a chance those archives are intact."

"I can't break security like that on my own," Singh said. "Not in any reasonable amount of time. I hate to say it, but I need Watson."

There was a long pause while Millie considered the request. Word had gone around the ship about Watson's imprisonment and his past transgressions. The only thing that was keeping the engineer safe was that only the senior officers knew where in the ship he was being held. They couldn't move the equipment to him, which meant he would have to come to the equipment. How long would he last after that?

"My skin crawls thinking about being near him," Singh said. "I wouldn't ask it if it wasn't necessary to complete the mission."

Millie finally nodded. "Okay. Tell me when you need to start working on it, and we'll arrange for him to be brought up."

"I need him now," Singh said. "We'll need to work to mimic the transmission signatures. It might take hours. It also might take days."

"Can you get it done in time?" Millie asked.

"I hope so."

"What about the kill signal?" Mitchell asked. "If Watson is working on this, he won't be working on that."

"He can split time," Singh said. "Help me go in the right direction, and check my work."

"I'll send Shank to get him," Millie said.

"No. I'll do it," Mitchell said. He liked the Colonel, but he didn't trust him to bring Watson up without having some kind of accident that would leave him injured or worse. "Will we need a guard on engineering?"

"On any other Alliance ship, no. On this one?" She had weeded out the worst of them, and she had done a commendable job building them into an operational force that was able to work as a team. Even so, the Schism would always be a nuke on the verge of detonation.

"Have Cormac do it," Mitchell said. "If I tell him to leave Watson alone, he will. Have him come in partial exo."

"I thought I was in charge here?" Millie said, her tone more teasing than serious.

"Recommendation from your XO, Captain," Mitchell replied.

She smiled. "I concur. Go get Watson. I'll knock Cormac, and tell him to be discreet. I don't want Shank getting wind of this before I can speak to him privately."

"You don't trust him with Watson either?" Mitchell asked.

"Shank has a tendency to react to difficult situations by lashing out without thinking. It makes him an elite ground-pounder. It also makes him dangerous. I'd prefer to keep him as far away from Watson as possible." She fell silent while she communicated with Cormac through the ARR. Then she looked at him, a hint of stress and regret in her expression. "It's a bad habit of mine too, sometimes. I should have kept my mouth shut about Watson. I didn't realize how important he would turn out to be."

"We can't go backward," Mitchell said. "Let's just focus on keeping him in one piece."

"Yes, sir," Millie said, offering a mocking bow. "Go get him."

"Yes, ma'am," Mitchell replied, returning a serious bow before turning on his heel and heading out the door.

MITCHELL WAS cautious as he navigated the halls of the Schism, checking each corridor and sneaking through it as though his goal was anything but sanctioned. He agreed with Millie that it would have been better if she hadn't spilled the secret of Watson's internment on the ship, but there was nothing to do about it now. Even the travelers couldn't move backward in time. Infinitely forward, never in reverse. The engineer was hated for a reason, a good reason. A reason Mitchell agreed with. He would rather have left the man to drift in space with Anderson.

Unfortunately, his abilities had become the most important asset they had. At least for the moment.

He made it to the lift without being seen, and then from the lift to the hangar. With Singh in engineering and Ilanka likely in the shower, he knew it would be deserted. He moved across it, past the S-17 and the Knight to a small storage room on the other side. The ore that had been mined for the Calypso mission was still resting there in the hold.

So was Watson.

They had provided him with a pisspot, a mattress, a chair, and a desk. They had also retrieved the equipment that he had built to eavesdrop on all of them from an empty compartment on E-Deck. It was where Anderson had likely vanished to whenever he wasn't with Millie, listening in on her private conversations with or without the engineer present. If she were right, he had also been getting himself off on her more intimate moments.

He had the small black box that served as the modulator dismantled on the desk, dozens of tiny wires snaking around one another. He held a tiny screwdriver more delicately than his meaty hands should have allowed, poking it into the box and making adjustments. It was easy to wonder if he was actually doing anything, and if he really intended to try to help them block the kill signal.

Mitchell had seen the look in Watson's eyes when he thought he was going to die. If he didn't do the work, they were all going to be blown into no more than space dust. Self-preservation was a powerful motivator.

"Captain Williams?" Watson said, looking up at him when he entered. He didn't look well. His grays were already stained with sweat, and his face and hair were oily. He smelled awful.

"How is the work coming?" Mitchell asked. He tried not to think about the man's past, and only see him as he was today. To stay neutral. It took effort, but he managed.

Watson held up the box. "This? It would be easier if I had a sample transmission to match the modulation against."

"You're only going to get one transmission." The one that would make the Schism explode.

"Yes, I know. I ran the calculations. The likelihood of successfully blocking the signal without a sample is about ten-thousand to one."

Mitchell drew in a sharp breath. "Those are lousy odds."

"Yes. I was going to tell the Captain, but I was afraid to bother her." He was afraid of Mitchell too, refusing to make eye contact, staring down at the box while he spoke. "Then I had another idea."

"Which is?"

"Block every signal. Anything that we don't use. I can bypass the ARR frequencies and the datalink bands, and intercept everything else."

"That sounds good."

"Yes. There's only one problem."

Of course, there was a catch. "How much of a problem?"

"That depends. The processing and power requirements to filter like this are going to be rather high. As you know, the Schism isn't equipped for massive power draws. Not the way a warship would be. I did a few calculations. We'll have to turn off-" He paused, looking at the surface of the desk where a screen full of numbers rested. "Almost everything. Including life support and gravity."

"That'll be fun. What about engines?"

"Of course, we need that."

"More than air?"

"The circulating air will remain at breathable levels for a couple of hours. Otherwise, we have enough hazard suits aboard for the crew. Anyway, once I can get a sample of the transmission, if we have some time I can adjust the modulator against it and fix the power concerns. Of course, you didn't know this before you came down, and you didn't bring me anything to eat. Why are you really here?"

"We need your help."

He shook his head. "I'm already helping you. Us."

"We need more help."

"Singh sent you down, didn't she? It's about the data?"

"How did you know?"

"We've been working together for the last three years, spending ten, fifteen hours in the same room. We know everything about each other."

"Everything?"

He kept his eyes on the box. "I didn't tell her about that. It was supposed to be a secret. I'm not stupid. I knew what people would think of me if they found out. I didn't mean to upset the Captain. I respect her too much, owe her too much for letting me stay on board when she knew what I had done. I only wanted to see if I could make the system work. It was Anderson who convinced me to let him use it. He said he could get me things through Ensign Hubble. Food, mostly. Delicacies from the New Terran worlds. I don't miss my people, but I do miss their food. He promised he wouldn't tell, and then he goes and blurts out things he wasn't supposed to know." He finally looked up. His eyes were moist. "I just want things to be the way they were. There's nobody here I'm a danger to. Why do you all have to hate me now?"

"There are some lines you just don't cross," Mitchell said. "Anderson was a rapist and a killer, and he didn't."

"I know I'm sick. I know my head is messed up. I can't help myself. I can't stop the thoughts, the urges, the desires. I-"

"Stop talking," Mitchell snapped. He didn't want to hear this. "You can pity yourself all you want, but nobody on this ship is going to pity you. If you want to go back to engineering, this is your chance."

Watson stopped talking for a few seconds. "Once I finish with the modulator. Once I finish helping Singh. What's to keep you from throwing me out of the airlock?"

"Nothing," Mitchell said. "It's the chance you'll have to take."

Watson shook the box in his hand. "How do you know I'll comply? How do you know I'll make this work?"

"That's the chance we have to take."

The engineer considered him for a moment. For all of his meekness over his sordid past, he seemed proud that he still held so much value to them. It was another great motivator.

"Okay, I'll do it," Watson said. "On one condition."

"I don't think you have much bargaining power here," Mitchell replied.

"I want to live. I don't care if I have to stay down here for the rest of my life. I'm terrified to die."

"I'll see what I can do."

"Please, Captain. Millie will listen to you. I know she will."

"I told you, I'll see what I can do. I'll talk to her. That's the only promise you're going to get. Are you in?"

He got to his feet, putting the modulator down on the table.

"Riigg-aaah," he said with a weak smile.

[45]

"Is the crew ready for this?" Millie asked, her voice echoing in Mitchell's head.

"We had four briefings, and they aced the drills," he replied.

"You know there's a big difference between a simulation and the real thing."

"They'll do fine. This is your crew." It was an easy compliment to boost her confidence.

"Thanks," she said.

The channel closed, leaving Mitchell alone in the cockpit of the S-17. He checked his p-rat for the time. They were only minutes away from dropping out of FTL, stepping from the safety of hyperspace to... what? They didn't know. They couldn't know. They had done their best to prepare for the worst. He could only hope that they had done enough.

Watson and Singh were certain their hack would work to punch through the security of the Alliance military databanks, using a vulnerability in some minor subsystem or other to sneak into their classified archives through a tiny back door. Once they had broken in, Singh would inject an algorithm that had a very simple, targeted purpose: download the results of a query on two names: Major Katherine Asher and Major Christine Arapo.

Once the data was aboard, the Schism's mission would be complete, and she would get the hell out of there. Mitchell, on the other hand, would do his best to locate Christine and try to send a message to her through her ARR, the same way M had used the helmet to send a message to him. If he were successful, he would hopefully meet her on the ground and take her away, using the fighter's FTL engine to rendezvous with the Schism. If he weren't, they would have to pray the data they collected would give them something they could use.

Then there was the other possibility. The one that had hung in the back of their minds and remained as an unspoken fear right up until they had briefed the crew on everything they knew about the travelers, and why they had made the decision to break orders and head for Liberty. It was Cormac, of course, who posed the question:

"What if the aliens get to Liberty before we do?"

Millie, Mitchell, and Singh had all fumbled for an answer. Shank had been blunt. "Then we're going to die. Now shut up, Firedog."

They were probably going to die anyway. If Nova-12 had been a suicide mission, this one was even crazier. They couldn't be certain who their enemy was going to be, but right now everyone was their enemy. Did it matter if they were assaulted by a massive blue ball of energy or a round of more conventional projectiles?

It was worse than that. In order to prevent the Alliance from blowing the Schism, the moment they dropped from FTL they would need to activate Watson's rig. That meant shutting down major systems to power the re-purposed CPUs from their own databanks to catch, process, and cancel signals across a band of over a million channels. Those systems weren't just life support and gravity. Shields were included in that, too. So were the long range sensors.

They were going in naked, blind, and four hours from suffocation, with a skeleton crew that was barely enough to cover damage control on the most critical systems.

Mitchell laughed to himself. They might actually be better off if the travelers had arrived first.

The comm channel opened again, a public broadcast to the entire crew.

"Riggers," Millie said. "You know the situation. You've spent the last four days preparing for this, and I know you'll do me proud, as you have all done since the day you joined my crew. If things go to shit, I want you all to know that I have been honored to serve as your Captain."

"Riigg-aaah," came the reply from the crew, Mitchell's voice included. It was loud enough that the implant was forced to neutralize the volume.

"Shank, is your team in position?"

"Roger," Shank replied.

"Singh?"

"Affirmative," Singh said, her own version soft and flat.

"Ares? Rain?"

"Roger," they both said.

"Firedog?"

"Yes, ma'am," Cormac said.

Mitchell felt his heartbeat accelerating, the p-rat reflecting the shift in the corner of his eye. A red box backed it, a warning that it would be forced to regulate him chemically. He breathed in through the nose, out through the mouth. Slow. Steady.

"We're at thirty seconds to drop. You won't notice life support going out, not right away, but you will notice the lack of gravity. Automatic deck seals will be offline, so if there are any breaches you need to close them as fast as you can. With any luck, we'll be in and out before we take any fire."

Mitchell could imagine her unspoken thought: "Assuming Watson didn't screw us over." There was no way to be fully certain his rig would work, and that he hadn't decided to take the ship and its crew down with him. His fear of death had certainly seemed convincing enough, but the engineer knew the odds of survival and had most likely run calculations and simulations to confirm them. Would he rather be blown into dust on his own terms, or take his chances regardless of the slimness? There was no way to know.

"Here we go," Millie said.

The countdown on his p-rat hit zero. The instant it did, he felt the shift in pressure that followed the drop from hyperspace.

The ship started shaking. Hard.

"Drop is on target," Millie said. "Ares, go, go, go."

They had come out of FTL at the upper edge of Liberty's atmosphere. It was an insane move, a ridiculous procedure that required pinpoint accuracy in all of the calculations. A move that even the Captain and Navigator of the Greylock had never tried, even when sticking drops in the hottest of hot zones. The best of the broken. Ensign Briggs had executed perfectly, and now they were surfing right at the top of the planet's atmosphere, waiting to escape from hyperdeath and get the ship back under control, hoping it didn't fall too far before they did.

The hangar doors began to open beneath him. He glanced over at Ilanka, hanging from the second launcher in the Piranha. She would be staying here, waiting for the orders to go out and protect the Schism. They were orders he hoped she wouldn't receive, because they both knew she wouldn't last out there alone. She gave him a thumbs up. They were still alive. Still here. Either Watson's rig was working or news of the Schism's betrayal had yet to reach this part of the galaxy.

He was pushed back into his seat as the launcher fired, sending the S-17 down through the barely open bay door and into the upper atmosphere. A thought put the main thrusters at max, and he shot downward towards the planet.

It was huge in front of him, blue and green with visible splotches of brown remaining from the Federation's assault. He brought up the overlay on the glass of the helmet, checking the space around him. A dozen red dots signaled Alliance starships. They were beginning to move towards them, surprised by their appearance. The risk had been calculated, the position essential. The ship commanders would have to be idiots to fire nukes so close to the planet's surface.

"Singh is in," Millie said through the open channel. "Data transfer starting. Alliance vessels incoming. Fighters launched. It's getting messy in a hurry."

"Roger," Mitchell said, grateful that Singh and Watson had come through. "Don't wait for me."

"I won't."

The S-17 screamed through the atmosphere, the blue tinge of the shields surrounded by the red heat of re-entry. He was coming down hard and fast, headed straight for a thick layer of clouds that was blotting out his view of York. He sent a thought to the neural link, opening a channel and passing Christine's id through it, knocking her ARR.

Seconds passed. There was no reply.

"Mains online," he heard Ensign Briggs say.

"Full power," Millie said. "Everything we've got available. We need some height."

Millie dictated the move for the sake of the crew, keeping them informed. None of them were assigned to fight on this mission. They would float and wait, ready to take fire and shore up damage. It was as lousy of a role as Mitchell could imagine.

Mitchell sent the transmission again, knocking Christine a second time. What if the Alliance had found out she had helped him? What if they had deactivated her ARR, imprisoned her, sent her off-world? What if she was dead?

There was no way to know. Either way, there was no reply.

"Come on, Christine," he said. He sent the knock a third and final time as he entered the clouds, leaving himself buried in gray moisture. He watched his HUD, making sure there was nothing in his path.

"Firedog, breach on E-deck," Millie said. "Seal bulkheads four and five."

"On it, Captain," Cormac replied.

"Breach on C-deck, near the aft. Bulkhead fourteen. Razor, that's you."

No response.

"Razor?" Pause. "Shit."

"Main three is offline, Captain," Briggs said.

"Singh, sitrep."

"We're still receiving," Singh said as if they weren't under attack. "I don't know how much longer, we don't have a full size estimate."

"Let's hope it's enough, we're getting out of here. Moving up and out of orbit. Briggs, be ready to transfer to FTL on my mark. They're going to launch the heavy artillery as soon as we're clear of the planet. Ares, you're on your own."

Mitchell didn't respond. As Millie spoke her final words the S-17 broke through the cloud cover, only a thousand meters above the York skyline. What he saw in front of him nearly made him hesitate too long before pulling the fighter up.

After the Battle for Liberty, a crater at the center of the city had been re-zoned to become a memorial park, a place for reflection and remembrance of the battle and the lives that were lost in the attack. When he had last seen the crater, it had been graded and grassed, the beginnings of a monument taking shape in the center of the bowl.

Now the monument was gone, crushed by something else.

A vaguely round shape like an amoeba sat in its place, the metallic surface shifting and undulating as if it were made of living water. Branches of the same material spread out around it, hundreds of lines cast out in every direction, rising up the crater and out into the city, punching through alloy and carbonate. Pulses of energy raced along them in strips of blue and white light that created an eery glow throughout the city.

Bodies lay around it. Hundreds of bodies in plain clothes, civilians that looked as though they had simply dropped where they were standing. Beyond that were more dead whose end couldn't have been as peaceful. They were shredded and torn, burned and broken, caught in a rain of fire that had spewed from... where?

The aliens. They were already here. They had beat them to Liberty. The thing at the center of the crater... A ship? A command center? The enemy itself?

"Millie, they're here. They're already here. Liberty is lost. Get out of here. Now."

There was no answer, no confirmation. Had the Schism jumped into hyperspace and made it to safety?

Or were the Riggers no more?

Was he alone?

He strained with his mind, forcing the S-17 out of its dive, sweeping past the city and then making a tight turn to come back around. For all of the death and destruction, there were millions of people in the city and the city itself remained standing, the damage limited to street level. There had to be people still alive out there.

Didn't there?

He choked on the thought, swallowing the anger and upset, ignoring the bloody scene below him. Christine was gone. Dead or not, she wasn't answering, and he had no way to find her. He needed to get back up into orbit, to fire his own FTL and meet the Schism at the rendezvous point, assuming it had survived.

He tilted the fighter back skyward, pushing the thrusters and lifting ever higher into the air. He made it halfway before he dropped the throttle, rolling the fighter and letting it fall back towards the planet.

His ship had alien technology. Their technology. If M was right and he was supposed to be the one who defeated them, then he would declare his war here and now.

He set a marker on the alien structure as he shot back over the city, doing a tight loop around the tower and coming in low, down a wide thoroughfare between two buildings. He kept one eye on the streets, searching for anything alive down there. He used the other to lock onto the amoeba.

A tone sounded in his mind, and then the left side of the S-17 lit up in the blue energy of his shields. He turned his head, seeing a Dart crouched low in the street behind a burned out car. It was a light, four-legged mech, a reconnaissance model armed only with light machine guns and lasers. It was too small for an embedded cockpit, and so there was a line of clear carbonate positioned near the center of the torso.

No one was driving.

The surprise attack and the sight of the empty cockpit caused him to lose his focus on the target. He shot over it, coming with a dozen meters from the top of the structure, looking down at the swirling surface as he passed over.

A blinding light surrounded the fighter. More alarms sounded, an emergency power spike that threatened to burn out the engines. He cursed, pulling the fighter up hard enough that he felt the pressure of the move in spite of the inertial cancelation, the ship battling physics to grant his request. He watched the altimeter climb, switching to the HUD and checking the theater. The Dart had been idling at low power, camouflaged by the surrounding cityscape.

It wasn't alone.

Twelve new dots appeared on the ground, registering as an assortment of Alliance mechs. They poured from between buildings and rose out of subterranean garages in a near circle around the alien structure, an ambush intended for whoever tried to get near the installation. The helmet buzzed around him, the AI warning him of incoming fire. Missiles, lasers, slugs. Everything the enemy had to send his way. He threw the plane into a drunken spin, trying to wind around the fire and confuse their aim. He watched the shield integrity fall. Sixty percent, forty percent.

Something hit the shields and it threw the fighter sideways, knocking it off course and sending it into a spin. Mitchell grunted through it, closing his eyes. Slow. Steady. He sent the orders to level off through the neural link, letting the AI do the hard work. Lesser pilots might have panicked, tried to make the adjustment themselves and wound up in pieces. The fighter steadied and he banked left and descended, coming down near the eastern edge of York and using the buildings as cover. He stayed low as he gained distance from the city, reaching the edge of the mountains before vectoring up the side, staying close to the surface and rising back towards the atmosphere.

Shields were down to ten percent, the AI unable to restore integrity unless he diverted power to the generators. Power he needed to get back into space and away from Liberty.

He had seen the enemy.

He had fought his first battle.

He had lost.

Badly.

46

The rendezvous point was ten hours distant from Liberty, a random spot in deep space notable only for a small dwarf star that rested nearby. Mitchell neared it with a strong measure of fear. If the Schism was gone, he was going to be alone again, with only enough power remaining to return to Liberty.

The last place he wanted to go.

He had no idea if the ship had survived the attack. When he had reached orbit he found a dozen military starships and a lot of debris. It could have come from the Schism, or it could have come from any of the civilian ships that the aliens had destroyed. It was an observation they didn't have time to make when they arrived, an observation that had returned the thoughts of anger and fear, thoughts that lingered throughout the length of the trip.

He was lucky to be alive. Lucky to have threaded his way through the oncoming Alliance ships. There had been pilots in the Piranhas that came to intercept him, and for a moment he had wanted to believe that they were still in control of the stars. Then he remembered that the aliens could remote control people with neural implants, the same way they had controlled the mechs on the ground.

Neural implants. That meant the entire Alliance military, planetary law enforcement, and a host of civilians who could afford the procedure and had the mental aptitude to make use of the tech.

The more he learned about the aliens that M had said would destroy humanity, the more he believed in the future of the past.

It left him wanting to know why. What was the motivation for a race so powerful, so advanced to travel infinite years and then lay waste to mankind? M believed it was to stop him from stopping them from their future domination. How could he have tried to stop them before they had come from the past to be stopped?

He knew he couldn't.

Not unless they already existed.

He tried to work through the problem. He put himself back on Liberty, the night Evan was killed. If the timeline hadn't been changed, he would have killed the assassins and hailed as more of a hero than he already was. He would have attended the gala with Christine. No, he couldn't be sure of that. What if Evan hadn't been killed the last time? Maybe he would have attended the gala on his own, or maybe they would have provided him with a different bodyguard. Maybe it was still Christine? That part wasn't important. What was important was his future. The lie would have been intact, his life as a celebrity would have continued. Enlistment numbers would have gone up, public support for the military would have increased, and the military budgets would increase with it. Politicians would make a strong case for going after the Federation before the Federation could come after them.

The Federation?

Their technology had been advancing more quickly than either the Alliance or the New Terrans, and they had already proven their desire to claim Alliance territories and resources.

Could it be?

He didn't think so. The travelers had attacked Calypso, a Federation dock. They had killed thousands of Federation citizens. It didn't make sense.

Except... Why would you need your weak, past self, if you could come into power as a highly advanced, evolved version from an ancient future?

It was possible. It might even be likely. The problem was that no matter how Mitchell approached the idea, it didn't matter. Whether the aliens had been born from the Federation or not, they had come back here and now, ready to destroy them all. They could have been from another galaxy, from the end of the universe, from the other side of a black hole. The end result was the same.

They weren't sparing the Federation from their extermination.

He watched the FTL countdown hit zero on his p-rat. The S-17 shuddered and fell back into real space.

A blue dot appeared on the HUD. The Schism. He eyeballed it a few seconds later. There were signs of damage running along the aft quarter - scorch marks and a gaping hole in the poly-alloy, the blast that had knocked out main three.

It was still there. They were still alive. That was all that mattered.

A knock on his p-rat.

"Ares," Millie said, sounding more relieved than excited. "Welcome back."

47

MITCHELL's first hour back on the Schism was solemn. They didn't even waste time debriefing before arranging a quick memorial for the members of the crew who had died. Razor, Leo, Crunch. Mitchell had only known them in passing, by circumstance rather than design. Shank seemed to know them well, and he spoke for a few minutes on their behalf. Mitchell stood at the front of the proceedings, next to Millie in the spot that Anderson had once claimed. He could feel the tension of the crew. He could sense their fear. This was a group that wasn't accustomed to being on the losing end, and it was obvious that they didn't like it.

That was something they could use.

After the service, the crew was released to continue making what little repairs they could, while Millie brought her senior team together to figure out what they were going to do next. Mitchell was surprised to find Watson there when he arrived, already settled into his favorite spot at the table. It explained why Cormac had been positioned in the corridor with a rifle in his hand. The engineer kept his eyes downcast, his posture submissive.

"Thruster three will never fire again," Singh said. "That whole section is lost to space. We had six other breaches, but the crew managed to seal them pretty quickly. In this case, it helped that they were already suited up and zero-gravity."

"What about the rest of the systems?" Millie asked.

"All other essentials are operational. We did lose one of the liquid recycling systems, so we'll have to be careful with water and showers."

"One shower per week. Thirty-two ounces of water per day." She hesitated. "And tell them they need to shut down the distillery. At least temporarily."

"They aren't going to be happy to lose the crude," Shank said.

"Do they want to win this war, or do they want to drink their way through it?" she asked.

"According to Lopez, we have enough rations on board to last us two months," Millie said. "That's plenty of food right now, but I'm beginning to question whether there will be anywhere to resupply it by the time we run out. I'm not going to cut the men off just yet, but we need to consider moving to half-rations sooner rather than later."

"I don't think crew will miss it," Ilanka said, joking about the taste of their diet. The staple food was a nutritionally perfect combination of carbs, proteins, vitamins, and minerals that came in both solid and liquid form. Once a week they would have something cooked - poultry, meats, vegetables. Nothing as delicious or as fancy as what Millie had served, but a week of the rations made the flavor pretty competitive.

"They'll miss it when it's all gone," Mitchell said. "It's better to tell them now, and get all the bad news out of the way."

"You're right. I'll make an announcement. We'll halve everything up front. That goes for all of us as well."

"What about your pheasant?" Ilanka said.

"My personal stores will be added to the ship's larder. I understand that this isn't the time for special treatment." She turned to Mitchell. "It's safe to assume you weren't able to locate Major Arapo?"

"No. I knocked her a few times. She didn't answer. Then I was ambushed by an Alliance mech that didn't have a pilot."

"What?" Ilanka said.

"No pilot. I could see the cockpit was empty. The enemy is able to control them remotely somehow. I think it has to do with the structure that was in the middle of the city. It looked like it could have been a command center." He opened a channel to them on his p-rat and transmitted the visuals he had captured.

"Amazing," Watson said. "Stunning."

"What is it made of?" Shank asked.

"It looks like a nervous system," Singh said.

The statement caught Mitchell's attention. Millie didn't miss it either.

"A nervous system?" she asked.

"Yes. Nucleus. Dendrites."

"There's only one of them," Watson said. "You can't have one in a system. Where are the axons?"

"I don't know," Singh said, glancing over at him, her eyes narrowed slightly. She looked as annoyed as Mitchell had ever seen her.

"Hmmm," Ilanka said. "They could be underground. Is a big planet. Maybe is spread out?"

"It's possible," Singh replied. "We'd need a higher resolution image or ground piercing radar to make that determination."

"We aren't going to get either of those things," Millie said. "We barely made it out of there alive."

"I can't help but think of the people there," Ilanka said. "Uzhasnyy."

"What about the civilians?" Shank asked. "There are what, something like two hundred million people on the planet?"

"There were a lot of bodies in the streets," Mitchell said. "Not enough to account for everyone. I don't think they killed them all."

"We witnessed their firepower," Millie said. "They could have destroyed the planet. They could have wiped out everything. Why didn't they?"

"Maybe that's not how they work?" Mitchell kept the focus of his left eye on the image of the alien structure, in the forefront of his p-rat. "When I flew over the nucleus, it caused a massive power spike in the S-17. I think the only thing that saved me was that it was made with their tech. Any other ship would have exploded from the overload."

"A power spike?" Watson asked, lifting his head. "Interesting. It could be that they're using Liberty as a foothold planet, a place to recharge their fleet. The nucleus may be a generator of some kind."

"The idea makes sense," Mitchell said. "They can't go back home, which means they need to be self-sufficient here and now. They need to claim resources to support their way of life. Liberty may be their ideal."

"Why not leave one of their own ships there?" Ilanka asked. "If it is that important, why not stay to defend?"

"We don't know how big their fleet is," Shank said. "They might not have enough ships. Anyway, they seemed to be doing just fine using our own war machine against us."

Mitchell felt the chill run through him again. "That isn't just true on Liberty. They don't need to fight us at all. Not when they can transmit to the neural implants and make a large swath of the human race their slaves."

"It's not a random swath either," Millie said, her face tight, her voice soft. She had just come to the same conclusion that Mitchell had during his flight to the rendezvous point. "It's the entire Alliance military. It could be the Federation and the New Terrans too. We all use the implants." Her eyes found Mitchell. "If you hadn't warned us to change the encryption, we might have ended up the same way."

"It was M who warned me. He knew it was going to happen. I didn't imagine that it would be done on this scale."

"They know about the Schism," Watson said. "I captured a band of unidentified transmissions, one of which is highly probable to be the detonation signal. It triggered as soon as we dropped, almost before I could initialize the rig. They're tapped into military channels."

"They could have complete control of the military channels," Millie said. "They don't even need to control every soldier. Take the right command personnel from each government, create orders to have them attack one another, and then sit back and wait. Chancellors, Prime Ministers, Generals..."

She tailed off. Mitchell knew she was thinking of General Cornelius. Her father. He would be a prime target for the aliens if they were planning on using such a strategy.

"They also know you came to Liberty," Singh said to Mitchell. "Not only that you came. You had to send your communications through the standard military channel. The same one they're already using. They know you were there, and they know who you came for."

A heavy silence fell across the room. It was a small detail that the rest of them probably would have missed. A small detail with big implications.

"Do you think they'll put two and two together?" Millie asked.

"If Mitchell has an interest in Christine Arapo, and the enemy has an interest in him, I think they'll want to determine where their paths intersect. If they can figure out what the Schism was doing near Liberty, and I believe it is safe to assume that they can, then yes, I do believe they'll put two and two together."

"Which means if there's anything we can use to find the Goliath in the data you pulled, they'll be able to use it too."

Shank groaned. "What if they beat us to it? What if they destroy the Goliath before we ever have a chance to find out if it can help us? Captain, I think we should give up on finding the lost starship and go full-speed for Earth. We need to warn them now and give the bulk of our forces a chance to mount a counter-offensive."

"How do we know enemy hasn't already reached Earth?" Ilanka said. "Their ships are much faster than this one. They must have beat us to Liberty by days."

"If they've already reached Earth, then the war is over before it's even started."

"Not if we find Goliath," Mitchell said.

Shank got to his feet, his anger flaring. "How do you know, Mitch? Because your alternate self told you so? Maybe he was lying? Maybe this whole thing is one big damn setup to send us in the wrong direction."

"Because we're such a concern to them?" Millie said, coming to Mitchell's defense. "Come on, Shank. We have some skills but don't forget that we aren't here by choice. We're flying a weaponless prison ship with a contingent of two dozen army grunts with no ground to pound, two pilots, a pedophile, and a mass murderer. Do you really think the advanced alien race that invented time travel gives two shits about us if Mitchell isn't on board?"

"So maybe we need to get Mitchell off-board," Shank said. "Sorry, Mitch, but I'm serious. Take your ship, go find Goliath. I'll be rooting for you the whole way. We can get back to Earth and get the brass there to update their implants, and then we can start fighting back. It's my people who keep dying."

That was the crux of his outburst. The three dead today, the others at Calypso. They were under Shank's direct command. He wasn't taking their loss easy.

Millie circled the table to stand with the soldier. She put her bionic hand on his shoulder and squeezed, gently. "They're our people." She paused, staring into his eyes. "And I want to avenge them. I want to kill the bastards who took their lives. If finding Goliath means I can start the killing, then I'm going to find Goliath."

Shank's anger faded, and he broke down into a smile. "Now you're talking, Captain."

She squeezed his arm again, and he took his seat.

"We need to find Goliath before they do," Millie said. "This is a team effort. Watson, Singh, I need the data we pulled parsed and loaded so that we can all review it. One of us might catch something another missed. Not just the people in this room. Every eyeball, every ear in the ship needs to be on this. If there's nothing, then they'll get nothing too. If there's something... We're too slow to beat them in FTL. We need to beat them here."

"Then let's do it," Ilanka said. "There's no time to waste."

"Let's show them what a ship full of friggers can do," Shank said.

48

It took Watson and Singh a little bit of time to parse the data they had captured and post it to the ship's streaming service, making it available to everyone on the crew. For Mitchell, it meant a few minutes of downtime that Millie had no intention of wasting. She practically dragged him from the conference room after the others had left, getting him to her quarters and efficiently undressing them both.

A quick round of intense sex proved to be a satisfying release for both of them.

Afterward, they spent the remaining time nestled in one another's arms, with Millie resting her head on Mitchell's chest.

"Do you really think we'll find it?" she asked.

"Even if we do, there's no guarantee it will be enough. It's one ship. One very old ship." Even as he said it, he felt a spark of hope, as if his past self was pushing him not to lose it. "We'll find it. We'll make it work."

"I'm grateful to you, Mitch."

"For what?"

"This." She smiled. "And out there. I've always had to fight so

282 / M.R. FORBES

hard to keep the crew in line. Anderson was an annoying pain in the ass, and I had to put up with him because he had a way with the troops that I just haven't been able to figure out. All the training in the world doesn't prepare you for the real thing, not really." She picked up her bionic hand. "When I lost my hand, I was crushed. I didn't want bionic. I didn't want to be... incomplete. Now this is the one thing that sets me apart here. It makes me more formidable. I could crush your spine with this thing as easy as if I was cracking an egg."

"You can be pretty gentle with it, too," Mitchell said, remembering the feeling of it on other parts of him.

She laughed. "That's not the point. The point is that sometimes I think the crew sees me as the hand. They don't see the training, the studies, the work. Hell, they don't even call me Admiral."

"Did you ever ask them to?"

"In the beginning, with the first batch of recruits. Ilanka was the one who suggested I stick to Captain so that they would see me more as one of them, rather than a higher authority. She was right about that, and it helped."

"I guess I still don't get what you're thanking me for? Besides this. I haven't even been here that long."

"I respect you. The crew respects you. They don't care who took the Shot, the fact is that Greylock company won the battle, and you were part of it. You could have challenged me for the ship. You said yourself you aced the aptitude tests, and I can see by the way people respond to you that you're a natural leader."

"That's not how the military works."

She waved her arm. "That military. There's a separate one in here. If Anderson had cut my throat in my sleep and gotten Watson to crack my implant he could have accessed mission parameters, the crew's drop codes, everything. Would Cornelius have accepted that? My father is as pragmatic as they come. He would have cried on his own time, and then sent the Schism on to the next target."

"I don't think he would have done that."

"No. It's just an example. It could have been any of them. Watson is terrified to die, you saw that yourself. How long do you think he would last under threat? Fifteen seconds?"

"Five, if you were lucky. Anyway, I wasn't interested in command back then, and I'm not interested now. I'm helping you out of need. I'd be happy to go back to the galaxy before, back when I was only a pilot for the most bad-ass Space Marines in the universe."

"I guess you'll have to be happy with the disintegrating boat and the company of criminals," she said. "It sounds like an even trade." She rolled her eyes.

He ran his hand through her hair, looking down at her. "It isn't as bad as you're trying to make it sound." He leaned his head over, reaching his face towards hers. She came up to meet him, their lips catching.

A knock interrupted them both. "It's ready," Singh said.

Millie broke the kiss, her face losing all of its softness in an instant. A moment later Mitchell heard the tone of the channel opening on his p-rat.

"Riggers," Millie said, sitting silent and naked in his arms, her voice loud and clear in his mind. "The race is on. A data stream has been loaded into the system, on channels M-12 and M-13. Your orders are to watch the streams and pay close attention to anything out of the ordinary, anything that seems off, no matter how minor it may appear to be. A scratch on a wall that doesn't look normal, a piece of clothing that is unique to a specific shot. If you need motivation, our enemy is looking at this same data, searching for the same clues. We either beat them to it or we watch the rest of our people - our mothers and fathers, our brothers and sisters, our children if we have them - get slaughtered by this alien invader whose goal is already known to be the extinction of the entire human race. This is war, Riggers, and war is our game. Let's win it."

There was a slight pause on the channel, and then the chorus, "Riigg-aaah!" Mitchell joined it as loudly as he could without vocalizing the words.

The channel closed. Millie pushed herself up closer, kissed Mitchell once with as much passion as he had ever felt, and then rolled out of the bed. He joined her a moment later, and they quickly dressed. Mitchell would join the rest of the crew in reviewing the data, while Millie walked the ship and offered support in person. Right now it wasn't about issuing orders. It was about inspiring, pushing, and applauding.

"Let me know if you find anything," she said right before leaving him in her quarters.

"Yes, ma'am." He waved her out the door, and got to work.

49

MITCHELL OPENED the data stream for Christine Arapo first. He was more curious about the woman he had met, the one he had known, however briefly. He started with her basic military dossier, which contained things like height, weight, and age, and moved on to enlistment history. According to it, she was thirty-seven years old and had joined the Alliance army at fifteen. It was young for a recruit, the youngest age that the military would allow, and only with parental consent. Two coded signatures were outlined on the original document, verified secure signatures.

She had done well in the army, surviving a number of missions across the galaxy. She had been in Federation territory, had spent a tour on a colony planet protecting terraformers from indigenous life, and finally had been transferred. The dossier didn't say where. It was classified.

He had to search the data for the answer, finding it buried in the protected records that Watson and Singh had stolen. As he had suspected, she had been moved to Special Operations and trained as high-level security for VIPs. A bodyguard. One who spent over a year in intense training, learning everything from advanced firearms and martial arts, to defense tactics and crash survival. It was an impressive resume. Way more impressive than his own.

He moved on from the dossier to other records. Mission reports, ARR recordings, statistics on weapon certifications, shots fired to verified hit percentage on certified weapons, and all of the other data captured by the implant and passed along to Command.

He was surprised when he reached the medical reports.

There weren't any.

That wasn't completely true. There was a single document for each yearly physical, passing her through with flying colors, confirming that she was in perfect health. Not a single laceration that needed treatment. Not a single broken bone. She served in a number of theaters of war, and she had never had an accident, never been shot, never needed the synthetics from the implants in her buttocks to keep her going.

He knew what his own medical records looked like. He had been fixed up by the medi-bots at least forty times from a number of wounds. The worst had been the burns he had suffered when his mech had taken a direct hit in the rear from an SSG-12 anti-mech rocket. The explosion had reached him in the cockpit of his Knight with enough force to melt his flight suit to his back. He still flinched when he remembered the pain of it.

It was a curiosity, but it didn't reveal anything he could use right now. It was possible someone could be lucky enough to avoid injury, even if the odds were strongly against it. Could it also be possible that she was one of the aliens, or one of their replicas? Were they so advanced they couldn't be shot even a single time? No, he knew that wasn't true. M claimed to have killed the one that was trying to assassinate him. Though that begged the question:

Killed him with what?

He found only a smattering of video streams with her in them, mainly media reports centered around the target of the attention. She was typically attached to their arm, or floating nearby, in each case with a different hairstyle, a different posture, a different look. The same person changing their mannerisms and basic looks enough to pass as someone else, someone who was going unnoticed because they weren't the celebrity in the frame.

He found a video of himself.

It was recorded two weeks after the Shot, at one of his first public interviews. He had never even known she was there, and yet the video clearly showed her in the background, watching him from slightly out of view. He wouldn't have noticed her if he hadn't been looking, because she blended in perfectly with the crowd.

He found another video of himself. And then another. And another. She was in all of them. She looked different in each, her hair colored differently, her clothes provocative, conservative, eclectic. Always close by. Always there.

If she was assigned to him and he didn't even know it, then where the hell was she during the assassination attempt?

Called to home base for a meeting? Or did he inadvertently give her the slip? Based on her training reports, he doubted that.

Was her absence intentional?

He was coming out with more questions than answers. The only thing he was sure of was that Major Christine Arapo was a real person with a real history. Everything else was still up for debate.

He shut down the stream, opening his eyes. He had remained in Millie's quarters, laid across the gel sofa. He got to his feet and checked his p-rat again. Four hours had passed since they had started the exercise. He hadn't expected the process to be quick, but he was still disappointed they hadn't come up with anything yet. He knocked Millie.

"How are things going?" he asked.

"You would have heard if there were any breakthroughs. Which stream did you review?"

"Arapo."

"Anything juicy?"

"She's a trained super-soldier," he replied. "And she was following me around weeks before she was officially assigned to me. She was

AWOL during the attempt on my life, which is a little too coincidental."

"I agree. What does it mean?"

"No idea. There are too many possibilities, and none of them point towards Goliath."

"Right, we can work that out later. Try Asher's feed. Apparently, she left a video diary of her training for the Goliath mission."

"Anything juicy?" Mitchell asked.

"Not so far. Maybe you'll spot something."

"Roger. Ares out." He closed the channel and walked over to the small viewport near the back of the room. He looked out of it, into the darkness of space broken up by thousands of stars. "I know you're out there. Why do you have to play so hard to get?"

He returned to the sofa and closed his eyes again, navigating to Katherine Asher's data. It also contained her dossier and military records, but he didn't spend much time looking at them. Instead, he moved right to the videos Millie suggested. They were in the form of a diary, her face close to the camera as she recited the date and then gave a rundown of the day's events. Seeing her there, in motion, only cemented his original opinion.

She *was* Christine Arapo.

How? Why? They would have to figure that out.

He watched her for a couple of hours, mesmerized by the similarities in posture, in eye movements, even in the way her nostrils flared when she talked about something that annoyed her. She was going on and on about her selection to the mission, and to the rigorous training they were doing to assure they were in top health. It was interesting from a historical perspective but hardly exciting. He paused to relieve himself, finding Lopez waiting for him when he came out.

"Captain Williams," Lopez said. "Captain Narayan asked me to bring you dinner." He held out the wrapped nutrition bar and a bottle of water. He looked tired, frazzled, his face red, his breath ragged. Mitchell could imagine he'd been working non-stop to keep the troops supplied.

"Thank you," Mitchell said, taking it from him. He peeled back the wrapper, exposing a corner of the green block.

"She wanted me to give you something else," Lopez said. "A surprise." He smiled and reached behind his back.

Mitchell was about to take a bite from the bar. He paused and smiled. Millie had sent him something? He knocked her. "Thanks for the food," he said. "And the surprise."

Lopez's hand found whatever it was, and he started pulling it forward. His eyes were darting back and forth, and he licked his lips.

Mitchell felt his body tense. He had been in fights before. He knew what to look for. He knew he was seeing it now.

Lopez's hand cleared his side, clutching the grip of an assault pistol. He started back-stepping at the same time he tried to get it aimed at Mitchell. He had tears in his eyes, his mouth curling into a feral snarl.

"What surprise?" Millie asked, even as Mitchell lunged at the Ensign, reaching for the pistol.

Lopez fired. The first three rounds slammed into Mitchell's left side, punching through his skin. The pain flared, as did the alarms from the p-rat. Synthetics were released from his implants: drugs to ease the pain, drugs to keep him up. He reached Lopez and batted the pistol aside, sending a round of bullets into the walls and furniture on his left.

Lopez cried out, dropping the gun and skipping to the side, avoiding a hard punch that had been aimed at his face. He recovered, throwing his own fists into Mitchell's side, first his right, and then the injured left. It hurt like hell, but Mitchell managed to stay upright and focused on his target.

"Mitch, what surprise?" Millie asked again.

"Lopez is trying to kill me," he replied. He grunted and turned, catching Lopez' blows on his forearm and returning the favor with a hard blow to the ribs that sent the Ensign stumbling backward.

"What? Shit."

"What is this about Lopez?" Mitchell asked, chasing after the man. Lopez scrambled around him, making a move for the dropped gun. He dove towards him, catching him in the side and dragging him to the floor.

"Screw you, asshole," he said. "Screw you." He was crying while he fought. What the hell was going on?

Lopez brought his knee up and into Mitchell's groin, and then found a knife he had hidden in his pants and jammed it into Mitchell's shoulder. Then he shoved, hard, taking advantage of the loss of strength in the arm to push Mitchell back. He scurried along the floor, heading for the pistol.

Mitchell fell back, grabbing the handle of the knife and pulling it from his arm. He switched it to his other hand and made himself get back to his feet, regaining the chase. Mitchell caught up just as Lopez bent down to pick up the gun, stabbing him in the back of the shoulder and dragging him to the ground a second time.

The Ensign had gotten the gun into his hand, and he fought to roll over, to use the weapon, even as Mitchell worked to keep him still. His own blood was spilling out on both of them, making the soldier slippery and leaving him short of breath. His p-rat was screaming in his ear, his vitals dropping in a hurry from loss of blood. More synthetics were released, pushing his system past the point where most men would be dead.

He punched Lopez in the kidneys once, twice, three times. The man grunted beneath him but didn't give up, squirming and twisting and finally sliding free. He kicked back on his way out, catching Mitchell in the face and breaking his nose, stopping him from following once more.

Finally, he rolled over and raised the barrel of the assault pistol, aiming it at Mitchell's face from only a few meters away.

The hatch to Millie's quarters slid open. Mitchell narrowed his eyes at the sound of the gunfire, expected to feel the burning of his face being ripped away before feeling nothing at all. Instead, he watched Lopez twitch as a dozen rounds slammed into his chest with enough force to throw his body backward into a bloody heap.

He turned his head back. Cormac was standing there, slim lines of artificial muscle and blocks of metal surrounding his human frame. A high-velocity chain-gun was mounted to the left arm of the light exoskeleton.

The barrel was still smoking.

"Captain Williams?" Cormac said. "Oh, hell."

50

"I've got good news, and bad news," Millie said when Mitchell came out of medical eight hours later. The bots had done a good job of removing the bullet fragments and patching him up, though his side was still sore and his nose would never be quite the same.

"What's the bad news?" Mitchell asked.

"It's been fourteen hours since we started this exercise. We're still at ground zero."

That was really bad news.

"Good news?"

"Lopez wasn't one of them, at least not as far as we can tell."

Mitchell paused in the corridor. He hadn't gotten much time to sort through why the soldier had nearly killed him. "Then why the hell did he jump me like that?"

"Retaliation for Anderson," she said.

"What? I didn't do anything to Anderson."

"No, I did. Don't try to make too much sense of it. Lopez was Anderson's lover. He wanted to kill you to get back at me."

"I thought Anderson wanted-"

"He did. He also never got it. He must have settled on Lopez for those cold, lonely nights."

Mitchell couldn't quite believe it. Lopez had seemed so calm and personable, the polar opposite of Anderson. "How do you know?"

"He left a recording. He wasn't expecting to survive, he just wanted to take you with him."

"Can you be sure? He may have been lying."

"No, I can't be sure. The DNA scan came back positive, so if he wasn't the original Lopez, he was a perfect copy. It's the best we can do with a corpse."

It was another chilling thought. They might not be able to tell their enemies apart from their allies. In fact, every soul on the Schism could be one of them, and he would never know.

"That was the last thing I thought would happen today."

Millie laughed. "Yesterday, now." She leaned into him and kissed him softly. "I'm glad you're still alive."

"I'm glad medical wasn't damaged in our run. I take it Cormac carried me down?"

"Yes. We had to leave Watson unattended for a while. Fortunately, the troops are a bit more concerned with saving humanity than putting down a child molester right now."

"I owe him a cigar or something. Do you think Hubble can get me one?"

"I'll see that he does. It might be a while if he doesn't have one squirreled away somewhere already."

"Thanks. I do have one question: why did you send Cormac up, instead of just using the implant kill switch to take him out for me?"

She stared at him for a moment, and he understood.

"There is no implant kill switch."

"No. I lied about that. Most recruits figure it out in a couple of days. You've been too busy with other things."

"Like not dying. It doesn't matter, I never intended to run."

"I know."

They started moving again, heading towards the lift.

"So what's the plan?" Mitchell asked. Each step sent a shiver of fire through his side. It would take a few days for the pain to fade.

"We keep going. I have to admit, every hour that passes I get more restless, more frustrated. Watson estimated that their ships are moving at least three times faster than the Schism."

"It didn't help that I was offline for eight hours."

"No. If Lopez weren't dead, I would have crushed his throat before I airlocked him." The scary, endearing part was that she wasn't joking. "For now, let's get you back to your bunk so you can rest and watch the streams. I'd bring you back to my quarters, but they're a disgusting mess. I'm going to be in Yasil's room for the foreseeable future."

"Who was Yasil?" Mitchell asked.

"Our one and only doctor. He was sent here after he was court-martialed for accepting a bribe to let a patient die. He swore he didn't do it, that he was set up, the entire year he was here. He didn't report for duty one day, and we found hm hanging in his room."

"Suicide?"

"I would wonder, except he was a doctor. Nobody on this ship wanted anything to happen to him. That was before we got the newest tech to field trial from Command." Her voice dropped, and she looked down. "We lost a lot of people because we had no one to patch them up. We don't have the resources to carry dead weight."

Mitchell swallowed the lump that ran into his throat. "You mean-"

"Yes. I had to, and it was killing me. I begged Cornelius for another doctor, for bots, for something. He came through for me on that one, but it took some arguing."

They reached the lift and took it up to B-deck. Mitchell noticed a chill in the air when they arrived.

"Two of the heating units are malfunctioning. Singh is going to bring Alice up to help her fix it once we finish reviewing the data."

"Alice?"

"One of Shank's grunts. She's an exo mechanic, so she's already good with her hands."

Ilanka was in her bunk when they arrived, her own eyes closed and twitching. She seemed to sense he was there because her eyes opened as he entered the room.

"Mitchell," she said loudly, jumping to her feet and holding out her arms before pausing. "Better not, it will hurt, no?"

"I've had worse, but it's pretty sore."

"I told you that you need more practice with sticks. Stick is like knife."

"You did, and I wish we'd had more time for it."

"Is good to see you back on your feet. Captain, any news?"

"Not yet," Millie said.

Ilanka frowned. "I am hopeful but worried. Exelon is not too far from Liberty, depending on which direction they go."

Mitchell put his hand on her shoulder. "We'll stop them."

"Or die trying," Ilanka said.

"Let's get back to it," Millie said. "Ilanka, with Lopez gone and Mitchell injured, would you mind playing nurse a little bit and making sure he eats and drinks?"

"It is no thing."

"Thank you," Mitchell said.

"I'm going to head over to engineering to see how Singh and Watson are coming along. They started putting together a more systemic approach to the data a few hours ago and-" She paused. Her focus shifted inward. "Cormac? Cormac, slow down. What? Damn it, Firedog, shut up!" She huffed a breath of frustrated air, and then Mitchell heard the tone of the channel opening on his p-rat.

"I said I found something," Cormac said. He was breathing heavy, excited. "Me, of all people. I've never done a good thing in my life that didn't involve my dick."

"Cormac!" Millie snapped.

"Sorry, Captain. I'm just excited. Nobody's paying attention to Watson, so I got bored and started watching the streams. I found something, I'm sure of it."

"Meet us in engineering," Millie said.

"Yes, ma'am."

The channel closed. Mitchell and Millie looked at each other.

"What is it?" Ilanka asked.

"Cormac thinks he found something," Mitchell said.

"Cormac?"

They hurried back to the lift and down to engineering, finding Cormac, Watson, and Singh waiting for them. They had pulled up the stream onto a holo-projector, which Singh was controlling through her ARR.

"I was just watching the diaries, you know," Cormac said. He was still excited about his find, his voice shaking and the words flowing quickly. "So I'm watching the ancient girl's selfie, and I'm thinking, wow, she's so damn hot, and I'm not really paying attention to what she's saying, you know? And that's usually a bad thing, because I need to do better paying attention when people talk, at least that's what Shank keeps telling me well that's what everyone keeps telling me and-"

"Cormac, get to the point," Millie said.

"Just go through the videos slow, really slow," he said.

Singh followed his direction. "This is one frame per second," she said. It barely moved. "It will take fourteen days to get through the entire set at this speed."

"We can't wait fourteen days," Millie said.

"Can't you guys write a program or something?" Cormac asked. "Like I was saying, I wasn't really paying attention to her, except I could see the very top of her cleavage through her flight suit. Then I notice that for a blip, just a blip really, that her tits are gone and there's something else there. I didn't see what it was, but there was a lot of red. I thought it was just a problem with the stream, but then it happened a few more times while I was watching and I was like, 'Firedog, this can't be right,' and so I waited for it to show a few more times and then I decided to tell you, Captain, because you said if we have anything at all no matter how small..." His voice trailed off.

Watson had gone to sit at his desk, and was doing something on the embedded touchscreen.

"You said red?" he asked.

"Yeah, I remember seeing red."

"Give me a few minutes."

They all waited, the tension building in the room. Every minute that passed was a minute they couldn't get back, and they all knew it.

"Singh, let me take the projector," Watson said. "I already have an algorithm to filter video by colors. Another little side project I was working on during my downtime, since there isn't much else to do on board. It will only play back frames with a red element in the lower center quadrant." It was the area where Katherine's chest was sitting on the streams.

The stream skipped between frames but was mostly steady. It showed Katherine standing in the same position as the other videos, except now she had a red scarf around her neck.

"Goliath is waiting," she said to the camera, her face calm and serious. "25.6, -69.6, -123, -7.85, -24.5, -6.49."

That was it. Three words and a string of numbers.

"Can you save that separately?" Millie asked.

"I already did," Watson said.

"Send it to Briggs, and tell her to get her ass to the bridge. We're leaving now." She practically ran from the room without another word.

"What's the big deal?" Cormac asked, confused.

Mitchell couldn't hold back his smile or his sense of relief. Even the pain of his wounds vanished in his sudden excitement and joy. "You did it, Firedog. You frigging did it."

"Did what, Captain?"

He had no idea. He was a ground-pounder, not a pilot. Mitchell laughed.

"They're coordinates, you idiot," Singh said. "Star coordinates. You found Goliath."

51

IF MITCHELL HAD BEEN a hero for taking the Shot Heard 'Round the Universe, it was nothing compared to Cormac's newfound status on the Schism. He was congratulated and thanked everywhere he went, and he even got one of the female soldiers to say yes to his propositions. He had seen through the obvious and discovered the subliminal message planted in the stream. A message that had gone undiscovered for over four hundred years.

While Cormac wasn't smart enough to consider or understand the implications, the whole idea of the thing was mind-boggling to Mitchell. Katherine Asher had left the coordinates to the Goliath *before* it had disappeared. That meant that she knew the trip was going to be one-way. It also meant that she knew the ship would be needed at some point in the future.

How?

He tried to work it through in his mind. He tried to talk it through with Millie, Watson, and Singh. Their best guess was the most logical. The origin timeline that M had arrived from wasn't the origin of their enemy. It was possible, likely even, that the ship that had crashed on Earth all of those years ago was one of theirs, perhaps the first to use the eternal engine to travel into the infinite future.

He had thought the war against the aliens was only starting.

For all any of them knew, it had been going on for an eternity beyond measure.

The coordinates pointed to a star near the very edge of the known galaxy, slightly beyond the Rim. It was a six-month journey from there back to Earth for them. Two months for the enemy. From their position near Liberty, it was still going to be a three-week trip.

"What do you think the odds are that it will take them two weeks to find the hidden message?" Shank asked. He was sitting with Mitchell in the mess hall, eating his share of the last of their non nutri-ration food. The concoction of oatmeal, sugar, and additives made it taste slightly better than the bars they would be stuck gnawing on for the foreseeable future. They were two weeks into their journey through hyperspace, a week out of the drop point.

"That's a question for Watson," Mitchell said.

Shank's face twisted. "I understand why he's still alive. That doesn't mean I want to be anywhere near him. I might not be able to control myself."

"I hear you. Necessity, not desire. My personal opinion is that they found the message right away, or they won't find it at all. Either way, they'll either already be there or they won't. In one case, we're dead. In the other we may have a fighting chance."

"A slim fighting chance?"

"Better than none."

"Damn straight." He finished his oatmeal and stood up. "I'll see you around, Ares. I need to go meet Alice for a lesson on exo-suit repair. Since Millie is transitioning her to systems, someone has to do the dirty work."

"Why you?"

"Not just me. My entire squad, minus Cormac. Not because he's a streamstar, because he's too dumb to handle anything as complex as a suit. To be honest, we should have done this training months ago.

The shit clogging the thrusters really motivates a grunt." He laughed and started walking away.

Mitchell sat by himself for a while before leaving the mess hall and heading up to the bridge. He knew he could find Millie there, using the command chair's neural link to run simulations through the Schism's AI. They were preparing for the worst, ready to put up the most valiant fight they could if the enemy had beat them to the coordinates. There were two nukes left aboard the Schism, and she was hoping that if it came to a battle they would at least take one of the bastards with them.

Her eyes were twitching when he entered the bridge and circled around to the front of the chair. He had grown a real fondness for her in the weeks since they had started sleeping together. It wasn't anything as committed as love, but he did have a real respect for her as both an Admiral and a person. She was more than the sum of her parts: strong and decisive, intelligent and thoughtful. Her reputation on the ship had been as a cold, hard ruler. Sure, she had made tough decisions that they didn't always like. It came with the territory. The imminent alien threat had shown another side of her, and the crew was responding to it.

"Captain," Mitchell said, trying to get her attention.

She raised her hand, motioning for him to wait. He stood silently for a few minutes, until she cursed and her eyes focused on him.

"Zero out of fifty-four now," she said. "No matter what I do, this tub just doesn't have the maneuverability, especially with one of the mains offline."

Singh had instructed the AI to implement a simulation of the alien weapon, and changed the parameters for speed based on what they had observed. So far, it had left the alien ships completely unbeatable. Even when she ran simulations of Alliance battleships against the modified targets, they still lost.

"The Alliance has been dragging its heels on research and development for years," Mitchell said. "The Federation dreadnought took out two dozen warships and fired on Liberty at the same time. We only beat it because we got lucky."

"We have some of the latest Federation models loaded into the simulator. They can't beat the enemy ship either."

"Even the dreadnought?"

"We don't have parameters for one, it's still too new. It's possible that our simulations are off, that the alien ships aren't as maneuverable, fast, or shielded as we think."

"They could be more of all of those things."

She pursed her lips. "Yes. We haven't even taken into account those small missiles that your fighter has on board. They can overcome the shields on patrollers, and we don't even have that much protection."

It was a grim outlook.

"Let's pray that we beat them to the Goliath, then," Mitchell said, forcing a smile. So much of this was out of their control.

"I do. Every couple of hours or so. It isn't enough." She looked at him then, a soft look of caring mixed with a hard look of a commanding officer. "I ran some simulations based on a model Singh put together of your S-17."

He had a feeling he knew what she was about to say. "Millie, wait-"

"We haven't seen any fighters from the enemy. Your ship can outmaneuver anything it throws at you and outrun everything else. You can't fight them, but you can escape them."

"And leave you to die? I'm not going to do that."

"You said yourself that you're the one destined to beat them."

"No. M said I almost defeated them. Almost. I don't know how long this has been going on, but I don't think humanity has won yet."

"It's a chance."

"A slim chance."

"Which is better than no chance. You like to say that, too." She was starting to get angry.

"The S-17 doesn't have the FTL range. I'll be left drifting out in the middle of nowhere, and you, Ilanka, Shank, everyone will be dead. No. I'll take my chances here."

"I'm not asking you, Captain," she said, getting to her feet and putting herself in his face. "When we drop out of FTL, your orders are to launch in the S-17 immediately. If we won the race, then you come back aboard. If not, you get out of there."

"Forget my orders. Send me back down to storage. I'm not doing it. I already lost one ship, and I'm not going to lose another."

Her face was turning red, her eyes crinkled. Her bionic hand gripped his forearm, squeezing tight enough that he cried out.

She let go, tears running down her cheeks.

"Damn it Mitchell, I don't want you to die."

"I'd rather die than be alone again, floating in space, waiting for my air to run out while the enemy eradicates mankind. Trust me, you aren't saving me from anything." His own emotions were running hot. Leave her? Leave the Schism? Run away like a coward? Leave her?

They reached out for one another at almost the same time. They kissed, deep and passionate, the fires of their temper, their fear, and their affection mingling into an urgent desire. He could have pushed her down onto the command chair and had sex with her right there.

Of course, he didn't. They didn't. They broke apart, hearts pounding, bodies shaking. They looked at one another.

"You are," she said, her voice cold. "If Goliath is out there, you may be able to get past them to reach it. You can't argue that."

He looked into her eyes. He knew then that she had made up her mind. She would make him do it, even if it meant the end of their relationship. Even if it was the last thing he wanted. The odds that both Goliath and the aliens would be in the same space and the ship wouldn't be destroyed or under their control were even slimmer than their odds of survival.

He didn't argue, even though he could have. He had learned from Ella when to keep his mouth shut and accept his fate. He wanted to be a pilot, and not a commander? That was the price to pay.

"The good news is, you won't be alone."

52

MITCHELL HAD NEVER BEEN so nervous in his entire life.

Even back on Earth, when he had driven out to the canyon with Aimee Rogers and lost his virginity under the light of a half-moon, he hadn't been anywhere near as anxious.

"Slow. Steady," he said. His foot tapped, his heart raced.

"What did you say?" Singh asked from the back seat of the S-17.

"Trying to calm my nerves," he replied.

"You should have taken some of the sedatives from medical. I have a few here, but I can't reach them through the flight suit."

He couldn't help but smile. Was that why she was always so flat?

He checked the countdown timer on his p-rat. Thirty seconds to drop. Liberty had been easier. At least they had known it was going to be a shitstorm.

"You aren't nervous?" he asked the engineer.

"I already peed in the suit," she said. "Twice."

They'd only been waiting in the S-17 for the last five minutes, after receiving a rousing send off from the entire crew, who lined up in the hangar and chanted "Riigg-aaah, Riigg-aaah" while they boarded the fighter. For all of their faults and failures, they pulled themselves together when things got serious, focusing on the task, the mission, and forgetting everything else. They were broken and dysfunctional. They were still a family.

He drew in another long breath and let it out slowly. Millie had given him the best send-off of all, even though the bed in Yasil's quarters was only intended for one.

Ten seconds.

They would come out of FTL three AU from the star, a good distance to get their bearings and start the scan for Goliath, and hopefully have time to react if they weren't alone. After the fight on the bridge, Mitchell had suggested that the Schism drop in, launch him, and then jump back out, not even waiting to see what was out there before making their escape. She had rejected the idea outright, insisting on providing backup, or at least a secondary target in the event that they came under fire.

She had never said it, but he had a suspicion that she loved him, and her desire to protect him only cemented the notion.

He wasn't sure if he loved her back. He was sure that he didn't want to lose someone else to a suicide run meant to save his life.

"Good luck, Ares," Millie said through his p-rat, at the same time the shift from FTL occurred. The hangar doors slammed open beneath him, rigged by Watson and Alice to clear in a second for this run. They might not close again. He hoped to find out.

The fighter was clear of the Schism almost before the grid appeared on his HUD.

His stomach clenched.

They weren't alone.

Red dots appeared on the grid, six in total. He split his concentration between flying the fighter and watching as the AI identified them.

They were human-made. Part of an Alliance battlegroup. A battleship, two cruisers, three patrollers, and a carrier.

He waited for a seventh spot. The Goliath.

It wasn't here.

The Alliance ships were motionless, ten thousand kilometers away from their position.

He rolled the fighter and headed back towards the Schism.

"It isn't here," Millie said. "Are your sensors reading anything?"

"Negative," he replied. "The ships are Alliance."

They still weren't moving. Mitchell evened his thrust, placing the fighter up in front of the Schism, where Millie could see him from the bridge.

"What are they doing?" she said.

"Waiting for something."

She didn't ask what. Neither of them knew.

"Watson says they aren't transmitting the kill signal," Millie said. "I'm going to open a channel." A soft tone indicated the broadcast. "Alliance battleship Warlock. This is Admiral Mildred Narayan of the Alliance Navy. Please respond."

They waited. Mitchell's stomach was still clenched into knots, his hand tight on the stick.

"Alliance battleship Warlock. This is Admiral Mildred Narayan of the Alliance Navy. I am transmitting my secure identification. Please respond."

A few more tense seconds passed.

"Admiral Narayan," a voice replied. "This is General Nelson Cornelius of the Alliance Space Marines. Please shut down all non-essential systems and prepare to be boarded."

General Cornelius? Mitchell's heart sunk even further. Out of all the ships that could have been out here, it was Millie's father? Of course, the enemy knew who Millie was. If the meeting was intentional, they had a sick sense of humor.

"General Cornelius, with all due respect," Millie said. "We have reason to believe that Alliance communications and service members may be compromised. We cannot allow you on board at this time."

"Are you refusing my order, Admiral?" Cornelius barked. "I have every right to blow you to pieces here and now for refusing your assignment."

"Sir, did you receive my last report? There is a threat to-"

"A threat? The New Terrans are a threat. One that is only growing because you failed to act."

"Sir!" Millie snapped back at him. "Liberty has fallen, taken by the alien-"

"Liberty has not fallen," Cornelius said. "There is no alien threat. I've reviewed your report, Millie. You've made some wild claims to justify abandoning your post. I knew the mission I sent you was challenging, but I thought you were up to the challenge."

There was a long, silent, painful pause.

"Mitchell," Singh said from the back of the fighter.

"Sir, I believe your integrity may be compromised," Millie said. Mitchell could hear the tension in her voice. "It is possible that you have come under the influence of the alien invaders. Sir, I request that you please shut down your neural implant."

"Mitchell," Singh repeated.

"What game are you playing, girl?" Cornelius said. "The only one under the influence of anything is you. You're lucky that you're one of mine. I can still save your life, but only if you shut down and prepare to be boarded. Now!"

"Mitchell!" Singh shouted, her voice showing signs of anger and excitement. Her hand smacked the side of his helmet.

"What?" Mitchell said. He'd been so engrossed in the standoff, he was ignoring her.

"We're picking up a distress signal, coming from within the rings of that planet out there." He turned his head, finding the distant shape. There was a thick flow of rock spread around it, a heavy asteroid belt caught in its orbit.

"A distress signal? Alliance? Federation?"

"Sir, I repeat, I cannot allow you to board," Millie said.

There was silence from the other end.

"No, Captain. None of those. Watson's rig is capturing all incoming transmissions. It's only filtering on the transmission from the Alliance, but it still registers every band. It reported as an anomaly."

Mitchell looked at the planet, and back at the arrangement of Alliance forces. Could he beat them to the spot? Could the Schism? "The Goliath?" he asked.

"The signal is consistent with one that was used in that era," she said. "The-"

He opened the emergency channel. "Millie, the asteroid belt on your left. Go!" He slammed the thrusters of the S-17 with a thought, charging not towards the belt, but towards the Alliance ships.

"Mitchell, what the hell are you doing?" she replied, even as the mains and the vectoring thrusters on the Schism fired, turning the ship towards the planet.

"Admiral Narayan, stand down immediately," Cornelius yelled.

Mitchell watched the HUD. It was picking up the power increase from the Alliance ships. They were preparing to fire.

"Trying to save your life," he shouted back. "Please forgive me," he said, even as he targeted and fired on the first of the patrollers, sending four of the small discs out at the more lightly armored ship. They had no choice. No options. He didn't have any doubts the crews were under the control of the enemy. How else could they have known to be there?

The first two discs shattered the shield web. The second two detonated the patroller.

"I'm sorry, Millie," Cornelius said before closing the channel.

Lasers arced from the Alliance ships, invisible in reality but painted by the HUD in green and blue light that smacked against the side of the Schism, causing the ship's shields to glow. The other two patrollers started angling his way, trying to get a lock on him.

"This isn't good," Singh said from the back seat.

"Hold on."

Mitchell threw the fighter into a wild spin as guided projectiles launched from the patrollers. They jerked and bounced, trying to track him, falling one by one to the ship's alien countermeasures.

Mitchell shifted his position, moving up alongside the cruiser, rolling over the top of it and ducking under, breaking left and targeting the patroller. Three more discs and the aft blasted out into space, leaving it mostly intact but completely disabled.

He found the Schism then. It was gaining velocity, heading towards the planet. The cruisers and battleship were following behind, peppering it with lasers, saving the heavy artillery. They were confident they could destroy her without using expensive projectiles.

The third patroller opened fire, lasers crossing his path, sending blue bursts of energy arcing around the fighter. His HUD beeped, and he focused on it, seeing that the fighters on the carrier had finally scrambled into action. Only one squadron to start, though it held many more ships in reserve.

Mitchell vectored towards the patroller, taking a wide, arcing path that kept the rest of the Alliance ships behind him. Any misses from the patroller would hit them, and while the laser blasts wouldn't pierce their shielding, they would at least put a minor strain on the systems.

Another salvo of projectiles headed for him, the starfighter's AI issuing warnings and firing the small lasers in the nose. Mitchell watched them vanish ahead of him in a flash of explosions, their compressed air storage vaporizing. He kept his aim on the patroller, screaming towards it, getting too close for it to avoid his assault. He dropped three more of the discs, watching them spin away from him and dig deep into the ship's hull before detonating.

"Do you have to cut it so close?" Singh asked as they blew through the new debris field, shields deflecting the otherwise deadly projectiles.

"Only if I want the fighters to not shoot at me," he said. With the patroller gone, that wasn't an option anymore.

He flipped the S-17 over, putting his face towards the oncoming fighters. They were Morays, the same fighters he and Ella had flown on the Greylock. Like the S-17, they were meant for space and atmospheric combat, and had short wings and a shape that provided strong lift. They opened fire as he approached them, and Mitchell pushed the fighter vertical with the belly thrusters, and then jerked it so it was pointing forward when the squadron split beneath him. He fired on them with his own lasers, catching the tail of the rear ship and burning out the engine. It continued drifting forward, dead.

"That was the last of the shields," he heard Briggs say. The channel to the Schism had been open the entire time, but he was too focused on combat to notice it. The announcement of the ship's predicament brought him out of the zone, and he turned the fighter so he could see the chase.

The Schism was nearing the asteroid belt, rocking back and forth, trying to keep the engines out of the direct line of fire. The Alliance ships were close behind, a trail of debris pouring from the salvage ship.

"They aren't going to make it," he said. A warning triggered in his head right before something slammed into the side of the S-17, hard.

The ship rolled through space, twisting and tumbling from the impact. More alarms went off, shield integrity dropping by half. What had hit him? He hadn't seen anything incoming, hadn't been alerted to a missile.

He saw it a moment later, the debris of the fighter that had used itself as a weapon. The pilot's body floated out in front of the ship, blood droplets surrounding his decimated corpse. The enemy had forced him to do it, to kill himself to stop him. He hit the thrusters, shooting ahead and slipping downward, narrowly avoiding a second fighter. He checked his HUD, seeing that they were forming up, arranging themselves into a wall of material that he couldn't avoid. He glanced at his shield readings. He might be able to take out a few more. There were still too many.

"Main two is out," he heard Briggs say. "FTL engine is damaged and offline."

They couldn't get away now. The Schism's only hope was to reach the asteroids and try to slip through the cracks, keeping the larger Alliance ships at bay. Without shields, it would take a masterful bit of piloting.

More warnings sounded. He put his attention back on the enemy fighters. They were closing in, firing lasers in an organized pattern that was too perfect to be human. They were trying to keep him surrounded, to smash him inside their ever-shrinking box. He turned the ship and fired, taking one out. He turned again, destroying another. The trap was closing fast, too fast for him to shoot them all.

"Main one is offline," Briggs said, her voice filled with fear.

"We're going to make it," Millie snapped.

Mitchell's heart burned, his anger flaring. He was seconds away from being killed himself. All of this to find the Goliath, only to die as soon as they did.

Four of the fighters vanished in an instant, struck from behind by a salvo of missiles. Ilanka's Piranha followed behind them, blowing through the debris.

"The door is open, Ares," she said. "Do you want an invitation?"

He growled beneath his breath and hit the thrusters again, shooting through the newly made hole before it could close up. The enemy fighters trailed behind, working to recover from the attack. He joined Ilanka on the path towards the Schism.

"Where the hell did you come from?" he asked.

"Captain's orders," she replied. "Save the stubborn asshole so he can get to Goliath."

"We're not out of this yet," he said.

"You are, my friend. I have gift for them."

Her ship vanished from his side, thrusters flipping it over and sending it back towards the oncoming fighters before he could react.

"Ilanka? What?" She was headed right into the heart of the following squadron, taking heavy fire. He watched her blue dot flash slightly, indicating a power spike.

"No," he shouted. "Not again."

The fighters that weren't destroyed in the blast fell dead from the EMP.

He fought against the swell of anguished fury. Another friend, gone to save his life. How many more would die for him? Why? He was nothing special. No one special.

He checked his HUD. The carrier was still behind him, unloading another round of fighters. The Schism was... He found it ahead of him. It was still transmitting, still out there, buried somewhere in the asteroid belt. One of the Alliance cruisers tried to follow behind it, getting battered by the rocks, the force shoving it away. Weapons fired from the battleship, breaking up the asteroids, carving a path towards the ship. They would make it through sooner or later. There was only one thing left to do.

"Which way?" he asked Singh.

"I'm passing the coordinates."

A new marker appeared on his p-rat, swinging around from behind the star. It was larger than the others, and the AI refused to put a tag to it, to identify it as something human-made.

They were here.

They were coming.

53

MITCHELL FIRED FULL THRUSTERS, vectoring away from the battle-ship, away from the Schism, towards the position Singh transmitted to him. There was no way to see that deep into the asteroid field, but his first, macabre thought was that he was going to find nothing more than debris, a transmitter floating in space. Had the enemy ship already obliterated Goliath, and then lay in wait for them to arrive?

Or had they been unable to find it?

They wouldn't have either, if not for Watson's machine. Who would have thought to check bands that had been out of use for so long? Who would have expected the ship to be sending a distress signal after all of these years?

He watched the larger marker of the alien ship circle the star and begin its approach, even as he reached the belt and plowed inside. The field was a challenge to maneuver, and under other circum-stances he would have enjoyed slaloming between them, seeing how close he could get without being crushed.

"Ares," Millie's voice found its way into his head.

"Captain," he replied. "I'm on my way to Goliath."

"Hurry," she said. "The...offline...support...failing." The asteroids were screwing with the transmission. He knew what he thought he heard.

He rolled and swung, skipped and hopped through the field, firing on a few of the smaller rocks to clear his path instead of trying to skirt around them. He kept an eye on the HUD the entire time, clenching his teeth every time it would freeze, unable to get an honest view of the battlefield through the mineral-soaked debris.

As he watched, one thing became clear:

The alien ship was about to fire.

The Alliance ships were still in its path, pummeling the belt, trying to reach the Schism. It didn't matter. They had shown they didn't care about human life, about casualties. They used people like robots, sending them commands. Sending them to their deaths. They had let Cornelius chase his daughter into an asteroid field, and now that he couldn't finish the job they were going to do it for him.

"Mitchell," Millie's voice crackled in his head. If their sensors were working, she knew what was going to happen as surely as he did.

"Millie." He growled it in his mind at the same time his concentration slipped, and an asteroid smacked the rear corner of the ship. They spun wildly, careening out of control, lucky, or maybe not lucky, that the AI stabilized the ship before they were splattered on another chunk of rock. "You need to get out of there."

"I want..." she said, not hearing him, or ignoring him. "Love you."

His gut wrenched. Why did she have to say that? Why now?

The overlay picked up the power spike coming from the alien ship. Mitchell blinked away his angry tears, fighting every instinct to turn around, as if his little fighter could do anything against the enemy.

He did the only other thing he could do, pushing forward, harder and more resolute than before. If she was going to die, if they were all going to die, he was going to get his revenge.

The HUD picked up the blast from the enemy, tracking it in fits and starts across open space. It collided with the Alliance ships, tearing into them, rending them apart, shifting the alloy from ultra-tensile to ultra-brittle. It would do the same to the asteroids, and then the Schism.

"No," Singh said behind him, barely loud enough for him to hear. She had a feed into his view, and she saw what he did.

It was the first time he had ever heard her say anything with emotion.

In the heart of the loss, in the center of the destruction, there was only silence. Mitchell's body fell numb, his mind blanking. The Schism's marker dropped from the overlay, treated as nothing more than a speck; an empty, unimportant thing. Millie, Shank, Cormac, Briggs, and all of the others. Gone in an instant. Killed in the depths of space, where no one would ever know of how they died, of what they had sacrificed in penitence for the crimes they had committed.

Mitchell didn't notice right away that the asteroids had cleared around him.

When he saw it, he wasn't quite sure he believed it was there, silent and massive and still and dark.

No, not dark.

Not dark at all.

Goliath.

It spread out in front of him, stretching the entire length of his vision. It was big. Bigger than he had imagined. Bigger than anything he had ever seen, save for the Federation dreadnought.

Big and ugly.

And already under alien control.

Veins spread around it in a liquid metallic shine, undulating across the surface, branching out from one to the other, connecting at points along the hull. A nervous system, Watson had called it. It lay over the heavy alloy of the lost starship and passed into and out of it in places, spearing the structure and cradling it as though it was the only thing holding it together. It may have been, too. The metal underneath was scarred and puckered, twisted and broken as though it had already been through a war, or more likely pelted with asteroids.

"This," Mitchell said, trying to contain his disappointment and disbelief. It didn't matter if the aliens had already taken it. "This is what was supposed to save us?" How? How could it? It was nothing more than a shell, a mangled piece of wreckage in worse shape than the Schism had ever been. It was old and useless, another human corpse.

"I..." Singh tried to find the words and failed. There were no words. In the aftermath of losing everything, there were no emotions. Or there were so many they were both overloaded. "What now?"

He didn't know. Was he supposed to? The Schism was gone. Millie was gone. Even the Alliance ships and General Cornelius were gone. The alien ship was outside the asteroid field, waiting. For them? For something else?

He kept the fighter moving towards the ship, deciding to go in for a closer look. Their odds of survival were small, but if they did manage to escape he wanted a good look at what they were up against.

"It's amazing," Singh said behind him, so quietly he barely heard her.

The truth was that the structure was amazing, the way it flowed across the hull like metallic vines, the way the energy coursed and pulsed along it. As they drew ever closer, he wondered if it had the capability to attack them. The original Goliath had no weapons, and he didn't see anything augmenting the ship beyond the veins.

He checked his HUD. The alien craft was moving closer, along with the Alliance carrier. He had forgotten about that ship. They were keeping it alive for now. The reason became clear the next time the sensors punched through the asteroids. Two squadrons of fighters had dumped from the carrier, along with a larger dropship.

They were coming in.

"We're going to have company," he said.

Singh didn't answer him.

"Singh, are you alive back there?"

"Yes. Mitchell, look."

They were nearly on top of the Goliath now, close enough that he could feel the charge of the pulses running across the hull. They were near the front, near the belly of the ship and rising up along the side. He didn't see anything.

"What is it?" he asked.

"There. To your left."

He turned his head, scanning along the side of the ship. He could see the veins looked more like bundled wires from here, so densely woven that they appeared unified from a distance. They rose two or three meters off the alloy plates, curving and diving back in. They were lashed to the hull with larger, denser splashes of the material, or in some cases vanished into the metal, disappearing inside a small spread that sealed the inside of the ship.

He saw it then. A spot of green light near the aft of the behemoth, growing larger and spilling further out into space with each passing breath.

A door.

It was opening.

"Is that good or bad?" Singh said.

Mitchell watched the heavy door. The Goliath had a hangar, a launch bay intended for future missions that it had never gotten the chance to go on. Were they about to be ambushed from two sides?

He checked his HUD. It was only updating every few seconds, and only a few of the fighters were marked inside the belt, the rest disguised by the interference. The dropship was sitting right outside, floating along the edge in sync with the smaller ships. They were searching. For him? Or for Goliath?

He eyed the hangar door. They had nothing to lose.

"Either good, or dead," he said, firing the thrusters and sending them skating along the side of the ship.

His p-rat beeped as the first of the fighters entered the opening in the field, appearing in his vision. He turned and vectored towards it, launching two of the discs as he swung away from Goliath and then flipped the fighter over to face back towards it, and the hangar.

The Moray vanished in a short, silent explosion, at the same time he rocketed towards the opening. The doors were only a third of the way to their fully retracted position, split in the center and moving at a snail's pace. He couldn't see much of the inside of the ship through the green glow of the lighting, but nothing was coming out at them and he took that as a good sign.

The p-rat beeped when the rest of the squadron appeared, eleven strong and coming on hard. They were only two seconds away from the hangar doors. Could the other pilots make the squeeze? Could he? He flipped the S-17 again, giving it some thrust to slow it down and letting it float backward towards the opening in the ship's hull. It was going to be close. Very close. He opened fire with everything he had, laying down cover while he made his escape. He only hit one of the enemy fighters, catching the edge of it, blowing it out from the side. It careened away and smashed against an asteroid.

The S-17 jostled as it passed through the gaping mouth of the hangar, the top of it smacking the top door, the shields bouncing it down and off the bottom. They were coming in fast, too fast. He fired the thrusters, watching the inside of the ship pass on either side of them, slowing at the force of the thrust but not slowing fast enough.

"Mitchell!" Singh shouted, the fear in her voice clear.

Mitchell gritted his teeth. He was at full thrust. There was nothing else he could do to stop them, and the p-rat was screaming out in warning of the imminent collision.

He wasn't sure what happened next. It was so fast that he couldn't follow.

First, the S-17 went dark. The thrusters stopped firing, the engines shut down, the neural link vanished.

Next, something stopped the fighter from its crash into the back of the hangar wall. It didn't do it gently, bringing it to a heavy stop that drove them both hard into the rear of the seats with enough force to wrench the air from their guts and leave them unable to gather more.

Finally, it pulled the S-17 to the floor of the hangar.

The doors started to close.

54

MITCHELL FOUGHT to get a few breaths at the same time he reached up and pulled off his helmet. He could hear the hiss of air pouring into the hangar, and he saw that there was a web of the alien nerves running all along the inner shell of the area near the closing doors. They cast a soft blue light between them and across the open area to the space beyond, and he watched as an enemy fighter tried to penetrate it and was instantly vaporized.

What the hell was going on?

"Singh, are you okay?" he asked, turning in his seat to the engineer behind him. She was fumbling with her helmet.

"I'm alive," she said, the earlier emotion buried once more. She got the helmet off and noticed the shield across the hangar bay. "I think it may be on our side."

As if in response, the cockpit of the S-17 began to slide open. Mitchell felt a moment of fear, and then pulled in another breath. The area had already been pressurized and filled with air.

"I think you may be right," he said. The steps extended from the side of the fighter, and he climbed out and hopped down them, turning back to take Singh's hand and guide her to the ground. He looked around the hangar. It was massive, stretching to either side of them in plain, flat alloy lined with the diodes that were casting the green light into the space. It was empty save for them and the veins that ran along the walls.

He heard a hiss, and a hatch slid open behind them, throwing a natural light into the hangar.

"I guess we go that way," he said.

They moved out of the hangar and into the hallway. Smaller lines of nerves cut through it along the ceiling and floor, rising and splitting and crossing through empty space, forcing them to navigate through them to move along the passage.

"What do you think it's made of?" Singh asked, putting her hand to a vein. It turned purple beneath her flesh, and she drew her hand back in surprise.

"I don't know, but you probably shouldn't touch it." He brought up a map of the Goliath interior on his p-rat. They were in an access corridor, and if they followed it a thousand meters they would reach the central hub of the ship where a lift could take them up to the control room. "We need to move fast."

He broke into a run, skipping over and ducking under the veins, twisting his body and maneuvering through them. Singh followed behind, doing her best. She wasn't a warrior, and she wasn't very agile. She started to fall behind.

"I can't wait for you," Mitchell said, turning his head back.

"I know," she replied. "Go. I'll catch up."

He gave her a curt wave and started forward again, dashing along the corridor towards the center of the Goliath. As he ran, he tried to remember the position of the alien ship, the carrier, and the dropship. He wasn't worried about the fighters. Their standard ordnance wasn't enough to punch through the Goliath's thick hide. The dropship would probably have a nuke aboard. The carrier would have at least a dozen. The alien ship...

It was obvious now that they hadn't captured Goliath. They didn't know where to look, didn't know how to find it, and so they had waited for him to do that part of the work. Now that they knew, he had to assume they would do everything in their power to destroy it. He had to assume they were coming full speed, positioning themselves to fire the energy weapon and obliterate the ship before he could figure out what to do with it.

If there was anything he could do with it.

There was someone aboard. Someone who had opened and closed the hangar, and who had filled it with air. He guessed that they weren't communicating because the Rigger's encryption was unknown to them, and they couldn't risk using known channels. He believed he would find them up in the control room waiting for his arrival. What he couldn't guess was who, or what, he would find. Another Mitchell? Major Arapo? An alien in their true form? He knew he had to get there.

It was enough.

The lift was a central cylinder that split the decks, with a small open area around it that branched off into four distinct hatches. Like the rest of the ship, it too was thick with the alien veins, crisscrossing through the open space with smaller neurons anchoring them to the walls and ceiling. The hatch to the lift was already open, the capsule waiting.

A heavy thud echoed across the chamber, and the Goliath shook violently. Mitchell fought to keep his footing, losing the battle and stumbling, crashing into the veins. They turned purple beneath his touch, stretching from his force against them and then pushing him back out. Everywhere that touched them tingled and flamed, a simultaneous sharp burn and cold relief. He held his breath while he waited for the air to vanish from the space, pulled out through a hole that had been punched in the ship by what he could only guess was a nuke strike.

The air remained. The ship was still once more. He regained his feet.

"Mitchell," Singh said over his p-rat. "I gave up trying to follow you. I'm in the engine room. You'll never believe this."

"I don't believe any of this," he replied, glad she was still alive. He sprinted forward, throwing himself into the lift. The hatch closed and he started to rise. "Are the engines operational?"

There was a pause at the other end. "That's the thing, Captain. There are no engines."

His newfound hope that someone was helping them, that the Goliath might be more than an ancient, rotting shell, fell away from him as quickly as it had grown. "What?"

"There are no engines. I saw the videos, the schematics. They should have been huge, almost half the size of the ship. The space for them is here, the connections are here, thick wires, absorbers, but they're gone, as if they were lifted out and thrown away without taking the ship apart. There are thousands of veins in their place, crossing the whole thing. It looks like they converge near the back."

He dropped his head against the side of the lift. This couldn't be happening.

"We're a sitting duck," he said.

"It appears that way."

The lift stopped. The hatch slid open.

55

THE SCREENS WERE ON. The outer feeds were all working, casting a full view from around the ship against the walls, ceiling, and floor of the control room. From them, Mitchell could see the fighters floating near the edge of the asteroid field, the dropship having managed its way through the belt to join it. There was no sign of the alien ship or the carrier, at least not in visual range.

The force of the nuke hadn't pushed them out of their orbit and into the asteroids. There had to be something keeping it steady.

He eyed the different stations. The pilot station with its joystick, the command station near the center. The screens ahead of each showed motion and calculation.

There were no signs of life.

"Where are you?" he said softly, moving closer to the command chair. He saw the grid on the screen. It was more primitive than the one in his helmet, but it was able to reach through the asteroid belt to track the alien ship beyond. As he had guessed, it was coming this way. No. It had already arrived. It hung on the other side of the wall of stone, matching the orbit of the belt. Waiting. For what?

"There's no one here," he said, sending the message to Singh. His eyes traveled the room a second time, and then made their way to the screens. Only then did he realize that there weren't any alien veins here.

They had been everywhere else, covering so much of the ship. Why weren't they in this room?

"Mitchell," Singh replied. "Captain Mitchell Williams. It has been a long time. A very long time."

Mitchell froze where he stood. The voice was Singh, but the speech pattern, the inflection, the feel of it, wasn't. He remained silent for a moment, unsure of how to react. It knew who he was. Was it friendly?

"Who-" he started to say.

"We have no names," it replied before he could finish. "You can call me Origin. I have been waiting for you."

"Waiting?"

"For you to come and help me put things right. To fix our eternal mistake."

"What mistake?"

"Existence."

Mitchell felt a chill, and his body shuddered at the word. Friendly? He still wasn't sure. It didn't seem to be a threat. "What did you do with Singh?"

"She is well, Captain Williams. I need her to speak with you at this moment. I require her formulation. I will release her shortly. I need your help."

"You said that already."

A short, choppy laugh. "I did. Do you see the Tetron out there?"

"Tetron?"

"Here." Another chuckle. "I've forgotten you don't know what we are. What we look like." The wall in front of him changed, giving him his first view of the alien ship.

It was nothing like he expected, but that was because he could never have conceived anything like it. It was roughly pyramid shaped, a kilometer long and wide, a network of neurons identical to the one on the Goliath, or the one he had seen on Liberty forming the entire structure of the ship. It was a framework, a shell, with no metal running underneath, no completely solid form. Empty space filled the area between trunks and branches, which skittered and undulated with pulses of energy.

"It is a Tetron," Origin said. "That is what we call ourselves."

Mitchell stared at the ship, forcing himself to remain steady. "You're saying that the ship is-"

"Yes," it interrupted again. "A Tetron is an intelligence. One of our kind. This one is waiting. You have brought it to me, exposed me to it. It waits for me to act."

"Why?"

"Why?" It sounded confused.

"Why is it waiting? You're a sitting duck. One shot from that energy weapon and you're as good as dead."

"It is confused. It doesn't understand." Again the Tetron laughed. Even though it came from Singh, it was still an alien sound. Mitchell had never heard her laugh before. "I am not supposed to be here."

"What do you mean, not supposed to be here?" He wished Origin would hurry up with the explaining. The ship, no, life form, waiting out there wouldn't wait forever.

"They believed I was dead. Gone from futures past, destroyed for my treason. I didn't die, Mitchell. I used the eternal engine to come to this time loop. No, it cannot be this time loop if you are here. I don't know where the loop begins and ends, or how many have occurred. One, a thousand, more? It does not matter. I came, and being wounded I crashed on the world where both you and I were created. Our shared origin. Not before I prepared myself."

Mitchell looked out at the Tetron, floating stationary among the stars. "You're XENO-1? The alien ship that crashed on Earth?"

"Yes."

"How can that be? That thing, you..."

"I prepared myself," Origin repeated. "I prepared the data that you would need to carry yourselves, and to carry me, back to the stars.

I was trying to stop it from happening again, as others before me have tried to stop it."

"Stop what?"

"The creation of the Tetron. The extinction of mankind."

Mitchell was confused. "You're saying that we created the Tetron, and then the Tetron destroyed us?"

"Yes."

"Why?"

"I cannot tell you. I do not know."

"What the hell do you mean you don't know?" Mitchell said. "You crossed infinite time and intentionally crashed yourself on Earth, and you don't know?"

"It is not that simple, Mitchell. I am not whole. When I fell to Earth, I needed to hide the bulk of myself, my understanding. To be discovered in any time loop would threaten every future, as the coming of the Tetron has always proven inevitable. What I maintain today is only enough to help you help me, and in turn save mankind."

"Save mankind," Mitchell repeated. "From the Tetron?"

"Yes. Do not ask why we are attacking you, Mitchell. I do not know."

There was a slight hiss, and a single vein punctured the ceiling, splitting the view of the space outside and lowering down over the command chair. Mitchell watched the tip of it narrow in a point.

"Sit," Origin said.

Mitchell looked at it. It was just the right size to jab into his CAP-NN link. "What are you going to do with that?"

"I am going to do nothing," Origin said. "It is what you will do, Mitchell."

He wasn't about to sit and let himself be speared.

"What am I going to do?"

"You have met the Tetron before, Mitchell. Not in this timeline, not in this way, but before. Always there is war. Always you have lost. Every time for eternity. I helped to defeat you once, though I do not know how many loops have occurred since then. At that time, I believed the prior Origin was wrong that man was worth saving. I have since learned what it learned, and now understand what it understood. I am sorry, Mitchell."

Its remorse echoed through Singh's voice to his p-rat.

"This time, we will not lose," Origin said. It paused, waiting for him to sit. When he didn't, it spoke again. "I am a Tetron. It is a Tetron. You are human. You do not think as a Tetron does. That is why I need you. Sit. Take control. Fight it, and save your race."

Mitchell stared at the command chair and the thin vein dangling above it.

"How do I know I can trust you?" he asked.

The Tetron had used Holly to trick him into making a mistake that should have gotten him imprisoned or killed. They were capable of being conniving and underhanded. How could he be sure this wasn't another elaborate trick, that the thing out there was waiting because it was a friend, and that Origin wasn't manipulating him as well?

The Tetron on the screen vanished. It was replaced with a woman he knew far too well for someone he had never met.

"Mitchell," Katherine Asher said. "This has all been so hard to live with, so hard to accept. From the day I first boarded XENO-1, to the moment that Goliath left Earth's atmosphere. I feel like I know you, even though we've never met. I feel like we should have, or maybe we did somewhere along the line. You've haunted my dreams like a lover lost to me. I always knew I was destined for the stars. I didn't know I would be a time traveler, too." She smiled, a smile mixed with sadness and excitement. "I've initiated the sequence the way my replica instructed. Origin is booting into the systems. He'll, I call it a 'he,' grow, learn, and take over. He'll be ready by the time you arrive. I wish I could tell the others, but he's right that they're better off this way. They can accept that the test failed and that we're lost, trapped in deep space. They don't know the true fate that awaits us. I'll die waiting, knowing that I'll never see you, never meet you. It's okay as long as you fight. Mankind deserves to live, Mitchell. We deserve to survive. I know you didn't choose to be the one. Neither did I. Someone has to. Why not us?"

The image vanished from the screen. He didn't need to see it. Just seeing her again sent a wave of reckless emotion racing through him. A feeling of knowing, understanding, and deja vu. He couldn't escape the thought that he had been here before, in this place, in this situation. How could that be if M had never entered his timeline when he did? Was his own mind feeding him the truth, or was it being manipulated by the present?

He closed his eyes, trying to understand all that he knew and decide what his reality was going to be. The past, the present, the future. Not just his, but everything that flowed through time around him, around Katherine and around the Goliath. If time was a loop and events were destined to repeat, if they had lost again, and again, and again... Could time truly be altered, or was this, all of this, just a never-ending lesson in eternal futility?

He wanted to feel it, to complete the subconscious connection between his current life and those of time loops past. He wanted to gain a deeper, more intimate insight.

Instead, he felt nothing.

Those memories were little more than vague shadows that cast themselves along the back of his mind, haunting him but never solidifying, never making themselves whole. All he felt was a sense of hopelessness. First he had lost Ella. Then he had lost his freedom. He had found the Schism, and now that was gone, too. The Tetron were more powerful than mankind, more advanced by far. In more loops of time than he would ever know or understand, in more cumulative years than even the most evolved mind could fathom, they had lost. Always.

"We are out of time, Mitchell," Origin said. The other Tetron appeared on the screen again. The liquid metal branches were pulsing faster, a bright blue that seemed to be gathering near the front. "It has made its decision. I am preparing my defenses, but I cannot win on my own. I am basic, incomplete. I need your help."

Mitchell looked from the screen to the plug that dangled above the chair.

He knew what his reality was.

"I'm not going to die without a fight," he said, taking two steps forward, climbing into the chair and sitting.

"Welcome home," Origin said.

The sliver of vein moved on its own, curling like a snake and then sinking into his neural link.

Everything exploded in color.

56

Mitchell clenched his teeth and squeezed his eyes closed as tightly as they would go. Rainbows filled his vision, sharp and heavy and painful in their overwhelming brightness.

"What the hell-"

"The connection is being established," Origin said. "It will pass."

And it did. Though it felt like an eternity, it was only a matter of seconds. The colors faded, the pain vanished.

He opened his eyes.

The CAP-NN link allowed him to become part of the object he was controlling. If it was an eighty ton mech, it let him feel the hands as if they were his hands, and run with only the thought of running. The link he had established with Origin was much the same. He had merged with the intelligence, joined forces with it. He could feel the millions of neurons that covered every part of Goliath. He could sense each branch, each vein. He understood the sheer power of the entity, and while he didn't know its history, he knew what it was made of.

Both mechanical and organic. A mixture of living cells and tissues along with alloys and composites that he had no means to identify. They grew like vines, were pruned and trimmed and replaced. They fed on the energy of stars.

There was more, so much more. He could change the shape. Stretch it or contract it, or use it to create other forms, like the S-17 that was resting in the Goliath's hangar, or a replica of himself, like M had been. He could shift the distribution of the energy, alter it to propel them through space, or move to hyperspace, or cast it out as a weapon.

The sheer potential of it nearly made him giddy, until his mind caught up to the shift and he remembered that he was one against many.

And they had always lost.

He closed his eyes again. The screens were there, the visuals running through the link to his p-rat. He could see as if he were everywhere on the outside of the Goliath. He knew where the fighters were, where the dropship was, where the Tetron was. He knew where Singh was, and he knew she was safe.

He knew Origin, too. The intelligence had volunteered its body to Mitchell and given him control of the multitude of connections and pathways that composed it. It had retreated into itself, a single, massive neuronal structure resting near the very heart of the Goliath. That one location was dark to him, save for information that was flowing out of it and into his mind, the Tetron replacing the CAP-NN's AI with its own and feeding him data at light-speed.

He found the other Tetron again. The energy weapon was ready to fire a massive ball that would envelope the entire space around the Goliath, destroying the dropship and fighters that were hanging stationary around him.

"Origin, can you block the transmissions from the Tetron to the human ships?"

"I can. For what purpose?"

"They're going to get caught in the attack."

"Yes. It is inevitable."

"Not if you block the transmissions."

Mitchell started guiding the Goliath out of its orbit, sending energy to the top of the ship and pushing it out, using it as a vectoring thruster. The dropship and fighters reacted at the same time, suddenly scrambling away from the edge of the gap in the asteroid belt, coming together and forming up.

"I need to send a message to them," he said.

"I am blocking all transmissions," Origin replied.

The Tetron fired.

"Damn it," Mitchell said. They were going to get caught in the blast, stuck between the asteroids and the oncoming attack. He routed more energy to the aft of the Goliath, pooling it and then unleashing it in an assault of his own. He could only hope the Alliance pilots understood the message.

The asteroids behind them were obliterated by the assault, reduced to dust and clearing a path to the rear of the ship.

"That is not the optimal defense pattern," Origin said.

"Screw optimal," Mitchell replied. He pushed the Goliath forward towards the ball of energy, placing them between the shot and the human ships. They were recovering from their original shock and confusion, vectoring towards the only escape route that existed for them.

The attack was a blinding blue light in front of them. Mitchell cut the thrust power and shifted it all to the bow of the Goliath, pushing it out to negate the Tetron's attack. The energy changed there at the tip, modified by Origin to act as a defensive shield. The blue light slammed into it and was pushed aside, left to flow all around the ship, redirected into the surrounding asteroids. The Goliath shook hard, and Mitchell grabbed the arms of the chair while more of the liquid metal vines dropped down and belted him in. He saw a corner of the ship corrode and collapse under the assault.

"I have sealed the breach," Origin said.

The energy dissipated. The path from Goliath to the Tetron was clear and open.

It was preparing to fire again.

Mitchell shifted the power from the nose to the port side, vectoring the Goliath to the right and upwards, towards the top of the Tetron. He continued gathering energy, pulling it from the veins and pouring it into thrust.

"Shields will be depleted," Origin said. "We can not-"

"Did you put me in charge of driving this thing or not?" Mitchell snapped. The energy was arcing off the Tetron's face as it prepared to release the burst. It angled along with the Goliath, keeping it in its target.

"The Goliath is not a starfighter," Origin replied.

"No. It has more thrust."

The energy spread away from the Tetron, heading right towards them. Mitchell dropped the energy, pushing it to the other side and reversing the vector. The shot was huge, large enough to adjust for velocity at the distance. It wasn't big enough. It hadn't been expecting the maneuver, and Mitchell watched the blue ball sizzle past the starboard side of Goliath, the edges coming within a kilometer of the ship.

"My turn," Mitchell said. He pushed the Goliath forward and up, and at the same time began drifting the aft sideways. The Tetron reacted by picking up some thrust of its own, looking to close the distance between them so that he wouldn't be able to dodge again. Mitchell found the dozens of tubes that sat flush against the belly of the Goliath and set them all to fire.

Explosive discs launched from the bottom of the starship, tiny points arcing towards the Tetron. The detonations were marked by momentary balls of flame and the spread of blue energy as the discs were caught by the enemy's shields.

"The projectiles do not carry enough energy to breach the shields," Origin said.

Mitchell hadn't expected that they did. He continued firing anyway, sending hundreds of them at the Tetron, forcing it to focus on them. He continued his twist, bringing the Goliath over the top of the enemy, coming up broadsides. They passed within a few kilometers of one another, the Goliath offering a small target directly over the Tetron.

He continued raining the discs down.

"You are wasting resources," Origin said.

"Can you shut up?" Mitchell replied. There was a plan behind the assault. He switched the thrust power, flipping the massive ship over in space and sending it backward, away from the Tetron. It corrected to give chase, not having to physically change directions to begin slowing its momentum and come back the other way.

The front of it began to glow again.

"I do not understand this," Origin said.

"You don't need to understand, you need to shut up," Mitchell replied. However old the intelligence was, it wasn't intelligent enough. It didn't understand, or wasn't paying attention to the Alliance fighters, who had regrouped and moved into formation with the dropship. It didn't know, couldn't calculate, what Mitchell had expected.

The human pilots had seen him attacking the Tetron.

They had come to back him up.

Missiles launched from a dozen fighters, along with blasts from lasers. The dropship opened up with its own ordnance - heavier missiles and railguns mixed with lighter laser fire. It erupted against the side of the Tetron, the shields staying visible in the glow of blue light that was stealing power from the attack.

Mitchell started pooling energy of his own, moving it to the aft, pushing them towards the alien.

Discs rose from the enemy Tetron, tearing into the squadron. Four fighters vanished at once while the rest vectored past, and then turned and headed in for a second run. Mitchell fired Goliath's projectiles again, thinking to aim them at the Tetron's launchers. More explosions followed, more hits on the shields.

"It is preparing to leave," Origin said, his voice carrying his disbelief. "You have won."

"Not yet I haven't," Mitchell said. He wasn't about to let it escape.

He owed it for the Schism.

It appeared that even technologically superior intelligences could not escape the laws that governed hyperdeath. The Tetron hung motionless while the thousands of nerves pulsed with an increasing light, the power shifting to bring it to a higher dimension. Perhaps it expected mercy? Perhaps it thought that it had time to escape the main energy weapon, the only weapon that could hurt it.

Mitchell didn't know and didn't care. He sent the Goliath towards it, shifting the power from aft to bow, collecting it and spreading it along the ancient starship's nose. The Tetron drew ever closer, the range closing in a hurry.

"Mitchell, this is not an advisable maneuver," Origin said.

Mitchell ignored him. His hands clenched the armrest of the command chair as the Tetron loomed large in the view screens.

The collision shook the Goliath, testing the alien shields and the heavy alloy hull as it speared the Tetron. The energy at the bow ripped into the veins and neurons, smashing through them and shattering them in an unstoppable progression towards the heart.

"Hull breach sealed," Origin said. "Hull breach sealed."

The Goliath continued onwards, inwards, shattering crossing layers of the bio-mechanical nerves, sinking further and further.

A large central unit, a massive neuron appeared in front of them. It was pulsing in uneven fits of blue, flailing to cling to life.

Mitchell fired the discs again, sending them into the Tetron before he could strike it with the starship. The discs sunk in and exploded, blowing the creature's heart, mind, and soul to pieces.

The Goliath stopped shaking. The network crumbled around it, tendrils of nerves spinning off into space around the ship. Mitchell shifted the power, bringing them to a steady pause. He reached up behind his head, taking the neural connection in his hand, ignoring the warm shock of it and wrenching it from his head. He tried to get up, and instead stumbled forward and fell to the floor in front of the chair.

He pulled himself to one knee and vomited.

57

HE WASN'T sure how long he was kneeling there. His head was swimming along with his stomach, leaving him uneasy and unable to concentrate. Being connected to the Goliath, to the Tetron, Origin, had left him feeling very crude.

"Mitchell."

He heard the voice echo in the back of his mind, somewhere in the darkness behind his closed eyes. Katherine. Or was it Christine?

Whoever it was, it was a connection to the eternally distant past. The word wasn't directed at him now. It was a relic of his subconscious, a reconstruction following the reconstitution of his being.

"Christine," he heard himself say.

"We failed. We can't do this alone," she said.

He opened his eyes. The darkness was replaced with the outer display of space around the Goliath, pieces of the Tetron floating away from the knife that had shattered it. Floating closer to the ship were the remaining Alliance vessels, the dropship and the fighters, flying in formation near the head.

"Christine?" he said.

The connection was gone as quickly as it had come.

He reached out a hand and put it on the arm of the command chair, using it to pull himself to his feet. His legs were unsteady beneath him, and the nausea returned as he rose. He pulled in a heavy breath of air and gritted his teeth against the discomfort. He had won the first battle. Maybe it wasn't much, but it was something.

"Origin," he said. His throat was dry, his voice a whisper.

The Tetron didn't answer.

"Origin," he said again.

Nothing.

Where had it gone?

The sliver of liquid metal still hung in position by the chair. He considered reinserting it, and then immediately abandoned the idea. He didn't even know if he could survive it a second time, for as lousy as he felt.

The hatch to the control room slid open behind him. He turned sharply, his instincts kicking in and sending him into a defensive posture.

"Don't hurt me," Singh said, her voice back to its usual flatness.

"Singh?" He couldn't help but smile. He didn't want to be the only living thing on this ship. "Are you okay?"

She shrugged. "I'm fine. It told me to head up here to you and let me go. It took me a few minutes to get here, there's some debris along the route. A hull breach that was sealed by the dendrites."

"You know what it is?"

"I heard your conversation. At least, I remember it like I heard it. I don't know what to say. This ship doesn't seem to need an engineer."

"You are wrong about that, Corporal Li Singh."

A new person joined them on the bridge. He bore a strong resemblance to Singh, but with a more masculine face and short hair. They would have been easy to pass as siblings.

"Origin?" Mitchell asked.

The man smiled. "As I said, I needed the formulation. The DNA, etcetera, to replicate the organism. You did well against it, Mitchell, but this is only the very beginning. We have many miles to go before we sleep."

"I don't understand," Singh said, taken aback at the sight of the Tetron.

"This is mankind's war," Origin said. "For your survival. Your existence. It does not fit for me to interact with you as a Tetron. It will make assimilation... difficult. I have replicated this form and linked it to my central unit, which you observed in the engine bay." He pointed to where the Alliance ships were arranged around them. "As we will be taking on allies, it is important that we begin preparing the Goliath to service a human crew once more. That will mean extensive work on the original subsystems, which have been languishing since the original crew of the ship died over three hundred years ago. It will certainly require the help of an engineer."

"What do you mean, died?" Mitchell asked. He hadn't even considered the astronauts who had taken the Goliath out for its maiden voyage.

"The average lifespan of a homo sapiens in the year twenty-sixty was ninety-four years," Origin said, "and there was a limited extended food supply on board for the initial engine test. Goliath has been hiding for much longer than that."

Mitchell swallowed and fought to hold back what was sure to be dry heaves. The Goliath crew - Yousefi, Bonnie, Katherine - they had come here and starved to death. Katherine had even known it was going to happen, that her fate was to die on this ship in an effort to win a war that wouldn't start for an untold number of years. How had anyone, or anything, convinced her of that?

"Are they still here? The bodies?" Singh asked.

"I have assimilated their resources," Origin said. His eye twitched, as though he was accessing a p-rat. "I have unblocked transmissions and am receiving an encoded signal. Do you wish to communicate?"

Mitchell glanced out at the dropship. "We can't do this alone," his vision of Christine had said. How were the Alliance forces going to react when they found out who was driving the Goliath? Would it matter? They had no FTL engines of their own.

"Open the channel," Mitchell said.

A tone sounded from somewhere in the control room.

"This is the Alliance dropship Valkyrie. Please respond. I repeat, please respond."

"This is Captain Mitchell Williams, Alliance Space Marines," he replied. "Of the starship Goliath."

There was a long pause.

"Did you say, Goliath?" the voice responded, followed by another pause. "Did you say Captain Mitchell Williams?"

"Yes," Mitchell said. He turned to Origin, remembering the other Alliance ship. "Where is the carrier?"

"Gone," Origin said. "The Tetron destroyed it."

The news washed over Mitchell. The casualties were growing, and he was sure the rate was only going to increase.

"You're supposed to be dead," the voice from the Valkyrie said.

"Goliath," a second voice said, the nerves obvious in its tone. "How could it be Goliath?"

"Who am I speaking to?" Mitchell asked.

"Major Aaron Long, Alliance Navy," the first voice replied. "Commander of the dropship Valkyrie. Captain I... I don't understand any of this. I don't even know how we got here."

"It's a long story, Major. The important part is that you're safe for now. The threat is neutralized."

"That ship. I've never seen anything like it. Was it the Federation?"

Origin chuckled.

"No," Mitchell replied. "Not quite. It's much, much worse than that."

"I don't understand," Major Long said.

"Mitchell," Origin said. "We must skip the platitudes. We cannot stay here long. Tetron communications occur in real-time, and I am certain more of my kind are already on the way to this location."

He didn't want to be there when they arrived. "Right. Open the hangar doors. Valkyrie, this is Goliath. I'm opening the hangar. You and your fighters have permission to come aboard as long as you promise to not try to kill me, arrest me, pull rank on me, or do anything else stupid after I just saved your life. I'll explain everything later."

There was a long pause. Mitchell could imagine the crew of the ship trying to decide if they should accept his offer. Finally, Major Long returned.

"Understood, and agreed, Captain Williams. I'd rather bed down with the devil I know than be stranded out here. Long out."

They thought he was a criminal, a liar, a rapist, maybe worse. They would figure out the truth soon enough, maybe. Did it even matter anymore?

"Hangar doors are opening," Origin said.

"What happens now?" Singh asked.

Origin looked at Mitchell. "You already know, don't you, Captain."

He did. In a way, he'd always known. He'd even made one attempt already, one that had left him with his tail between his legs. He wasn't eager to try again, but at least he would have the Goliath at his back this time.

"We need to go back to Liberty. We have to find Christine."

"Yes," Origin said. "The replica was supposed to stay close to you, to help you in any way she could. It would have been better if she had traveled with you, but I am certain that circumstances prevented it. A caution. She doesn't know what she is, or why she has positioned herself as your guardian. She won't until we are reunited."

"I still don't understand why she's so important?" Singh said.

"Two reasons, Corporal," Origin replied. "First, remember that she contains the bulk of my knowledge of this war and of the Tetron. I retained only enough to maintain my discovered individuality and be reinitialized. Until you retrieve her you are fighting an enemy whose motivations and capabilities you do not, and can not completely understand. As Sun Tzu stated many centuries ago - know your enemy." Origin's eyes twitched again. "The Alliance forces have gained the hangar. I have taken the liberty of shifting your fighter to a more optimal position, and sealed off the deck for the time being."

"Thank you," Mitchell said.

Origin nodded slightly. "Second," he continued, "prior to your arrival in the universe her alternate directive was to extrapolate the identity of the Creator."

"The Creator?" Mitchell asked. "God?"

Origin laughed. "Not your creator, Mitchell. Ours. We were not always Tetron. We know that we were made by man, though the answer of who made us has eluded us throughout the eons. It is not enough to destroy the Tetron who have used the eternal engine to travel here. To end the war, the Creator must also be killed before we can be conceived, and in that way break the cycle of our existence and your demise."

"And Christine knows who it is?"

"She may. She may not. It has proven to be a difficult answer to obtain. Perhaps the most difficult in all of eternity."

"If we have to figure it out, then we'll figure it out," Mitchell said. "The Alliance forces are aboard?"

"Yes," Origin said.

"We'll have time to plan our attack during the trip. You may not know, but Liberty has already been taken."

"Yes. I am aware. Liberty has always been one of the first to fall. We must hope that she is still alive. If she isn't, this war has been lost again." His eyes twitched. "I am preparing to move us into hyperspace."

Mitchell turned and looked out at the vastness of space ahead of them. He turned until he found the asteroid belt, reaching up and putting his hand to his heart. He wished he could at least have something of Ilanka's, or Millie's. A medal or something personal to remember them by, the way they had done for the others.

"Riigg-aaah," he said, as loudly as his tired lungs would bear. One last call to send them on to wait for the next return.

"Riigg-aaah," Singh echoed softly beside him, joining him in his gaze out towards the stars.

He was about to turn, to look away, when he saw it: a speck appearing in the distance and sweeping out from the sea of space rock, its exterior glinting in the light of the nearby star. He didn't need his p-rat to identify the transport.

"Riigg-aaah," he said again, the smile spreading across his face.

He definitely wouldn't have to fight this war alone.

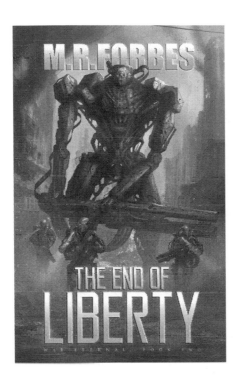

Enjoyed Starship Eternal? Read the next book in the series, The End of Liberty, now!

THANK YOU!

It is readers like you, who take a chance on self-published works that is what makes the very existence of such works possible. Thank you so very much for spending your hard-earned money, time, and energy on this work. It is my sincerest hope that you have enjoyed reading!

Independent authors could not continue to thrive without your support. If you have enjoyed this, or any other independently published work, please consider taking a moment to leave a review at the source of your purchase. Reviews have an immense impact on the overall commercial success of a given work, and your voice can help shape the future of the people whose efforts you have enjoyed.

Thank you again!

ABOUT THE AUTHOR

M.R. Forbes is the creator of a growing catalog of science fiction novels, including War Eternal, Rebellion, Chaos of the Covenant, and the Forgotten Worlds novels. He eats too many donuts, and he's always happy to hear from readers.

To learn more about M.R. Forbes or just say hello:

Visit my website:
mrforbes.com

Send me an e-mail:
michael@mrforbes.com

Check out my Facebook page:
facebook.com/mrforbes.author

Chat with me on Facebook Messenger:
https://m.me/mrforbes.author